J.-K. Huysmans

The Oblate
(*L'Oblat*)

T0018199

Translated with an introduction and notes by
Brendan King

Dedalus

This book is supported by Arts Council England

ARTS COUNCIL
ENGLAND

Supported using public funding by

Published in the UK by Dedalus Limited
24-26, St Judith's Lane, Sawtry, Cambs, PE28 5XE
email: info@dedalusbooks.com
www.dedalusbooks.com

ISBN printed book 978 1 912868 95 7
ISBN ebook 978 1 915568 06 9

Dedalus is distributed in the USA & Canada by SCB Distributors
15608 South New Century Drive, Gardena, CA 90248
email: info@scbdistributors.com   www.scbdistributors.com

Dedalus is distributed in Australia by Peribo Pty Ltd
58, Beaumont Road, Mount Kuring-gai, N.S.W 2080
email: info@peribo.com.au   www.peribo.com.au

First published in France in 1903
First published by Dedalus in 2022

Translation, Introduction, and Notes copyright © Brendan King 2022

The right of Brendan King to be identified as the translator of this work
has been asserted by him in accordance with the Copyright, Designs and
Patent Acts, 1988

Printed by Clays Ltd, Elcograf S.p.A.
Typeset by Brendan King

This book is sold subject to the condition that it shall not, by way of
trade or otherwise, be lent, re-sold, hired out or otherwise circulated
without the publisher's prior consent in any form of binding or cover
other than that in which it is published and without a similar condition
including this condition being imposed on the subsequent purchaser.

A CIP Catalogue record for this book is available on request.

About the Translator

Brendan King is a freelance writer, reviewer and translator with a special interest in late nineteenth-century French fiction. His Ph.D. was on the life and work of J.-K. Huysmans.

His previous translations of Huysmans' work for Dedalus include *Là-Bas: A Journey into the Self, Parisian Sketches, Marthe, Against Nature, Stranded, The Cathedral* (a revised and updated edition of Clara Bell's 1898 translation), *The Vatard Sisters, Drifting, Modern Art* and *Certain Artists*.

He also edited Robert Baldick's definitive biography *The Life of J.-K. Huysmans,* which was published in paperback by Dedalus in 2005.

CONTENTS

INTRODUCTION

Published in 1903, *L'Oblat* (*The Oblate*) was J.-K. Huysmans' final novel and brought to a close his trilogy (or quartet if you include *Là-bas* of 1891) that chronicled the spiritual journey of his alter-ego protagonist, Durtal. Its position in the canon of Huysmans' works is an anomalous one: it was overshadowed commercially and in the public imagination by its predecessors in the series, especially *La Cathédrale* of 1898 which was a runaway bestseller, and it remains the least well-known of his novels.

La Cathédrale – famously a book in which, almost literally, nothing happens – owed some its popular success to the fact that it deliberately didn't engage with the contemporary political issues that were tearing France apart at the time. Although the Dreyfus Affair was in full swing during the novel's composition, and it was published in the same year as Émile Zola's *J'accuse*, you would get no idea of this from reading it. By contrast, *L'Oblat* could not be accused of shying away from the political controversies of the day, with the fallout from the Dreyfus Affair and the Republican government's subsequent move to separate Church and State, and thereby effectively curtail the Catholic Church's political influence, featuring centre stage. The novel's characters not only discuss ongoing contemporary political events, they live out the consequences of the government's radical political decisions.

Of course Huysmans' view of the Affair – that it was, as Christopher Lloyd puts it in *J.-K. Huysmans and the Fin-de-Siècle Novel*, 'a conspiracy got up by Jews, Freemasons and Protestants with the aim of subverting the Church' – is not one that is accepted today, but however misguided his opinion was, it nevertheless reflects the attitude of a significant part of the French population at that period. It helps us to understand why passions surrounding the Affair were so high, and why the social divisions that resulted were so deep, traumatic and long-lasting.

Huysmans was not primarily a political novelist. He was not a writer like Zola, who could take social situations of great moment and deliberately weave them into the metaphorical web of his fiction. While other novelists might have found sufficient material to craft a dramatic narrative from such contentious events, that was neither Huysmans' style nor his intention. His focus of interest lay elsewhere, as Robert Baldick explains in his biography:

> One of Huysmans' objects in writing *L'Oblat* was to present a vivid but accurate account of the life of a French religious community at the beginning of the century. He wished, in fact, to emulate the Flemish sculptors who, in the figurines in Dijon Museum which are described in the book, had represented 'the monastic humanity of their time, merry or melancholy, phlegmatic or fervent'.
>
> (*Life of J.-K. Huysmans*, Dedalus Books, 2006, p. 427)

Huysmans' previous two novels, *En Route* and *La Cathédrale*, were similarly didactic in this sense, introducing his readers to plainchant and Christian symbolism respectively. In *L'Oblat* he aimed to do the same for the splendours of the liturgy. It's true that fiction and the liturgy were not obvious bedfellows, but Huysmans had started out as a writer in Zola's Naturalist school, in which research and documentation were considered integral to the writing process. As Elizabeth Emery puts it:

> For Huysmans, the novel was a form that allowed him to transmit information to his readers, while giving them a bit of entertainment. He understood all along that he would have to push the limits of the genre, but he was willing to take his chances in order to initiate his contemporaries into the medieval practices of the Catholic Church. [...] Huysmans saw the novel as the form best positioned to resuscitate the moralizing function of medieval art in the modern world.
>
> (*Romancing the Cathedral*, University of New York, 2001, p. 123)

Indeed, one contemporary critic was so struck by the documentary aspect of the novel that, in an otherwise hostile review, he conceded:

> It seems to me that the best chance *L'Oblat* has to last is that, in four or five hundred years, it may be used as a convenient document on the life of religious communities. Armed with *L'Oblat* an expert scholar could even reconstruct, in its entirety, the liturgy of some Benedictine ceremonies. I'm not making a joke: that's a great thing.
>
> (Léon Blum, *Gil Blas*, 9 March 1903)

Nevertheless, Huysmans was aware that presenting such specialised and often abstruse material wasn't going to be easy, and that to make it palatable to the reader he had to sugar-coat the pill, so to speak, through various fictional devices. As he told his friend Henri d'Hennezel, who was also writing a book on a similar theme:

> The devices that can be used, conversations, soliloquies, or personal chapters, are not very varied, but after all they suffice. Obviously, as we've said before, a novel conceived in this way is a 'mongrel' and a hybrid, but there's nothing else to be done. Otherwise your book is certain to be a flop, because no one will read a brochure on the liturgy, least of all the clergy, and besides, we're doing a useful job in masking the taste of technique with an appetising sauce.
>
> (Huysmans to Henri d'Hennezel, 26 June 1903)

L'Oblat does indeed contain some of the trademark 'devices' of Huysmans' earlier novels, albeit in a slightly lower key. There is the phantasmagoric blending of art and mythical history in the description of Khosrow's palace, for example, or the often comical interludes with Monsieur Lampre and Mlle de Garambois, which serve a similar function as the scenes with Carhaix and his wife in *Là-bas*, or with Madame Bavoil in *La Cathédrale*.

Undoubtedly one of the ingredients of the 'appetising sauce' for many readers is the identification of Durtal with his creator.

Introduction

En Route, La Cathédrale and *L'Oblat* are generally taken to constitute a faithful account of Huysmans' own conversion, or more accurately re-conversion, to Catholicism. Contemporary reviewers especially tended to see the fictional Durtal and Huysmans the writer as practically interchangeable:

> Durtal, the mystic in *Là-Bas,* is no other than M. Huysmans himself, and he makes no secret whatever of the fact. He appears again in *En Route* and in *La Cathédrale*, both of which have been translated into English, and he will finally be seen in *L'Oblat*, a forthcoming study of the Benedictine life upon which M. Huysmans is at present engaged.
>
> (*Academy,* 28 August 1898)

But as with most autobiographically inspired novels, the relationship between life and fiction is rarely so simple. It's true that *L'Oblat* tells the story in broad outline of the two years Huysmans spent at a monastery in Ligugé, and it's also true that, like the sequence of novels that preceded it, *L'Oblat* is a *roman à clef,* with many of its characters and settings based on real-life originals. The Burgundian abbey of Val-des-Saints in the novel, for example, is a thinly disguised description of the abbey of Saint Martin in Ligugé where Huysmans took his vows as an oblate. Madame Bavoil, who also appears in *La Cathédrale*, was based on Huysmans' housekeeper, Julie Thibault; Mlle de Garambois was a fictional portrait of Madame Godefroy, a 'sister oblate' who Huysmans had somewhat begrudgingly come to respect at Ligugé; and fictional monks such as Dom Felletin and Dom de Fonneuve were based on monks that Huysmans actually knew, such as Dom Besse and Dom Chamard. Even so, Huysmans was keen to make a distinction between himself and his fictional alter ego:

> *L'Oblat* is sort of my story, or rather it's the story of an imaginary character in a milieu which I've known and which I've loved, and which I miss.
>
> (*Gil Blas,* 1 February 1903)

Introduction

As Elizabeth Emery points out, the differences between Durtal and Huysmans, and between the settings of the novels and those of Huysmans' life, are as significant as the similarities:

> Huysmans wrote at work and during vacations; Durtal lives from his writing and has no other obligations. Huysmans went to churches accompanied by his friends George Landry and Gustave Boucher; Durtal is always alone in *En Route,* a solitary observer of church art and ceremony. While Huysmans shared a house with a married couple, the Leclaires, during his time as a Benedictine oblate at Ligugé, in *L'Oblat* Durtal lives with no one but his housekeeper. Durtal is a purified, simplified version of Huysmans, with no responsibilities. Although the outline of their conversion is similar, Durtal is not Huysmans, but an idealized alter ego from which all complications except the spiritual have been removed.
>
> (*Romancing the Cathedral,* p. 96)

If the line between fact and fiction is not always easy to determine, what is clear is that with *L'Oblat* Huysmans had reached the end of his spiritual journey, or rather his presentation of it in the guise of fiction. Some critics, such as Jean-Marie Seillan, have nevertheless argued that in the wake of *L'Oblat* Huysmans was ready to shift direction again, and that while there is no evidence he was planning to write a novel of 'de-conversion', there are certain thematic and stylistic signs in his later work that allow us to speculate 'that an evolution of this sort was likely to happen'. Whether Huysmans would indeed have found further terrain in which to explore his alter ego's psychological and spiritual state had he not died in 1907 at the age of only fifty-nine, must however remain a moot question.

The Writing of *L'Oblat*

Huysmans conceived the idea of writing *L'Oblat* many years before its eventual publication, indeed before he had even finished *La Cathédrale*. In an interview given to *L'Echo de Paris* in 1896, the author laid out his plans after the publication of *En Route* the year before, explaining how *La Cathédrale* would continue Durtal's story, and centre on the symbolic aspect of religious architecture:

> Ultimately, whatever happens, the influence of the cathedral on Durtal will be such that it will inevitably lead my hero to the Trappists, where he will enter definitively, though without taking the definitive vows of a monk. That will be the subject of *L'Oblat*.

(*L'Echo de Paris*, 28 August 1896)

In what might be considered a case of life imitating art, the experiences that primarily form the backdrop to *L'Oblat* would date to the two-year period Huysmans spent at Ligugé in the south-west of France between 1899 and 1901, three years after the novel's initial conception. It was here, at the abbey of Saint Martin, that Huysmans and his friend Gustave Boucher began their year-long novitiate in March 1900, and where both made their professions of oblatehood on 21 March 1901. Boucher, who had first introduced Huysmans to Ligugé in 1898, also helped to arrange the purchase of land and the construction of a house there, which the author bought jointly with his friends Léon Leclaire and his wife. The newly-built house, named the Maison Notre-Dame, was effectively divided into two apartments: Huysmans occupying the upper floor, with a view of the monastery situated conveniently close by, and the Leclaires occupying the ground floor, though as it turned out the couple would spend relatively little time there.

Following the success of *La Cathédrale,* Huysmans was increasingly seen as something of a literary celebrity, and his plan to become an oblate was the subject of news reports, profiles and even cartoons in the press. Inevitably, expectations regarding his new novel were raised, particularly among Catholics who felt that the work of high-profile converts such as Huysmans could present their embattled cause in a positive light. As the secretary to the bishop of Poitiers, Canon Omer Péret, told the writer during his negotiations to buy the house:

INTRODUCTION

Yes indeed, my dear Huysmans, you have promised *L'Oblat* to
your public: you must live it and write it here!
(Quoted in Baldick, *Life of J.-K. Huysmans*, p. 372)

When Huysmans moved into the Maison Notre-Dame during
the summer of 1899, his intention was to spend the rest of his
life there and write; he had even formed plans to found an
artistic religious community there. As it turned out, however,
his stay would be short-lived. In the wake of political and social
divisions exacerbated by the Dreyfus Affair, the newly-formed
Republican coalition government of 1899, led by the anticlerical Réne Waldeck-Rousseau, sought to neuter the political
power of religious associations, particularly those allied to the
Catholic Church. Consequently, with the passing of Waldeck-
Rousseau's Law of Associations in 1901, the monks of Saint Martin
were effectively forced to relocate to a monastery in Belgium.
Huysmans had little alternative but to move out also, and by the
end of 1901 he had reluctantly returned to Paris.

Ironically, Huysmans only got around to starting *L'Oblat* a few
months before he was due to leave Ligugé. The delay was no doubt
the result of having to complete a number of other works he was
already committed to, principally his hagiography of a fourteenth
century mystic, *Sainte Lydwine de Schiedam* (1901), which he'd
begun working on in 1897, but which was mostly written during
the summer and autumn of 1900 in the Maison Notre-Dame. By
the time he started collecting notes for *L'Oblat*, therefore, he was
aware that the rapidly evolving political developments would play
a decisive part in shaping the novel's narrative arc. As he told his
Dutch friend Arij Prins:

I'm still plunged into studies on the liturgy for *L'Oblat,* which
I'm hoping to write; basically, I'm living it every single day,
and the end of the book will be furnished to me by events.
(Huysmans to Arij Prins, 1 August 1901)

Around this time, Huysmans decided he was going to set his
novel not in Ligugé, which he had come to dislike, but in Dijon,

which he had first visited in 1895, in the company of Boucher. The city's Carthusian monastery, together with its Musée des Beaux Arts which contained a number of Flemish devotional works dating from the fifteenth and sixteenth centuries, no doubt offered the novelist more scope to explore medieval lore, art and history than Ligugé.

By the autumn of 1901 Huysmans and the Leclaires were finalising their plans to quit the Maison Notre-Dame. A diary entry written at the time shows how much the move and the current political events were affecting the author:

> I feel utterly forsaken... truly it's time that I went. One week more. My head aches and I feel sick at heart, as though I were suffocating. I didn't know that this disaster the monastery has suffered would affect me so deeply. Ah! however weak he may be, the Abbot was Jesus Christ being driven away – was Our Father himself. I kissed his hand and was close to tears. Even Houllier [the monk left behind as caretaker to look after the land and buildings], mediocre though he is, seems lovable now that he's there alone, for he represents monk and monastery. Never would I have suspected that I loved them so much, that they had entered so deeply into my life.
>
> (Diary entry for 29 September 1901)

For Huysmans, the return to Paris was a huge disruption. He had to find a new place to live, and arrange the transportation of the thousands of books he possessed, not to mention his numerous pictures and *objets d'art*. Unsurprisingly, all this prevented any serious work on the novel, however by the start of 1902 he was definitively installed in Paris, at 20 Rue Monsieur, in a large apartment in the annexe of the Benedictine convent there:

> Finally, by the grace of God. I can get back into my new book *L'Oblat*, perhaps I'll be able to finish it in peace in this place...
>
> (Huysmans to Arij Prins, 5 January 1902)

In February, however, Huysmans laid aside work on *L'Oblat* again in order to devote himself to a short life of the Italian priest Don Bosco, who had dedicated his life to helping the disadvantaged youth of Turin. However, this brief hagiographical essay, which was published later that same year, did not take up much of his time, and by the end of spring he was back at work on the novel:

> I am hitched into my book *L'Oblat*, but it progresses very slowly. The subject is so specialised that I ask myself, aside from me and a few monks, who the devil could it possibly interest? It's true that for a number of years I've only done books of this sort, and that nevertheless there's a public that finds it interesting – many of them, I believe, out of disgust at the state this unfortunate country of France is in, and out of hatred of the persecutors and the sectarians.
>
> (Huysmans to Arij Prins, 17 May 1902)

During the summer of 1902 there was another delay, this time the result of a bizarre incident involving a supposed legacy, a Satanic doctor, and a young misguided woman in Marseilles. The affair of the mysterious Dr Rodaglia and his attempt to marry his goddaughter to Huysmans, which resulted in the author having to travel to Marseilles to sort the whole matter out, is recounted in full by Robert Baldick in his biography.

Despite this, work on the novel continued throughout the rest of the summer:

> I'm still working on *L'Oblat*, but it's long and difficult to put together, and it will be a bit boring with the work on the liturgy of the Middle Ages – but I've a public who I can fortunately make swallow it all. If they've accepted *La Cathédrale* and *Sainte Lydwine*, there's no reason why I can't make them devour all this too.
>
> (Huysmans to Arij Prins, 25 July 1902)

In August, Huysmans moved once more, this time to 60 Rue de Babylone, a fourth floor flat less than five minutes away from the Rue Monsieur. Initially at least, he found the new apartment more peaceful and comfortable, but even so he continued to find work on the novel difficult, aware that his book was likely to stir up controversy. As Huysmans saw it, the Catholics of France were no less guilty than the Republican government, and in a letter to Leclaire he told his friend that he intended to pillory everyone, laymen, priests and monks alike, for having failed, as he saw it, in their duty to God and the Church:

> This guttersnipe government hasn't sprung from a self-sown seed, but from the general cowardice and stupidity of the Catholics [...]. By heaven, but the Catholics are going to cop it in *L'Oblat*! They may howl as much as they like, but they, the clergy and the religious Orders are all going to hear a few home truths.
>
> (Quoted in *Life of J.-K. Huysmans*, p. 427)

At one point, Huysmans even lost patience with Pope Leo XIII, who in his opinion should have threatened the French president with excommunication. Consequently, he extended the scope of his indictment to the Vatican, telling Leclaire:

> Before the year is out there won't be a monastery left in this filthy country. I'm slating it, the government, the Pope, the clergy, everything, in *L'Oblat*. The book is going to create a tremendous stink.
>
> (Huysmans to Léon Leclaire 28 August 1902)

By October, the book was nearly complete, and Huysmans informed Prins:

> I'm working hard and I've only got two chapters left to do, but everything will have to be recopied and tidied up. I'm trying to get it ready for the start of the year. And then it will be a right storm on all sides! Because *L'Oblat* is the most violent book I've ever written. In it, everyone gets it in the neck, the Catholics who are behind everything, as much as the government of crooks who lead us.

Introduction

Since that diabolical Dreyfus Affair, France has become a
right sink of corruption. It's impossible to see how it will all
end, if not in total bankruptcy or a war.

(Huysmans to Arij Prins, 18 October 1902)

On 24 November, Huysmans told Leclaire that he had just
written *finis* to the book. The first three weeks of December
were spent revising and copying out the manuscript, and it was
delivered to his publisher, Stock, on Christmas Day. At the end of
the year, Huysmans gave Prins another update on the book and
predicted how it would be received:

I've finished my book which has gone off to the printer. I'm
hoping it will appear in the first months of the new year. I'm
expecting a general uproar with it because everyone, the Pope
and President Loubet, gets it in the neck. I'll be lucky this
time if I avoid getting put on the Index in Rome, which I
narrowly escaped before with *La Cathédrale*.

I'm exhausted. *L'Oblat* is a big book, and the enormous
amount of research was a real headache...

(Huysmans to Arij Prins, 29 December 1902)

On its publication in March, *L'Oblat* received a significant
amount of coverage in the press – Lucien Descaves refers to more
than a hundred articles in the space of four months in France and
Belgium alone – and though it sold relatively well initially, its sales
tailed off and it never reached the sustained levels of *En Route* or
La Cathédrale. For the most part, the critical response to the novel
was respectful, but muted. As always, there were those who took
issue with Huysmans' style, or found his invective too strong for
their tastes. Huysmans himself was more concerned about what he
saw as the hostile reaction in the Catholic and Benedictine press:

There's an unleashing of fury against *L'Oblat* here. The
Catholics above all, exasperated that one of their own has

told them such harsh truths. As for the Benedictines, they feel they haven't been flattered enough, and are protesting against the book. What can you say about the pride and incomprehension of these people!

It's always a continuous stream of attacks against me. But I don't care. I write books to tell the truth, to say what I think; I am loyal to no party and never will be. Let them shout! [...]

What a country of idiots and scoundrels this beautiful France is.

(Huysmans to Arij Prins, 21 April 1903)

After the novel's publication, Huysmans travelled to Lourdes to stay with the Leclaires, who had set up house there after leaving Ligugé. A week later he reported to his friend Georges Landry:

I'm living next to the Leclaires, in a villa belonging to the Carmelite monastery located close by, and I've got a view from my window of the Basilica, the Grotto blazing with light day and night, and the chain of the Pyrenees [...]

I'm going to stay here for the rest of the month. I've worked hard enough to deserve a little holiday.

(Huysmans to Georges Landry, 11 March 1903)

Despite feeling overwhelmed by weeks of proof-reading and the complicated legal arrangements involved in setting up the Académie Goncourt, of which he was the president, during his stay at Lourdes Huysmans had already started making notes for his next and final book. This time he had no thought of using his experiences there to continue the Durtal cycle, and the book, entitled *Les Foules de Lourdes* (*The Crowds of Lourdes*), would be framed as a piece of reportage. It would be published in October 1906, less than eight months before his death.

TRANSLATOR'S NOTE

L'Oblat was first translated into English as *The Oblate of St Benedict* in 1924 by Edward Perceval. This translation was, however, not particularly well received at the time, as the text contained a number of errors and omissions. This new translation is based on the edition of *L'Oblat* in Volumes XVII and XVIII of Huysmans' *Oeuvres complètes* (Crès, 1928-34). A section of Notes is included at the end of the book to provide additional information for references or allusions in the text that might be unfamiliar to the reader.

The Oblate
(*L'Oblat*)

Ut quid, Deus, repulisti in finem ?
Iratus est furor tuus, super ovees pascuæ tuæ ?
Memor esto congregationis tuæ...
Psaume LXXIII.

O God, why have you cast us off unto the end?
Why is thy wrath enkindled against the sheep
of thy pasture?
Psalm 73

CHAPTER I

For more than eighteen months now, Durtal had been living in Val-des-Saints. Tired of Chartres, where he had provisionally settled, and plagued by desultory longings for the cloister, he'd left for the abbey of Solesmes.[1]

Recommended to the head of the monastery by Abbé Plomb, one of the curates at Chartres who had known his reverence for a number of years, Durtal had been cordially received and had stayed at the monastery on several occasions for more than a fortnight, but he always came back more ill at ease, more uncertain than before. He would meet up again joyfully with his old friends, Abbé Gévresin and his housekeeper, Madame Bavoil; he would return to his lodgings with a sigh of relief, and then the same thing would happen: little by little he was seized again by memories of the conventual life at Solesmes, so utterly different from that which he'd experienced at La Trappe.[2]

Indeed, there was none of the iron rule of the Cistercians, the perpetual silence, the rigorous fasts and never-ending abstinence, the sleeping fully clothed in a dormitory, the getting up in the dark at two in the morning, working at some trade or labouring on the land; the Benedictines could speak, and on certain days eat meat; they could sleep undressed and each had his own private cell; they would rise at four, and devote themselves to intellectual work, toiling away in a library rather than in a workshop or a field.

The Rule of St Benedict, so inflexible among the White

Monks, had been tempered by the Black Monks;[3] it easily adapted itself to the dissimilar needs of the two Orders, the aims of which, indeed, were not the same.

The Trappists were more particularly devoted to the work of mortification and repentance, whereas the Benedictines, properly called, to the divine service of praising God; consequently, the former, under the impetus of St Bernard,[4] had emphasised all that was strict and harsh in the rule; whereas the latter, on the contrary, had adopted, and even relaxed, the more appealing and indulgent dispositions it contained.

Guests and those on retreat would keenly feel this difference; to the same degree that his reception had been curt and austere when Durtal had first visited La Trappe – already ten years ago now – in order to convert, so his welcome at Solesmes, when he'd gone with a plan to test out his vocation, had been affable and friendly.

He'd profited when at the Benedictines from the good-natured aspect of their observances; he had been given almost complete liberty as regards getting up in the morning, going out for a walk, or attending services; he would eat his meals with the monks, not, as at the Cistercians, in a room apart; he was no longer kept at a distance, on the outskirts of the community, or on the fringes of the cloister, but was right inside it, living with the fathers,[5] talking and working with them. The duties of hospitality, so expressly recommended by the Order's patriarch, were truly carried out to the letter by the Black Monks.

This paternal characteristic made him smile when he got back to Chartres; over time, the image of Solesmes clarified in his mind, would become idealised in proportion to its distance.

'There's no place like Solesmes!' he would exclaim, 'the only monastic life possible for me is there.'

And yet he couldn't forget that every time he'd left the abbey and was sitting in the cab that would take him to Sablé station, he'd exhaled deeply, like a man relieved of an insupportable burden, and once installed on the train would say to himself: 'My God, what luck, here I am free again!' – and yet he would continue to miss the embarrassment of being with others, the relief of fixed hours with no unexpected amusements and no unforeseen disturbances.

He found it difficult to analyse these changing impressions, these opposing feelings. 'Yes, certainly,' he would declare, 'Solesmes is unique in France; religious art shines here like nowhere else; its plainchant is perfect; its services are conducted with a matchless pomp; and what's more nowhere else would I come across an abbot of Dom Delatte's stature, or musical palaeographers more skilled or learned than Dom Mocquereau and Dom Cagin,[6] and I could also add, monks that were more helpful and pleasant – yes, but...'

But what? And then, by way of response, his whole being seemed to recoil with a sort of instinctive repulsion for this monastery, whose splendidly illuminated façade, by contrast, made the unlit outbuildings that adjoined it darker still; and so he advanced with precaution, like a cat that sniffs around a strange appartment, ready to bolt at the slightest alarm.

'But that doesn't make any sense,' he admitted, 'I don't have a shadow of a proof that the inside of a cloister differs in spirit to that of its façade; it's strange what's going on inside me.'

'Come on, let's have it out: what is it that I don't like?' And he answered himself: 'Everything and nothing.' Nevertheless, certain observations stood out in the light, came to the fore as regards the setting of the abbey. First of all, the grandeur of this monastery and its army of monks and novices, which detracted from the intimacy and charm possessed by less-imposing retreats, such as La Trappe at Our Lady of the Hearth,[7] for example. With its huge buildings, and the crowd of monks that cluttered them, Solesmes inevitably took on the air of an army barracks. It felt like you marched to a service as if you were on parade; like the abbot was a general surrounded by his staff, and that the others were no more than humble privates. No, one could never feel at ease, and one could never be sure of the morrow, if one belonged to that religious garrison, which has something uneasy and fearful about it, always on its guard; and indeed, one fine morning you could, if you ceased to please, be sent off, like a mere package, to some distant cloister.

Then, what was there to say about the unutterable dreariness of those recreation periods, of those supervised and inevitably gloomy conversations, the irritation produced over time by the lack of the solitude that is so delightful at La Trappe, but which is impractical at Solesmes, where there are neither ponds nor woods, and where the garden is flat and bare, with no winding path, no alcove where one could mediate, hidden from sight, alone.

'That's all well and good,' he continued, 'but to be fair, I ought to admit now that, with the exception of the place itself – and again everyone except me likes it – my other grievances are devoid of meaning. Indeed, how would it be possible to get the effect of Solesmes as a whole, the solemnity of its services and the glory of its plainchant, without that serried mass of monks? How, without a grip of iron, could you direct an army of nearly a hundred men, whose different temperaments, by dint of constant contact, are ready to burst into flame? So it's essential that discipline be as strict in a monastery – more even – than in an army camp; and lastly, it has to help out other monastries in the congregation that are less well staffed, sending them those they lack, whether it's a director of liturgy, a precentor, or a nurse – in short, the specialist they need.

'That the inmates of Solesmes dread such an exile proves that they are happy in their abbey, and isn't that the highest praise you can make? In any case, such enforced departures are, for the most part, less down to disgrace than loans from monastery to monastery, necessitated by the very interests of the Order.

'As to the repugnance I feel about living among that ever-changing crowd, a priest to whom I spoke quite openly about it judiciously replied: "Where would the merit be if we didn't suffer from being rolled around like a pebble on the shore of the great cloister?"

'Well, yes, I can't deny it, but that doesn't stop me from preferring something else...'

And Durtal would reflect and then bring out more substantial

CHAPTER I

arguments, more conclusive reasons to justify his apprehensions.

'Suppose,' he said to himself, 'that the abbot allows me to work on my books in peace, and agrees not to interfere in literary matters – and he is so broadminded he would no doubt allow this dispensation – it would count for nothing because I'd be absolutely incapable of writing a book in this abbey.

'I've tried the experiment on several occasions, but the mornings and afternoons are so chopped up by services, it makes all artistic work impossible. This life, divided into little slices, may be excellent for collecting materials and for putting together notes, but to work on actual pages, no.'

And he remembered those sad occasions when, escaping from a service, he'd wanted to get down to work on a chapter, only to be discouraged by the thought that as soon as he started to get underway, he'd have to leave his cell and go back to the chapel for another service, and he concluded: 'The cloister is useful when preparing a book, but it's best to write it elsewhere.'

And what did it mean to be an oblate anyway? He'd never been able to get a clear answer. 'It depends on the goodwill of the abbot, and consequently can change according to the monastery; but was that seriously the case? The profession of oblate among the Benedictines has existed since the eighth century, and is governed by age-old regulations, but where were they? No one seems to know.

'The goodwill of an abbot! But that would be to surrender oneself, bound hand and foot, to a man who, in short, one knows only by hearsay; and if the man in whose monastery you were interned was either old and narrow-minded, or young, arrogant and unpredictable, it would be worse than being a monk, because a monk is at least protected by strict ordinances that his superior can't infringe. But what an ambiguous state of affairs – neither flesh nor fowl – is that of an oblate in a monastery! Halfway between the fathers and the lay brothers, he would in all likelihood be accepted by neither one nor the other.

'Being an oblate in an abbey is not therefore something to be envied.

'Ah, and then there's always the heavy, rarefied atmosphere of the cloister; no, that's definitely not for me.' How often had he repeated this phrase to himself; but he would nevertheless return to Solesmes, because as soon as he was settled back at Chartres, he was overtaken by a nostalgia for the divine office, for those days that are so precisely and wisely split up by the liturgy to lead the soul back to God, to prevent those who don't work from drifting too far away.

At Chartres, in the evenings, he had the impression that he hadn't prayed, that he had wasted his time, and the haunting plainchant he had heard came back to his mind in snatches, fuelling his desire to hear them again, stirring up, along with the recollection of those splendid services, his regret at having lost them.

Never had he so well understood the necessity of communal prayer, of liturgical prayer, of that prayer for which the Church has appointed the time and decided the text. He would tell himself that everything was in the Psalms, joy and contrition, adoration and ecstasy; that their verses adapted themselves to all states of the soul, corresponded to every need. He began to realise the power inherent in these supplicatory prayers, by virtue of the divine inspiration they possessed, by the fact that they were formulated by the Son to be offered to his Father by his faithful precursors. Now that he was deprived of them, he felt a weakness in his whole being, a feeling of implacable discouragement, of overwhelming dejection.

"Oh, yes," he would say to his confessor, Abbé Gévresin, "yes, I'm haunted by fantasies of the past; I've inoculated myself with the seductive poison of the liturgy and I've got it now in the blood of my soul and I'll never be rid of it. I'm a morphine addict of the divine office; what I'm telling you sounds stupid, but that's the way it is."

"And the abbot of Solesmes, what does he think of these hesitations?" the old priest asked.

"Dom Delatte's eyes smile and his mouth puckers with just a hint of scorn when he listens to the history of my fickleness. Perhaps he thinks it's a matter of temptation in my case, as I myself used to believe in the past."

Chapter I

"And me too," said Abbé Gévresin.

"But you no longer think that surely? Don't you remember how we implored Our Lady of the Crypt to enlighten us; and every time I went back to Solesmes the feeling was the same, but yet again, no; it was aggravated by an unreasonsble aversion, a recoil. Certainly, it was neither a sign of vocation, nor an invitation…"

After a pause, Durtal continued: "There is, of course, the fearful argument put forward by some of the good Lord's henchmen: reason proves to you that the monastic life is superior to any other existence, so there's no need to know anything more, that suffices; you must therefore start off down that path and have the strength of will to suffer the disillusions it entails and the sacrifices it demands.

"Obviously, this is a theory pitched at a very high level; it assumes an exceptional generosity of spirit, a complete renunciation of the self, an infallible faith, and a rare firmness of character and power of endurance. But that's like jumping into the sea for the love of God and forcing him to fish you out.

"It's also to put the cart before the horse; it puts our Lord after and not before; it's to deny vocation, the touch, impetus, and attraction of the divine; it's to obey without waiting for the call of Christ, on whom one claims to inflict one's views.

"I'm not getting mixed up in any of that; besides, I haven't been led in that way by the Holy Virgin, my Mother."

"And you're not mistaken in not wishing to tempt the Lord," said Abbé Gévresin, "but let's look at the question, please, from another angle. Nothing obliges you to don the habit of an oblate or shut yourself up in a cloister; you can lodge outside and still attend the services.

"I've told you before that this is the only solution that would suit you; you're past the age of illusions; you're too keen an observer for living side-by-side with monks to be good for you, you'd become aware of their hidden failings too quickly: live near them, not among them. Public opinion about the monks runs from one extreme to the other, and both extremes are equally foolish. Some people imagine them like those coloured engravings you've seen, chubby-cheeked and fat, holding a pie in one hand and clutching a wicker-covered wine bottle against their heart with the other, and nothing could be more inaccurate or more stupid. Others imagine them as angelic beings, hovering above the world, and that's no less inaccurate and no less stupid. The truth is that they are men, better than most laymen, but still just men, subject therefore to all a man's frailties when they are not absolute saints, and Lord knows…

"But no, to go back to what I was saying, prudence consists in adopting the middle way, in becoming an oblate, outside but in the vicinity of the cloister at Solesmes."

"At Solesmes? No. There's not a single habitable house to rent. Abbé Plomb, who went there, knows it; what's more, Solesmes is a bit of a hole; living outside the cloister would be horrible, because there aren't even any paths where you can wander around in the shade in summer. Added to which, the nearest town, Sablé, is of the worst sort, and the slowness of the trains to get to Le Mans or Paris! No, at Solesmes, there's no middle ground, it's the abbey or nothing."

"Then go to another monastery, in a region that's more attractive and easier to reach… Burgundy, for instance, at Val-des-Saints, which Abbé Plomb told you about."

"Well, that remains to be seen…"

And in due course it did end up being seen. One of the fathers from the abbey passed through Chartres and stayed with Abbé Plomb, who had immediately put him in touch with Durtal.

The two men were made for each other.

Dom Felletin was a monk over sixty-five years old, but still young and active, tall and strongly built, a ruddy complexion with cheeks flecked with crimson spots like the skin of an apricot; his nose was large, and when he laughed the tip of it wiggled; with light blue eyes and firm mouth, this priest diffused a feeling of tranquil gaiety, the joy of a healthy, selfless soul, a soul at ease with itself. Full of enthusiasm for his Order, enamoured of the liturgy and mysticism, he dreamed of groups of oblates forming a community around his own.

Chapter I

He pounced, so to speak, on Durtal, and as if by magic all questions were swiftly resolved. All that was left was to rent, at a good price, a house near the monastery, with an old garden; and he boasted of the paternal aspect of his abbey, the probity of its services.

"Obviously," he said, "with us you won't find the refined art of Solesmes; we don't have a master like Father Mocquereau to direct the choir; but even so, the Mass is beautifully sung, and the ceremonies are, as you'll see, magnificent; and lastly, not far from Val-des-Saints you have a town full of medieval treasures and ancient churches, and what's more, a town that is very lively and well-stocked with all modern conveniences, Dijon."

And Durtal, won over by this jovial priest, undertook a retreat at his convent for a fortnight, and on the advice of the abbot he'd rented the house and garden adjoining the cloister.

And life there was indeed very pleasant.

The abbey was homely, with none of the feeling of crowdedness and dull panic that had so oppressed him at Solesmes; indeed, Val-des-Saints went a bit too far in the opposite direction, in that everyone had almost too much freedom, though Durtal, who benefitted from it, wasn't about to complain. The abbot, Dom Anthime Bernard, was an old man of nearly eighty, well-known for his saintly character and, in spite of his incessant problems, his attentive benevolence and unfailing cheerfulness. He welcomed Durtal with open arms, and after a month told him that the monastery was now his home, and to assure him this wasn't an idle phrase he gave him a key to the main entrance. It meant that, even aside from the friendship that soon bound him to some of the inmates of the cloister, Durtal could take advantage of his exceptional position as a postulant, then as novice oblate; it would introduce him, on terms of equality, into the Order of which he would become a member, as soon as his term of probation was over.

The obscure question of the oblate's status had indeed come up almost immediately; but if he hadn't completely resolved it, the abbot at least dealt with it by a simple, common-sense solution.

"Begin your novitiate," he told Durtal, "we'll discuss it afterwards. Like that of the monks, it will last a year and a day;

during this period you will follow a course of liturgy with Dom Felletin and attend the services. In the meantime, we shall no doubt have unearthed the regulations and the texts which you can study yourself with the novice master."

And Durtal having accepted this arrangement, every feast day now served as a pretext to invite him to dine at the monastery.

The work, the services, the discussions, and his researches in the monastry's library, which contained nearly thirty thousand volumes, occupied him sufficiently that it was impossible to be bored. Then, on certain days when life seemed a little dull to him, he would take the train to Dijon; at other times, he liked to daydream in the garden, part of which had remained fallow, despite the protests of the gardener; this was a veritable wilderness of weeds and wild flowers that had sprung up from nowhere; and Durtal enjoyed himself amid this tangle of vegetation, limiting himself to pulling up only nettles and briars, hostile plants that threatened to choke the others; and he imagined that, in spring, he would nevertheless prune some of these intruders in order to establish in their place a liturgical garden with a small enclosure of medicinal herbs, copied from the one that Walafrid Strabo[8] had, in days gone by, planted near the outbuildings of his convent.

Only one thing was left to be desired in the solitude of his refuge: domestic service. Mother Vergognat, a peasant woman from the hamlet who kept house for him, was quite impossible. Lazy and with a fondness for drink, she made the pitiful quality of the food even worse by her lackadaisical way of cooking it; she was a stranger to moderation, you'd either gum up your teeth in a gelatinous paste or shatter them chewing something as hard as wood. Durtal, unable to do anything else, had chosen the path of offering up to the Lord the penitential misery of these dishes as an expiation for his former sins, when he learned, via telegram, of the sudden death of Abbé Gévresin. He hurriedly threw himself onto the express train to Paris, and from there reached Chartres in time to see, one last time, on his death-bed, the man he had perhaps loved the most. He had stayed in town for a few days, and

Chapter I

seeing that Abbé Plomb, one of their mutual friends, couldn't take the deceased's domestic, Madame Bavoil, into his service – having six months previously appointed his aunt to run his house – had offered to take the good woman to Val-des-Saints in the capacity of housekeeper and friend.

He had left Chartres without a definite answer, because she couldn't make up her mind; then, a few weeks after his return to Val-des-Saints, he'd received a letter from her announcing her arrival.

He'd gone to meet her at Dijon station; he was fully expecting to see a somewhat comical descent from the train, because Mme Bavoil was devoid of all preconceived ideas in matters of dress and couldn't take into account the bizarreness of her outfit, but even so she amazed him when he saw her waving in the doorway of the carriage, wearing an astounding black frilled bonnet and brandishing a grey umbrella; then she alighted from the train, dragging after her a sort of carpetbag from beneath the flaps of which the neck of an uncorked bottle emerged; and this, along with her luggage, greatly amused the porters unloading her strange trunk, a cross between a sideboard and a sarcophagus, an enormous long object which was also hairy, because on closer examination one noticed that bristles of hog's hair were sticking up on the lid, sprouting in large patches over the worn planks of wood.

"What have you got in there?" he cried in alarm.

"Why, my linen and my things," she replied calmly.

And while, a little embarrassed, he entrusted this absurd monument to the station attendants, she got her breath back, drew from her pocket a handkerchief as big as a tablecloth, chequered in a Nankin-yellow and brown pattern, and proceeded to dust the tin crucifix that was swinging on a chain against her blouse.

"Would you like to have something to eat or drink?" Durtal suggested. "We have time."

"You must be joking!" – and from her carpet-bag she extracted a crust of bread and pulled out her litre bottle of water, which was still half full. "I ate and drank on the way, and here's the proof..."

– and she calmly poured the remaining water over her hands, which she then shook, on the platform, to dry them.

"Now, my friend," she said, "I'm at your service."

Durtal, not without a few misgivings, somehow doubted it. The arrival at Val-des-Saints had been a noisy one. The villagers stared in amazement on their doorsteps at this thin little woman, dressed in black, who would gesticulate and stop to kiss their children, asking them their names and their ages, and then bless them, making the sign of the cross on their foreheads with her thumb.

Chapter II

"Well, Madame Bavoil, aren't you surprised to find yourself sitting here with me, two steps from a monastery?"

"But why should I be surprised, my friend? It's a long while since anything surprised me. When the dear Abbé Gévresin died, I said to God: Should I stay at Chartres, return to Paris, or rejoin my good friend Durtal who offers me a home? What seems best to you? Since you are the appointed steward of my poor soul's effects, direct them in your own fashion and guide me on my new path without too many hitches. However, if this is an act of your goodness my diligent Lord, I'd rather not be messed about by long delays, so if it pleases you act quickly."

"And here you are."

"Well, unless I'm mistaken, that's the answer I believe I heard; but that's beside the point. If I'm here, with you at Val-des-Saints it's to look after your household and be of service to you, so let's talk a bit about this place, the sort of life they lead here, the resources it has at its disposal, so as to organise our daily routine and feed ourselves."

"The village you've seen as you came out of the station; it comprises one street and a few lanes bordered by thatched cottages; it contains some two hundred dwellings, possesses a butcher's shop, a baker's, and a grocer's where you can also buy tobacco and haberdashery; such are its resources; food is available, but while it's not expensive, it's also wretched quality and you have to go to Dijon every week in order to get provisions. But in any case, Mother Vergognat, who to date had prepared my meals, will be able to inform you better than I about the choice and price of food; she's coming this evening, so you can question her at your leisure."

"The house isn't bad, as far as I can judge at first glance, and

35

the garden is spacious and planted with fine old trees," replied Mme. Bavoil after a pause, "so all is for the best; and what about your Benedictines?"

"They live over there; look out of the window, you can see the long row of casement windows of the monastery and the steeple of the church… you won't be long in getting to know them, because it's rare that any of them crosses the village without passing through here to shake my hand; they are pious men and their company is a great comfort."

"Are there many of them?"

"About fifty, including novices and lay brothers."

"So, my friend, it's a big abbey, this convent of Val-des-Saints!"

"Yes, it's one of the most important institutions that Solesmes has ever founded; it's the finest cloister in Burgundy."

"Is it of ancient origin?"

"Yes, there was once a priory on this site that was part of the illustrious abbey of Saint-Seine, located about five leagues from Dijon, whose restored buildings – or rather altered from top to bottom – have been transformed into hydropathic factories and warehouses for patients in need of a water cure. Saint-Seine, which was founded in 534 by the saint of that name, counted among its monks St Benedict of Aniane,[1] who reformed the Order of St Benedict in the ninth century; his priory at Val-des-Saints was flourishing at the time; it still existed up to the period of the Revolution, but it was dragging along in languishing piety and ultimately its life drained out in obscurity. It disappeared in all the turmoil. It was exhumed only thirty years ago. Dom Guéranger,[2] the abbot of Solesmes, to whom its ruins were given, rebuilt it and populated it with monks, and from the insignificant priory it was in its beginnings, it's become an influential abbey."

"And that friend of Abbé Plomb, the one who came to see us at Chartres, Dom… what was it…? Ah, I've no memory for names…"

"Dom Felletin."

"That's the one, is he here?"

"Yes, he's the novice master."

"I'd be happy to meet him."

Chapter II

"You'll see him, I told him you were coming."

"So, for company you have the monks; and aside from them, who else?"

"Aside from them? Well, the list is fairly short. In the village there's an old bachelor, very odd and somewhat gruff, but a good fellow, Monsieur Lampre. He lives in a rather fine house next to the monastery. He's always criticising the Benedictines, but he adores them, it's only his way of talking; when he says of a father that 'he's a pious dolt', you have to translate it: it means he's a monk whose ideas don't absolutely coincide with his; the main thing is to understand him."

"How do the monks get on with him?"

"They know him and are fully aware that no one is more devoted to them; he has proved it time and time again; first of all by gifting them the abbey itself, of which he was the owner, then by supplementing their income with considerable sums of money when they were going through a difficult period; the truth is that he dreams of an ideal perfection that cannot exist, and the human side that every monk inevitably has irritates him. Nonetheless, despite this shortcoming he's a helpful and pious Christian; he's very knowledgeable, moreover, about monastic usages and customs, and he possesses a specialist library of monographs on the monastic life, and an exceptionally fine collection of rare illuminated manuscripts.

"Aside from this layman, who is the only person it's a pleasure to visit, there's a lady oblate, Mademoiselle de Garambois, who is really the most charitable creature and the most indulgent of old maids. Beneath her exterior, this stout, somewhat elderly lady, conceals a soul as youthful and innocent as that of a little child; people laugh a bit at her in the village and in the abbey, on account of her mania for wearing clothes that match the liturgical colour of the day; she's a living *Ordo*,[3] a walking eccesiatical calendar; she's a regimental pennant; you know you're going to celebrate the feast of a martyr when she decorates her hat with red, or that of a confessor when she bears a white ribbon; unfortunately the number of ecclesiastical colours is limited and she laments it so often they tease her about it; but everyone is in accord when it comes to admiring her good nature and her indefatigable kindness.

"You'll meet her and it won't take long to discern her two ardent passions: fine cuisine, and the divine office; she is crazy about dainty dishes and liturgical pomp; and on these matters she could teach a thing or two to the most accomplished of chefs and the most learned of monks."

"So, my friend, she's no commonplace person, this lady oblate of yours…"

"And how fond she is of her Benedictines! In times past she had a vocation to be a nun, and she did her novitiate at the abbey of Saint Cecilia at Solesmes, but before she completed it she fell ill, and on her doctor's orders had to abandon it; she consoles herself now by living in the vicinity of a monastery; the wilted nun has bloomed again as an oblate."

"But to understand the liturgy like that she must be a scholar?"

"She knows Latin, she learned it during her novitiate at Solesmes, and I believe she has worked on it since; but outside treatises on plainchant and the Mass, nothing interests her; nevertheless, as I mentioned, she rejoices when it comes to tasty cuisine; so she's a convent *cordon bleu*, a Mother Blémeur of the stove;[4] she can just as easily recite recipes from cookery books as antiphons from the Psalter."

"Why doesn't she live at Solesmes where she began her novitiate?"

"Because, like me, she couldn't find a suitable house to rent in that town; added to which, she's the niece of Monsieur Lampre, the old character I told you about; he's her only living relative, and she came here to be near him and the monastery."

"And they live in the same house?"

"No, although they're fond of each other, if they lived together side by side they'd be at each other's throats; I leave you to imagine how she'd fight tooth and nail with him whenever he maligns her dear monks.

"With the exception of these two people, there's no one – and I'll say it again – worth meeting in this hole; the peasants

Chapter II

are greedy and devious; and as for the bloated aristocracy, those noblemen rotting away in the surrounding châteaux, they are undoubtedly, from an intellectual point of view, even more inferior than the rustics; you say hello to them when you meet them, but that's all."

"How do they get on with the monastery?"

"Badly; they abuse it for reasons which if they're not exactly worthy, are very human; in the first place the Benedictines run the parish here, in other words, the parish priest is one of the monks, the church of Val-des-Saints being both an abbey church and a parish church. Now a priest who is a monk cannot accept invitations from the gentry and frequent their drawing rooms, like an ordinary priest could do; so the squires have no minister of their own, over whom their wives can take control and influence to suit their own interests; that's grievance number one; then, among the local nobility here, there's a pompous old dotard, decked out in his heraldic garb, who likes to sing opera arias adapted for church use by some pious villain; on several occasions this trumped-up baron has tried to get permission – in May, the month of the Virgin Mary – to croon this codswallop in the church; the monks naturally rebuffed him, the music of these second-rate Gounods and Massenets not yet being, thank God, allowed in the cloisters. So his friends have taken up his cause and they'll never forgive the abbey for having prevented this aforesaid dotard from desecrating the walls of our sanctuary with the shrill sound of his cracked voice; that's grievance number two, and by no means the least."

"Well, they seem like a fine bunch, these nobles of yours…"

"They are the quintessence of imbecility, concentrated stupidity; we're in the provinces, Madame Bavoil…"

"And the peasants, are they also as ill-disposed towards the monastery?"

"They make their living from it; they receive its benefits and so consequently they hate it."

"But this is a land of scoundrels you've brought me to!"

"No," replied Durtal, laughing, "there are no scoundrels in

Val-des-Saints, but a lot of paragons of vanity and models of stupidity; when all is said and done that's perhaps worse, but you only have to imitate me, to refuse absolutely to get to know them, and you'll have peace."

"What's that ringing?" asked Madame Bavoil, who was listening to the prolonged chiming of a bell.

"They're the first strokes of vespers.[5] It must be ten minutes to four... a minute fast," said Durtal, looking at his watch.

"Are we going to vespers?"

"Certainly, in as much as these are for the Exaltation of the Cross[6] this evening."

"So, for my introduction, I'm going to see a fine service?"

"See? no; hear, yes. This feast day is a major double,[7] so doesn't entail the splendour that you can admire in a double of the first class, such as at Christmas, for example; but even if you don't witness a magnificent ceremony unfurling amid the candlelit maze of the choir, you will at least hear a most splendidly composed service, with its wonderful antiphons and its fiery hymns all dipped in blood."

They arrived, still talking, in front of the church.

"Oh, but it's old!" Madame Bavoil exclaimed, looking at the porch which looked like pumice stone and sprouted moss the colour of orpiment and green lacquer.

"Yes, the belfry and the porch date from the fifteenth century, but the rest of the church is modern. The interior has been restored as best as it could, but it's disfigured by terrible Stations of the Cross, and is lit by plain windows, except at the back; the church of Val-des-Saints is nothing but a vague memory of what it was in its earlier days; nevertheless, the apse, with its old choir stalls which came from another abbey, and its altar which, though modern, is well executed, is not too offensive, judge for yourself..."

They went in; the nave extended in front of them, vast, without pillars, and cut in quarters by a transept containing on one side a chapel to the Blessed Virgin, and on the other, a chapel to St Joseph; it was poorly lit, almost dark. At the back, two rows of pews stretched out to the right and left of the sanctuary, running from the communion table to the Gothic stone altar, which stood out against a wall painted, *trompe-l'oeil* fashion, to resemble a brown curtain.

Modern 'stained-glass' windows rose up at the top of the walls, their straight panes of glass, painted with figures, the tones of which were both garish and insipid. When the weather was not too overcast, one could make out our Lord and his mother, dressed in a ruched fabric of an acid redcurrant red and a crude Prussian blue; then there was a St Benignus of Dijon, wearing a pumpkin-coloured sugar-loaf mitre, and decked out in a sorrel green chasuble; there was also a St Bernard swathed in a white cloak the colour of rice water, a St Benedict, a St Odilon of Cluny, a St Scholastica and a St Gertrude dressed in habits the colour of dried black grapes.

All this had been stained and kiln-fired twenty years ago by some undistinguished Lavergnian.

These affronts to the eye did not disturb Madame Bavoil at all, and when she finished her inspection, she knelt down at a *prie-dieu*, took out a pair of spectacles with circular lenses from a huge case, and began to read a book stuffed with images of saints which she kissed.

The bells continued to peal for a time, then fell silent; a few minutes afterwards, four o'clock sounded and they began to chime again. As the last waves of sound died away, the measured tread of feet was heard. Madame Bavoil looked round; through a door at the back of the church the monks were coming in, two by two, followed by the abbot on his own, recognisable by the golden cross on his chest; ascending a couple of steps to the choir in front of the communion rail, they genuflected in pairs before the altar, then, rising again, acknowledged each other and went to their places, one to the left, on the side of the Gospel, the other to the right, on the side of the Epistle;[8] and then all, on their knees, made the sign of the cross on their foreheads and lips, and at a signal from the abbot who tapped his lectern, they all stood up and, bowing deeply, waited for a second tap to begin the service.

First, nones was chanted in simple psalmody, and when the

monks had finished, they remained standing, still bowing their heads in silence, until the abbot gave the signal to intone vespers.

The psalms were the same as those on Sundays, so frequent in the liturgy that Durtal obviously knew them by heart; the interest for him resided in the antiphons, in the short responsories, and the hymn; but that evening he was lost in thought, not about the service itself but, since the service was the very cause of his musings, about his surroundings; he recalled the story of the Exaltation of the Cross which he had read that morning, in a collection of medieval legends.

At first, it was a vague evocation of Asia, hazy, distorted, almost mad; then the vision grew clearer, honed in on that usurper of the sacred gallows, that astonishing Khosrow II,[9] who in the seventh century invaded Syria, stormed and looted Jerusalem, seized the high priest Zachiariah, and brought back in triumph to his kingdom in Persia the wood of the True Cross,[10] which St Helena had left in the very place where Christ had suffered.

Once back in his own kingdom, the incommensurate pride of this man exploded; he wanted to be worshipped like the Lord and calmly decreed that he was no more nor less than God the Father.

In order to devote himself wholly to this new role, he abdicated in favour of his son, and built a tower whose outer walls were covered in sheets of gold, and he shut himself inside on the ground floor, in a strange hall panelled in precious metals and incrusted with jewels; then like the Almighty, he wanted to have his own firmament, and he raised the ceiling up to a vertiginous height, illuminating it during the day by a cleverly manipulated sun, and at night by an artificial moon, around which twinkled the coloured fires of fake stars; but this was not enough; the unchanging sky, engineered by hundreds of slaves, bored him; he demanded the rain, showers and storms of real seasons, and he installed at the top of the tower hydraulic devices that would, at will, dispense the fine rain of a day that turns for the worst, the wild downpour of a thunderstorm, or the light raindrops of a summer evening; he also primed darts of lightning, while heavy chariots in the subterranean passages of the tower rolled over metallic slabs and shook the walls with the noise of their thunder.

So he believed himself to be the indisputable personification of God the Father, and at the bottom of this well encased in gold and studded with gems, and enclosed by the dome of a theatrical firmament, he sat permanently on his throne, to the right of which he planted the Cross of our Saviour, while to the left, on an imitation dunghill made of burnished silver filigree, he placed a rooster.

He intended these to represent the Son and the Holy Spirit.

And his former subjects paraded before this crowned and painted idol, immobile in his golden cloak, darting sparks from all its jewels that burned with the rays of light from fake stars, dazzling, ever burning, amid this inferno of gleaming walls and fabrics.

Between the Cross and the rooster, beneath the flaming mitre, one pictures in one's mind that wizened face, creased with wrinkles lining the forehead and cheeks under a plaster of make-up, the ringleted and braided beard, the hollow, vacuous eyes, the only things that seemed alive in this golden statue, venerated by the prayers that rose around it amid dizzying clouds of frankincense, prayers that invoked, in the name of Jesus, God the Father.

How long did this masquerade last? Fourteen years, according to legend; nevertheless, there came a time when the Emperor Heraclius managed to raise a huge army and set out in search of the Holy Cross. He engaged the usurper's troops near the Danube, defeated his son in single combat, and pressing on into Persia, encountered the old monarch in his tower.

Khosrow did not know that his son had been defeated, because everyone hated him and no one dared to tell him the news. He almost died with anger when he saw Emperor Heraclius enter, followed by his entourage, and sword in hand said to him:

"King, thou hast in spite of all done honour in thy fashion to the Cross of Christ; if thou therefore consent to confess that thou art but a man, and that thou art but the humble servant of the Most High, thy life shall be spared. I will simply carry away the Cross of Our Redeemer and let thee reign over thy people in peace. But if thou refuse these conditions, it will be the worse for thee, for I will slay thee forthwith."

As he listened, Khosrow's eyes burned as red as the eyes of an old wolf at night, and he stood up to curse his opponent and scornfully reject his offer. Then, with a stroke of his sword, the emperor decapitated the old man, whose head flew off and bounced on the paved floor, balanced for a moment on its neck, wobbled as if to say 'No' again, and finally toppled over on one side, and the light in his eyes was extinguished just as the golden mummy fell, streams of blood pouring from the gaping hole of the neck, as if through the uncorked bunghole of a wine barrel.

And Heraclius had the king buried, and destroyed his tower.

"*Gloria Patri, el Filio, et Spiritui Sancto.*"

All the monks standing in their places were bowing low, their foreheads almost touching the pews in front of them; they straightened up, responding: "*Sicut erat in principio,*" and sat down again, finishing with: "*Et in saecula saeculorum. Amen.*"

'It's ridiculous to get distracted like this,' thought Durtal. 'I would do better to follow my vespers than to go chasing after legends regarding this feast day that are, moreover, made up; the real story is much simpler:

'In 611, Khosrow, the king of Persia, subdued Jerusalem with the help of the Jews, who claimed they wanted to rebuild the Temple; he cut the throats of the Christians, took the high priest Zachariah prisoner, and carried off the wood of the True Cross. So then there was a Catholic crusade against this unbeliever.

'Emperor Heraclius lands in Cilicia, wins the battle of Issus, returns to Constantinople, and with the support of tribes from the Caucasus invades Trebizond where, to avenge the murder of the priests of Judea, he massacres the Zoroastrian magi; then, after having allied himself with the hordes of the Volga, he once more marches against the Persian army, defeating it at Nineveh, and withdrawing to Taurus. There, proposals for peace are presented to him by Sheroe, the king's son, who has just assassinated his father; the peace proposals are accepted; the priest Zachariah is freed, and the Cross and the Roman Eagles captured in Jerusalem by Khosrow are restored.

'Khosrow had therefore been murdered by his son, without

there being any question of a mechanical tower or a rooster.

'As for Heraclius, he resolved to bring back the symbol of salvation to the Holy Sepulchre; when he arrived in Jerusalem he hoisted the Cross on his shoulder, intending to begin the ascent of Golgotha; but when he reached the city gates leading to the hill, he found it impossible to take another step. Then the patriarch Zachariah pointed out to him that when Christ entered by that gate, he was not adorned in regal clothes, but simply dressed and mounted on a donkey, thus giving an example of humility to all his followers.

'The emperor immediately stripped off his purple robes, took off his sandals and dressed himself in the ragged clothes of a pauper, after which he easily climbed the hill of Calvary and replaced the Cross in the very spot from which Khosrow had taken it.

'This didn't prevent the brave Heraclius from coming to a bad end,' Durtal concluded, 'because he spread the heresy of the monothelites – which is to say those who, while acknowledging that Jesus had both a divine and a human nature, attributed a single action, a single will to these two distinct natures – and he died leaving a line of successors famous for their debauchery and their crimes.

'And now that's enough; let's return to the service.' It was easy for him this time to get back into it; the choir was singing the hymn by Fortunatus, the *Vexilla Regis*,[11] and the magnificent soaring of this sequence, the succession of impassioned verses, bearing aloft the holy spoils, gripped him to the marrow. He listened in ecstasy to those cries of victory: "The Royal Banner forward goes, The mystic Cross refulgent glows," and those war-like apostrophes, those shouts of joy: "O beautiful and radiant tree, adorned in regal majesty! How blest thine arms, beyond compare, Which Earth's eternal ransom bare, O Cross, all hail, sole hope abide!"

Then came the long antiphon of the *Magnificat*, repeating the acclamations and praises of the poet: "O Cross, more radiant than the stars, Sweet wood, sweet nails, bearing a weight that's sweeter still," and the *Magnificat* itself, chanted in a solemn tone, and the *Salve Regina*, reminding the human creature of the reality of sin, imploring, after these liturgical hurrahs, his forgiveness…

"They're very appealing, you know, your services," said Madame Bavoil as they left the church.

"Aren't they, it's something different from the cathedrals of Paris or Chartres; what's lacking in these Benedictine choral services is a boy's voice, but you can't have everything; I ought to be bored with these services having attended them for so long, but no, every day they seem new to me; I still listen with pleasure to those four Sunday psalms, which we're inundated with because they continually repeat them almost every feast day."

"Why does the liturgy attribute so much importance to these psalms? And, indeed, why do you have four instead of five, like us, because the last one's missing?"

"Yes, the Benedictine vespers leave out the last Roman psalm, but add a short lesson, which is generally a model of thoughtful and affecting melody; why? I don't know; no doubt because the monastic service has been kept intact since its origin, whereas the Roman service has been improved over the ages, and only stopped when it reached its definitive form, its highest point; as to the reasons which motivated the choice of the first four Sunday psalms in preference to the others, to print the words of the psalmist on so many feast days, they are explained in a more or less confusing manner by the manuals. For the opening psalm, *Dixit Dominus Domino meo*, this is understandable; our Lord cited it to prove his divinity to the Pharisees, so it's natural that this Messianic hymn should occupy a place of honour in the vespers. The third, *Beatus vir qui timet Dominum*, for its part, was mentioned by St Paul in his Epistle to the Corinthians to encourage them to give alms generously, this is another reason for its privileged position; less clear are the motives to be found for the other two; however, the second, *Confitebor tibi, Domine, in toto corde meo*, contains, in speaking of the manna Jehovah distributed to the Hebrews in the wilderness, an allusion to the paschal food; perhaps that's why it was set apart; finally the fourth psalm, *Laudate, pueri, Dominum*, is a beautiful hymn of praise which fittingly closes the series.

"It's equally true that vespers don't have that well-defined character of evening prayer, so particular in the admirable service of compline. It's quite possible that Dom Cabrol[12] is right when he states in his book *Antique Prayer* that the psalms of vespers, which are numbered consecutively in the Psalter, were chosen as they came, without regard to their meaning or purpose. These explanations don't seem to satisfy you…"

"Well, my friend, I don't know anything about it, but it seems to me, at least in my humble opinion, that you're looking for difficulties where there aren't any. Isn't it simpler than that? The first psalm represents our Lord, to whom it is more personally addressed; the *Beatus vir* applies to the righteous, to St Joseph, who is referred to thus throughout the office devoted to him; the *Laudate pueri*, which in its wording recalls the *Magnificat*, applies to the Blessed Virgin. As for the second psalm, the *Confitebor*, I wouldn't have guessed it, but since you say that it relates to the Blessed Sacrament of the altar, that's all the better; with these psalms I can specifically pray to Jesus in his own person, and under the Eucharistic versions to St Mary and St Joseph; I don't ask for anything more, and it doesn't worry me at all to know if this office is more or less well adapted to the needs of evening prayer. But to change the subject, here we are in the middle of the village. That rather ugly-looking shop sticking out at the end of the street, is that the butcher's where you buy your meat?"

"Yes, but I must warn you now that we eat the same things here as they do in the cloister. One day the butcher kills an ox, or let's be more precise, a cow; another day, a sheep, and another day, a calf; the greater part of these animals is naturally reserved for the monastery, which, not counting guests, has fifty mouths to feed; so we have to take what remains of the cow, the sheep and the calf served in the cloister; because you can well imagine that they won't slaughter an animal expressly for you, Monsieur Lampre or Mademoiselle de Garambois; so we all feed, monks and lay people, on the same fare, on the same day; this wouldn't matter so much, despite the lack of variety in these dishes, if the butcher didn't kill his beasts the night before, or even on the very morning he sells them; because, well, one has to chew the most indescribable things that are both rubbery and stringy at the same time."

"Up to a certain point, cooking can improve meat that is too fresh," said Madame Bavoil, "but in these instances it means one has to say goodbye to grilled chops or rare steaks; indeed, one has to stew for hours in a casserole those pieces of… what did you call the leg of lamb you hated so much at Chartres?"

"Tough and leathery, Madame Bavoil; those are the inelegant synonyms for intractable meat."

Madame Bavoil smiled, and then slapped her forehead.

"Come now," she said, "if Mlle de Garambois is such a gourmet she wouldn't use that leathery meat you're talking about. So what does she do?"

"Oh, she and her maid are always going into Dijon to bring back provisions."

"Well, we can do the same as them if need be; how long does it take to get there by train?"

"A good half-hour, but the train times are inconvenient. The timetable is this: 6.30 and 10 o'clock in the morning; and 2 o'clock in the afternoon. Coming back, 6 and 11 o'clock in the morning, 3 and 6 o'clock in the evening, and that's all."

"Fine, and you, do you go to Dijon often?"

"Sometimes. Dijon is a charming city, very cordial and jolly; there's a museum with some Flemish primitives, an admirable sculpture, *The Well of Moses*, some quaint side streets and churches that I like; and it also possesses an excellent Black Virgin."

"Ah," exclaimed Madame Bavoil, coming to a halt, "so it has a Black Virgin? I hesitated a bit, I have to admit, about leaving Chartres because of Our Lady of the Cave and Our Lady of the Pillar…[13] so, I'm going to find them here; but it's not a modern Madonna is it?"

"Rest assured, Our Lady of Provisions, or of Good Hope, dates from the twelfth century, if I'm not mistaken. In 1513 she saved the city of Dijon, which Louis II de la Trémoille,[14] at the head of a small number of troops, was defending against the assault and pillage of the Swiss. In memory of this event a procession was held every year, on 12th September, in her honour; this lasted until the middle of the eighteenth century, then stopped, I don't know why; what is certain at any rate is that Our Lady of Good Hope is held in great esteem in Burgundy; if her detailed history interests you, I'll lend you a book that recounts her miracles, it's a rather stodgy volume by a certain Abbé Gaudrillet,[15] who calls himself part of the 'society of priests' in the parish of Our Lady of Dijon."

As they chatted, they arrived at the house. Mother Vergognat was waiting for them. Durtal introduced the two women to each other, inwardly amused by the contrast between them. Madame Bavoil had hardly changed; her hair had however become thinner, and those hairs that hadn't deserted her had become whiter; her face was still bony and spotted with freckles; her profile had become more angular with age, but her dark eyes hadn't changed, inquisitive and calm at the same time; she still had something of the peasant and the church candle seller about her, but she still also had that indefinable look when her enraptured soul, lost in prayer, caught fire.

The other had turned out to be verbose, red-faced and bumptious; she had pig-like eyes, and grey and white bristles sprouted beneath her coarse nose; her mouth, crenellated with a row of rust-yellow teeth, could laugh, but when closed it was thin and pinched; she was a mixture of a bibulous weaver and a crafty rustic; you could plumb the depths of her soul in a mere second.

Madame Bavoil examined her with her black eyes, then, with a sigh that said much, she politely told her that she intended to maintain friendly relations with her, and that she reckoned on employing her often for some of the tougher housework; and with this assurance, Madame Vergognat's scowling face relaxed, but she nevertheless felt bound to appear more stupid than she really was, so as not to compromise herself in her replies.

"Now, let's see," insisted Madame Bavoil, "are you telling me that at Madame Catherine's here, they sell needles and thread, and all kinds of haberdashery?"

"Well, that depends, my good lady… there's thread and there's thread; Madame Catherine is most obliging, as to that, you can ask around, everyone says so."

Madame Bavoil searched in vain to unravel the meaning of this reply. Unable to do so, she asked another question, relating to the shape of the bread sold in the village. Mother Vergognat didn't seem to grasp the meaning of the words, and she hesitantly stammered out: "I really don't know what to tell you."

"I'm just asking you a simple question," continued Madame Bavoil. "Is the bread your baker makes round or split, is it a loaf or a roll? Why, there must be some left in the kitchen, bring it to me so that I can look at it."

The peasant brought back a crust.

"That's a split loaf, that's all I wanted to know."

"Maybe it is," said Mother Vergognat.

"Oh my," exclaimed Madame Bavoil after she had gone, "are they all like this in Val-des-Saints?"

"No, the others are worse; she's the best; you can see from this example how easy it is to extract a 'yes' or 'no' from these people."

"Really, my friend, the confessor must have a fine time with this sort of parishioner; how they must try to deceive him and beat about the bush!"

"They don't beat about anything at all given that they never go to confession."

"What? In this monastic region, are the inhabitants non-practising…?"

"A phrase you'll often hear spoken here is 'I'm a good Republican, that's why I don't go to Mass'; as for the morals of the peasantry, they are so despicable it's better not to talk about them. They've been corrupted by the town's political agents, rotten to the bone."

"Lord!" exclaimed Madame Bavoil, clasping her hands, "what are we coming to? Now here I am, compelled to live among the wicked companions of the Prodigal Son, because if what my friend is saying is correct, that's what these people are!"

"You're part of the monastery now, so I'm not going to wash your hands[1] any more," said the abbot laughing to Durtal and Monsieur Lampre. "Go straight through to your places."

And the abbot stood aside to let them pass and stopped on the threshold of the refectory.

Next to him were two monks; one was holding an old earthenware ewer and bowl, and the other, a towel. A visiting priest came forward, the abbot took the ewer, and as a sign of welcome, poured a few drops of water on his fingers, then the guestmaster gestured to the clergyman to follow him, and placed him next to Durtal.

The refectory was an immense room with a beamed ceiling, supported on corbels that were curiously carved with marmosets and flowers. It belonged, like the Chapter Hall, the oratory, and the reception room for guests, to the monastery's original buildings, which dated back to the fifteenth century. These were all that remained, alongside a great winding staircase and the old cellars, of the original abbey; the other parts of the building had either been constructed in the seventeenth century, or more recently.

Beneath the white walls of the refectory, panelled halfway up with pine, ran long benches and tables, separated by enough space to pass between them, which were fixed to a slightly raised floor, like wooden sidewalks on either side of a street whose surface was paved its whole width with red tiles. It was illuminated by six large windows with lozenge-shaped panes of frosted glass.

At the back of the room stood the abbot's table; it was similar to the others, but the panelling on the wall behind was topped by cone-like points and surmounted by a cross. This table was flanked by two others, one on the right for the prior, and one on the left for the sub-prior, who like the abbot ate their meals alone.

Facing them, at the other end of the room next to the door, was a lectern near the wall, occupied that day by a novice, who was preparing to read aloud during the meal.

Everyone was standing.

"*Benedicite*," said the abbot.

"*Benedicite*," repeated the two lines of monks.

"*Oculi omnium.*"

"*In te sperant, Domine, et tu das escam illorum in tempore opportuno. Aperis, tu, manum tuam et imples omne animal benedictione.*"

And the *Gloria* of the doxology bowed all the heads like a puff of wind. They rose up again at the *Kyrie Eleison*, and bowed again during the *Pater*, recited *sotto voce*, only to rise again when it was over.

In a voice that swelled in volume towards the end, the abbot continued:

"*Oremus. Benedic, Domine, nos et haec tua dona quae de tua largitate sumus sumpturi. Per Christum, etc.*"

"*Amen.*"

And in the silence, the fresh voice of the novice at the lectern chanted in a solemn but also joyous tone: "*Jube, Domine, benedicere.*"

And the abbot responded:

"*Mensae caelestis participes faciat nos Rex aeternae gloriae.*"

"*Amen*," said all the monks in unison, and they took and unfolded their serviettes, in which were rolled a knife, a fork and a spoon.

The table for guests was in the centre of the room, near that of the abbot, which faced it and looked down on it, because unlike his, which was on the raised wooden platform, it was on the floor. It was separated by a large empty space from that of the lay brothers, which was also on the platform, but at the other end of the room, near the lectern.

Two fathers in blue aprons served the monks and the lay brothers. The guestmaster looked after the guests.

Chapter III

The guests' dinner – because in a monastery lunch is called dinner, and dinner, supper – consisted of meat broth thickened with semolina, boiled beef, mutton with haricot beans, a salad with a tart vinegar dressing, full-cream milk that was drunk with a soupspoon, and some cheese.

That of the monks was the same – minus the mutton and the full-cream milk. Some drank water with a little red wine, and others just water; silence was the rule; everyone ate concentrating on what was on their plate.

And invariably, after having chanted at dinner a passage from the Bible – or, at supper, some articles from the Rules of the Order – the weekly-appointed reader would launch into some religious or semi-secular work, preceded by this announcement: 'Here follows the story of so-and-so, from chapter such-and-such…'

He read in a monotonous tone, deliberately – something imposed by tradition, no doubt to prevent his listeners from deriving pleasure from it or himself from showing off – and it was like a drizzle of grey words. One paid little attention to it at first, but when the first cravings for food were satisfied, heads were lifted, chairs would lean back against the wall, and if the story was interesting, one would listen.

It was, unfortunately, extremely tedious. One had to swallow insipid slices of history, or, what was worse, fragments from the lives of the saints, written in that oleaginous style dear to Catholics; and then occasionally a fleeting smile would cross the faces of the monks on hearing for the thousandth time the same tired expressions in these oft-repeated tales.

Those who had finished their meal would wipe their knives and their cutlery, and after having washed them wrap them up again in their napkins. The abbot looked about to see that everyone had eaten his portion of cheese, and then, with a smart rap with his little gavel on the table, he would stop the reading.

The interrupted lector would change his tone, and in a modulated and plaintive voice launch into the words:

"*Tu autem, Domine, miserere nobis.*"

And everyone, with much shuffling of feet, would stand up

and reply in the same tone: "*Deo gratias.*"

The abbot, in a voice that was somewhat tremulous, but which became more assured and louder towards the end of the prayer, would begin:

"*Confiteantur tibi, Domine, omnia opera tua.*"

"*Et sancti tui benedicant tibi,*" came the response.

As with the *Benedicite*, all heads would bow at the *Gloria*, and the abbot would pronounce the prayer:

"*Agimus tibi gratias, omnipotens Deus, pro universis beneficiis tuis, qui vivis et regnas in saecula saeculorum.*"

"*Amen.*"

Then they would turn around, and in single file leave the refectory, the monks first and the abbot last; they passed through the cloister, reciting the *Miserere*, until they reached the chapel, where the office of grace would end.

After leaving the church, the abbot, as was customary, invited his guests for coffee.

The room intended for this kind of reception was situated at the foot of the staircase leading to the two floors of cells, in a short corridor connected to the vaulted arcade of the cloister via a small door.

It was a solidly built room with enormous walls so thick that in the embrasures of its two windows looking out onto the garden you could have placed a bed. These walls, whitewashed and arrayed with photographs representing views of the old parts of the abbey, were adorned with a fireplace, on the painted plaster chimney-breast of which hung a crucifix, the same colour as the tinfoil that covers a bar of chocolate.

The furniture consisted of rush-bottom chairs and a huge white wooden table, covered with a striped oilcloth.

Around this table were gathered Dom Bernard, the abbot, Dom de Fonneuve, the prior, Dom Felletin, the novice master, Dom Badole, the guestmaster, a visiting priest, Monsieur Lampre and Durtal, invited in honour of the feast of St Placidus.

Dom Badole was looking around in search of a sugar bowl that was right in front of him. He was short, of compact stature, and his ivory-coloured face, lined with a thousand wrinkles could – if

CHAPTER III

it had been topped by a mob cap – have been mistaken for that of some ultra-devout old maid, whose benign fixed smile he also had. His habit of keeping his arms folded in an X across his chest when he greeted you, his affected politeness and his obsequious manner were embarrassing; and what was curious was that this man, so outwardly friendly to others, was so severe as regards himself. When his day of talking and bowing was over, he was unsparing in his self-discipline, chastising himself for being unable to keep up his inner life amid this existence that was necessarily frittered away by the coming and going of guests; he couldn't bring himself to reconcile his duties as host with his own spiritual contemplation as a monk, and at times one wondered, looking into his eyes, with that cold, pale blue, almost cruel look like those of a Siamese cat, if he would not also have willingly flagellated those visitors who unwittingly caused him so much remorse.

As a monk he was exemplary, and as a priest very pious, but slow of comprehension and of limited intelligence. After trying him in various other jobs which he'd shown himself incapable of carrying out, he'd been delegated to the easy task of taking care of the guests. He acquitted himself pretty well when there were no more than two guests, but more than that and he would panic and ask for help.

The prior offered a singular contrast to him. Dom de Fonneuve carried his seventy years lightly and the lucidity and vigour of his mind, his knowledge, celebrated in the world of historians, made him the abbey's most eminent personality. In summer, people came from all over the world to consult him; texts were submitted to him which he deciphered effortlessly. He could correct a copyist's blunders, detect interpolations, and re-establish the original text in the blink of an eye. Moreover, he was like an almanac, he knew the monastery library volume by volume, and in a second could track down information that it would have taken anyone else a week to discover.

At the present day, he remained one of the last survivors of that great generation of monks trained by Dom Guéranger; along with Dom Pitra[2] he had travelled to all the libraries in Europe, searched through all the archives.

But what was even better than his incomparable scholarship, was his ardent kindness; he was a lover of souls; he threw himself on them, embraced them passionately, cried for joy at the notion that he'd been able to save one. They would call him, jokingly but not unjustly, the 'Grandmother' of the cloister, the one to whom you would go and speak about troubles and who would console you. He'd lived in several monasteries, and had also been the victim of many intrigues, but he had nevertheless preserved his childlike spirit, never believing evil of anyone, sincerely loving his brothers, as the Rule requires, always ready to embrace, without even a shadow of resentment, any monk who might have done him an injury. From the depth of his being there welled up a flood of affection that carried all before it, a need to believe only good about people, a sensibility such that a simple affectionate expression would move him to tears.

With his big, round head, his eyes that sparkled in his wrinkled face, he gave the impression of sturdiness with a touch of mischief, but a gentle mischief that loved to laugh, which was content not to go too far when having fun. His only flaw was his short temper. It would rise…and rise, like milk in a saucepan, whenever he noticed that the monks were not observing the rules. He would reprimand them furiously, banging his fist on the table; then, when the culprit had gone, he would run after him, embrace him, and beg him to forgive his vehemence; and his tenderness, his desire to make amends for what, in his fatherly kindness, he believed to be his act of humiliation, was such that the delinquent could subsequently neglect his observances with impunity. He was so fearful of losing his temper again and wounding the feelings of his brother, that he would fall silent for a while and bite his tongue.

The abbot was calmer, his benevolence a little more even-handed. He closed his eyes to everyone's foibles and would watch his prior play the role of whipper-in-chief, knowing full well that his reprimands were but a prelude to being spoiled; so he would smile on both the one and the other.

At nearly eighty years old, he limited himself to setting an example. He would come down to church, freshly shaven, half an hour before anyone else, and he would meditate and pray until matins; and the younger monks, who had a little difficulty in getting out of bed during the winter at four o'clock in the morning, venerated this tall, emaciated old man, a little stooped, who, with his nose and his spectacles, resembled the cardinal archbishop of Paris, and they admired his resolution to accept none of the comforts or dispensations that would have been amply justified by his age and the infirmities from which he was suffering.

There was, moreover, a good deal of finesse beneath the good nature of this excellent man, so eager never to get angry. He knew too well of the faults of his children and sometimes he would describe them in an amusing way.

"Father Titourne," he would say of a monk just out of his novitiate, who was always in a daze and always late for services, "Father Titourne has his head in the clouds, what do you expect me to do about it?"

"The monastery is governed too leniently," growled the severe Monsieur Lampre.

"But you must admit that this leniency proves how virtuous the monks are," replied Durtal, "because after all, in the outside world any institution governed in such an easy-going way would collapse, and here, however, everything works."

Monsieur Lampre was obliged to admit it, but he continued to grumble nonetheless. This small man of seventy, paunchy, with a flushed face, a wild beard and hair that was completely white, was grumpy albeit also obliging and generous. He was also very pious, though he wasn't averse to ribald jokes and liked to laugh. Among all these men who had spread out willy-nilly from different regions, he was the only Burgundian within the monastery enclosure.

"Now, let's see," said the guestmaster who came in holding a coffee pot, "the stove had gone out and I didn't want to offer you cold coffee so that made me a little late, please excuse me and help yourselves to sugar."

He filled the tiny cups, and poured a few drops of white

cognac into liqueur-glasses the size of a thimble.

"Well," said Dom de Fonneuve to Durtal, "were you satisfied with the ceremony this morning?"

"Yes, father, the novices acquitted themselves wonderfully."

"I must tell them, because that will make them happy!" exclaimed the good prior.

The feast of St Placidus was in fact an important event in Benedictine monasteries; this saint was the patron of novices, and on this day they would replace the fathers, who stepped aside for them. They would perform the service, intone the antiphons, sing the choral music, and were, in short, the masters of the choir.

"Nevertheless, my dear Durtal," said Monsieur Lampre, "you must admit that, if the cantor hadn't come to their aid during the *Gloria* and the *Gradual* they would never have got through it."

"But you must also admit," replied Durtal, "that the plainsong in this Mass is difficult to sing, and what's worse it's irritatingly pretentious and ugly.

"Is there anything in art less musical and more incoherent than this so-called deluxe version of the *Gloria,* a floor to ceiling *Gloria*, a Russian switchback railway of voices with its ups and downs? Added to which, the dancing *Credo*, sung on great feast days, is far inferior to the ordinary *Credo*. It's really only the second phrase of the *Gradual* and the *Alleluia* that are any good in this service.

"How different to those honest, frugal Masses, to that truly celestial plainchant that's sung on lesser feast days. Indeed, the more I hear it, the more I'm convinced that Gregorian music is not at all something that's suited to grand ceremony. The *Kyrie Eleisons* of the normal Mass, so tender, so plaintive, so gentle, become convoluted as soon as they're dressed up for bigger, more important feast days; you could say that they've grafted trills[3] and grace notes running up and down the stave onto pure Gothic melodies.

"Indeed, isn't it true that the solemn Masses are, musically speaking, vastly inferior to the familiar Masses used on the feast days of lesser saints; and recall, too, those Saturdays not devoted to any particular saint, when the simple Mass of the Blessed Virgin is celebrated. The *Kyrie*, No. 7, brief, plaintive, sounding a bit like a death knell, and the *Gloria*, so calm in its profound joyousness, so deliberate in the certitude of its praise; the *Agnus Dei*, evoking the idea of a child's prayer, with its simple melody which almost coaxes the Lord in an embrace; all that is admirable in its sobriety and candour; far above those complicated airs, those cantilenas that have been distorted in order to stretch them out, and which we have to endure under the pretext of a superior rite, of a more eminent hierarchy of saints!"

"The fact is," said Dom de Fonneuve, "that plainchant was made to be sung by the people; it therefore has to be easy to learn and remember, with no useless vocal ornaments or difficult combinations, not to mention pleasurable; and your observation is correct, they made it ugly by trying to expand it and dress it up in courtly regalia. What's more this is so true that the young men and young girls of the village, who have been instructed by Father Ramondoux, sing very well at High Mass on Sundays, when it's a question of a simple double, but they stumble if the office is of a higher grade, a double of the first class for instance."

"Ah," Durtal exclaimed, who was recalling certain offices, "the second phrase of the *Gradual*, which is generally the choicest morsel of a Mass, certain jubilant *Alleluias* that are wholly divine, and some entire Masses, from the *Introit* to the *Ite, missa est*, those for the Blessed Sacrament, those for the Blessed Virgin, that for an abbot, or the *Dilexisti* from the Virgins' liturgy – what sovereign finds, what radiant marvels!

"There, the ornamentation is perfect; to my mind the 'Common of Saints'[4] can be compared pretty well to a series of boxes in which jewellery is arranged; sometimes on red velvet for the martyrs, sometimes on white velvet for the saints who aren't designated under this title; each jewel case contains a collection of pieces, *Introit, Kyrie, Gloria, Gradual, Alleluia, Offertory, Sanctus* and *Communion*, a musical whole that corresponds to a complete jewelley box, earrings, necklaces, bracelets and rings, the stones and settings of which match and harmonise in tone."

"In short, mediocrity is the exception, and the admirable dominates," said the abbot. "You can cite an execrable *Gloria*, or a few hymns whose melodies are muddled or dull, but what is that when set beside the superb, imposing mass of our offices?"

"You're right, my most reverend father, our criticisms can only apply to a limited number of pieces, and, I would add, to those that are the least ancient or most reworked, because it seems that the simpler Gregorian chant is, the older and more intact it is. The only misfortune is that, on major feast days when one would be happy to see music equal in beauty to the pomp and ceremony of the service, you're condemned to hear precisely nothing but the quintessence of bad singing."

"It will be no less to the glory of Dom Pothier and the school of Solesmes to have resuscitated these ancient cantilenas which are the true music of the Church, the only music in short, because all the great musicians, from Palestrina down to the masters of our own day, have never succeeded, when they've tried to translate liturgical prose, in equalling the excellence of certain of our *Kyries*, our *Paters* in the vespers, or even our *Credos*. And I'm not even going to mention the *Te Deum*, and the lessons and gospels of Holy Week," enthused Dom de Fonneuve.

"The first question to ask," Monsieur Lampre added, "is whether Palestrina's music, which has been dinned into our ears ever since the fashionable success of the St Gervais choir, is church music at all. And personally, I doubt it. That system of overlapping voices which gallop along, one after the other, till they catch up in a dead heat at the end smacks too much of the art of steeplechase; it's music fit for the paddock and the weighing enclosure, not for the house of Christ; when all is said and done it has no relation in any shape or form with a cry from the soul, or with a prayer."

"These excesses of counterpoint and the fugal form say nothing to me either," replied Dom de Fonneuve, "that art smacks of the theatre and the concert hall; it's too individual and vain. So how can this music in a state of sin really be of interest to the faithful or the priest?"

"It panders to the anti-liturgical taste of both," said Durtal, laughing.

"To go back to our novices," resumed Dom Felletin, who

thought it best after this last remark to change the conversation – which in any case the visiting priest, who was discussing the winemaking crisis with the guestmaster, didn't hear – "you have to take into account that, due to the lack of time, they only had two rehearsals, and admit that apart from the failed Gloria, they pulled it off admirably."

"Yes, father, and how wonderful and charming Brother Blanche looked in his heavy cope and with his precentor's baton…"

The abbot smiled.

"He's a good boy, isn't he? And so are the others; to have such youths as those in an abbey is a blessing." And he listed his charges: "Brother Blanche is as pious as an angel; he loves archaeology and is crazy about the liturgy, and what's more he's endowed with a very beautiful voice; we will direct his studies in this direction and he will truly do credit to our monastery; Brother Gèdre is equally faithful to God and works away valiantly at his Greek; if we could find in him the makings of a good Hellenist that would be perfect, because that's what we lack. Brother Sourche is the most intelligent, the most able of them all, but he has a troubled mind and leans towards rationalism, but in the atmosphere of the cloister this will pass. Brother Marigot and Brother Vénérand, by contrast, are not so quick; they struggle with theology and make little progress, but they're very submissive and very obedient; later on they'll be given various household chores that require neither intellectual effort nor any special aptitude; as for the novices who were already priests when they entered, they're excellent and we can only praise them."

"You're forgetting, my most reverend father, Brother de Chambéon," said Dom Felletin.

"A saintly man! And what a proof of the mysterious workings of a late vocation," added the abbot after a pause.

"Monsieur de Chambéon withdrew from the world where he'd occupied a distinguished position in order to be admitted, at the age of fifty-five, into our novitiate. He became a child again and lived with lads between seventeen and twenty, and he set an example. He's the 'waker-upper', the brother who's up first in the morning to ring the bell and wake the others; he polishes the stairs and trims the lamps; he still does all the more menial tasks. And he does it so simply, almost apologising for monopolising these unpleasant tasks: 'I don't need as much sleep at my age, and I'm more used to housework than these young fellows.' In short, he always invents excellent reasons for imposing on himself the most humiliating of chores."

"It's profoundly edifying to me," said the prior in his turn, "when I see him, with his grey hair, laughing and joking with our young novices."

"By the way," said the guestmaster, who had finished bemoaning the drop in sales of wine with the visiting priest, "what do the newspapers say? Are they still talking about choking us in the trap of some new law?"

"Indeed they do, father," replied Monsieur Lampre. "They're talking about it more and more; the Masonic press is turning the screw and a diabolical persecution is approaching."

"Bah!" exclaimed Dom de Fonneuve with great assurance, "they wouldn't dare; parliament would never vote for such a law; to interfere with the religious Orders is a bigger mouthful than they could swallow. If you ask me, they're just entertaining the idle reader with threats that won't come to anything."

"That remains to be seen," replied Durtal, "note how the attack on the Church has been pursued for many years now, with a methodical determination that nothing can stop. The sphere of freedom left to Catholics is getting smaller; the Dreyfus Affair[5] has advanced the cause of Freemasonry and Socialism by twenty years; in short, it was nothing but a pretext to jump down the throat of the Church; the Jews and Protestants are all up in arms; their newspapers are already sounding the monk's death knell; do you think they'll stop there? And then there's that sectarian who, in order to spur on the zeal of the Masonic Lodges, curses God like a demon…"

"The Right Honorable Monsieur Brisson…"[6] said Monsieur Lampre.

"What miserable deeds," said Dom de Fonneuve slowly, "what miserable deeds this man must have committed in his pitiful existence to hate our Lord like this!"

"No matter," concluded the abbot, "I agree with the prior, the storm is not ready to break yet; moreover, our prayers will avert it. In the meantime, I think we can sleep safely in our beds."

The cups and the liqueur glasses had long been empty. The abbot, getting up from the table, gave the signal to leave, and he went back to his cell, as did the prior; the guestmaster accompanied the visiting priest, while Monsieur Lampre and Durtal followed Dom Felletin, who led them for a walk in the garden.

The monks' recreation break, prolonged on account of the feast day, hadn't ended. The fathers strolled in two lines, walking alternately down an avenue of hornbeam trees, first one way, then the other; and the novices were doing likewise at the other end of the garden, down another avenue.

The garden, forming a sort of quadrangle, was situated behind the abbey, and extended well into the countryside beyond. Coming out of the cloister, on the same level, you passed several square plots of land where beans and cabbages alternated with flowers, and these squares, planted at their four corners with spindle-shaped pear trees, were cut in two by small paths bordered by boxwood which then led to large avenues of trees, at the end of which meadows and orchards could be seen, flanked in the far distance by a hedge of poplars and behind which stood the boundary wall.

The view was a little too rectilinear, but the vegetation was vigorous, the meadows were fresh and green, and everywhere vines climbed in nonchalant profusion over the walls, the corners of which were covered in emerald green moss and sulphur-coloured lichen.

The avenue assigned to the novices was on the right; formed simply by a straggly cradle of vines, it ended in a grotto, topped by a mediocre statue of St Joseph. This grotto was divided into two compartments separated by a grill. Ravens were kept in one, in memory of St Benedict, who liked to give food to one that had become his pet; in the other were doves, in honour of St Scholastica, whose soul had flown to heaven in that form.

It was an afternoon of reds and blues, one of those days when the smile of an old springtime is reborn on the barely furrowed lips of a youthful autumn. The veil of the heavens was suddenly rent asunder, and through a screen of vine leaves the ground was covered with large drops of light and shade. It was as if one was walking over a piece of black lace lying on a floor of pale pebbles. The novices were sheltering from the sun, some by lifting up their hoods, others by pulling the back part of their scapulars over their heads. They were laughing with Father Emonot, the under-master, or the father preceptor as he was called.

Formerly curate at a church in Lyons, Father Emonot was a small, nervous man, with a bald head seated well back on his neck, a bilious complexion, and eyes that darted here and there, so you could never fix on them directly underneath his spectacles.

The evening service, which the novices were again to conduct, was naturally the subject of conversation.

"What can you do," sighed Blanche, the youthful novice, "I'm scared… when you have to intone the antiphon I get confused… I'm only good in the choir; besides, as you know, when you hear your own voice, alone, in the silence of the church, it immediately gives you the shivers."

"Don't be so modest, little brother," said Durtal, surrounded by novices, "you sang very well."

The youth blushed with pleasure.

"All the same," he continued, looking down, "I really felt it inside, my throat felt woolly, I was suffocating. Oh, and that cope, when you're not used to it, it weighs on your shoulders and arms. You feel strange, very awkward inside it."

"Like a bored recruit standing in his sentry box," blurted out Brother Aymé.

"You always find comparisons that recall the barracks, and your expressions have nothing monastic about them," said the father preceptor to this brother, whose working-class Parisian appearance stood out a little in the group.

He was only a postulant, and there was a chance he would leave before he started his probation period. He was intelligent and pious, but after his year of military service in the army he'd come back with a somewhat knowing demeanour, and a mania for imitating military music, which infuriated such a scrupulous and straight-laced man as Father Emonot.

Indeed, he would already have got rid of him if Dom Felletin hadn't pleaded the culprit's cause in the Chapter. "Come now," he'd said, "let's not take things so seriously; Brother Aymé will mend his ways in time; the environment here will have its effect, so let's wait and see."

The bell for the end of the recreation period sounded. The novices fell silent, and led by the preceptor returned to the abbey. Dom Felletin stayed with Monsieur Lampre and Durtal, and took them to the meadow.

"Those two will never get along with each other," exlaimed Monsieur Lampre.

"What do you expect," replied Dom Felletin, "Dom Emonot can't abide frivolity, and yet there has to be some relaxation for youthful spirits after the strain of such prayer; that this postulant has a bad attitude is undeniable, but it's improving; the most annoying thing is his habit of imitating the tuba with his cheeks, and of saying the first thing that comes into his head and laughing. His jokes are, I'll admit, innocent enough, but that doesn't alter the fact that, only the other day, hearing one made the father preceptor red in the face with anger, and he complained to the abbot, who fortunately just smiled.

"— 'What tomfoolery has he committed now?'

"— 'Well, I'd just been lecturing them on chapter thirty-three of the Rules, which states that no one should be so bold as to deem anything as belonging to himself, or even speak of it as such; it explains the way of speaking used by the monks, who shouldn't say 'my book', 'my scapular', 'my fork', but 'our book', 'our scapular', 'our fork'. It goes without saying that this impersonal way of designating things only applies to utensils intended for our use. But no sooner was the lecture over, Brother Aymé at once trod on little Blanche's foot, and apologised with these words: 'I believe, my brother, that I stepped on our foot'.

"Father Emonot, who overheard this, saw this joke as a lack of deference, I ask you!"

"It's a somewhat feeble joke, but it's not enough to hang a cat for," said Durtal.

"But why," exclaimed Monsieur Lampre, "why the devil do you have such a narrow-minded man as a novice master?"

Dom Felletin laughed.

"We complement each other; Father Emonot has what I lack as a director of a noviate. He's disciplined, observant, and always on the alert; and these qualities are indispensible in an environment which is necessarily two groups: that of novices of a certain age who are already priests, and the youngsters, the babies, who aren't. It's a cause of friction; the former thinking themselves superior to the others, and the others quoting the Rules and rejecting any such pretention. Now, the father preceptor is very skilful at preventing these petty discords from arising. There haven't been any since he came here. He treats everyone as equal, but with such fine tact that no one complains. Moreover, you, my dear Durtal, in your capacity as a novice oblate, have the run of the novices' quarters, and you must admit that the corridors are well polished, there's not a speck of dust, and all the cells are clean and tidy. Father Emonot keeps it well aired and clean everywhere; he makes the novices do manual work, which is essential for their health and was prescribed by our founder, whereas before he came, work was limited to making them clean the fathers' shoes on Saturdays. In short, he has made all his pupils conform to a discipline that is excellent for body and soul alike."

"He's a drill-sergeant…" Monsieur Lampre grumbled.

"Well, they're necessary. As for me, I'm getting old, and if I'm still good for lectures and as a spiritual director, I'm absolutely incapable of looking after the practical side. It would all be laxity, dirt and disorder if I wasn't seconded by this preceptor, who may be scrupulous and narrow-minded, but who is nonetheless, when it comes to it, a very holy monk."

"In short," said Durtal laughing, "if they didn't have him to scold them, your pupils would be too happy; the cloister would then be an Eden!"

A bell rang. "That's the first call for vespers, goodbye," said

Dom Felletin as he withdrew.

After the service, once they were outside the church, Monsieur Lampre walked part of the way with Durtal, and resumed the conversation where the father had left off.

"Believe me," he said, "Dom Felletin will, in his turn, be in big trouble if he persists in wanting to keep that precentor. I know his type inside out, this Emonot; he's a model of religiosity, a holy man, I'll admit. I know things about him that you would describe as admirable. He'll go to any lengths to save his disciples from temptation; when he makes them too miserable during the day, he goes and prays outside their door at night; but despite all his virtues he, like the guestmaster, is consumed with scruples and the others suffer for it; what's worse in my opinion, is that his conception of Benedictine life is frightening for the future of the Order. In his eyes, a vocation is summed up by passive obedience..."

"But what of it?" exclaimed Durtal.

"Allow me to finish; it's summed up above all in the attempt to emphasise the solemnity of the choir. Those of his novices who fulfil, to the satisfaction of Dom d'Auberoche the ceremonial director, the office of candle-bearer, who know how to carry a candle upright, between fingers that are sufficiently spread apart to reveal the sham turquoises and imitation gems that adorn it, those are the ones that possess a vocation for the Benedictines!

"He dreams of producing others as futile as himself; he advocates the investiture of men you wouldn't want to see in the worst seminary; his recruiting methods are beneath contempt; he admits students who have been refused by all other institutions, individuals who want to become monks because they're unfit for anything else in life; and yet these he marks out for the priesthood, as long as they comply with all his idiosyncrasies. There's no point Dom Felletin defending him, he's managed to impose this type of novice on the abbot, who imagines that the prosperity of a monastery lies in an ever-increasing number of postulants.

"It'll be a fine thing for the intellectual level of the Benedictines in a few years' time, if this carries on!

"And note," Monsieur Lampre continued, after a pause, "that it's not just here that the level of intelligence is dropping. In the other abbeys it's the same. Most of them, along with a few more or less scholarly ecclesiastics, recruit men who work in trade, gentlemen, officers, naval lieutenants and lawyers. Obviously, these people are far superior to Brothers Marigot and Vénérand, those recruited by Father Emonot, who the reverend father admitted to us just now were completely unintelligent; but are they suited by their primary education to become what I call true Benedictines? Come off it! Novices such as these will never give us a Dom Pitra, a Dom Pothier, a Dom Mocquereau, a Dom Chamart or a Dom de Fonneuve, monks worthy of continuing the tradition of Saint Maur.[7]"

"My God," said Durtal, "if only they became saints… Don't you think that's worth more than becoming a scholar? We hear a lot about Saint Maur, of which the modern congregation at Solesmes is the heir, but just think, there was a Father Jean Mabillon,[8] a Father Bernard de Monfaucon, a Father Edmond Martène, a Father Luc d'Achery and a Thierry Ruinart, to name just five, but there's no St Mabillon, St Monfaucon, St Martène, St Luc d'Achery, or St Ruinart; the community of Saint Maur hasn't given a single saint to heaven, is that something to be proud of?

"Any yet… and yet… Benedictine learning – isn't it the case that, with the exception of musical paleography, the National Charter School[9] surpasses it utterly? – the truth is that its place is now taken by the laity.

"It's not to learning but rather to art that the Order of St Benedict should look, if it wants to uphold the standard of its former reputation; it needs to recruit artists to revive the religious art that is languishing; it ought to do for literature and art what Dom Guéranger did for the liturgy, and Dom Pothier for plainchant. The abbot of Solesmes understood this, and pointed the way as best he could in this direction. He had a talented architect among his monks and commissioned him to construct new buildings for the monastery, and Dom Mellet hewed out of granite a monument admirable in its simplicity and strength, the only example of monastic architecture that has been created in our time. What we need now is men of letters, sculptors, painters… in a word, what we need is to revive the tradition not of Saint Maur, but of Cluny… it's true that this scheme, in my humble opinion, is far more likely to be realised with the oblates than with the fathers."

"Perhaps you're right, but putting aside this question of art, allow me to tell you that the preference you have for piety rather than learning can hardly be justified in an abbey; because when all is said and done, nothing is more risky than to admit and ordain an unintelligent man as a father simply because he leads a godly life. Piety, even saintliness, can disappear, but stupidity, now that remains!"

"Essentially, when you think about it, it's a fruitless discussion, because the future of the Order is threatened with dangers far more serious than what we've been talking about. In spite of the abbot's optimisim, I greatly fear that his monks will soon be dispersed and driven out of France. All they can do is to pray, day after day, while waiting for the catastrophe…"

"Alas…" exclaimed Monsieur Lampre.

They parted company. As he walked along, Durtal thought to himself: 'He's astonishing, all the same, is Monsieur Lampre; he can't convince himself that a monastery is a microcosm, a society in miniature, an image in small format, of ordinary life. In a convent there can't be only St Benedicts and St Bernards, any more than there can only be men of genius or of talent in the world. The mediocre are necessary in order to accomplish mediocre labours; it has always been so, and it will always be so. We are constantly being told of the greatness of the monks of Saint Maur, but how many of them were neither scholars nor researchers; how many, by performing servile tasks, have enabled the Mabillons of the world to work in peace, and have helped and supported them by their prayers? And where, or in what class of society, could Monsieur Lampre find such an assemblage of virtues like those in our cloister? Because there are only devout monks here. I'm not even talking about the abbot, Dom de Fonneuve or Dom Felletin, but of the other monks, too; that there are, among them, some that are ignorant and incapable goes without saying, but they are nonetheless excellent priests; and before abusing them, it would be as well to know if our Lord doesn't delight more in those souls who escape the perils of the mind and the dangers of vainglorious learning? And as for the novices, how charming they are. When I see that lad of seventeen, little Brother Blanche, with his frank, open face, clear blue eyes and youthful laugh, I can imagine the innocence of this soul, imbued even to its most secret fibres with the joy in God, and he's not the only one of his kind; how many in this novitiate are as delightfully simple and as exquisitely pious as him.'

And Durtal continued his solitary walk down the road; 'There's a look that rarely deceives. A novice arrives; look at him, he's nondescript, an undistinguished face, eyes like everyone else's; but wait a few weeks; let the phase of dull boredom pass, the crisis of homesickness that for some lasts a fortnight, for others a bit more or less — because almost all have to go through this stage, and you warn them because there's no way for them to avoid it — well, once this depression is over, his face is unrecognisable. It becomes brighter, cleaner as it were, or rather what makes him so different is his eyes; you could almost recognise whether there's a chance of a vocation or not by this change alone; it's in the special clarity of the pupil that this can be discerned. It really seems as if the cloister has filtered the water in their eyes, that previously looked so cloudy, as if it has cleared it of the gravel deposited there by the images of the world; it's very curious.

'And how happy they are these lads! For the most part, they don't know anything about life; they flourish, slowly, sheltered in an admirable greenhouse, on prepared soil, removed from the frost and away from the wind; that does not of course stop the demon from attacking them, like a worm burrowing into their roots, but the horticulturists here are skilled, and Dom de Fonneuve and Dom Felletin know all the old secrets of their trade necessary to cure them.

'My God, how stupid I am,' he exclaimed suddenly, stopping on the spot. 'I forgot to get what Madame Bavoil asked me for; I'll have to go back to the monastery.'

He retraced his steps and exchanged hellos at the porter's lodge with Brother Arsène, a lay brother who combined the functions of tailor with that of concierge of the abbey.

CHAPTER III

"Is the father pharmacist in?"

"Of course, Monsieur Durtal; when there's no service, he prepares his herbs in his room; he never stirs."

In order to allow the country women to enter the pharmacy, which would fulfill their prescriptions for the greater glory of God, Father Philigone Miné's cell was located near the porter's lodge, outside the enclosure.

Durtal lifted the latch, but in spite of Brother Arsène's assurance, the room was empty.

Thinking that the monk was probably not far away, Durtal sat down on a rush chair and whiled away the time by making a mental inventory of the cluttered room's contents.

It was indeed the most bizarre clutter you could imagine; this cubicle, with its lime-washed walls, was the former kitchen and was still equipped with its stove, on which disturbing broths were simmering in copper saucepans. Along a whole section of the wall, shelves of white deal contained phials and labelled packets; opposite the window, the cracked panes of which were bandaged with star-shaped bits of paper, a floral cotton curtain, greasy as a dish-cloth, hid a small iron bed next to which, on a box containing a disused sewing-machine, was balanced a basin and a stoneware jug, the whole thing being propped up on the uneven floor by a piece of wood; but where the father's ingenuity was particularly noticeable was in a series of comical details. From an old set of pan scales, which he'd hung onto a slat sticking out of the wall, he'd made a soap dish; he would put a similar sized piece of soap in each pan and use the two pieces alternately, one on one day the other the next, in order to keep it balanced. A rod fixed into the stone of the wall by a clever system of hooks and spikes bristled with bent nails on which towels were drying. No space was wasted in this den; planks climbed up on uneven brackets; opposite the shelves filled with the flasks and packets, they formed racks no two of which were the same; they were held together, no one knew how, by patched-up pieces of wood, joining together when they weren't too far apart, one to the other by added slats of cardboard. And there was a mishmash of bottles and pious statues, antique engravings and modern colour prints were pasted onto the hood of the stove, so blackened by smoke that you could no longer make out the faces; and then there were the strange utensils, flasks and retorts, broken lamps and leaking bottles, mortars and bowls, with bits of charcoal, under a layer of dust, in every corner.

'All the same,' thought Durtal, 'when Father Miné ran a pharmacy in Paris before becoming a Benedictine, what sort of customers can he have had, if his shop was in as dirty and untidy a state as this?'

'Here he is,' Durtal said to himself, hearing the shuffling of feet and the muffled sound of slippers.

The monk entered.

He was the monastery's most senior inmate, older indeed than the abbot, being over eighty-two. Like the forgotten stump of an extremely old tree, his skull was covered with bumps, freckles and wrinkles; his eyes evoked the idea of frosted glass because they were dulled by a white film of cataract. His nose curved over a firm mouth, crenellated with teeth; his complexion was fresh and his cheeks not overly lined with wrinkles. Apart from his hazy eyesight and his tottering legs, he was absolutely fine. His hearing was intact and his speech unimpaired, and he was affected by none of the usual infirmities of an octogenarian.

He looked both venerable and comical. In the cloister they called him 'Dom Alchemist', not because he was trying to find the Philosopher's Stone – in which he nonetheless believed – but because his bizarre look, his perpetual air of abstraction, his studies on the pharmacopoeia of the Middle Ages, his rage against the prescriptions of modern doctors, and his contempt for new remedies, justified, up to a certain point, this nickname.

He propped his staff in a corner and wished Durtal good day.

"Now, father, I've come to ask you for a gauze bandage for my housekeeper, who has grazed her finger."

"Very well, young man," – Father Miné referred to everyone under sixty in this way – and while searching for the gauze in his boxes, he said, more to himself than to Durtal:

"How would they have used that powder, so highly praised by the medical men of the Middle Ages, and which they labelled 'Lamprey powder,' because it was made of the calcined head of that fish?"

"I've no idea," replied Durtal.

"Yes," continued the old man, following his train of thought, "that inventory I discovered in a fifteenth century Dijon apothecary is a most curious one. We find in it those old-fashioned medicaments which certainly had their uses, and at any rate didn't poison people like the alkaloids used by modern chemists; but not everything is clear in this grimoire. By heaven, I know that the ointment called 'Anthos' is nothing more than rosemary ointment, and that 'Goliamenin' is Armenian fuller's earth, but 'Samenduc'? What's that? And what was Samenduc used for?"

And he looked at Durtal, nodding his head.

Unthinkingly, in order to at least say something, Durtal blurted out:

"But father, perhaps this information is recorded in one of the books up in the library…"

The old man gave a start and then the flood gates opened:

"The library?" he shouted, "is that a joke? Have I ever been able to get them to buy a collection of our ancient codices and formularies? Whenever I tell them that one of these books is coming up for auction they are always deemed 'too expensive'. Too expensive! I'm ashamed to say that we Benedictines don't even possess that volume by one of our greatest ancestors at Saint Maur, the *Botanical and Pharmaceutical Dictionary* by Dom Nicholas Alexander! The pharmacy…? that doesn't interest them, the fathers; now their health, that interests them when they come and ask me for a cure. Then they think there might be something worthwhile in the science! But isn't pharmacy part of the work of our Order? Wasn't it us, the monks, who in times past used to cure the sick in the villages that sprang up around our monasteries?"

Durtal, who had already heard this indictment before, attempted to beat a retreat, but the old man barred his way. He was about to continue his complaints when Father Ramondoux, the choirmaster, came in. He shook hands with Durtal who, though he detested the cantor's overbearing manner, liked him as a person because he had qualities of frankness and friendliness one could rely on. It was just that while his soul was amiable, his physical appearance was less so.

Father Ramondoux was a native of Auvergne, loquacious and jovial. He had a bull-neck, a broad chest and a beer-belly. His glaucous eyes bulged above a short snub nose, his jowls were sagging and huge tufts of red hair sprang from the pits of his ears and the cavities of his nose.

"My voice is worn out," he said to Father Miné. The latter just shrugged his shoulders.

"Listen," he said.

He opened his huge mouth and an alarming wheezing sound came out.

"I saw in this newspaper here," he continued after he'd stopped trying to sing, "an advertisement for pastilles that are supposed to strengthen the vocal cords and to cure hoarseness in singers; could you get me some?"

"Pastilles!" Dom Miné exclaimed contemptuously, "pastilles! What are they, just antiseptic sweets that's all. I don't keep that kind of stuff, and on no account will I sell any; but if you really want to cure yourself – though I can't see that there's any need – I'll make you some nitrated lemonade."[10]

"Do you think I want to poison myself with your old potions…?" Father Ramondoux exclaimed.

Durtal, not wanting to hear any more, took advantage of the discussion that had started up between the two monks and slipped out the door.

Chapter IV

The house in which Durtal lived was an old building the colour of pumice stone, topped with brown tiles and chestnut-coloured shutters; it was laid out in a very simple fashion. A rickety porch with three steps, a door with a brass peep-hole and a bell-pull made from a deer's hoof, and behind it a hallway, off which two large rooms opened on the right, and two small ones on the left. These latter two were, in fact, smaller by the width of the stairway situated between them and leading up to the first and only floor.

Logically, the first ground-floor room on the left was intended to be the dining room and the next, after the stairway, the kitchen, furnished with a door opening onto a courtyard; on the right would have been the living room and a bedroom. But Durtal had moved upstairs because of the humidity oozing from the damp walls downstairs; the first floor was laid out in the same way as the one below, two large rooms on the right and two smaller ones on the left, because the staircase, even though it was sort of converted into a ladder, continued its course right up to the garret under the roof. So the rooms were redistributed as follows: downstairs on the left as you came in, the dining room had become an unoccupied guest-room; the living room was the dining-room, and the bedroom was Madame Bavoil's room, as it was next to her kitchen. Upstairs, the study corresponded to the dining room below, and Durtal's bedroom to that of Madame Bavoil; in place of the kitchen downstairs, he had fitted up a bathroom, and in the empty room above the guest room, as well as all along the hallway, there were shelves for books that overflowed on all sides.

In effect, he lived in his study, which was huge, lined from floor to ceiling with books. The kind Abbé Gévresin had left him his library which, joined to his own, covered the walls of several rooms, and even two walls of his bedroom were lined with a mass of old volumes.

From one of his windows he had a view of the garden, and the church and abbey a short distance away, and from another the countryside undulated, as far as the eye could see, in lines of black stakes and clumps of vines, to a horizon of thin red hills.

That morning, which was All Saints' Day, was grey and cold, and the landscape looked melancholy. After lunch, Durtal strolled around the garden with Madame Bavoil, in order to choose where to put certain plants that had been ordered in Dijon and which were due to arrive in a few days.

This spacious garden, enclosed by ancient dry-stone walls, was planted with silver poplars, chestnut trees, cypresses and pines of various species; but one gigantic tree towered over them all, a magnificent tree, a cedar with bluish leaves. Unfortunately, it had created a void around itself and killed all the trees that grew too near its roots or its branches, so much so that it stood alone on a barren patch of soil strewn with its dead leaves, where no plant, no flower ventured to grow.

The garden began in front of the house, with a lawn behind which clumps of shrubs and flowers intertwined, cut across by little paths edged with thyme; but the really charming part was that which ran along the walls; here, the paths meandered, bordered on one side by a wall invaded by saxifrage and valerian, which in certain places ended in climbing branches of bryony with white flowers and red berries, and on the other by laburnum trees, enormous boxwoods, chestnuts, limes and elms; and the year before, to replace the old dead tree stumps, Durtal had planted rowans, quinces, medlars and some of those maples whose leaves seem to be coated in blood each year and turn bronze as they get older.

In spring, sprays of lilac perfumed these paths, and towards the end of May you would trample the fallen flowers of chestnut and laburnum seeds underfoot; you would walk on them like a carpet woven in white and pink, speckled with drops of gold; in summer, you could rest there in the shade, amid a humming of bees, a chirruping of birds chattering in the undergrowth; in the autumn, when the wind blew, you could hear the sound of the sea in the poplars, and cavalry charges in the pines; the damp earth, covered with rotting leaves, smelled of wild boar; the flowers grew less, the thickets became less dense, and dead branches of wood littered the ground.

One seemed far away from everything in these 'breviary-walks', as Durtal called them, and indeed they really seemed to be designed to help one meditate on the lives of the saints which those books condensed into exemplary lessons.

Their charm consisted in not having been tidied up or raked; the clearings, the paths under the trees, contained the most diverse plants, carried there either by birds or by the wind; and during different seasons Durtal would carry out excavations there, discovering Honesty plants, commonly called Pope's Pennies, whose stems swayed with green silicles spotted like dominoes by the seeds inside, and which became like disks of silvered parchment when dried; a basil plant that stank of kitchen grease, of burnt butter mixed with an indefinable smell of lemon balm and sage; rough and hairy borage with star-shaped flowers of the exquisite blue of an arctic sky; mullein rose up like Indian pagodas with their pale leaves and washed-out, sulphur yellow flowers, but the leaves were ragged, all were covered, as if sprinkled with flour, with caterpillars that resembled the skin of a Bondon cheese, caterpillars that were constantly tearing and gnawing at them; there was everything in this abandoned corner of nature; rosehips and brambles; dandelions whose stalks, full of sap the colour of limewash, infected the fingers that touched them, and coltsfoot, with its monumental leaves in decorative shapes, whose flowers were like the shaving-brush heads of purple thistles, flowers with a soft mane dipped in the lees of a cheap red wine.

But that particular afternoon, Madame Bavoil, insensible to the intimate delights of these pathways, said to Durtal as soon as they left them:

"All that's very pretty, but it would nevertheless be useful to point out the place you intend for your vegetable garden, because at the end of the day it's silly to have to go as far as Dijon to buy vegetables when they could be harvested here."

But Durtal did his best to defend his wilderness, while agreeing that his housekeeper was not wrong.

Eventually, they ended up vaguely agreeing on a plot of ground at the bottom of the garden, but Madame Bavoil wouldn't give up without a struggle.

"That section you've left uncultivated," she said, "I can use that too, can't I?"

"Certainly not! That's where I'm going to put my liturgical flora and Walafrid Strabo's medicinal herbs."

"Come on, my friend, be reasonable, you don't need a lot of space to grow a few herbs; give me the list, it won't be hard to figure out how much is enough for them."

Grumbling, Durtal handed Madame Bavoil a bit of paper which he took out of his pocket; she cleaned her glasses by breathing on them and rubbing them vigorously with her handkerchief, then proceeded to read:

"Sage, rue, sunflower, cucumber, melon, wormwood, horehound, fennel, iris, lovage, chervil, lily, poppy, clary, mint, fleabane, wild celery, betony, agrimony, hemp-agrimony, ephedra, catmint, radish and rose."

"Twenty-four plants," she continued, counting on her fingers, and then she laughed. "Flea-bane and catmint… what are they and where would you find them?"

"Father Miné assured me that fleabane is none other than daisy, and catmint is Nepeta, so there'll be no difficulty in finding them; but what made you laugh?"

"I was laughing because this garden of yours will be terribly ugly. Except for the parti-coloured sage you bought, which is very pretty with its pink, white and green leaves, the poppy, iris, rose and lily, all the rest of your herbs are very dreary, they're the runts of the meadow, they'll be choked by the melon and especially by the cucumber which will entwine them and strangle them in its trailing stems and tendrils."

Chapter IV

"Well, all the more reason to make the plot bigger, to protect these unfortunate flowers from the cucumber's assaults."

"As for your little liturgical wild garden," Madame Bavoil went on, ignoring this last remark, "it'll need even less space, seeing that when one plant is growing, another will be dead, because these plants don't all bloom in the same season; you'll never have your rows all filled at the same time. So why waste so much space when they'll never manage to fill it?"

Durtal ignored this observation in his turn, because what he hadn't admitted to Madame Bavoil was that he'd already made an experiment of this sort the year before, with lamentable results. However, he stuck to his idea, saying to himself, 'I'll start the project again on a new basis; the issue is to find some perennial plants that are easy to grow, and which can, from a liturgical point of view, serve as synonyms for those that can't thrive in this soil, in this very mild climate; but for that it'll be necessary to delve more deeply into Migne's *Patrologia*,[1] and that's no small matter...'

"In short, there's no hurry with the garden," he continued, "I've got to think about it a bit more and we'll see later; for the moment, Madame Bavoil, lets deal with Walafrid Strabo's."

"But who is he, may I ask, this Strabo you've been going on about for the last few months?"

"Strabo, or Strabus, which means 'squint-eyed', is the name, or rather the nickname, of a monk, a disciple of Rabanus Maurus[2] who in the ninth century was abbot of the monastery in Reichenau, located on one of the islands of Lake Constance. He wrote numerous works, including the lives of two saints in verse, that of St Blathmac and that of St Mammes; but only one of his poems has survived, *Hortulus*, the very one in which he describes the little garden in his abbey; as a side note, it's to this poem that I owe this memorable phrase from Father Philigone Miné, who when I asked him for an explanation of some of the virtues of the various plants mentioned by Strabo said: 'That author would be totally forgotten if he'd written nothing but religious poetry and liturgical studies; it's to his pharmaceutical poem alone that he owes his fame. You, who have embarked on writing, meditate a little on this truth for your future's sake, young man.'"

"Young man? You're over fifty, and you're going grey, my friend!"

"You're not wrong," Durtal replied, laughing.

"Well, go on then, since you're set on your Strabo garden, but in his list of herbs and flowers there are some that have never been cultivated for medical purposes: radish, cucumbers and chervil, for instance, those aren't suitable for a pharmacy, they're articles for the kitchen."

"On the contrary, Madame Bavoil, the apothecaries of the Middle Ages did use them in certain cases; melons, gherkins, cucumbers – the whole *Cucurbitaceae* family in fact – possessed, according to them, properties that are not perhaps entirely imaginary. They believed that a melon plaster would cure an inflammation of the eyes; that young gherkins were apt to ease vomiting caused by over-heated ventricles of the stomach; and that their leaves, steeped in wine and applied as a liniment, fend off an attack of rabies. As for the virtues of the radish, they are doubtful; on the other hand, chervil is well-known as a diuretic and as a restorative used to cure the engorgement of milk in the breasts; and the melon, aside from its other qualities, has long been known as a laxative, and its reputation as far as that goes hasn't changed...

"What's more, you don't realise that it's all the same to me whether Strabo's favourite plants have medicinal properties or not; I look at it in a different way: this flowerbed, whether it's more or less attractive with its colours and shapes, is for me just a springboard to the past, a vehicle to take me back to my dreams. I'm just the man to imagine myself looking at the good Benedictine abbot Walafrid, pruning and watering his 'students', giving a course in medical and celestial botany to dream monks and saints, in the middle of this enchanted site, in an idealised abbey, whose inverted image is reflected, rippled by the breeze, in the azure waters of a lake."

"Well, if that amuses you that's fine by me," replied Madame Bavoil, "but in the meantime, if we get another day or two of bitter weather like today, the garden will be completely withered."

CHAPTER IV

They walked slowly down one of the paths.

"We'll still have the late-flowering plants, the chrysanthemums," said Durtal, "and those untamed plants that you hold in such low esteem are very hardy, Madame Bavoil," and he pointed out to her the wild campion, the white stars of which looked as if they'd bloomed in the neck of a pale green bottle, streaked with dark green stripes, the pink and white gladioli, the blue veronicas, and splendid holly-bushes, with their vermilion berries and their dark-leaves; but if these plants still persevered, others were dying or already dead; the sunflowers had withered and looked horrible. They stood there, as if after a fire, on charred stems, at the end of which hung black leaves and disks shaped like the head of a shower, and the weight of these burnt disks caused them to sway in a gloomy salute at the slightest breeze.

"Well, at least the juniper berries are ripe," explained Durtal, who began to nibble on these little blue pellets which tasted of turpentine and sugar.

"You could at least wait until the frost has wilted them," said Madame Bavoil. She fell silent and then, after a pause, went on:

"You must admit that it would be better to tidy this up," and she pointed to the flowerbeds where all the cultivated flowers had disappeared, at the wild flora, the knotweeds with red stems and elongated, black-spotted leaves; the euphorbias swaying at the end of their small, flesh-coloured peduncles, like green eyelids with yellow-green pupils; the blueweed bristling with white cilia, whose purple flowers, shielded by rough leaves, tapered into long spikes.

"Pull this up? But you're not thinking; these flowers are the last ones still here. What's more, even though they don't figure on Walafrid Strabo's lists, they're medicinal flowers too, these poor little things you despise so much...

"Knotweed is full of tannin, and is therefore an excellent remedy for stomach upsets; euphorbia, or devil's milk, or little lightning, or asp milk, cauterises the skin and removes warts; blueweed contains potassium nitrate, and can be consumed as a sudorific like borage; they're all useful, even that faux nettle they call purple laurel that smells like a damp cellar when you crush its leaves between your fingers – here, just smell that – it was used in the Middle Ages, ground up with some salt, for bruises…"

"That smells so bad," exclaimed Madame Bavoil, pushing away Durtal's hand. "But, my word, how learned you are, my friend!"

"It's all book learning. The truth is that, having a garden, I amused myself by buying horticultural dictionaries, old and new; and thanks to their coloured plates, I recognised the names of the flowers; it's nothing cleverer than that; moreover, I have to admit that outside of this specialism in pharmaceutical flora, my knowledge of ordinary botany is nil."

"Was it in Dijon that you found these books?"

"Not all, I receive catalogues from all the second hand booksellers in Paris, the provinces and Belgium, and I do my hunting for books from here; besides, it's the only sort of hunting I understand. It's also great fun; but dear me, how often you miss the game you aim at from such a distance, and which is brought down by another hunter at close range; but the pleasure one feels when a parcel of books arrives, and you take out the brace of birds that you've been stalking from afar. Besides, aside from the monastery and the garden, what other entertainment do you expect there to be in Val-des-Saints?"

"That's fair; and was it you who planted the Christmas roses all along these paths?"

"Yes, I was thinking about the winter. With its cedar and its pines, the garden would remain green up above, but on the ground it looked melancholy with its brown earth and dead leaves; so I bought this species of hellebore from Dijon, which has been very successful. There are also some of a different species, with their jagged leaves like a child's lace cuffs; these ones grow green flowers from leaves that are almost black, or rather they're not growing at all because they're dying."

"My word, you'd think you were trying to assemble a collection of poisonous plants!"

"Well, if you were to add to the euphorbia and hellebore the deadly nightshade over there, with its redcurrant-like berries, and the hemlock that springs up everywhere, despite my not having sown any, there would indeed be enough here to poison a whole regiment."

"I'd like to think that among this crop of plain Janes you have a favourite?"

"Of course, and that favourtie is swallow-wort, or, if you prefer, celandine; and look, there it is," continued Durtal, pointing his finger at one of the plants that had outlived its brethren, which for the most part had wilted this late in the season.

"My compliments, she's pretty!"

"Well, she's not as down-at-heel as you seem to think, Madame Bavoil; her leaves of muted green, heavily infused with blue, have an elegant cut, and craftsmen in the Middle Ages carved them on the capitals of cathedral pillars; her star-shaped flower is of a bright yellow and her fruit is a tiny pod, inside which, when you open it, are dazzling rows of little pearls; and lastly, look, when you snap her white, hairy stem the most beautful orange-coloured blood comes out, which is even more efficacious than the sap of the euphorbia in curing warts; in the Middle Ages, in the 'Court of Miracles',[3] the beggars, who simulated their infirmities in order to excite the pity of passers-by, would mix the juice of these two plants, and cover themselves with terrible-looking, but quite painless wounds; so to malingerers, celandine was indeed a blessing!

"During that same period, she was also the subject of the most bizarre legends; people were convinced that, if placed on a sick man's head, she would sing if he were going to pass away, and weep if he were going to recover; which is not, I admit, exactly to her credit; it was also thought that if fledgling swallows lost their sight their mother could restore it to them just by smearing their eyes with the juice of this plant; celandine is therefore both decorative and medieval, disreputable and useful; so Madame Bavoil, is it any wonder I'm mad about a flower like that?"

But Madame Bavoil was no longer listening to him; from where she stood on a little mound, she could see over the wall to the road below.

"Look," she cried, "there's Mademoiselle de Garambois!"

Together, they went to meet her, arriving at the door at the same time as she did.

"Hello brother," she said to Durtal, "and hello Mother Bavoil; "here, let me give you this," and she held out a parcel; "I've brought you something nice."

"Oh, you little beggar!" cried Madame Bavoil, laughing. "These are some more sweet things, and packed in little pots… yes, I can feel them under the paper; that must be some jam at least."

"No, you're a long way off," replied Mlle de Garambois, who, at Durtal's invitation, went up with Madame Bavoil to the study.

"I'm so tired, I feel quite stupid," she said, making a funny pout as she looked at herself in the mirror before she sat down. "Now then, let's talk seriously. Would you believe it, a friend who lives in the Midi sent me some potted meat, which she prepares herself and which is so delicious!"

"Rillette?"

"Goose paté, if you prefer; now pay attention, because I'm going to tell you the various ways in which they ought to be served. The most common way is to spread it, with some butter, on cornbread, that's been toasted first."

"And where the devil do you think I'll find cornbread!" exclaimed Madame Bavoil.

"Well, in the absence of this kind of bread," continued Mlle de Garambois imperturbably, "you cut thin slices of ordinary bread, spread your butter and your paté on top and then you toast them; but real gourmets disagree as to whether it's better to toast the bread before or after the paté has been spread on it; it's up to you to decide this important question…

"Other people, I have to confess, just eat them cold, without any preparation whatsoever; but these people are unworthy to taste such an inestimable dish; as for real gourmets, they refuse to touch them unless they are prepared according to the following recipe, so listen well Madame Bavoil.

"First, you prepare some slices of bread the thickness of a finger; you toast them but don't burn them and then moderately sprinkle them with some old red wine and a few spoonfuls of consommé; then you spread a layer of paté over the slices, and cover them with a very thin mixture of mustard and butter; you add some pepper and nutmeg to taste, and put the slices back on the grill, just long enough to reheat them underneath.

"Finally, you serve them on a warm plate, after having soaked them generously in brandy, which you ignite; your slices blaze like a pudding or a soufflé omelette, and they are just divine," concluded Mlle de Garambois, who leaned back in her armchair and gazed heavenwards.

"Good God, how is it possible?" sighed Madame Bavoil, clasping her hands together.

"How is what possible?" asked Mlle de Garambois, laughing.

"That such a God-fearing woman should be thus tempted by the demon of gluttony, and be able to invent such things…"

"But I didn't invent anything, I'm simply spreading the word, Madame Bavoil."

Durtal was studying his sister-oblate with a smile. Her physiognomy was always a surprise to him, because he never managed to explain the incomparable grace and youthfulness which, at certain moments, transformed the face of this woman of fifty, who, at other times, looked her age.

Mlle de Garambois was very stout and walked with a 'rolling gait' as they say. Dressed by the best Paris dressmakers, she was very elegant and wore clothes that would have suited a young woman, though in her case this didn't seem so ridiculous, because she looked seventeen when she smiled. She had been very pretty, and still retained her wonderful silky complexion, her bright childlike eyes, and above all a mouth and chin whose mischievous charm was truly exquisite.

It was enough for her to be happy for the crow's-feet and the wrinkles to disappear. Marvellous teeth would light up her little mouth; and a dimple would dance, innocently and yet with a slight air of irony, on her chin. Leaning forward a little, her two hands on the arms of the chair – a pose she often adopted – Mlle de Garambois would toss her head and the look of an amiable, impish girl, whose soul she possessed, would suddenly appear on her face. She had in fact all the happiness and innocence of a child; and above all she was so kind and charitable that she, for whom walking was so painful, would run the whole length of the village to bandage the wounds or change the linen of the sick. This woman, so fastidious as regards herself, who, at home, would have no doubt hesitated to do the washing up, lost all sense of distaste, or rather overcame it, when it came to being of service to others; and God alone knows what unpleasant tasks she had to perform when visiting sick peasants or abandoned women and children!

"You missed your vocation," her uncle, Monsieur Lampre, would sometimes say to her, "you ought to have been a hospital nurse."

"But then I'd have missed out on the divine office," and then, making fun of herself, she would add with a lively smile, "and on my nice little dinners!"

She was on good terms with Madame Bavoil, though at times she drove the latter to despair. "She has all the makings of a saint," Madame Bavoil would say, "and yet the devil, who's got a hold of her through that damned gluttony, blocks her progress; I'm forever telling her so, but she's so blinded by it, she doesn't hear me." And gently, kindly, tirelessly, she would keep trying to cure her; but Mlle de Garambois took all the admonitions in good spirit, and even pretended to be more of a gourmand than she really was, in order to tease her.

"Well," she continued, "now you've absorbed all the finer points of my recipe, let me sum up: toast the slices of bread, moisten them with soup and wine, smear them in butter and mustard, put them back on the grill, soak them in brandy and set light to them like a punch; is that all clear?"

"If you imagine we're going to inflict a rigmarole like that on ourselves... Our friend will eat them quite simply, fried in butter."

"That wouldn't be so bad, even so... oh, one other thing, you were at High Mass this morning; don't you think the abbot conducted the service well?"

"Yes," said Durtal, "with his tall stature, his diaphanous complexion and his long slender fingers, he looked as if he'd just stepped out of a stained-glass window."

"I presume," Madame Bavoil added, "that those jewels blazing on his mitre are imitations?"

"Think again, they're genuine; a monk, now dead, who entered the monastery after the death of his wife, donated all the jewels she owned – and there were a lot – to make this mitre. That explains why it's encrusted with diamonds, aquamarines, sapphires, valuable gemstones and other choice gems."

"Ah…"

"By contrast, the other two mitres – because the rubric states that abbots, like bishops, should have three mitres – the other two were paid for from the funds of the abbey, which isn't rich, so they are quite mediocre. The one that comes after the ceremonial mitre – referred to as the *pretiosa* – is called the *auriphrygiata* in liturgical language; it's quite simply cut out of a fabric that is more or less pure gold; as for the third, the *simplex*, which consists of cardboard covered with satin or silk, it looks like a sugarloaf made out of white paper.

"When do they use that one?"

"The abbot wears it for services for the dead, during Holy Week, and when candidates are taking the habit; in other words, for minor occasions or for mourning."

"It's indisputable that in terms of beautiful services we do as well here as they do in Solesmes," said Mlle de Garambois, "but, my word, we are lucky to have got such an incomparable liturgy director, so knowledgeable as to his role."

"And what's perhaps better still, a man of taste…" added Durtal.

"That tall, slightly bald man who has such a distinguished air?" asked Madame Bavoil.

"Yes, Father d'Auberoche. He's devoted to his work and never spares himself. You can be sure he spent a sleepless night in order to make this All Saints' Day a success; but then not a thing was overlooked; his little group of choir boys and novices learned their parts without the slightest hitch. He knows how to impose hieratic attitudes on the assistants; he knows how to conjure up the old smell of the cloister of the Middle Ages; take for instance that little detail of the *vimpa*, the satin scarf worn over the shoulders of the crosier- and mitre-bearers, which hangs down at the front, like a shawl, in two wide flaps inside which they hide their hands when they have to bear these insignia. As for the crosier, that presents no great difficulty, but for the mitre, it's another thing altogether. It has to be folded and held, in the same way that St Denis held his severed head; it's a very minor thing if you will, but if this pose is poorly observed, the medieval character of it disappears; well, Dom d'Auberoche not only taught the mitre-bearer the right attitude, but he himself organised the folds in the scarf, lifting it and creasing it just like a thirteenth-century sculptor; he could teach a thing or two to costumiers in Paris; there's no one like him in the whole congregation."

"He's still quite young," remarked Madame Bavoil.

"He must be about thirty-four at most. He was born into a large saintly family; he has what we call in art, a 'line', and always seems to have stepped out of a stained-glass window. Besides being a mortified monk, he is a very interesting scholar to listen to when he deals with the liturgy and symbolism; but one rarely sees him; first of all, he's very busy with his studies and his ceremonial rehearsals, and he's also what they call a 'solitary', in other words, a monk who lives apart, in his cell."

"Ah, if only the singing in this abbey was at the same level as the ceremonial, I'd have no reason to miss Solesmes," sighed Mlle de Garambois.

"Yes, but Father Ramondoux is a bit of a barker; it always seems to me, whenever he opens his mouth a street cry comes out: 'Roll-up! Roll-up!' The curious thing is that he's by no means ignorant of his profession; he teaches plainchant to his pupils very well, but he himself practises exactly the opposite of what he professes in his lessons.

"But despite these imperfections, how the less important monasteries still envy us... what a magnificent ceremony we had this morning! What a splendid liturgy it was today! That epistle taken from Revelations is a photograph of Heaven, or, rather, a perfect painting by one of the Flemish primitives; indeed, how the old Flemish painters interpreted this text of St John, with its procession of angels, elders and saints! And the opening *Introit*, the famous *Gaudeamus*, sung only on the most joyous feast days, how fine it is! That melody, which dances and can barely contain itself for joy, and which nevertheless stops before the end of the phrase, at *Gaudent angeli,* as if it can do no more, and perhaps also as if gripped by a vague apprehension of not being sufficiently deferential, but which then resumes, overwhelmed despite itself, in a rapture, to end in prostration, like that of the elders in Revelations, prone, their faces to the ground, before the throne; these notes of jubilation, it's surely the Holy Spirit that inspired them. It's of a simplicity that is admirable and caresses the ear with marvellous artistry. What musician could ever express the exaltation of the soul like this?"

"Here's our brother getting carried away again," said Mlle de Garambois, laughing, "but to return to the ceremonial side, are you aware, Madame Bavoil, that your friend and employer is one of Dom d'Auberoche's best pupils?"

"Certainly," she continued, smiling at Durtal, who was looking at her a little surprised, "I'm not saying this lightly, because though I didn't see you officiate, the day when you took the habit, I heard from the father himself immediately afterwards that you looked the part wonderfully well; in short, you had what you called just now a 'line'."

"All right, go on. I can see you're laughing at me, Mademoiselle Oblate."

"Yes, go on," cried Madame Bavoil, "because this tight-lipped man has never told me how that ceremony went. All you can get out of him is, 'Yes, it wasn't so bad,' and that's all; so come on, seeing as you're in the know, give me all the details."

"You'll correct me if I make a mistake," said Mlle de Garambois to Durtal, who was rolling a cigarette and affected the disinterested air of a man unconcerned by such stories.

"It was last year, on the feast of St Joseph, that's to say nearly eight months ago, the day before the feast of St Benedict; they'd chosen that day for the taking of the habit so that the ceremony of profession could take place the following year on the feast of St Benedict itself, the novitiate lasting, like that of the monks, a year and a day. Is that right?"

Durtal nodded his head.

"After the second vespers of St Joseph, they went into the novitiate's chapel, which no one can enter except the monks – and even then fathers who are not carrying out their function, have to be authorised, with the approval of the novice master and the abbot – because the novitiate is closed to everyone without distinction…"

"For us women particularly," said Madame Bavoil.

"Women? the Rule is unbending, if they were to even put a foot within the enclosure of the abbey, they are punished with excommunication, *ipso facto,* by that fact alone… but, to go on… consequently the chapel, where the scene I'm telling you about took place, is unknown to me; nevertheless, I hope that our brother will agree to describe it for us after I've finished. There were gathered there a few professed monks, the novices, the novice master and the father preceptor, and in the absence of the abbot, the prior, who was officiating. Is that still right?"

Durtal again nodded assent.

"The candles were lit; the great black scapular of the Order, a little shorter however than that of the fathers, was folded on a silver platter on the altar, and covered with flowers…"

"With anemones," Durtal interrupted, "the choice of this species was due to the graceful suggestion of Dom d'Auberoche, who believes, as I do, that this *Ranunculous* was the true lily of the scriptures, the symbol of the Blessed Virgin."

"Well, well, our friend has decided to talk," remarked Madame Bavoil, who was eagerly drinking it all in.

"I might add," continued Durtal, "that the reliquary containing the holy relics of St Benedict had been transferred to the chapel for the occasion; it stood on a cabinet, to the right of the altar, surrounded by a flaming bank of candles."

"Good, now I know, because the same ceremony was performed for me, but in one of the chapels of the church… so, to resume, Dom de Fonneuve, in a cowl and a white stole, stood on the predella of the high altar, between Dom Felletin and Dom

Chapter IV

d'Auberoche, and you, you were kneeling on the lowest step.

"The prior began with the *Adjuterium nostrum in nomine Domini*, and went through all the verses, the responsories being chanted by the monks and novices present; then, with some lengthy prayers, he blessed the scapular, and after having sprinkled it with holy water he turned to you, and you now stood up, and after bowing ascended the altar steps, where you knelt down again. He then vested you with the monastic habit, saying to you in Latin: 'May the Lord clothe you a new man, created in the image of God, in justice and in holy truth; in the name of the Father, the Son, etc.'

"After which, he turned back again to the altar, and you went back and knelt on the lowest step. The sequence of verses and responsories began again, followed by the *Kyrie Eleison*, the *Pater*, and accompanied by short prayers that alternated between the celebrant and the monks, and then finally came the long prayer: 'O God, whose will it was that our Blessed Father, St Benedict...' I've forgotten the rest; but it was something about the saint protecting you and granting you perseverance... you know the sort of thing...

"To close the ceremony, you kissed the holy relic that Father d'Auberoche held out to you, and while your name was being inscribed in the monastic register you embraced – at least I presume you did – each of your new brothers in turn."

"Yes, it's done as in the theatre, you simply lean and touch cheeks together, then you shake hands and bow. And that's it. Now, if you want to know exactly what I think, well, this ceremony is an imitation, in other words, it's modern. The ritual was conceived by the prior of the monastery of Saint Mary in Paris; it was he who, after the Pope's letter urging the Benedictines to re-establish oblature, founded and organised the meetings of oblates. That's the principal thing, since in the ceremony of profession the oblate has to recite the famous *Suscipe*, which is in a manner of speaking the 'open-sesame' into the Order, opening wide a door that was hitherto half-closed; but, in the end, however skilful the choice of liturgical prayers was for these offices, it's still not the authentic thing, the true one, the one that was used in the Middle Ages – which it's just a matter of finding!"

"Dom Guéranger himself has also drawn up a rite," said Mlle de Garambois, "extracted, no doubt, like that for his monks, from ancient ceremonies, principally those of the Congregation of Saint Maur."

"I doubt it. I believe that what Dom Guéranger wrote was merely a draft, which he would have reworked if he'd lived. Father du Bourg was inspired by it to draw up his own and he improved it by instituting two ceremonies, because Dom Guéranger's work was only comprised of one; you became an oblate without any probation by taking the habit. And the novitiate established by the prior of Paris has some benefits, because it offers a guarantee for the postulant and for the community."

"But you've done some research, haven't you; what did you discover?"

"Some interesting material about the life, habits and customs of the oblates in the Middle Ages, but almost nothing on the liturgy; there, my harvest was practically nil."

"Come," resumed Madame Bavoil, who wasn't very interested in this discussion, "since our friend has agreed to open his mouth on the subject, I'd really like him to finish the details; what's the novitiate chapel like?"

"It's a very small room where the novice master, the father preceptor, and the novices who are priests, say Mass every morning. Dom Felletin, backed by Dom d'Auberoche, who in his capacity as liturgy director, lives as much in the novitiate as in the cloister, wanted the things that were acquired for this chapel to be suitable. The altar is of oak, but of an antique form; the reliquaries are very simple but copied from old models; the same with the pale brass candlesticks; and lastly, the statue of the Blessed Virgin and that of St Benedict are seventeenth-century carvings; they're mediocre statues but even so they're far superior to those you can buy now in the Rue St Sulpice.

"From that point of view, it's only fair to praise these two monks who did their best to counter the unrefined tastes of Dom Emonot, the preceptor, and to counter that of a lot of other monks.

"But to finish this story, Madame Bavoil, I will tell you that the next day, after matins, I went to holy communion with the novices in that selfsame chapel; so now that you know everyhing, are you satisfied?"

"Why certainly, my friend; but it has to be said, without in any way reproaching you, that you could have given me this satisfaction earlier. So, when are you making your profession?"

"On St Benedict's day, next year, in five months' time."

"And yours, Mademoiselle de Garambois?"

"Oh me, I'm an old hand; I finished my novitiate and made my profession more than a year ago already; and you know, as far as that goes Monsieur Novice, you need to treat me with some respect."

"Have I ever failed in that regard?" replied Durtal, laughing.

"Yes, indeed, by assuming that slightly mocking air when your sister in St Benedict was telling you just now about some admirable cookery recipes."

"Don't be under any illusions on that subject, good Mother Bavoil here has forgotten every single word of the method you gave her of that glorious way of preparing the paté; however, I want to show you how much I value your opinion, so if you would be so kind would you come and help with the plan, in other words, have lunch on any day you'd care to mention; we'll see if we can drag your uncle along at the same time; the unfortunate thing is that we won't be able to have our director, Dom Felletin, join us."

"I've got it!" Mlle de Garambois shouted joyfully, "let's have lunch on Thursday, the day the monks take their walk. Dom Felletin can either ditch his novices, or bring them along with him, and if he can't eat lunch, he can at least drink some coffee with us."

"Why can't he have lunch?"

"It's forbidden, Madame Bavoil, if we lived in another village it might perhaps be possible with a bit of goodwill, but in the very place where the abbey is located the Rule is strict; it's impossible."

"If it bothers Dom Felletin to ask for permission, I'll go and see the abbot myself, who I know in advance will say 'yes'," said Durtal.

"That's settled, but now I'm going, because it's nearly time for vespers. Goodbye."

On these words, Mlle de Garambois left them, but she had hardly got beyond the garden gate when she came back, and called out:

"Don't forget this detail, which is important: don't add any salt to the goose paté, it's already seasoned."

"Don't worry about that, you gourmand you," cried Madame Bavoil, shaking her head in despair as she watched her disappear.

"What's worse," she continued, turning to Durtal, "is that it's growing on you."

"What do you mean it's growing on me?"

"By dint of hearing her talk about good food and dainty dishes, your mouth ends up watering."

"The funny thing would be if it grew on you, too…"

Madame Bavoil made an indignant gesture, then shrugged her shoulders with a smile.

CHAPTER V

"Friend," said Madame Bavoil to Durtal on Wednesday evening before the lunch party, "I can't be both in Dijon and tend to my stove at the same time; so you'll have to take the first train tomorrow and bring back a pie and some cakes."

"And a bottle of green Chartreuse because that, I believe, is the only liqueur that Mlle de Garambois deigns to drink."

"And a bottle of green Chartreuse…" Madame Bavoil added.

The next morning, Durtal got out at Dijon. 'The most important thing,' he thought on coming out of the station, 'is to go and hear Mass at Our Lady of Dijon; after which I'll spend some time in front of the Black Virgin, as I've lots of time to kill; then, last of all, so I don't have to drag them around with me all day, I'll make a few purchases before I go."

As usual, whenever he set foot in this town on a fine day, he felt blessed and soothed, almost joyful, in spirit. He liked Dijon's intimate atmosphere and its cheerful gossipy nature; he liked the attentive and friendly welcome of its shops, the bustling life of its streets, the rather quaint charm of its old houses and its squares, planted with tall trees and adorned with pretty flowers.

Unfortunately, this town was beginning to be like other towns that contrived to imitate the needless ugliness of modern Paris; the old streets were disappearing; new quarters were springing up on all sides; with insolent buildings, bow windows jutting out in the English style, decorated with coloured tiles, a checkerboard of diamond-shaped leaded-glass, all surrounded by iron railings; the impetus had been given; in the last thirty years Dijon had changed more than in several centuries; it was now crisscrossed with wide avenues bearing the hackneyed names of Jean-Jacques Rousseau and Voltaire, of the Republic and of Thiers, of Carnot and of Liberty, and to top it all, a statue of that loudmouth idiot

Garibaldi had been erected at the corner of a peaceful intersection, in memory of that infamous warmongering charlatan.

The truth was that the old Burgundian, religious and lively, quick-witted and independent, had been replaced by another Burgundian, who had preserved his native characteristics, but who had lost his stamp of originality when he lost his faith. Dijon became apathetic and atheistic at the same time as it became Republican. The good nature and the alacrity remained, but that flavour of naive piety mixed with Rabelaisian jubilation had gone, and Durtal couldn't help but deplore it a little.

'But despite everything, this town is still one of the few in the provinces where one can stroll around pleasantly,' he said to himself as he walked down the Avenue de la Gare; he threaded his way through the Place Darcy, where a bold bronze statue still recalled the half-forgotten fame of the sculptor, François Rude, and, passing through the Porte Guillaume, he went down the Rue de la Liberté as far as the Rue des Forges, where he turned and arrived in front of the façade of Our Lady of Dijon.

There, he stopped to contemplate one more time this solemn and baleful church; despite the renovations it had undergone, it had preserved a character of its own, quite unlike the art of the thirteenth century; with its double row of arches, forming open galleries above the three deep bays of the great porch, it didn't resemble any other church. And in a series of friezes there were rows of gargoyles[1] on each storey, gargoyles that had been restored, and some even completely redone, but very skilfully by an artist with a real sense of the Middle Ages. It was quite difficult, at the height they were at, and without retreating a considerable distance, to see them properly, nevertheless one could make out, as in the usual troupe of monsters that nestle on the towers of a cathedral, the two series of ill-defined devils and men.

The devils, in the conventional shape of fallen angels, with wings feathered with scales, and heads bristling with horns, sported a Gorgon's mask between their legs; or else they were extravagant animals, a lion crossed with a heifer, beasts with the muzzle of a leopard and the hair of an onager or a goat; oxen with almost human physiognomies, smiling with the grin of a drunken hag staring at her pint of beer; unspeakable monsters descended from no specific breed, taking elements from panthers or pigs, from calves or Hindu goddesses. The men, writhed in painful and comical attitudes, with heads twisted backwards on their shoulders and wild eyes; others had snub-noses, flared nostrils and funnel-shaped mouths; others still had baroque faces, the hilarious and salacious look of an old burgess, or of libertine monks, overly jolly and well fed; and last of all others with the grimacing faces of gnomes, topped in pie-shaped caps, straining open their gullets as if they'd been forced to swallow a tricorn hat;[2] and in the midst of all these mad creatures, of all these nightmarish beings, a real woman praying, in panic, with clasped hands, a face of terror and faith, imprisoned in this menagerie of monsters, imploring the prayers of passers-by, pleading desperately that someone help to save her, to find mercy.

Hers was the single cry from the soul that escaped from this church, whose rectilinear façade, unknown to Gothic art and borrowed from the memory of Roman constructions that survived during the Middle Ages in Burgundy, would have been too uniform, too austere, and very little suited to the mocking temperament of the people of Dijon if the intrusion of a teratology into this edifice hadn't interrupted its monotony and severity.

Without this circus of buffoons and devils, Our Lady of Dijon would have seemed to belong to another region, foreign to this country that built it.

However, ogival art would reappear with its customary look, with those long and thin turrets, topped with candle-snuffer roofs, that stood on either side of the façade. On that of the left, stood the famous automata[3] captured in 1381 by Philip the Bold at Cambrai; but this Flemish fellow charged with striking the hours on a bell with his hammer, was no longer shut up in a gilded bell tower amid a motley of lively colours, as he was previously; he was now confined in a black iron cage and had been given a companion, then one child, then two. To tell the truth, they looked like dolls clumsily cut out of an Épinal print[4] and magnified, but without sufficient artistic ingenuity.

Even so, these little mannikins were amusing and Durtal recalled, as he examined them, the only word-artist that Burgundy made no attempt to be proud of, Aloysius Bertrand,[5] who in his *Gaspard de la Nuit,* had lauded these figures in distinctive and singularly colourful terms; but this town, smug in its belated devotion to its great men, to La Monnoye and Piron, Crébillon and Rameau, Dubois and Rude, and deprived of that of Bossuet whose fame had been stolen from it by the town of Meaux, seemed to be ignorant even of the very title of Bertrand's book.

As for the rest of the edifice, with its sensible stanchions and its rational flying buttresses, it was quite ordinary in character; its central tower, as well as the four turrets with their pointed caps, were modern; there were no more figures carved under the vaults of the portal, because they'd been destroyed during the Revolution by the rabble that comprised, as it did everywhere else, the municipality. All in all, Our Lady of Dijon's exterior charm resided in its façade, and was limited to that.

On the other hand, in spite of all the retouching it had endured, the interior retained the familiar charm of its former times. Our Lady of Dijon didn't convey an impression of mystery and immensity as great, dark churches do. It was bright and well-lit, and always had something of the month of Mary about it, even during Holy Week; the disappearance of the old stained-glass windows perhaps helped to suggest the impression it gave of youthful celebration and ease. Obviously, one couldn't compare its nave and its aisles with those of immense cathedrals, but it was, in its compact size, slender and light, well matched with its girdle of pillars their capitals decorated with arums and crosier-like ferns, and when you got to the transept it made a final effort, with its stone lantern tower, rebuilt on a new plan, springing up into the void.

Stopping there at the choir, behind the altar was a round apse illuminated by stained-glass depicting a panoply of shields and swords. There was no circular gallery allowing one to wander around the choir; the church ended, as far as the faithful were concerned, at the communion table. At the end of each arm of the transept were two hollowed-out niches, each containing an altar. On the right, an altar of gilt bronze, covered with flowers and glittering with candles was that of Our Lady of Good Hope, surmounted by a small figure of the Virgin, black as soot, as if charred by the flames of the candles; she was dressed in a white robe and a large cloak strewn with stars, her feet resting on a tuft of vine leaves and golden grapes. The statue, dressed in this fashion, was triangular in form and had the allure of Spanish Madonnas of another age. On the left, was an altar dedicated to St Joseph, above which a fifteenth-century fresco had been discovered in 1854 underneath a painting that was hiding it. It represented a Calvary scene, but there was something about the figures that was unexpected in such a subject and made it enigmatic and truly strange.

The scene was arranged, in fact, according to the fashion of the time, but between the two thieves hanging on their T-shaped gibbets there was neither Christ nor cross; the mother, a Madonna of the school of Rogier Van der Weyden, already old and draped in a blue robe, is about to collapse, supported by St John, dressed in a wine-coloured robe and a bluish mantle. He holds her up, but mechanically, staring very distractedly into the air; behind him are two women, one, wearing a vermilion and white turban, is decked out in yellow with a black girdle, and raises her eyes to heaven; the other, dressed in a red skirt and a white veil, closes her eyes, overwhelmed with grief like the Virgin; further off, three skeletons in their shrouds study the sky and pray.

Lastly, in the foreground, a strange, kneeling figure, a woman with the common, bony face of a boy from the slums, a headscarf round her neck, holds out her arms in profile, and she too scrutinises the clouds.

And while this is going on, the two thieves on their instruments of torture are in their death agonies. The penitent thief, resigned, unable to take it any longer, is dying; the unrepentant one, a bearded Hercules with flesh the colour of brick, is writhing, one leg bent back behind the cross; he is heavy, stocky, exhausted, and a small black horned devil, tail curled like a trumpet, pounces on him with outstretched claws, ready to seize the soul as it leaves his mouth and carry it away.

If to this brief description we add a town with gabled houses and castles in the distance, and on the back of a wall on the right side of the fresco, three banners – one red, bearing initials, and two white, one of them emblazoned with a crayfish or scorpion, and the other with a two-headed eagle – flying from poles like reed-pipes spiralled in pink and black, then you get a vague idea of this unexpected and curious panel.

What's immediately striking about the uniqueness of its arrangement is that all the figures, except Mary and the woman in a red skirt who are absorbed in their distress, are looking or pointing, either with a glance or gesture, at someone in the air that we don't see.

Christ, evidently, but if so, it must be Christ in the clouds and with his cross. Another conjecture is, on the face of it, possible: between the crosses of the two thieves, there perhaps used to be a third, in relief, bearing a carved Christ on it, and this piece, at a later period, could have been removed because it jutted out and interfered with the painting that had for many years been placed over it; but even admitting that the proof of this theory could be provided by archival documents, or even by the traces of that excision which no doubt remain in the mortar scraped off or sticking to the stone, the expressions of surprise and direction of the eyes and the gestures of the participants would still require explanation; and it's precisely these attitudes that are reflected in a very exact fashion in the *Introit* of the Mass for the Ascension – "Men of Galilee, why gaze ye thus in wonderment at the heavens?" – which seems to me to confute this second hypothesis.

'What is certain in any case,' thought Durtal, 'is that this Calvary, overly retouched though it is, is a very interesting specimen of that mystical realism that was brought to the court of Burgundy by Flemish painters; this fresco clearly smacks of Bruges; there's no doubt about its paternity.'

And, while waiting for the Mass to start, for which they hadn't yet rung the bell, he walked around the church and went to look at the other frescoes, discovered in 1867 in the side aisles, when they'd scraped the surface of the walls.

CHAPTER V

Beneath the falling flakes of whitewash, fragments had reappeared of a beautiful looking *Circumcision* and a *Baptism*, but they were so expertly restored and so visibly repainted since their rediscovery that the result was embarrassing. The painter who had retouched these frescoes, Louis-Joseph Yperman,[6] had been really too skilful and they looked like forgeries; by contrast, the other frescoes were more discreetly restored; two especially were exquisite, one representing three holy figures, a saint and two benefactors, and another, situated near the main entrance, of a Virgin holding an infant Jesus on her knees.

The most attractive of these works, that of the three saints, may be outlined as follows:

In the centre, St Venissa, with the martyr's palm in one hand and a book in the other; she was dressed in a pale lime-green robe and a faded rose cloak with sulphur-yellow lining; on her right, also standing, is St Guille, a bishop wearing a white mitre and holding a crozier; a heavy red cope studded with two rows of pearls covers his shoulders; on St Venissa's left, denoted by her usual attributes of a sword and a wheel, is St Catherine of Alexandria, tight-laced in an ermine bodice, with pale olive sleeves, over which a blue mantle, intensified by a creamy white, had been thrown.

St Venissa is looking down at her book, while St Guille stares fixedly in front of him, seeing nothing; both are ashen-faced and full of sorrow; as for St Catherine, she has the head of a decapitated woman who is still alive and suffering.

Lastly, low down in the foreground, two benefactors are kneeling – a burgher with clasped hands and a woman wearing a large headdress and draped in a prayer-shawl. 'I've seen that face somewhere before,' thought Durtal, 'that posture, that style of headdress and those coarse features of a stout matron remind me of a fifteenth-century sculpture by Jeanne de Laval, in the museum at Cluny. The two women look as if they were related.

'Now, St Guille is evidently St William of Bourges, but who is this Venissa, a saint unknown in the list of hagiographies? Her name is written in Gothic characters above her halo. Should one read a 'D' in place of the 'V' and suppose her to be St Denissa or

Denisa, who would be the saint of this name who was tortured in Africa in the fifth century? I don't know, but what is certain is that these melancholy figures, suddenly reawakened, have preserved a spectral aspect in their features. They have come out of the grave, but the colour of life hasn't yet returned.'

And it was the same with a fragment found in the other aisle of the church, a St Sabina, virgin and martyr, her neck a circle of purple and carrying her head in the same way as St Denys, a head whose tresses of blonde hair fall like tears; and also with a Madonna located very close to the door, a languid and sad Madonna, with her child on her knees, looking at a priest in a surplice kneeling in front of her; all of it washed out, pale and dying, in a vague landscape that faded into the stones of the wall.

In a way, it was as if Durtal was visiting a cemetery of Flemish art; these were sepulchral frescoes; these unexpectedly resuscitated beings had not yet regained their senses, and above all they looked tired and distressed at coming back to life; and by a natural association of ideas in front of this exhumation of the dead, Durtal was assailed by the memory of that passage, so suggestive and so prophetic, in which St Fulgentius comments on the raising of Lazarus in the Gospel of St John, and very clearly says: "Jesus wept not, as the Jews thought, because his friend was dead, rather he wept because he was going to recall one that he loved to the miseries of life."

'And the fact is that once is enough, quite enough,' sighed Durtal, as he returned to the chapel of the Virgin where the candles were lit, and he heard Mass there; then he sat down in a corner and tried to collect his thoughts and think things over more clearly.

What was uppermost at the moment was an immense fatigue. Even though liturgical prayer acts virtually independently, and through the strength of purpose it possesses – even if one's mind is elsewhere when reciting it – in order to be powerfully effective, to be productive, it demands undivided attention, a prior study of the text, a comprehension of the meaning it assumes, particularly when it's placed in this or that office. So, every evening, he

CHAPTER V

prepared an itinerary for the following day.

For the Mass it was easy; there was a missal for the Roman Rite, perhaps the only really complete one, the *Missal of the Faithful*, in two volumes, by a Benedictine from Maredsous, Dom Gérard Van Caloen,[7] who afterwards became abbot of the monastery at Olinda in Brazil. By combining this with the *Supplement to the Monastic Breviary* published by the Benedictines of Wisques, it was easy, after having looked up in the *Ordo* of the congregation of France which feast day it was, to avoid mistakes; then all he had to do was to check the Mass, whether it was the right Mass for a feast day or for a saint; the others, owing to their frequent repetition, had long been familiar to him.

But it was another matter as regards the offices. Without speaking of matins and lauds, and leaving aside the lesser hours which varied only on Sundays and Mondays, that left vespers, which, unlike compline, was always changing; and with these, unless you wanted to carry around the unwieldy Solesmes prayerbooks with you, it was a veritable headache.

The little diurnal which he generally used had been compiled by the English Benedictines for their own use, and was not commonly found in a French cloister and was very inconvenient. First of all, a host of English saints, venerated by monasteries across the Channel weren't even mentioned in our breviary, and many of ours were absent from their calendar; so one always had to consult the French supplement inserted at the end of the book; what's more, in order to cram a great deal of material into a small space, the volume was printed on thin paper, in close type, and with such an excess of rubrics in red that one's eyes danced between the lines and found it difficult to focus; and then there were a whole series of cross references and incomprehensible abbreviations for which there was no key; lastly, apart from the offices that were recently agreed on, many were doubled, such as that of St Pantaleon,[8] who the English church favoured, while with us he was listed in the series of simple martyrs, with no separate antiphon and merely honoured with an ordinary service; and to top it all and add to the incoherence, it was paginated in three sections, and the notes in the supplement, referring to such and such a page in the diurnal, were frequently inaccurate.

But he had little choice: either use this little portable volume or a massive French tome, the abbey at Solesmes not having published a breviary for use when travelling.

"What a mess," Durtal would say to Dom Felletin, who laughed, replying: "All the information I can give you will be of no use whatsoever; practice alone will guide you through the labyrinth of the hours, which, I admit, are frankly confusing."

And Durtal had, in fact, ended up grasping the thread, and by using a number of bookmarks between the pages had managed to find his way around in this jumble of texts, but only if he traced his steps carefully, because with the verses and the responsories of the commemorations it was often a mad race from one end of the book to the other, and you were lucky if you didn't stray into a double octave,[9] or into a season such as Advent, which complicated everything.

That done, and the reference markers established, the next thing was to study the text of the office, to understand its meaning, and to discover what, aside from the divine service of praise and the prayers of special intention, one could draw from it for the benefit of his own soul.

The difficulty that imposed itself first was this: to become sufficiently imbued with the spirit of the Psalms as to be persuaded that they were written for you personally, so exactly did they correspond to your thoughts; to recite them, as if they were a prayer handed down from the elders, in a word, to appropriate and assimilate the language of the Psalmist, to use the very same form of prayer as Christ and his precursors.

It was perfect in theory, but in reality it wasn't always so easy, because if you could see, reproduced in the sacred text, whenever the need arose, a map of your soul, if you suddenly discovered verses whose meaning had hitherto escaped you, but which now seemed clear and which so exactly matched your spiritual state at that moment that you were amazed and asked yourself how you hadn't understood their significance before, the terrible solvent of routine would appear in its turn, forcing you to recite the Psalms like an automaton, no longer imbuing it with any meaning.

And this routine, it must be admitted, was made inevitable by the very way in which the office was recited; in order to grasp all its implications, in order to thoroughly discern its meaning, even after a preliminary study of it, it would have been necessary to sing or to chant it slowly, religiously, to listen to it and reflect on it; but this wasn't possible, because it would have made the service interminably long and soporific, devoid of its rhythm and momentum, free of all its beauty, pruned of all its art.

'So,' Durtal concluded, 'one must accept the talismanic character of the liturgy, or else don't get mixed up in it at all; its power exists in a latent state; you don't feel the force of its current when you are experiencing it, but it reveals itself as soon as you're deprived of it.

'These excuses don't, alas, justify my wandering thoughts or prevent my imagination from running wild while I'm paying lip service to prayer. I am, it's true, called to order in those moments when I'm... I don't know where... but certainly very far from God, he supports my soul with a brief touch, and I return to him; then I really want to love him, but then everything collapses again, worldly preoccupations take over until suddenly, a propos of nothing, God knocks at the door of the heart once more and it opens to him.

'Ah, the truest image of myself has always been that of an inn; everyone comes and everyone goes; it's an open door to passing thoughts; but fortunately, despite its smallness, this hostel is not like that of Bethlehem always full; a room is reserved for the coming of Christ, an uncomfortable room, poorly cleaned, a hovel if you will, but ultimately he, who had a cross for a bed, would perhaps be content with it, if only the host was more attentive and more obliging. Alas, that's where the sore spot lies! The sad, begrudging welcome that Christ receives when he announces himself! I reply to every passer-by, I rush to answer calls from useless intruders, I haggle with purveyors of temptation, and yet I don't give him any more thought than if he didn't exist, and he says nothing or he leaves.

'How can I remedy this confusion in my pitiful soul?

'I feel less empty, however, less arid here, and also less absent-minded than at Chartres; but I've had enough of prayers, my head is spinning with devotions; I'm overwhelmed with fatigue, and fatigue breeds boredom, and boredom engenders despondency; therein lies the danger, and it's imperative I fight it. Oh, I know very well, Lord, that the dream is simple enough: erase the old traces, rid my mind of its imaginings, empty myself so that your son may be pleased to dwell there, become indifferent to pleasure or care, uninterested in what surrounds me, so as to limit my feelings to those expressed by the liturgy of the day; in a word, to neither weep, nor laugh, nor live, except in you and with you. Alas, that ideal is unattainable; no one can self-exile themselves in that way; you can't kill the old sinner within, at best you can make him sleep, but the slightest thing wakes him up.

'Yet the saints managed it with the help of special grace, and still God left them their faults in order to save them from pride; but for ordinary mortals, nothing of that sort can be achieved, and the more I think about it the more I'm convinced that nothing is more difficult than to transform oneself into a saint.

'True, many people have tamed the flesh; they practise humility and the love of Jesus; they no doubt repress the worst distractions; they are on the watch for God's coming; they're not far off being saints... but there's a banana skin on which they slip, which makes them fall and throws them back into the mass of holy men, but holy men are not saints, they are those who stop at the top of the hill, and unable to go further, rest and very often come back down.

'Now the touchstone of saintliness is not in bodily mortification and suffering – these are but means to an end – nor is it in the extinction of sins great and small, with the aid of heaven, every truly pious man of goodwill can aspire to this; it lies above all in the reality of that declaration in the Lord's Prayer that we repeat so glibly when we should be trembling: "Forgive us our trespasses as we forgive those who trespass against us." Indeed, to endure deceit and insults, to hold no grudge over injustices – even when they are prolonged and the hatred that stirs them ends up making life intolerable – to almost desire them, out of a need for humiliation and a desire for divine love, to not only wish no harm to one's torturer but to love him more and to ask without any ulterior motive, sincerely and from the bottom of one's heart, that he be happy, and of course on top of that to excuse his way of acting, to attribute all the blame to oneself – well, that, unless there's a very singular act of grace, is beyond human strength!

'And indeed, the amount of humility and charity that such self-effacement entails is disconcerting.

'People who possess virtues to a heroic degree recoil and are taken aback, even if only for a minute, in the face of an insult, but a sudden, brutal insult is bearable when you compare it to the slow turning of the screw of vexations and mean tricks; you recover after a short sharp blow, but you become agitated and panicked if you endure repeated pinpricks; their persistance exasperates, they irrigate, so to speak, the arid soil of the soul, gives the sins of resentment and anger time to grow – and God knows their offshoots are perennial!

'And what's more curious, if you manage to harden yourself, to restrain yourself, and in default of loving your tormentor, to achieve forgetfulness and silence, or at least retreat into yourself, if you manage even to stifle your complaints, to curb resentment as soon as it appears, what happens? You get agitated over little nothings, you get riled over trivialities. You avoided tumbling into the ditch, but you sprain your ankle in a little pothole, and you end up sprawling headlong on the ground all the same.

'Pride may be dead, but self-esteem, poorly interred, survives; the tide of sin may have ebbed, but the sludge remains, and the devil takes full advantage of it.

'These lapses would obviously be very ridiculous if one didn't know the tactic the Evil One employs: it's simple, everyone understands it, yet it always succeeds. Against those whose faults have become benign, he struggles and concentrates his efforts on a single point, and what's so lamentable is that if, in defiance of his ruse, you fortify that point, you expose others, and so he simulates the assault of an armed rampart, he even consents to retreat, to admit defeat, but during this time he enters by the back door which you've left defenceless, because you thought it closed and safe from danger; and so you don't notice his presence until he's already strutting around the place.

'Ah, saintliness, how rare it is! but what's the point of talking about it? If only one could find silence in oneself, and not fall back into old faults just at the moment when you're assuring the Lord that you want to avoid them at all costs. Alas, these are the resolutions of a drunkard, and such pious castles in the sand can never stand!

'The humiliation of these frequent confessions, where you constantly repeat the same thing, where you keep trotting out your crimes, where you chew the cud of your old sins over and over. You line up, once and for all, your sins in the usual order, you release the catch and the mechanism turns. Because when it's not a matter of the flesh, they are of trifling importance – which is an error anyway, but one imagines it to be so – there are moments when you no longer notice them, or you no longer know if since your last absolution you have committed them again, and from fear of deluding yourself and not being open with God, you confess them once more, without conviction, without repentance; and then... and then, an even more embarrassing question presents itself: when temptation arises, where does the fault begin? Did you dismiss it fast enough? Doesn't one always give in to it a little? Isn't there at least a suspicion of the sin of morose delectation,[10] even as one flinches under the lash?

'Carnal visions assail you, they spring up unexpectedly, like a bolt of lightning before you; you stare in surprise, then they become clearer and a terribly sweet languor flows through you; it's a narcotic that numbs you. In short, there's a moment of bewilderment followed by a moment of indulgence; you manage to recover yourself, but not quick enough for this fleeting pleasure, the result of a brief moment of forgetting oneself, not to make itself felt; too much so, in fact, because sometimes a hint of regret creeps in from having to reject, out of a sense of duty, the seduction of her charms. All this happens in the blink of an

Chapter V

eye, without one having the time to admit it to yourself, and it's only afterwards, on reflection, that you can breakdown the whole process and discern the details. Did you sin and to what degree? God alone knows.

'As a consolation, it's good to tell yourself that the devil has no power over the will, very little over the intellect, but complete sway over the imagination. There, he is master, and it's there he unleashes the sabbat; but this bacchanalia is of no more importance than the din of a military band passing your window. The panes rattle, objects in the room shake, and you can't hear anything else. You just have to keep quiet and wait until the racket of the brass and the drums moves off and fades away. This tumult is happening outside us, we submit to it, but we are not responsible – unless, of course, we go to the window in order to better hear it, because then there would be assent. Yes, that's easy to say, but...

'Another very unclear question is that of charity; it's right to observe it towards one's neighbour, that's agreed, but in certain cases where does it start and where does it end? And at certain moments, under this cover of charity, what becomes of truth, of justice, of honesty? Because in the end hypocrisy, idleness and iniquity are very often only separated from it by a thread; you help evil under the pretext of sparing people; you do harm to one person, under the guise of not judging another, and cowardice and the desire not to create problems for oneself gradually get mixed up in it. The boundary line between this virtue and those vices is usually so thin that you never know, in relation to this or that response, whether you've crossed it or not. Yes, I'm aware of the theological theory, which says: be ruthless as regards reprehensible acts, but merciful to those who commit them; but how, this general principle in no way resolves special cases, and in matters like this there are only special cases! The border that must not be crossed therefore remains ill-defined and obscure, and there's no fence to protect you from danger, or prevent you breaking your neck when you fall.

'How wretched is the soul hemmed in by petty faults! And the distress it experiences to see that it's constantly going over the same ground and making no headway against them!

'In order to console yourself, however, you have to tell yourself that due to our fallen nature it's impossible to remain unscathed, that there are specks and spots of sinfulness, like the motes of dust that, whether you like it or not, fill a room. They can be swept away by frequent confessions, but once this cleaning is done, others appear – it always has to be done again; and you're lucky if these 'crumbs' of carelessness don't accumulate without you knowing it into those 'mortal sins' of a room – those little rolled-up balls of who knows what kind of fluff which congregate under the furniture, and which common people refer to as 'sheep'!

'Enough of that, what time it is?' Durtal said, looking at his watch. 'Let's see, instead of daydreaming and mulling over doubts and moaning, suppose I go for a walk to kill some time?'

He set off at random down the street; here and there, old buildings arrested his attention: the houses in the Rue des Forges, the Hotel de Vogué,[11] the Maison de Cariatides in the Rue Chaudronnerie,[12] the oriel window in the Rue Vannerie;[13] but soon he reached the commercial part of the town, and then the wide, lifeless avenues where there was no Touring Club,[14] no Bon Marché,[15] no more Parisian emporiums bearing names that were now obsolete in Paris but still new in the provinces, such as the 'Poor Devil'[16] and the 'Hundred Thousand Overcoats';[17] no specialty gingerbread, liqueur, or mustard shops, which at least give an original stamp to the shopping quarter of Dijon. There were no stores or shops on these wide streets: they were rich, solitary, sullen looking, and ugly.

He came out at the Place du Trente Octobre, where, to glorify the memory of the National Defence, they had erected a statue to the resistance, seemingly modelled on a streetwalker standing on a barrel.[18]

'Ah,' he said, getting his bearings, 'there's the Boulevard Carnot; well, this would be an opportunity to visit the Carmelite chapel, which I've never been to before; Monsieur Lampre told me it was opposite the synagogue, so therefore it won't be difficult to find.'

CHAPTER V

He went down the Boulevard, and indeed glimpsed on his right the dome of the synagogue, which had become necessary since the number of Jews importing cheap goods from Paris had increased in Dijon; and on his left he saw one of those high perpendicular walls that seem to have been built to a uniform model by the Carmelites. A small postern door was half open, he pushed it and entered a little monastic garden, carefully raked with diligently kept flowerbeds, he walked over to a large open door beneath a Gothic building which could only have been a church, and indeed he stepped into a chapel.

This modern sanctuary, built in the ogival style, consisted of a simple aisle and no transept. At the far end near the altar, next to the lectern containing the Gospel, was the black iron grating of the enclosure; this tiny church was neither beautiful nor ugly, but what made it a little strange was the brown and grey light filtering in through its stained-glass windows, inhabited by large figures of male and female saints in the robes of the Order, robes of brown turning to plum purple, with white mantles. Names designated the personages who stood opposite each other on either side of the nave: among the men, Elias, John Soreth, St Albert and St John of the Cross; among the women, St Teresa, St Magdalene de Pazzi, Blessed Archangela, and Mother Mary of the Incarnation.

The chapel was warm and empty; you couldn't hear a sound. Durtal remembered some details about this Carmelite chapel that he'd read in an interesting book by Henri Chabeuf, *Dijon Through the Ages*. Its nuns had settled in the town at the beginning of the seventeenth century, under the direction of a disciple of St Teresa, Anne de la Lobère, in the Place Charbonnerie; then they had been transferred to another building which was converted into a barracks during the Revolution; finally they had ended up here, on Boulevard Carnot, opposite a synagogue.

'No doubt Providence placed them here on purpose,' thought Durtal, 'just as eucalyptus trees are planted near noxious marshes to destroy their miasma. Dijon little suspects it, but this humble cloister is a blessing to the town. Did they come here, as at Chartres, where the gatehouse of the convent in the Rue des

Jubelines was always full of good people looking to pray for sick children, for conversion, for help winning the lottery, for religious vocations, for everything in fact? And simple peasant women pulling on their purses, asking for a couple of *sous*; and the good Carmelite nuns were so conscientious that, every day, after having gone over the prayer requests written out by Sister Louisa, the gatekeeper, they would recite an additional prayer for those noted on the register, from fear that one had been overlooked...

'Those saintly women. But what a fool I am!' Durtal exclaimed suddenly, 'my mind is wandering aimlessly, I'm complaining about distractions, that I can't find a remedy anywhere, and St Teresa has already resolved this question. Indeed, I remember now that I'm in her house, having read in her correspondence a letter addressed to one of her confessors, a certain Dom Sancho, I believe, in which she essentially told him: "The distractions you're complaining about, I experience them as much as you, but there's nothing one can do about them, it seems to me, moreover, to be an incurable disease." Succinct, at least. She demolishes a passive soul in two words and with such certitude that, when she has spoken, there can be no mistake.

'What a woman! Her regime seems almost superhuman, and yet it was the most well balanced of them all. The divine machines she wanted were fitted with safety valves: recreations afforded the soul under pressure to find some relief, to relax, allowing the excess to be drained off; the only thing was, she needed to have nuns with cheerful, resolute characters. A melancholy nun would indeed have either despaired or gone mad in her cloister. As she was called to take on herself the temptations and ills of others, she could expect to endure the worst of sufferings, to struggle under the onslaught of those terrible sins that she draws to herself, like the metal tip of a lightning conductor, in order to resolve them.

'To be able to withstand such shocks,' Durtal said to himself, 'her body must be able to smile when her soul is in torment, and her soul must be cheerful when, in its turn, her body suffers. It is so much beyond human nature it's frightening.

'And yet, it could be worse; in a Carmelite convent, you are not alone, you share your trials, you support and help one another; there are also lulls in the conflict, diversions; but in the Middle Ages, and especially before that period, there were expiators and expiatrixes living in solitude, voluntary hermits in the darkness, kneeling in caves, with neither light, nor scenery to look at, buried alive between four walls.

'In the past, recluses had abounded in the Valley of the Nile; anchorites had considered that life in the open air – in a thebaid, in a cave that was often near an oasis, which brightened up the youthful light of the dawn and the fiery sparks of the setting sun – was too easy-going, and they cursed these temptations of nature that prevented them from suffering too much; there were those, like St Anthony, Peter Gelatinus, and Alexandra the Virgin, who hid themselves in abandoned sepulchres; others, like Simeon Stylites, buried themselves at the bottom of a dry well,[19] others again, like Acepsimas, St Thaias and St Nilammon, walled themselves up in a cellar with only a hole through which food could be given them; still others banished themselves in caverns from which they had driven out the wild beasts.

'This solitary hermit life which, like monasticism, originated in the East, spread to the West.

'The first recluse in France whose name has come down to us was St Leonianus, who in the fifth century shut himself up in a cabin, first at Autun and then at Vienne; during the same period one could also cite St Aignan, who died bishop of Orleans; St Eucherim who, before occupying the episcopal see of Lyons, sequestrated himself in a hut on the island of Léro. In the sixth century, St Friad and St Caluppo withdrew from the world, one near Nantes and the other near Clermont; St Leobardus, who shut himself up in a rocky cavern at Marmontiers; Hospitius, who immured himself near Nice; St Lucipinus, who shut himself up in the walls of an old building and by way of penance bore on his head an enormous stone, which two men could barely lift; also Patrolla, whose miracles are recounted by Gregory of Tours; St Cybardus, who built a cell for himself in the vicinity of Angoulême; St Libertus, who was incarcerated and died at Tours in the year 583. In the seventh century there was St Bavo and St Valericus or Vaury; the former secluded himself in the trunk of a tree and then in a hut in the middle of a forest near Gand, the latter lived entombed, in the Limousin. In the eighth century, there was St Vodoal and St Heltrude; one shut himself up in the outer court of a convent of nuns at Soissons, and the other in Hainaut, and Bauduin Willot's *Martyrology or Hagiography of Belgian Saints* notes that she died and was buried at Liessies; and how many others there are whose names I can't remember...' Durtal said to himself.

'But,' he went on, continuing his train of thought, 'it seems that up until the ninth century withdrawal into a solitary life wasn't subject to any precise rule, and it was up to the conscience of everyone to make it as severe or lenient, temporary or permanent, as they felt fit. Inevitably, there were abuses, some defected after having presumed too much on their strength, and had to retreat. To guard against such things, the Church decided that every postulant for claustration should first undergo a novitiate of two years in a monastery cell, and then, if he persevered in his resolve and was deemed fit to lead such a life, he should be bound not by temporary vows, but by perpetual vows.

'Indeed, in the ninth century we find a set of rules that applied to all male recluses. These rules, later published by Dom Luc d'Achery,[20] are presumed to have been written by Grimlaicus,[21] a priest or a monk, no one knows for sure.

'After having noted the two-year probation and the irrevocability of the commitment – which could, however, be broken in the case of severe illness – he goes into the details, decrees that the cell, adjoined to a church, should be built of stone and surrounded by high walls, having no communication with the outside except by a sort of peephole cut into the wall, just large enough to allow a tray of food to be passed through. The cell should be ten feet long and the same in width; a window, or rather a sort of porthole, was to open into the church and this would be hung with two curtains, to prevent the faithful from seeing the captive and to prevent him from seeing them. These curtains were to be drawn aside only before God, which is to say before the Holy Eucharist, which was to be administered every day to the prisoner if he was a layman. If, on the contrary, he was a priest, he was to celebrate a daily Mass alone, in a small oratory annexed to the cell; in other words, he was allowed to say Mass, but without a server or an assistant to offer up responses.

'The recluse was allowed to eat two prepared or cooked meals, but only during the day and never at night or by lamplight; for the first meal, some vegetables and eggs; for the second, some small fish, but only on the bigger feast days; he was allowed the half-measure of wine mentioned in the Rule of St Benedict, and he was to wear a habit similar to that worn by the monks of that Order. He was to lie on a bed made of wooden planks and a mattress; and he was to have a cloak, a hair shirt, and a pillow. He was also to sleep fully clothed.

'He had to wash his face and his body, and not let his hair and beard to grow for more than forty days. If he became dangerously ill, the seal of his cell was to be broken in order to treat him.

'These rules, conceived in the spirit of St Benedict, are lenient; with them, we are a long way from those anchorites feeding on herbs and roots in their caverns and tombs. But what totally contradicts the idea that everyone has about recluses is that, according to Grimlaicus' prescriptions, the inmates should never be less than two or three; each would live separately, in his own cell, but he could communicate with his neighbour by means of sort of cat flap, cut into the dividing wall; and so it was permissible, at certain times, to discuss the holy scriptures and the liturgy, and receive spiritual instruction from the eldest and most learned among them.

'If we add that each residence was adjoined to a garden in which the recluse could cultivate a few vegetables, we find ourselves singularly close to the Rule of St Bruno, where every Carthusian possesses a small house and garden.

'As Monsignor Pavy,[22] who was the first to carry out serious research on recluses, rightly remarks, this type of claustration in the ninth century was, in short, nothing but a convent in miniature.

'These ordinances, already quite lenient, became even more so later on, among the Camaldolese.[23]

'In the tenth century, St Romuald, their founder, declared that the right to pronounce on the validity of the vocation of those of his monks who wished to isolate themselves in a hut, would belong to the general chapter of the Order; and no one could be proposed to the chapter if he hadn't spent at least five years in the monastery after his profession. He also ruled that seclusion would no longer necessarily be perpetual.

'The cell of a chartered monk contained a bed, a table, a chair, a fireplace and a few pious images; it looked out onto a walled garden; the recluse had the right to converse with his brother monks, on the feast day of St Martin, and on Quinquagesima Sunday; every Friday and Saturday he would also attend Mass and nones, and during Holy Week he would leave his hermitage and take part in the services and the meals of the community.

'On other days he would recite the canonical hours in his cell, but not at any hour he chose, only when the bell for each service called the monks to chapel.

'We are getting closer and closer to the Rule of the Carthusians,' Durtal observed, 'and also to that of the Carmelites, because ultimately these monks are people seconded to hermitages for retreats of varying lengths, like those which took place at certain epochs in the monasteries of St Teresa; what is equally certain is that we are moving further and further away from the heroic era of hermitic life.

'And this slackening also occurs, in its turn, with women, despite their being more courageous than men.

'In the twelfth century, a treatise by the Blessed Aelred,[24] abbot of Rievaulx, covering the internment of nuns appeared. It is divided into seventy-eight chapters and abounds less in precepts than in advice. The female recluse should, he tells us, abstain from wine as much as possible, nevertheless, if she judges this drink to be beneficial to her health, she will be given a half-pint daily; she is to eat one dish only of vegetables or bread, and if she has a collation in the evening she must be

CHAPTER V

content with a little milk or fish, to which she can add some herbs or fruit if necessary; she must fast on bread and water on Wednesdays and Fridays, except in cases of indisposition, and she may not, under any pretext, decorate her cell with pictures or fabrics.

'She may speak if she wishes, but on condition that she doesn't engage in unnecessary conversations; she is not obliged to serve her own food, and if she wants she may have a servant to carry water and firewood, to prepare beans and other vegetables.

'This set of rules that Aelred had written for his sister sanctions among recluses the indulgence of an irrevocable decadence; they call to mind none of the rigorous habits of earlier centuries; certainly it's no longer a question of immurement, of anticipating the grave, a foretaste of the sepulchre.

'As to the ceremony used during the good old days of claustration, we only know it in outline and the precise details of the liturgy are lacking.

'Ideally, the recluse, whether male or female, would have been solemnly led to their cell on a Sunday before High Mass. They would prostrate themselves at the feet of a bishop if the cloister was attached to a church, or to an abbot or abbess if it was attached to a monastery, and they would attest out loud to the stability, obedience, and transformation of their morals. During the sprinkling with holy water they would stand in the choir of the church, and immediately after the *Exaudi* the procession, headed by the cross, would lead them, chanting the litany, to the door of their cell, which was then walled up or sealed with the sign of the cross, while the bells would ring loudly as if for some important festival.

'Almost always, when the conventual recluses, male or female, were taking their vows of obedience at the hands of the abbot or abbess, they would offer to hand over the ownership of all their goods, receiving from them in return a subsistence for the rest of their lives; and here the resemblance is striking with the typical ceremonies in the Middle Ages for the admission of the oblates of St Benedict.

'Moreover, it should be said that the more lenient the rules of the recluse's life were, the more the Benedictine institution of oblature came to the fore.

These recluses, when they weren't monks, were by any other name oblates. Many of them lived near Benedictine cloisters. Indeed, Mabillon notes that this kind of penitent, who followed the services of the community from their cell behind the curtain of the opening cut into the wall of the church, had become customary in the Order by the eleventh century.

'If one can judge by the inscriptions conserved in archives and in obituary lists, the number of these voluntary captives was considerable, and the institution spread with surprising rapidity throughout the ages.

'Male and female recluses abounded in Germany and in Flanders; we find them in England, Italy, Switzerland, and also in France, in Orleans, in the Chartres region, in Limousin, in Touraine, and in almost all the provinces. There were eleven hermitages at Lyons; in Paris, aside from Flore, the recluse of Saint Séverin, we are informed about Basilla, the recluse of Saint Victor, then Hermensande, the recluse of Saint Médard, Agnes de Rochier at Sainte Opportune, Alix la Bourgotte, Jeanne la Vodrière and Jeanne Painsercelli at Saint Innocentes, the Egyptian of the parish of Saint Eustache, a certain Marguerite at Saint Paul, the unknown recluse of the Church of Sainte Geneviève, and the succession of male and female hermits of Mont Valérien: Antoine, Guillemette de Faussard, Jean de Houssai, who died in the odour of sanctity, Thomas Guygadon, Jean de Chaillot, Jean le Comte, the Venerable Pierre de Bourbon, Seraphim de La None, and lastly Nicolas de la Boissière, who died there on 9 May 1669 at the age of forty-six.

'After him, there were only hermits living communally at Mont Valérien, under a rule that was almost exactly the same as that of the Cistercians. However, it contained a clause that hermits who wished to lead the stricter life of the earlier solitaries would, after examination, be permitted to occupy a special cell, for life, for a year, six months, three months, a fortnight, or a week, and were at liberty to rejoin the fraternity at the end of this time.

Chapter V

'The Rule of Grimlaicus must have fallen into disuse after a certain number of years. Was it ever even generally applied? This has by no means been proved. The importance attributed to it is mainly due to the fact that we don't know of any others, because that of St Romuald was, in short, really just the abbey's own internal rule.

'It was the same with Aelred's regulations; we don't know if it ever had the force of a law among women; what seems probable is that, while following these instructions in their broad outline, many of these recluses, male and female, tightened them or softened them, according to the more or less proven resilience of their health, or the more or less elevated level of their fervour. There were no doubt also local statutes, adding to or subtracting from the text of these edicts, but what seems certain in any case is that from the ninth century onwards the extreme conditions of the early recluses had disappeared. The cave had become a cell, where one worked or prayed, as in the neighbouring cells of the monastery. We possess a few details on this point.

'Hildeburga, who lived in the twelfth century, retired to a little house built for her by the abbot of Saint Martin in Pontoise, on the northern side of the church of her abbey, and here she occupied herself in making vestments for priests and in sewing monks' habits. At the Abbey du Bec in Normandy, the mother of the abbot, the Venerable Herluin, was lodged in a room adjoining the monastic chapel, and she would wash the community's garments and was responsible for many of the domestic chores. Mabillon also speaks of the Blessed Harduin, a recluse at the abbey of Fontenelle, who transcribed or composed numerous works. These hermits would therefore communicate with the inhabitants of the monastery, and lived in well-lit rooms and were supplied with the furniture necessary for their work.

'It seems to be true, on the other hand, that at the end of the fifteenth and beginning of the sixteenth centuries, certain hermitages fell into a shameful decline; in this regard one can cite a priest by the name of Pierre, a recluse of Saint Barthelemy at Lyons, who would calmly leave his cell and scandalise pious folk by strolling about the town.

'Hermitages continued to exist, however, until the end of the seventeenth century. In volume three of his *History of the Monastic Orders*, Hélyot[25] tells us about Jeanne de Cambry, who founded the Institute of the Presentation of the Blessed Virgin in Flanders, and who wanted to end her days in solitude, near the Church of Saint André at Lille, where she died in 1639; and he also gives us a few details about the liturgy used at that time.

'Mother de Cambry, he says, dressed in a natural, grey woollen robe and accompanied by two of her nuns, one holding a blue cloak, the other a black veil and a purple scapular – the colours of her Order – prostrated herself at the feet of the bishop of Tournai who was waiting to receive her on the threshold of the church. He helped her up, led her to the high altar, blessed the two garments, and imposed them on the postulant, who made her vows of perpetual confinement and was led in procession, while they sang the *Veni, Sponsa Christi,* to her cell, where the bishop shut her in and sealed the door with the sign of the cross. After Mother de Cambry, we next find Marguerite la Barge, who was immured at Sainte Irénée in Lyons, where she died in 1692. She is the last recluse who we have any knowledge of.

'Today,' Durtal continued with a smile, 'a travesty of the old hermitages exists near Lyons. I remember having once visited, when I was passing through the town, the hermit of Mont Cindre. We went there, in part, for amusement. The hermit was a worthy man, dressed in a cassock, and dwelling in a little house that had a garden adorned with an imitation rockery and hideous statues. He sold medals and seemed pious. No doubt he did a good trade, because a rival was building a shack close to his hut. It's difficult, I think, to equate these modern professionals with the wild hermits of earlier times.

'This now defunct practice of hermitic living has furnished hagiographers with a number of celebrated saints: St Heltrude, St Hildeburga, St Drago of Epinay, St Simeon of Trèves, St Viborada, St Rachilda, St Gemma, Blessed Dorothea, the patron saint of Prussia, the Blessed Agnes de Moncada, the Blessed Julia della Rena, the Venerable Yvette, or Jutte, of Liege, St Bavo, the Blessed Millory, the first recluse of the Order of

Vallombrosa, Blessed Diemona and Yulla, who had St Hildegarde as a pupil, Blessed Eve, who with Juliana of Cornillon instigated the feast of Corpus Christi, and how many others whose names escape me!' Durtal said to himself.

'To conclude, the hermitic way of life ended, as did the monasteries that were crumbling into dust when the Revolution swept them away, from a failure of love for God, a lack of the spirit of sacrifice, a lack of faith. It had been arduous at first, then lenient, and the images of La Sachette, the recluse in a rat-infested cell in *The Hunchback of Notre-Dame*, seem inaccurate at the period Victor Hugo was writing.

'Personally, what interests me most, apart from the fact that during the centuries of fervour the pinnacle of the contemplative life, the supreme effort of the soul wanting to melt into God, was surely produced in these confined cells, it's the resemblance I find between the two eras, between hermits and oblates.

'But time is getting on; enough dreaming, we have to think of material things and become the humble servant of Madame Bavoil. What an affliction it is all the same, to have a bobbin in one's brain and to unravel all one's recent reading in this way! It's the fault of those good Carmelites, whose severe observances reminded me of the ancient anchorites… but come, that's enough, let's go.'

And Durtal, after having made his purchases, headed towards the station. He hated packages and cursed the bags, the strings of which were cutting into his fingers. 'Too bad,' he said, 'I'm going to unload that bottle of Chartreuse by stuffing it into my coat; though Madame Bavoil will moan and reproach me yet again for ripping the lining of my overcoat pockets.'

And as he got into the train, his thoughts again turned to this woman. She was living now in the dark – no more visions, no more colloquies with God – all divine manifestations had suddenly ceased; she had once again become like everybody else; she accused herself of having evidently deserved this disgrace perhaps through having talked too much about these favours, and she was eaten up inside by this idea, even as she resigned herself to it.

'Who knows if,' thought Durtal, 'after the death of Abbé

Gévresin, who had been her spiritual director for years and who had been obsessed by the origin of her visions, she wouldn't have experienced serious problems with her new – and possibly arrogant, ignorant, or even too learned – confessors, because they would no doubt have made her drink a bitter cup of obedience and humility.[26] Who knows if it wasn't in the interests of her peace of mind that the Lord withdrew this privilege, which moreover had no bearing on the salvation of her soul, in order to prevent her from having to talk to them about it. Well, if she starts to get too sad about it, I'll try to console her with this theory.'

Chapter VI

"Serves you right for being greedy," said Madame Bavoil, laughing.

"I hereby renounce goose paté," said Durtal, as he placed on his plate something that looked like a thin slice of sponge, the edges of which were burnt to a crisp.

"It's my fault,' confessed Mlle de Garambois, looking crestfallen. "I grilled the toast badly, but it also needed a different bread than this soggy dough prepared by the village baker."

Madame Bavoil took away the disappointing delicacy and brought in a leg of mutton, which Durtal set about the job of carving.

"This light wine pleasantly titillates the tastebuds," remarked Monsieur Lampre. "You get the impression that the *terroir* that produced it is similar to Beaune…"

"Is that so?"

"I didn't have time to go to High Mass," said Madame Bavoil, as she served the boiled potatoes to go with the mutton. "I don't suppose there was anything unusual?"

"No, or rather, yes, there was just a little incident; Father Titourne came in during the *Introit* and had to go and kneel in front of the altar until the abbot gave him permission, by rapping his gavil on the pulpit, to get up and explain his reason for being late; and it seems that his excuses weren't considered satisfactory, because instead of going to his stall he had to sit in the back of the choir, on the bench for latecomers."

"Oh," said Durtal, "Father Titourne, who isn't quite right in the head, is always late; I confess it amuses me to see this lanky fellow with his black skullcap and his pallid Pierrot-like face, rushing into church at full speed. He has a way of swinging the sleeves of his cowl, which fly up and twirl round him like a whirlwind. He looks like Deburau[1] floundering in a bath of ink."

"What that man has to put with in the way of penances!"

"What do you mean?" asked Madame Bavoil.

"Well, two times a week, Monday and Friday, every monk has to confess the faults they've committed against the Rule, in front of the whole chapter. It goes without saying that such faults are very minor. One might reproach oneself for not bowing quickly enough at the *Gloria* during the Psalms, for having torn one's habit, or spilling one's bottle of ink… you see the sort of thing I mean. The reverend abbot inflicts on the delinquent a punishment that generally consists of a prayer, and the obligation to do a penance in the refectory – which is to say, he has to come and kneel in front of the abbot's table for a shorter or longer time according to the gravity of the offence; but in these cases the good father abbot doesn't leave his children to rot on the ground, because they barely have a chance to bend their knees before he gives them the sign to return to their seat."

"And are all the monks subjected to these punishments, which are humiliating if you have to endure them in front of guests?"

"All – professed monks, novices, postulants, and lay brothers, even the prior is not exempt, and the abbot, too, after the monks have finished their penance before the chapter, has to apologise to them for his own breaches of the Rule, and give his reasons."

"A slice of lamb, Monsieur Lampre? No? A potato then?"

"No," said Mlle de Garambois, replying to a look from Durtal, "I'm saving myself for some of that pâté I can see over there; in the meantime, hand me the accompanying salad, so I can toss it."

And when they got to the dessert, while she was nibbling some cake and gingerbread, Mlle de Garambois continued:

"We don't have to hurry because we have to wait for Dom Felletin to arrive before we have coffee and he's never early. Since we have plenty of time, brother, perhaps it might be good to keep the promise that you've always dodged up until now, and show us the documents you have on the history of oblature. At least tell us what it was in the past, since we know what it's like now."

"So it's a lecture you're asking me for?"

"Not at all, just take your notes, which are carefully arranged I'm sure, and simply read them to us, that will be enough."

"I'd be happy to, but I warn you there'll be no rigorous chronology and no careful attention to the sequence of events in this impromptu unpacking of material. You've caught me unawares, so you can't complain, you'll have to accept that this lesson will probably be incoherent."

"That's understood, on condition however that you don't bore us too much."

Durtal went out and after a few moments returned with a bundle of notebooks.

"Now, let's see," he said, "where to start? OK, with this first… that oblature is by no means, as many believe, an invention of the Benedictines. It bore fruit before it was grafted onto our institution among the Premonstratensians, the Templars and in other religious Orders; you could almost say it was in the blood of the Middle Ages, so much did it respond to the religious conceptions of the period.

"At any rate, we find it in the sixth century when the abbot of Agaunum, Severinus – one of the two saints by that name who serve as patrons of that fine church, Saint Séverin in Paris – ran a sort of community where men and women lived in separate houses, and led a quasi-monastic life, without being bound by vows; we come across it again in the following century, established by the rules of St Isidore and St Fructuosus. The latter decreed that, if a layman applied to one of his monasteries along with his wife and little children, he and his family were to be subject to the following rules: they would both submit to the jurisdiction of the abbot, who would dispose of their property; in return, they would not have to worry about food or clothing. They were to be forbidden to talk to each other without permission, though the children could see their parents whenever they liked until such time as they were old enough to be trained in the customs of the cloister.

"I should add, still by way of preface, that oblates were referred to in monastic chronicles and death lists under these names: *oblati, offerti, dati, donali, familiares, commissi, paioti, fratres conscripti, monachi laïci,* and that the documents I've collected on their account are taken from Mabillon's *Annals of the Order of St Benedict,* from Mittarelli's *Annals of the Camaldolese,* from du Cange's *Glossary of Writers in Medieval and Late Latin,* and especially from a collective work by Dom Ursmer Berlière, published in 1886 and 1887 in *The Faithful Messenger,*[2] a little review produced by the Benedictines of Maredsous; unfortunately, in this dense and detailed study there's an obvious confusion between oblates, lay brothers and recluses; and in fact it's difficult to differentiate them, their lives often being identical, and the texts sometimes using terms that apply indiscriminately to one or the other; and it's the same for the female oblates, who are often referred to in these terms: *oblatae, conversae, inclusae.*

"For the Cistercians, I found information in Manrique and in Le Nain, in the *Annals of Aiguebelle Abbey* and in Arbois de Jubainville's *Studies on the Interior Life of Cistercian Monasteries in the Thirteenth Century.*[3] I also unearthed details in some other old books; it's a bit of a mixed salad, but rather less well tossed than the one our sister-oblate prepared earlier.

"Now, after this exordium…"

"What a word!" interrupted Mlle de Garambois, laughing.

"After this exordium, I will tell you that there were two kinds of oblates: those who lived in the monastery, and those who lived in its environs. The regulations of the Cistercians are almost silent on the latter, and are almost wholly concerned with the former, but even then only in a general way.

"They preferred to call the resident oblates 'familiars', to distinguish them from those who remained in the world outside and were not bound to celibacy. They were tonsured, wore a habit that was almost identical to that of the monks, took a vow of obedience and could not change domicile without the authorisation of the abbot; but this kind of hybrid life became a cause of dissipation in the cloisters and in 1233 the General Chapter compelled them to take three religious vows like the fathers – and in 1293 suppressed them altogether. They have since been re-established… but I'm getting lost in my notes," continued Durtal, shuffling his papers.

Chapter VI

"I'll go on, we can look for them later if necessary.

"About the Benedictines proper, details are numerous, but most of the time too brief. We know that at the end of the eighth century St Ludger donned the habit and cowl at Monte Cassino, and that he remained there two and a half years without binding himself by any monastic vows; the same thing happened the following century at Fulda Abbey. Guntram, a nephew of the abbot Rabanus Maurus, even though he wasn't bound by any conventual vows and was therefore only an oblate or familiar, was appointed by his uncle to preside over a priory connected to the abbey, which, by the way, proves that at this time oblates were no less regarded from a religious point of view than professed monks.

"Finally, while mentioning the abuses that resulted from the oblature of those who took refuge in the monasteries in order to escape serving in the army, one of Charlemagne's decrees authorised laymen to reside in the cloister of Saint Vincent de Volturne after making a donation of their property.

"In the ninth century, at the Synod of Aix-la-Chapelle, St Benedict of Aniane tried to prohibit the entry of oblates into monasteries, but his opinion didn't prevail, because we see at the same time laymen and clerks, after having taken the habit, continued to live attached to the communities of Monte Cassino, Fulda and St Gall, and in this last location a well regulated and numerous oblature was still flourishing a hundred years later.

"But it was above all from the eleventh century onwards that it achieved its incredible expansion. What sort of life did the oblate lead in the cloisters? We know that he came into existence before the lay brother, but as to his way of life among the fathers we have only scraps of information.

"At Hirschau in the Black Forest, fifty oblates fulfilled duties that were later devolved on lay brothers. They helped to construct buildings, clear land, harvest crops, and tend the sick. They seem to have been the very first lay brothers, the *converti barbati*[4] of the cloisters; then, when these brothers were established and organised, they must have begun to occupy that halfway position between fathers and lay brothers that they still retain.

"The oblates who were called *paioti* in the fourteenth century underwent a two-year novitiate; they were not granted the title of brother, and they kept their name and wore the ordinary clothes of the period; they were committed only by vows of stability and obedience, and like the lay brothers, they had no seat either in the chapter or the choir. On the other hand, they were admitted to the refectory, where they had a separate table, and they enjoyed all the immunities and privileges of the Order."

"So they had no special dress?" asked Mlle de Garambois.

"Hold on a moment…" replied Durtal, who was leafing through his papers. "According to this note on the *paioti* which I got from Madame Félicie d'Ayzac's *History of the Abbey of Saint Denys*,[5] they indeed had no special dress, but there are other documents which aver that this was not always so. In his book on the customs of Cluny, Ulric tells us that the oblates wore a special livery, and the Council of Bayeux, quoted by du Cange, insisted that they had a distinctive sign on their habits; for his part, Mittarelli, in his *Annals of the Camaldolese*, thinks that the oblates of this branch of the Benedictine Order wore a white tunic and scapular, and a black hood; lastly, among the plates in Hélyot's *History of the Monastic Orders* is one that shows a Benedictine oblate in his habit. He's dressed in a robe that's shorter than that of a monk and topped by a hood that isn't attached to the habit like theirs is; in short, this hood is a cap, but less pointed than the headgear of the fathers."

"Yes, but in the community at Hirschau which you mentioned just now," said Monsieur Lampre, "the oblates didn't discard their worldly clothes and so consequently didn't wear the habit you're talking about."

"The whole thing's as clear as ink, because customs changed from abbey to abbey, and from century to century. It's also evident that the duties of oblates in the cloisters varied according to their capacities and according to age; manual labour was reserved for the illiterate, and intellectual work was, on the contrary, destined for those who could be of service as translators, copyists, or authors; common sense determined it; some were pseudo lay

Chapter VI

brothers, others were pseudo fathers.

"Later, in the sixteenth century, as the *Declarations of Saint Maur* tells us, each abbey of royal foundation had a monk called an 'oblate' or 'lay', who was nominated by the king. He would usually send an old soldier who was infirm or wounded; his duties consisted in ringing the bells, sweeping the church, and opening and closing the main door; he was a simple domestic; the abbey provided him with board, lodging and clothes, or else he could, if he chose, claim a pension of between sixty to a hundred pounds a year. This type of oblate disappeared in 1670, at the time the Hôtel des Invalides was founded in Paris."

"So you were the forerunner of the home for war veterans!" exclaimed Monsieur Lampre.

"Yes, and for young seminarians, too. Old age and childhood, the two extremes, because Chapter 59 of the Rule deals with children offered by their parents to the cloister, and in fact the Benedictines raised little oblates in their monasteries for centuries; they were nurseries for future monks; at present, this system has fallen into disuse in our country, but it still exists, to my knowledge, in an abbey run by Dom Guéranger: Santo Domingo de Silos, in Spain."

"It's unfortunate in terms of the ceremonies, and above all for plainchant, that we no longer have boys in the cloisters," said Mlle de Garambois.

"Of course, but communal dormitories are subject to dissipation and noise in a monastery, which has need of silence and peace. As this type of juvenile oblate has no relation to those that interest us, I'm not going to dwell any more on them, and to finish with the others I will just note that the claustral form of oblature continued until the end of the eighteenth century. At this period, we still find oblates at Monte Cassino and Subiaco in Italy, in Germany, and in France, where they were suppressed along with the monks by the Revolution.

"The institution of oblature was reborn with Dom Guéranger, when he re-established the Benedictine Order at Solesmes. At the present time, oblates living inside monasteries have a choice between taking the monastic habit, and then their life is the same as that of the fathers, or keeping their secular clothes, in which case their life is that of retreatants or guests. Étienne Cartier,[6] who translated St Catherine of Siena and Cassian, and who wrote *The Life of Fra Angelico,* and some dense studies on religious art, lived as a layman in this way for years at Solesmes.

"This, roughly speaking, is the information I've garnered about oblates living in cloisters. Let's now move on to the second category of affiliates, those who resided near or in the environs of priories and abbeys.

"This class can be subdivided into several groups: those who took the vow of obedience, without making any pecuniary arrangement; those who subjugated themselves to the monastery, while nevertheless remaining with their families and retaining the ownership and use of their property, on condition of paying a tax at a rate fixed by the abbot; those who donated their assets to the abbey, which then returned it to them in kind, either by leaving them the usufruct, or by granting them in exchange the legal subsistence in their own home…"

"I'm confused!" cried Mlle de Garambois.

"But no, listen, there were those who paid and those who didn't pay. For those who kept their money, that speaks for itself; as regards the others, it's only the conditions that vary; some paid a tax, others signed away the ownership of their money but retained the use of it during their lifetime; the former gave with one hand only to take back with the other; the latter practised a sort of exchange, and here I call your attention to these reciprocal contracts, which are absolutely the same as those used for recluses.

"Among the Cistercians I discovered an entirely different procedure; married oblates would allocate a sort of retirement pension to the abbey, which then maintained them during their lives, and their property would devolve to the monastery, half on the death of the husband and half on the death of the wife.

"The first category of these external oblates, those who didn't sign any financial commitment and were bound only by the vow of obedience, was most numerous in the eleventh and twelfth centuries. We find these oblates of both sexes residing near the main centres of the congregations of Cluny and Hirschau.

"The second category, those who subjugated themselves in exchange for rent and who continued to be resident outside the monastery walls, were called in vulgar parlance 'fourpenny serfs'. In his *Glossary*, du Cange provides us with detailed information on their account. The ceremony of initiation was an imitation of that of feudal servitude.

"The postulant presented himself, barefoot, with some kind of rope, usually that used for bells, wrapped around his neck; he would place four pennies on his head, which he would then deposit on the altar, along with his weapons; then, prostrate before the abbot, his hands clasped between his, he would swear obedience to him; women usually left a piece of jewelry on the altar as a sign of fealty; and a charter specifying the reasons and the terms of their vassalage was then filed in the abbey's archives.

"Here's one transcribed by the *Benedictine Review*, extracted from the cartulary of the Austrian cloister of Melck. It dates from the thirteenth century:

"'Let it be known to all the faithful that the parents of Adelaide, being entirely free and of noble birth, and having never been bound to any man by bonds of service, have given themselves to God, to the Holy Cross and to St Pancras, whose relics rest in this monastery consecrated in honour of the holy apostles Peter and Paul, and to St Coloman, martyr, under the Abbot Conrad and his successor Dom Reginald, in consideration of a yearly payment of five pence to this monastery; on condition also of finding a house of refuge among the aforementioned saints if ever an attempt be made to reduce them to serfdom. The witnesses, both those deceased and those yet alive, are inscribed in the cartulary of the said monastery.'"

"So they had to pay five pence, not four," remarked Monsieur Lampre.

"Yes, it's likely that nobles and rich people agreed to an increase in this type of tax; the four pence was no doubt the minimum required, at least that's what I think. To continue:

"Sometimes the nobles would even free their serfs, on condition that they paid a fee to an abbey. Here's an example of this kind of contract, this one dates from the eleventh century and comes from the *Thesaurus anecdotorum novissimus* by Bernhard Pez:[7]

"'Adelard gives to the abbey of Saint Emmeran at Ratisbon, his serf Theoburga with her two sons Harold and Enold, on condition that this serf shall pay every year the sum of twelve pence at the altar of Saint Emmeran, and her two sons, on the death of their mother, an annual fee of six pence.'"

"As for the third category, that of the beneficiaries and usufructuaries, it seems to have been a numerous one, and was justified above all by the fact that, apart from the desire to participate in the prayers of the monks, the oblates wanted to obtain the right to be buried in the cloister after their demise.

"And these were no vain promises that the abbots made to their affiliates. The proof is that in the twelfth century, the two abbeys of Admont and Salzburg agreed that as soon as they learned of the death of an oblate who was dependent on either of these monasteries, they would sound the death knell and recite six psalms in service of the deceased: *Verba Mea, Domine ne in furore, Dilexi, Credidi, De Profundis, Domine exaudi*; plus the Lord's Prayer, the versicle *A porta inferi* and the prayer *Absolve Domine,* and this for seven consecutive days, not to mention a conventual Mass, and six tapers being lit for the repose of his soul."

"Well," exclaimed Monsieur Lampre, "with all due respect, if you think for a moment that the congregation of Solesmes is going to revive this charitable practice of yesteryear in your honour, you can think again…"

Durtal laughed.

"We're not asking for as much as that are we my sister-oblate?"

"Why not? This custom seems very natural to me; but for all that I still don't see what, apart for the monetary tax, the obligations of an oblate were."

"They varied according to the monastery; however, there was one condition, a *sine qua non* that figures on every schedule of oblature: that of obedience."

Chapter VI

"And yet now you don't even mention it!" cried Monsieur Lampre. "That clause, the only obligatory one, the only one we can be sure of, isn't even referred to in your ritual of oblature; no, as I told you when you asked me why I – one of the oldest table companions of Val-des-Saints – am not one of your brothers in St Benedict: oblature as the monks today conceive it is a real joke…"

"Oh, come now…" protested Mlle de Garambois.

"Absolutely it is, and mark this well, both of you: there's nothing to expect from the French Benedictines. In order to develop the branch of an Order, you must first love it, and then have the spirit of proselytism. The Franciscans have it and their lay associations serve as real brothers for them. But the glorious Benedictine brotherhood will never allow you to get too close to it. You don't believe me, but you'll see… you'll see…"

"I'll go on," continued Durtal, who didn't consider it necessary to respond, "sometimes the vow of chastity was added to that of obedience, and please note that these vows, like those of professed monks, were for life. Those who broke them were looked upon as renegades and could be forced by ecclesiastical law to return and submit to their superiors. A case of this kind occurred at the abbey of Saint Saviour's in Schaffhausen. Dudo, an oblate – one who lived inside the monastery – decided one fine day to give up his oblature, took his belongings and left the cloister. The abbot appealed to Pope Urban II who threatened Dudo with excommunication if he didn't retract his apostasy and sacrilege. A synod at Constance was convened on the orders of His Holiness to judge the culprit, who was condemned to return to the abbey, and to restore his property with no hope of getting it back, and in addition, he had to undertake a punishment for his crime, inflicted on him by the abbot. There were no half measures in those days!"

"Yes, I know that oblates were regarded as ecclesiastics by canon law, and that they were granted the privilege of exemption from the Ordinary's[8] jurisdiction," said Monsieur Lampre. "And on the subject of the liturgical rite of profession and the taking of the habit, have you finally unearthed any details about them?"

"Not yet; however, it follows from Mittarelli's text that among the Camaldolese the profession made by oblates was often identical to that of the monks, the only difference being that the Church didn't recognise them as solemn and indissoluble vows.

"We might also add – to bring this slightly incoherent unpacking of my notes to an end – that oblates could be celibate or married, laymen or priests, and that male oblates could be attached to a nunnery, and female oblates to a monastery. Here, details are plentiful. To indicate just one source, you can read in Mabillon's Treatise that a number of male oblates made promises of obedience, continence and continual fidelity to the abbess of St Felicita in Florence."

"It springs from all this, my brother, that oblature was a very serious matter in the Middle Ages."

"Yes, and the Popes held it in high esteem. Listen to this, from Urban II's Bull addressed to the abbot of Hirschau: 'Oblature deserves nothing but praise, and is worthy to endure, because it is a mirror of the primitive state of the Church. We therefore approve it, call it a holy and Catholic institution, and confirm it.'

"His Holiness Leo XIII could only repeat the eulogy of his eleventh-century predecessor when, in his Brief given on 17 June 1898, at the request of Dom Hildebrand de Hemptinne, abbot of Saint Anselmo in Rome and primate of the Order of St Benedict, he extolled the institution of Benedictine oblates, and declared that it should be assisted and encouraged.

"These are all the documents I have concerning oblates who live outside the cloister; I've told you all I know, my sister, so please don't ask me for more."

"But can't you tell me a bit more about the female oblates specifially? As you can imagine, it's them I'm most interested in…"

"You know as much as I do, because, as I told you, there was no difference between them and oblates of the other sex… there you go, you're in luck," continued Durtal, who was leafing though his papers as he was replying to her: "Here are some extracts relating to them, which I copied from Mabillon's *Annals* in the abbey library.

"As early as the seventh century, one finds these female affiliates living near monastic communities, but it was mainly in the tenth century that they started to become numerous, especially at St Alban's and St Gall; in the eleventh century they were attached to monasteries in Swabia, and they flourished in France. At Flavigny, the mother of Guilbert, abbot of Nogent, withdrew to a cell built near the church; at Verdun, the mother of St Poppo of Stavelot, and Blessed Adelwine settled near the monastery of Saint Vanne. St Hiltrude resided next to the abbey of Liessies, of which her brother, Gondrad, was the abbot; two sisters of St William lived near his monastery at Gellone. The chronicles of St Gall conserve the names of Wiborada, Richilda, and Wildegarda. St Wiborada, the best known of these, took refuge near the abbey where her brother Hitton had become a monk; she learned the psalter and would bind manuscripts and weave fabrics for robes and habits. The mother of the Blessed John of Gorze, the reformer of the cloisters in Lorraine, was allowed to occupy a building adjoining the monastery in which her son was interned; she got her living from the monks, and in return occupied herself by sewing and mending their clothes.

"Most of these were both oblates and recluses, and if you want my opinion, well, the more I think about it the more I'm convinced that the first form of oblature was reclusion; and here, I'm able to give you an endess list of names: Walburga, who, before being abbess at Juvigny, had been one of the oblate recluses at Verdun; Cibelina, who lived in similar conditions near the monastery of Saint Faro in Meaux; and also Hodierna near that of Saint Arnoul at Metz; but a litany of all these pious women, whether Benedictines or cloistered, would serve little purpose."

"It is indeed very difficult," said Monsieur Lampre, "to distinguish between those oblates who were recluses, and those who weren't."

"For the most part, it's impossible; nevertheless, there are others who certainly can't be reckoned as recluses; Agnes, the German empress of the eleventh century for example, who became an oblate in the monastery of Fructuaria; she spent her days there in prayer, making clothes for the poor and caring for the sick, who she visited frequently. Since she would leave her convent to perform these acts of mercy, she wasn't a recluse.

"In general, the female oblates, who were often the mothers or sisters of monks and who wanted to live near their son or brother, used to wash and darn the linen of the community, embroider the priest's vestments or make the hosts, while some tended the sick of the neighbourhood. They usually wore a monastic habit and a black veil.

"Here's another note," continued Durtal, "again taken from Mabillon. At Fontenelle, when the body of St Wulfram was discovered, the Benedictines entrusted the care of his relics to a lady who had renounced the world and donned a nun's habit."

"You know, it's quite flattering for us to count an empress of Germany among our ancestors," said Mlle de Garambois, smiling.

"Oh, she wasn't the only one; several of her brother oblates were monarchs. Louis the Debonaire was an oblate at Saint Denys; King Lothaire at Saint Martin of Metz; King Garcia of Aragon, at San Salvador of Leyre; King Conrad of Germany, at Saint Gall; King Alfonso of Castille, at Sahagún; King Louis the Young of France, at the monastery of Christ Church in Canterbury; King Henry, your patron saint, at Saint Vanne in Verdun…"

"They were no doubt more honorary than real oblates," remarked Monsieur Lampre.

"It's possible, but the fact remains that oblature attracted quite a few people… and now, that's it, the meeting is adjourned, and I'm putting away my notes."

"But what about St Frances of Rome, our patron saint, have you forgotten about her?"

"Ah, yes, that's true; she was a great saint and a wonderful visionary; but her community of oblates, which was linked to a branch of the Olivetans, is a little special and has only a distant connection to oblates living in and around the cloister.

"Her oblates were really nuns, leading a conventual life and forming a separate Order, devoted to the nursing of bedridden invalids. You know their rules, they're still followed by the nuns who carried on her work after her death, at the Tower of Mirrors[9] convent in Rome.

"Four periods of abstinence a year, and outside this time they are permitted to eat meat on three days of the week, but only at dinner.

Fasting on Fridays and Saturdays; six hours of sleep in total; they are not cloistered, and can go out to distribute relief to the needy and the bedridden, but only in a closed conveyance; they still wear the same widow's mourning clothes as their founding saint did; they recite the divine office, and work in their cells.

"I sometimes wonder why, enamoured as you are of oblature, you didn't enter this convent, or, if you felt that the Italian climate was too harsh, why you didn't become a nun in France, where a similar community exists in Angers and in Paris, that of the 'Servants of the Poor, the perpetual oblates of St Benedict'?"

"Thank you, but as far as I'm concerned, my community is that of Solesmes; I have nothing to do with those twigs grafted onto the trunk of St Benedict; strictly speaking they aren't really Benedictines."

"What…!"

"I really must compliment you, my niece," said Monsieur Lampre ironically, "you're a worthy daughter of the French congregation. Outside it, there's no salvation, and only those who come through Solesmes are Benedictines."

"Obviously…"

"Well, what about the Benedictine nuns at Jouarre, who I believe restored a certain well-known and ancient abbey? Are they not Benedictines?"

"They're independent, they hold classes, sing services badly, and aren't under the direction of the Benedictine fathers. It's not the same thing."

"And the priory of the Benedictines of the Blessed Sacrament in the Rue Monsieur in Paris?"

"They're Sacramentines…"

"By heaven!" exclaimed Monsieur Lampre, "but they observe the Rule of St Benedict more strictly than your young Benedictines do; they have night services, more fast days, and sing plainchant according to Dom Pothier's method… what more do you want?"

"Nothing, except that the divine office isn't their principal function; it all boils down to that."

"There you are," said Monsieur Lampre to Durtal, "these are the notions my niece has brought back from her stay in the cloisters!"

Durtal laughed at this argument between uncle and niece; besides, it wasn't the first he'd witnessed.

Whenever it was a question of the Order of St Benedict, a quarrel would begin between the two of them, each ending up by exaggerating their opinion in order to annoy the other; the truth was that Mlle de Garambois was just repeating, and taking them seriously, the theories of Father Titourne, the crackpot who everyone at Val-des-Saints made fun of; both of them believed, in good faith, that they were enhancing the prestige of the French congregation by diminishing the others.

"With that approach," cried Monsieur Lampre, "you'd end up refusing the Benedictines at the Pierre-qui-Vire[10] monastery, which was founded by a saint, the right to wear a black cowl; but Father Muard's successors, who are attached to the Monte Cassino congregation, follow the ancient observances, getting up in the night for matins and lauds, practising perpetual abstinence; their regime is almost as harsh as that of the Trappists; and besides reciting the divine office, they preach, they harvest souls in the New World – in a word, they're St Benedict's most faithful disciples. Isn't that true?"

"Yes," replied Durtal, "but, personally, I must confess that the higher ideal of Dom Guéranger enthralls me. I don't see what use it is for Benedictines to preach and to teach. There are particular Orders whose task this is; for their part, the penitential Orders figure among the direct descendents of St Benedict; the Black Monks therefore don't need to duplicate their work. Dom Guéranger set a limit to their mission and defined their goal; he has marked them with an original stamp, precisely differentiating them from other institutions.

"His conception of the *Opus Dei,* of Masses and canonical hours performed artistically and celebrated with great pomp, that idea of luxury for God is, in my opinion, very beautiful; it demands that the monks charged with carrying it out be artists, scholars and saints, all at the same time; it's asking a lot I know, but ultimately, even allowing for human shortcomings, the work itself is nonetheless magnificent."

"At last," cried Mlle de Garambois, "someone who does justice to Dom Guéranger!"

"A tree is known by its fruit," retorted Monsieur Lampre. "What has the French Benedictine congregation ever produced?"

"What do you mean 'ever produced'? Why, you know as well as I do. Is it necessary to repeat that Dom Guéranger revived the study of the liturgy, Dom Pothier the study of plainchant, and Dom Pitra the study of symbolism, his *Spicilegium Solesmense*[11] constituting precious volumes for anyone who wants to understand the spirit and the art of the Middle Ages; and lastly, there's Dom François Le Bannier's exquisite translation into French of St Bonaventure's *Meditations on the Life of Christ*, as powerful in its own way as Balzac's *Droll Stories*."

"And more recently?"

"Recently? Well, I don't suppose for a moment that the Order has run out of steam. In any case, it can claim to have produced a master work, *The Treatise on Prayer* by the abbess of Saint Cecilia; among many other unforgettable pages, remember those where she explains the degrees of the mystical life by the petitions in the Lord's Prayer, taken in reverse order, that's to say, beginning with the last and ending with the first. Another book that's worth citing, which is very informative, very lucid, and, what's more, written in a vigorous, thoroughly modern style, is *The Book of Ancient Prayer* by Dom Cabrol, prior of Farnborough. Well, it seems to me that's already something!"

"My dear friend, if you really want to know my opinion, it's that deep down you and my niece are not Benedictines at all, you're Guérangists!"

"Now then, who's this arguing about us!" said Dom Felletin, who had just come in.

"Take a seat, father."

"And here am I with the coffee," said Madame Bavoil, who, turning to the monk, added: "it's true, you arrived just in time. I could hear from my kitchen someone being run through the wringer, as they say."

"So what is Monsieur Lampre accusing us of now?"

"Everything," replied Mlle de Garambois. "He reproaches you for bearing no fruit, for being consumed with arrogance and thinking yourselves the only Benedictines in the world; and lastly, he complains that you don't follow the patriarch's rules."

"That's a lot of grievances in one go. As to fruit, I don't think our tree can be called barren; to assure yourself of this you have only to open the *Bibliography of the Benedictine Congregation in France,* edited by Dom Cabrol. In history, you'll find the learned and patient works of Dom Chamart and of Dom de Fonneuve; in hagiography, the lives of St Cecilia, of St Hugh de Cluny, of St Frances of Rome, of St Scholastica, and of St Josaphat; in monasticism, *The Monks of the Orient,* by Dom Besse;[12] in the liturgy, there are learned articles by Dom Plaine; in musical paleography, the works of Dom Mocquereau and Dom Cagin; and in the field of symbolism there's Dom Legeay's magisterial studies."

"Yes, I'm familiar with the latter," said Durtal; "those works on the allegorical meaning of the scriptures are indeed pithy and engrossing; unfortunately, they're scattered in pamphlets and reprints from journals; no publisher, not even the monasteries that have a printing press like Solesmes and Ligugé, has had the courage to collect them, and yet this would add more to the glory and renown of the Order than those lives of the saints you spoke about."

"As to arrogance," continued Dom Felletin, "don't confuse that with *esprit de corps*, a sort of pride which is sometimes misplaced or unjust, but which stems from the solidarity of people living an enclosed life together, and whose field of vision is necessarily restricted. In the army, the dragoon thinks himself superior to those in the service corp, and because he is on horseback, judges himself to be much above the infantryman. It's inevitable; in order to get novices to like the profession for which they're being trained, you have to persuade them it's the finest and the best of all. It's not so very wicked, after all."

"No, and it's inevitable," said Durtal "In all the Orders, whatever they are, there's a sort of special microscope which magnifies motes into beams. A word, an insignificant gesture, of no importance anywhere else, assumes alarming proportions in the cloister; one ruminates over the simplest act to uncover the hidden meaning beneath it; the most well-intentioned criticism and the most harmless joke are looked on as attacks. On the other hand, a monk has only to produce a work of some kind, for all the bells to immediately ring in praise. There are bigwigs in a monastery, just as there are bigwigs in the provinces; it's childish, and yet it's touching, but, as you rightly say, it derives from that *esprit de corps*, and from an enclosed existence, ill-informed about the world outside."

"As to not following the Rule of St Benedict," continued the monk, who smiled at Durtal's last remark, "that charge is more serious. In what way, my dear Monsieur Lampre, do we not follow them?"

"That's plain enough: the Rule of St Benedict, like most of the rules of other institutions elsewhere, consists above all in general precepts and advice. Apart from liturgical prescriptions, the points it specifies as having to be strictly observed are relatively few. Now these are precisely the ones that you don't really care about. So, monks should sleep fully dressed and in a dormitory; they should say matins before dawn; they should abstain, unless ill or infirm, from eating the flesh of four-legged beasts at all times – yet you sleep undressed and in a cell, you recite the office after sunrise, and you eat meat."

"Four-legged beasts?" cried Mlle de Garambois, "so poultry, which has only two legs, is permitted!"

"Accusations of this sort," said Dom Felletin, smiling, "have long been brought against us. Not to mention the quarrel between St Bernard and Peter the Venerable, on this subject you will recollect that in his essay written to prove that the measure of wine allotted each day to the monks was half a *sextarius*, Dom Claude Lancelot, one of the Solitaires of Port-Royal,[13] reproached the Benedictines of the seventeenth century for cheating on the times of meals — as we do, too, during Lent – and he declares that nothing should be eaten till after the hour of vespers, that's to say, in the evening.

"Now the Trappists, as strict as they are, can no longer endure such abstinence. It is in fact impossible to get up at two o'clock in the morning as they do, or even at four o'clock as we do, and not eat a single thing until four o'clock in the afternoon; giddiness, neuralgia and gastric disorders become widespread. It was therefore necessary to cheat, and to move vespers, during Lent, before noon, that's to say before the usual mealtime; and believe me, despite this mitigation, I still exempt most of my novices from fasting till noon. In the morning I allow them to take a *frustulum*,[14] even if it's only a drop of black coffee and a scrap of bread, it suffices to prevent giddiness and headaches. You have no idea how much health is weakened by a life deprived of exercise, especially when the food is not very tasty, lacks red meat, and is too stodgy and full of starch. By the end of Lent, when even our bread is rationed and no one has enough to eat, people's characters change. Everyone loses their patience and starts getting worked up; sins against charity rise in proportion to the increase in austerity. Is that desirable?"

"Roast beef soothes the soul, and fish irritates it!" said Durtal, laughing.

"Alas, our bodies' weakness has been passed down from father to son, and this infirmity is echoed in our morale; it's a humiliation that the Lord inflicts on us, and it's therefore prudent not to neglect it, otherwise there'd be nothing left to do but send the best of our pupils away because they can't endure the fasts, or else transform the monastery into a hospital!

"And what's more, you imagine the Benedictines eat meat every day, and that's absolutely false; the truth is that we usually have some kind of fatty food a few times a week, except during Lent and Advent. Add to these two seasons, in which we're committed to fasting, Ember Days, vigils, Holy Week and certain festivals, you'll find that we practise abstinence for two-thirds of the year, and endure at least a hundred fasts.

"In any case, these dispensations – that have the sanction of the Church, which also relaxed the observances of the faithful – were anticipated by our Rule and are amply justified by our weakened constitutions and by our life of sedentary study, which it would be impossible to lead on a diet of vegetables and water.

"Take note also that if I'm very indulgent towards those of my novices who have a delicate disposition, I'm much less so with the others. I allow Brother de Chambéon, one of the good Lord's yeomen who has an iron constitution, to fast as much as he likes, and to splatter the walls of his cell with blood whenever he chastises himself. He's no less fit and cheerful for all that; it's perfect; but I will always forbid this kind of thing for the others, until it's demonstrated to me that they can endure it without harm."

"Is it on Friday that you discipline yourselves with the whip[15] while reciting the *Miserere*?"

"Yes, and Wednesdays, too, on days of penance; and each of us can choose to wear the hair shirt if his health allows it. We're not, therefore, as free from mortification as Monsieur Lampre seems to believe.

"As to a system of cells replacing the dormitories mentioned in the Rule, that was in no way an innovation by Dom Guéranger. It already existed in the fifteenth century in the congregations of St Justina and Valladolid, and has continued to this day; moreover, the dormitory has more disadvantages than advantages, and it's the same for the practice of sleeping fully dressed; the monks are free to do as they see fit in this regard, nevertheless, for those who are careless of their personal hygiene, the uncleanliness that results from not undressing makes one wish that it was proscribed; lastly, as regards the change in the hour for matins, you should note that it consists in a simple transposition of the timetable, and we don't gain even a minute extra in rest. Those who rise at two o'clock in the morning, like the Cistercians, go to bed at seven in winter and eight in summer, but then they have an hour's siesta in the afternoon. As for us, we never go to bed before nine and we are up at four in the morning. If you work it out, you'll see that it's seven hours sleep, and that's the same for both.

"And then, you see, in order to judge the Solesmes congregation fairly, you have to look at its origins. Dom Guéranger, who founded it, died in poverty after having struggled all his life with issues of money, and it needed the robust and cheerful soul of this monk to not despair and to carry on his work undaunted. Well, when he died, he hadn't yet succeeded in producing the sort of monks he'd imagined; his dream was only realised at the nunnery of Saint Cecilia, and this thanks to the abbess, who he had trained. He passed away and his successor, Dom Couturier, was an excellent man, but didn't have our founder's breadth of vision; and then came the expulsion of the monks in 1880. The Benedictines lived in the village, unenclosed, deprived of the formation that cloistral life gives. Dom Couturier died in his turn, and through the energy and intelligence of the new abbot, Dom Delatte, the monks, who had now returned to their monastery, resumed a regular monastic life.

"Consequently, if you take note of its shaky beginnings, the situation of the novices who became professed monks only after being dispersed to all four corners of the town, you have to admit that after trials such as these, the French congregation hasn't done so very badly after all."

There was a silence.

"Pardon me if I change the subject," continued Dom Felletin, whose face had suddenly become serious, "but your discussion perturbed me so much I forgot I've got some bad news to tell you."

"Bad news?"

"Yes, first of all Father Philigone Miné had a stroke this morning; the doctor from Dijon came and he assured us that he will survive, but that his brain, which was already a little unstable, will be affected."

"Oh, poor man!"

"And then there's a rumour running round – and it is unfortunately well-grounded – that the government is going to deprive us of the parish of Val-des-Saints."

"Is it going to appoint a parish priest here?"

"Yes."

"But the church," cried Monsieur Lampre, "being at once abbatial and parochial, will have to be split in two; half to the parish and half to the monks! It's absurd!"

"I'm afraid so…"

"And what does the abbot think of it all?" asked Durtal.

"He's very sad about it, but what can he do? He can't fight against the department for religion and the bishop."

"Oh, the bishop is in on it too…"

"Well, he also had to submit to the government's will. He wouldn't have made this change on his own – his hand was forced; all the same, he's old and infirm and doesn't want any trouble."

"By the way," said Monsieur Lampre, "do you know about the neat trick that was played on him when he was still a vicar in another town?"

"No…"

"A priest who, rightly or wrongly, had a grudge against him and accused him of having betrayed the cause of the religious Orders with the prefect, sent a paragraph to the newspapers, which was quite innocently inserted in the Paris papers, and reproduced by the provincial press, stating that Vicar General Triourault had just been appointed the titular bishop of Akeldama."

"The field of traitors, where Judas hanged himself!" cried Mlle de Garambois.

"The funny thing was that he received numerous visits and cards congratulating him on his elevation to the bishopric. He almost died of fury."

"Only a priest's hatred could come up with something like that," said Durtal.

"Well," continued the monk, "that's the news; and very distressing it is; as to what the *modus vivendi* will be between the new parish priest and the Benedictines, I've no idea. Who will be appointed to Val-des-Saints? I don't know that either; the only thing certain is that the nomination won't be long in coming."

"Father," said Madame Bavoil, who had just come back into the dining room, "won't the villagers protest and defend their monks?"

Dom Felletin laughed.

"You have to understand, Madame Bavoil, that here our Benedictine priest gets no stipend from the government, it's therefore a saving for the taxpayer; nor can he accept – our Rule forbids it – the fees to which all parish priests are entitled. So, we bury and marry the poor *gratis pro Deo*, and the money received from the funerals and weddings of people who have the means to pay are set aside for the purchase of firewood that is distributed to the needy when winter draws near. The peasants in this village are therefore lucky; but they are so stupid, so hostile to the monks, they'll be delighted to see our priest removed. Why? They don't even know themselves, it'll only be later, when they realise that the change affects their pocket, that they'll understand their stupidity.

"As for the squires, for them it's a triumph. They'll at last have their own parish priest, but I like to think that as long as we're here, the Baron des Atours and his family will be prohibited from singing profane music in our church…"

"Well, we shall see!" said Durtal. "Now then, a drop of Chartreuse, sister? What? You're refusing?"

"You are ferocious; my eyes water when I drink it, it's so strong…" This complaint was accompanied by an angelic smile as she drained the last drop in her glass.

"We're going through a troublesome period at the moment," resumed Dom Felletin, who was still lost in thought.

"What, is there something else?"

"There is… there is… I'm afraid I'm obliged to send away my cleverest novice, Brother Sourche."

"Why?"

"Because of his ideas, alas, he's a perceptive and intelligent lad, and he's also obedient and pious; he has all the qualities, but he radiates agitation around him; he scares me at certain moments, when I see him running, puffing like a steam engine down the corridors; he's got an exuberant nature and is prone to losing his temper when you try and restrain him. I'm afraid that by keeping him here he'll go mad. On the other hand, explain this… his very real piety is matched by a scepticism that's disconcerting. He's a rationalist to the very marrow; he's one of those people who attach themselves to a text with the idea that you're not learned unless you succeed in proving that the text is false, and he immediately denies anything that goes beyond his powers of reason. When he came here he was very taken by his reading of Monsignor Duchesne's works, and was always quoting Abbé Vacandard's *Life of St Bernard*.[16] 'He disproved several of the saint's miracles,' he would cry in admiration; we tried to respond, but it was in vain.

Chapter VI

Now, this novice is confusing the others with his suspect views and his quibbles over the transcendent; therefore, I consider that in the interests of the novitiate it would be dangerous to keep him here.

"Unfortunately, he's without means or position, and it would be cruel to dismiss him without having first provided for his future. He's determined not to go back into the outside world and still wants to become a priest, so we're going to try and get him into a seminary; perhaps his new masters will have more success than us in saving him from himself."

"But," said Durtal, "he won't do any harm to the seminarists, for, as you know, the real peril of the present time is that the most intelligent pupils are all rationalists."

"Alas…" said Dom Felletin.

"This new generation," continued Durtal, "understands faith in its own way; it accepts some things and rejects others; it no longer has confidence in the lessons of its masters; these young people are too easily duped by appearances. Fear of what people may say, pride, and the desire not to seem more credulous than the godless – all this unsettles them. Everyone of them has read Renan. They dream of a sensible, reasonable religion, one that doesn't shock the good sense of the middle-class with miracles. Unable to deny those in the gospels, because then they would cease to be Catholics, they fall back on those of the saints, and they twist and turn and force the various texts in order to try and prove that the eyewitnesses and writers who narrated them were imagining things, or were all impostors. Ah, what a nice sort of clergy we'll have soon. And what's strange, and will be the characteristic of our time, is that a movement towards mysticism is currently taking shape among the laity, and an inverse movement is occurring among the priests; they're retreating down the path along which we're advancing; the roles are reversed. It'll end with there being no agreement possible between the pastor and his flock."

"And this movement will spread to the cloisters," added Monsieur Lampre. "Brother Sourche is not alone, you may be sure; he's candid and says what he thinks, whereas the others, who are more prudent, will keep their ideas secret until they feel they are numerous enough to dare to express them; a day will come when, in order to show his learning and broad-mindedness, a bad monk will outdo the new school in destructiveness. We've already got partisans who are freethinkers in scriptural matters, the democratic abbots; we'll end up with Protestant monks."

"God preserve us," said Dom Felletin.

"A priest and monks devoid of mysticism, what a troupe of dead souls!" cried Durtal. "The monks would then be no more than curators of a museum of old traditions and rituals; and the priests nothing but celestial admin clerks, employees assigned to the office of the Sacrament."

"Fortunately, we're not there yet," said Dom Felletin, getting up from the table, "but all the same, I can't help but tremble when I think about the future. Who knows what the Lord has in store for us?"

"Perhaps the law on religious associations[17] won't be passed…"

"Hmm…" and the novice master made a gesture of incredulity as he left them.

"Do you think they'll be caught off guard when parliament passes this law?" said Durtal.

"The Benedictines?" declared Monsieur Lampre, "they imagine that France understands them and will be sorry to see them go! What a delusion! If they knew how little this wretched country that ignores them cares whether they stay or go, they'd be aghast!"

CHAPTER VII

Winter had come; a terrible cold held Val-des-Saints in its grip.

In spite of the fireplaces crammed with logs and the blooming gladioli-flames singing and dancing amid the cinders, the house was cold, because the north wind found its way through every crevice in the windows and doors. Draught excluders and screens proved to be useless, while your legs were being grilled, your back would freeze. "Every opening needs to be caulked, sealed like a bottle with melted wax and tallow," Durtal would grumble; and Madame Bavoil would calmly reply: "Wrap yourself up in blankets; that's the only practical way to get warm here." And she set an example, accumulating so many layers she looked like a bell made of skirts, and swaddling her head in such a mass of hats and shawls you could see nothing but the tip of her nose; she looked like a Samoyed[1] peasant, only instead of snowshoes she wore enormous clogs with upturned toes like the prow of a boat.

Nevertheless, by dint of piling up big logs in the hearth from early dawn, the rooms would end up becoming quite tolerable, almost mild by the late afternoon; but as for the outside! In spite of coats, scarves and hoods, it was as if your ears were being pricked by hundreds of needles, and there was a pincushion in your nose, at the end of which it felt like someone had added a pouring spout, as one does to the neck of a bottle in a wine merchants; eyes streamed with tears, and moustaches, fogged by breath, dripped; one's face looked aquatic and rubescent at the same time. But worse than this dry and harrowing cold was the thaw. Then Val-des-Saints turned into a cesspool; one waded in mud with no hope of escape. Durtal had tried clogs, but he twisted his ankle and couldn't walk in them; experiments with other kinds of footwear had little more success, he had to make do with simple goloshes; but in these he kept slipping about in the watery compost of mud, or else the galoshes refused to follow him, and if he insisted, they angrily spat out the coffee-coloured mire they'd drunk in the puddles, and finally parted company with him, the boot remaining stuck in the mire.

The most painful moments were in the mornings, when you had to make your way, in a darkness you could cut with a knife, down to the church.

Waking around half-past three, he would curl up under the eiderdown and dream, in the warmth, until four o'clock. Then a bell rang far away in the night, the cloister bell commanding you to get up; five minutes later, the summons from the bells was reiterated; ten minutes went by, and one heard nothing more, and then the bells would begin again, slowly dripping out their hundred strokes, one by one.

'That must be where the expression "at the hundredth stroke" comes from,' Durtal thought, imagining the jostling in the cells, the monks rushing downstairs, 'because by the hundredth stroke, everyone had to be in church. It's true that good St Benedict, having foreseen that some would be late, declares in his Rule that, in order to allow the laggards time to arrive, one should recite Psalm 66 a little slowly; this is the very reason it was called the Psalm of the Lazy, because after it had been recited those who hadn't got to their place must do a penance.

'As for me, there's no need to hurry,' thought Durtal, because he more or less knew, from having checked which feast day it was the night before on the *Ordo*, how long the office of matins and lauds would take. Sometimes, it was longer, sometimes shorter; on certain semi-doubles, it would last until ten past five; other days, such as on bigger feast days, it might not be over until a quarter to six; the end would be announced by the ringing of the *Angelus*, and then the Mass would begin straightaway.

'I'm only bound in conscience to go to the first Mass on days of communion, but I should be sorry to miss lauds,' and so saying he ended up dragging himself out of bed.

When the weather was fine and the sun had risen, it was easy

Chapter VII

enough to be present at the early morning canonical hours, but in the winter, on those days when the night lasts forever, and in that church with its bare stone floor, which was never heated and atrociously damp because it didn't have a crypt underneath, it was particularly painful; even so, Durtal would consider himself lucky as he sheltered in the nave, which seemed warm and cosy when you took refuge there after having been flayed alive by the north wind outside.

Then there were those sinister, moonless country nights, where you would stumble around, where you bumped into walls that you thought were further away. On these nights he would lose his way, his lantern would mislead him more than it illuminated him, seeming to push back the darkness two feet in front of it, and making the gloom beyond it even thicker; and on rainy days he advanced blindly, at the mercy of the storm, swapping the lantern from hand to hand in order to warm his numbed fingers in his pocket, squelching through the mud and struggling to keep his galoshes from disappearing into the puddles. The quarter of an hour's walk to the church seemed endless. But one way or another he nevertheless reached the church porch. There, he was guided by a point of light, the keyhole that glittered like an ember against the darkness of the door, and it was with a feeling of joy that he extinguished his lantern and lifted the latch.

Coming out of the shadows at the far end of the dark nave, the apse seemed to be glowing. The shades of the lamps above the choir stalls threw a gleam of light on the motionless monks, and the impression of their chants of pity and of praise, ringing out in this sleeping village, far away from everything, while the snow dulled the noise of the storm outside the door, was almost as radiant and overwhelming as if it were the work of angels and superhuman beings.

Durtal generally arrived towards the end of matins, when the monks were standing and intoning the short hymn *Te decet laus*, and immediately after the prayer, they began to sing lauds.

This office – comprised like that of vespers, of psalms and antiphons, a canticle from the Old Testament that varied according to the day, then three psalms of exultation with no intervening doxology, a reading from scripture, a short responsory, a hymn that differed according to whether it was summer or winter, and lastly, in place of the *Magnificat*, the *Benedictus* and its antiphon – was superb, superior to that of vespers in the sense that its psalms have a precise significance lacking in those of the evening service.

Aside from the psalms of praise, from which the name of 'lauds' was derived, the others all made allusion, in effect, to the rising sun and to the resurrection of Christ; and there was no morning prayer that was more concentrated, more specific or more beautiful.

If Durtal had ever seriously doubted the power of liturgical prayer, he would have had to admit that it existed in this splendid service, because after having listened to it, one felt a sublime enthusiasm, an exhilaration of the soul, a sort of impulse to participate more actively in the holy sacrifice, to penetrate more deeply into the eloquent mystery of the Mass.

And at the end of lauds, amid the silence that had fallen like death over the choir, with the monks kneeling, heads in their hands or with foreheads gleaming in the light on the pulpit, the *Angelus* would unleash its three peals from the bell tower, and then as the last stroke resounded through the night, all stood up and the priests went to get ready to say Mass. The lay brothers and sometimes the novices served them; often it was the abbot, assisted by two monks, who celebrated the first Mass at the high altar.

Madame Bavoil was very fond of this one, because she could kiss the abbot's ring when taking communion; and, more courageous than her master, she went down to the church each day; it's true that she was contemptuous of both lanterns and inky skies alike; she was in this respect like a cat, who can stare at the sun without blinking and see in the dark; she would walk with her little steps that no storm could halt and no frost could hasten; moreover, she wore so many wraps, so many cloaks and shawls piled on top of each other, that she was impervious to even the bitterest rain.

"After you've drunk your coffee, my friend," she said as they walked back together from the church, "you won't feel so cold." And, indeed, it was an exquisite moment, that moment when, delivered from this race through the frost and the gloom, Durtal would sit down in his study, in front of a fire in which pine cones crackled and their red-hot scales crumbled amid the orange flames of the logs; and already feeling warm again he would savour an uplifting cup of black coffee while eating a slice of bread.

"For once there's a change in the time of the service," Madame Bavoil said one morning, "because here we are on Christmas Eve. Do you know what time matins will be?"

"Ten o'clock this evening."

"Is the service in the breviaries that Abbé Gévresin left us?"

"Yes and no; it is, but I have to warn you that the monastic matins differs from that of the Roman breviary; the psalms vary, as do the antiphons, and though the readings are the same, they are split up differently; then there's the chant of the genealogy and a short hymn which the Roman text leaves out. So you can't follow the service with our good abbot's book, but if you like I can lend you an old eighteenth-century breviary in Latin and French, used by the Benedictine nuns of France. It's a bit bulky, but it's correct."

"If it gives the French, then it'll suit me. So we'll go down at about a quarter to ten?"

"No, I have to go to confession; I'll make my way to the cloister at nine in order to join Dom Felletin in his cell."

And indeed, Durtal lit his lantern that evening, and wrapped up in an omnibus driver's overcoat, he paddled through the muddy slush.

'I don't know,' he said to himself, 'if Brother Arsène will be at the gatehouse at this late hour, it's unlikely, so it would be wiser to go through the church and use my key to open the door under the belfry that leads to the monastery.'

He managed to get to the church. There, in the depths of the choir illuminated by a censer, Dom d'Auberoche was going through a rehearsal of the ceremony with his novices. He was making them advance, turn, bow, genuflect and kneel before the abbot's throne, then file past the altar, showing them how deep their bow should be, how emphatically they should incline their heads, at this or that place.

And he was also teaching them to give a little flick of the hips as they were genuflecting, in order to swing their habits back to hide their feet; and when they didn't get this movement of the body right, he would kneel in front of them to show them the way it should hang, and would point out to them, with a turn of his head, where it covered his heels.

'Oh, I'm fine,' Durtal murmured, 'there won't be any hitch tonight, but what a lot of bother the poor father is inflicting on himself!'

He went down the few steps leading to the first door of the belfry, the one which was kept shut only by a latch; he plunged into a kind of vestibule, with an enormously high vault, and along the walls of which hung huge ropes for ringing the bells, and with his master key he opened the second door that communicated directly with the cloister.

It was deserted with no oil lamp to illuminate the arcades. Durtal's hooded shadow, immense and comical looking, bounded over the walls in the gleams of his lantern. He walked along the refectory; a ray of light was running under the door and he could hear the sound of footsteps.

'Goodness me,' he said to himself, 'are they having supper? If so, I'm not going to meet Dom Felletin.' He reached the stairs, went up to the first floor and knocked gently at the novice master's door. No one answered.

He raised his lantern to check the sign screwed on the door that indicated where in the monastery a monk might be found if he wasn't in his room; but the peg which was usually stuck in the hole opposite the name of the designated room mutely hung at the end of its string.

As he was authorised to enter the father's cell when the latter had arranged a meeting, he turned the key that was still in the lock, placed his lighted lantern on the desk, sat down on a chair and waited.

He looked around this little room, where he had come so many times before, a whitewashed room with two doors, one joining the room to the landing by which he had entered, and the other opening onto the novitiate. Between the two doors stretched a shabby iron bedstead with a straw mattress but no sheets, on which a plaster-coloured blanket had been thrown. Looking at this pallet, it was evident that his friend slept on it fully dressed; there was also, beside a zinc washstand, a *prie-dieu,* two rush-bottomed chairs, and a fairly large desk, littered with books and papers; on the walls were nailed a wooden cross, without a Christ, and a pine frame containing a colour print of the Virgin by the Beuron school,[2] a pious, reserved-looking Madonna, a little insipid, but pleasant and attractive; and that was all.

'How bitterly cold it is in here,' murmured Durtal, 'I hope he hasn't forgotten the appointment.' The scuffing of slippers in the corridor reassured him.

"I'm late," said the monk, "but we were just drinking a bowl of mulled wine in the refectory, as is the usual custom, to stir the blood, because we're going to be on our feet and sing until dawn. Are you ready?"

"Yes, father," replied Durtal, who knelt at the *prie-dieu* and made his confession. After having given him absolution, Dom Felletin, calmy, thoughtfully, and speaking as if in a conference with his novices, talked about the Advent that had just ended and the feast of Christmas to come.

Durtal had sat down and was listening to him.

"Those four weeks," he said, "that represent the four thousand years before the coming of Christ are finally over. The first day of the civil year, the first of January in the Gregorian calendar, is a day of jubilation for the world; for us, the first day of the liturgical year, which is the first Sunday of Advent, is a day of sorrow. Advent, the symbol of Israel fasting in sackcloth and ashes, and calling for the coming of the Messiah, is indeed a time of penitence and mourning. No *Gloria*, no feast day organ, no *Ite, missa est,* no *Te Deum* in the night service; we have adopted purple vestments as a mark of sadness, and in the past, as a more forceful sign of anxiety and desolation, certain dioceses, like that of Beauvais, would wear vestments covered with ashes; others again, like those at Le Mans, Tours and the churches of the Dauphiné, went even further in the signification of mournful colours by draping themselves in black, the colour of death.

"The liturgy of this period is splendid. To the distress of souls bewailing their sins is blended the fervent cries and hurrahs of the prophets, announcing that forgiveness is near: the Masses of Ember Week, the O Antiphons,[3] the vespers hymn, the redemptive *Rorate coeli*, the responsory in the matins of the first Sunday, may be reckoned among the most precious jewels in the office's treasury; only the settings of Lent and Passiontide contain goldsmith work of such perfection; but now we have put them back in their casket for another year. The anxieties of the coming of death give way to the joy of wishes fulfilled; and yet all is not over, because Advent refers not only to the birth of Christ but also to his final accession to the throne, which is to say the end of the world, when according to the Creed he will come to judge the living and the dead. Consequently, it is only proper to remember this, and to temper our reassuring joy at the Saviour's birth with the salutary fear of the judge.

"Advent is therefore both the past and the future; and it's also in a certain sense the present, because this liturgical season is the only one which must remain immutable within us; the others disappear as the cycle turns; the year itself ends, but so far the universe has not disappeared in a final cataclysm; and so from generation to generation we pass on our anguish; we must always live in an eternal Advent, because, while awaiting the supreme disintegration of the world, it will have its fulfilment in each one of us, with death.

"Nature itself has undertaken the task of symbolising the worry this season subjects us to; the shortening of the days is like an emblem of our impatience and our regrets; but the days grow longer from the moment Jesus is born; the sun of righteousness dispels the shadows; it's the winter solstice, and it seems as if the earth, delivered from the pervading gloom, rejoices.

"Like nature, we should therefore forget for a few hours the menacing thought of punishment, and think only of that inexpressible event, of God who became a child to redeem us.

CHAPTER VII

"My dear friend, you have carefully prepared your office, I assume? You've already read the exquisite antiphons of matins; you spoke to me earlier during confession about your doubts and distractions during the singing of the psalms; you complained of the sadness you felt at not believing yourself to be sufficiently imbued by the spirit of the moment; you asked youself if routine didn't destroy the efficacy of our prayers? You're always trying to short-change yourself. But come, I know you well enough to know that, tonight, as soon as you hear that admirable *Invitatorium* you will quiver with pleasure. Do you really need to dwell on every word, to weigh every response? Don't you feel the presence of God in that enthusiasm which has nothing to do with discussion and analysis? Ah, you're not simple enough with him. More than anyone I know, you love the inspired prose of the canonical hours, and yet you try to convince yourself that you don't understand them well enough to love them! It's madness. With such suspicions you'll end up breaking any kind of momentum; and take care, because it's the sickness of procrastination – from which you suffered so much at La Trappe – which is returning.

"So try and be more indulgent towards yourself, and less stiff in your dealings with God. He doesn't expect you to dismantle, like the pieces of a clock, the subject of your prayers, or that you puzzle out their meaning before you start to say them. He only asks you to recite them; take an example: let's choose a saint whose authority you can't question, St Teresa; she didn't know Latin and had no wish that her nuns should learn it, and yet the Carmelites chant the office in that language. According to the logic of your theory, they were praying badly; but the truth is that they know by doing so they are singing the praises of the Lord and imploring him on behalf of those who don't pray at all, and that's enough; they saturate these thoughts with those words whose meaning they don't exactly grasp but which nevertheless express their desires in an absolute manner; they remind Jesus of his own promises and of his own complaints. Their prayers present him – if I may say so – with a draft signed with his blood which he cannot repudiate; indeed, are we not the creditors of certain promises in his gospels?

"Except… except…," the monk continued after a pause, as if talking to himself, "these promises, due to the immensity of his love, require, if they are to be realised, that we offer him a just return – measured nevertheless by our own yardstick – because what a miserable echo of the infinite we carry within us. This love can only be obtained through suffering. One must suffer to love, and suffer still more when one loves.

"But forget all that; let's not overshadow the joy of these few hours; we'll recover ourselves soon enough; let's think first of this incomparable eve, of this Christmas Eve which has moved all ages to tears. The gospels are brief; they recount the events without comment and without detail; 'There was no room at the Inn', and that's all; but what marvellous flesh the liturgy has wrapped around this skeleton which seemed so dry! The Old Testament serves to complete the New; and here it's the reverse of what usually happens; contrary to all precedents, these earlier texts put the finishing touches to those that follow; the oxen, the donkey… it's not to St Luke we owe them but to Isaiah, and they stay with us forever in the *O magnum mysterium*, one of the most magnificent responsories in that night's second nocturn.

"Oh, the radiant beauty of theophany! Even though Jesus has just been born and can't yet speak, he symbolises in an immediate way, through this material act, the teachings he will proclaim so clearly later on. His first care is to put into practice and confirm by example his mother's song of glory, the *Exaltavit humiles* in the *Magnificat*.

"His first thought is a thought of deference towards her. He wants to justify before all men the Virgin's cry of victory, and indeed he immediately attests that he prefers the meek, and that they must come to him before the mighty. He certifies that the rich will find it harder than the poor to be admitted to his presence, and he makes this clear by imposing a long journey on the kings and wise men who are the Magi, while he frees from fatigue and danger the shepherds, who are the first he summons to adore him, and he enhances the hierarchy of the humble by delegating, in order to lead them to him, not the silent gleaming of a star, but a rapturous choir of angels!

"And the Church conforms to the intentions of the Son. On this night of Christmas, the Magi only have a walk-on part, as it were, and it's not really a question of them, they don't have an office devoted to them until the feast of Epiphany. Today, it's all about the shepherds. And one should add that Mary, in her turn, has always confirmed this sign, because in the most celebrated of her apparitions, she always spoke to shepherdesses, not to wise men, or to monarchs, or to rich women."

"No doubt, father," said Durtal, "but permit me, nevertheless, to make an observation. The lesson in humility you mentioned earlier has been lost a little, all the same. The Middle Ages, which invented many legends about the Magi, never invented a single one about the poor shepherds; the relics of the Magi, who were promoted to the rank of saints, are still venerated at Cologne, but nobody has ever bothered to find out what became of the remains of the lowly shepherds, or wondered why they weren't also saints."

"That's true," said the monk, smiling. "But what do you expect, mankind loves a mystery; the Magi were so enigmatic, so strange, that everyone in the Middle Ages dreamed about these potentates, who represented for them the peak of wealth and the apex of power; but they forgot the good shepherds, because they couldn't conceive of them as being different to those they saw every day. It's the eternal refrain; the first in the eyes of God are the last in the eyes of man.

"Now go in peace, take communion my dear child, and pray for me."

Durtal got up to leave.

"By the way," said Dom Felletin, "I've received some information about the effect produced on the public by the Pope's letter concerning the law on religious associations. Everyone clearly understands that it sets out in milder and more diplomatic terms, what was asserted more rigorously in the interview with Henri des Houx[4] published in *Le Matin*. Leo XIII will withdraw the France protectorate over the East if she touches the religious Orders; so this is to tell you that faced with such an ultimatum the government will back down and the danger that the Freemasons were threatening us with is receding."

"But what if the government, convinced that His Holiness will back down at the first alarm, persists in passing this law?"

"Ah, you're very difficult to convince!"

"Well, let's hope the Lord hears you..."

Durtal shook hands with his confessor and went down the stairs leading to the cloister. He noticed a candle moving under the arches, and he recognised the candle bearer, little Brother Blanche. He was walking in front of a hooded Father d'Auberoche, who was carrying the relics on a salver covered by a veil, and they too were heading towards the church.

The apse looked like a hive: novices were putting the last touches to the preparations for the feast, and in the dimly-lit choir, it was like a black swarm of bees. They all moved aside and the humming ceased as Dom d'Auberoche passed through and laid his salver on the altar; he removed the linen cloth and placed the brass and gilded bronze reliquaries between burning tapers, and novices lit pale gold nightlights at the corners of the altar to honour the relics and to apprise the faithful of their presence.

And Father d'Auberoche, before retiring, made due obeisance to these holy remains, then genuflected before the tabernacle; and the sacristan began to light the lamps and the candles. Soon the back of the sanctuary was a blaze of light.

Draped with an oriental carpet which covered the steps and slabs of the choir, the altar, adorned with candles and green plants, was gleaming; on the table, the abbot's sacerdotal vestments were arranged, and the two mitres, the gold mitre and the precious mitre, sparkled, one on the Epistle side and the other on the Gospel side.

The choir was decorated with white, fringed hangings, and on the left, raised up on three steps, was the abbot's throne, its red velvet seat surmounted by a canopy that stood out against the white drapery, and with a painted plaque, like a sort of skylight, representing the abbot's coat of arms, above the back of the throne.

The abbot's usual seat, a little in front of the monks' stalls, was

Chapter VII

decorated like the throne in red velvet with a gold trim; there was also a *prie-dieu* covered in green baize standing before the altar.

'Ah, yes,' said Durtal to himself, 'those are signs of an important day, because the Smyrna rug and the green *prie-dieu* constitute the summit in the hierarchy of feast days!'

The bells were ringing. At dawn, a line of monks, the prior at their head, left the sacristy and made their way towards the church door opening onto the cloister to present the abbot with holy water. The nave was filling with village folk, the priest was ranging the children on benches; the loud clatter of clogs and boots filled the church. Monsieur Lampre pushed his way through the crowd and took a seat next to Durtal. The most noble Baron des Atours, accompanied by his family, entered. He cast a patronising glance at these peasants, who moved aside to let him pass; after he knelt down in the front row of pews, he buried his old army quartermaster's face in both hands, but they soon went their separate ways, one tugging at the toothbrush bristles of his moustache, the other caressing the smooth ball of his skull. His wife was of somewhat dubious distinction, but the ugliness of his daughter was certain; she resembled her mother, but with something even more provincial and idiotic; and the son, a fine young man, educated in the most devout institutions, was swaying backwards and forwards, his gloved hands grasping the knob of his cane, the other end of which was buried in the rotten straw of the chair in front of him.

It made you wonder if these people knew how to read, because they didn't have any prayer books and confined themselves, whether it was a Mass, matins or vespers, to fingering their costly rosaries, the silver chains of which made a jingling noise like that of a horse shaking its bit.

And suddenly the organ burst into a triumphal march; the abbot entered the nave, preceded by two masters of ceremonies; between them walked the crosier bearer, wearing an alb, his shoulders covered with a *vimpa*, a white satin scarf lined with cherry-coloured silk, the ends of which, folded back across his chest, were wrapped around the stem of the crosier. The abbot, the long black train of his habit borne by a novice, gave his blessing as he passed the kneeling worshippers, who crossed themselves.

He himself went to kneel at the *prie-dieu*, and his whole court of attendants, cope bearers, and monks in albs, also knelt, so that all one saw was a golden crook dominating a field of dead moons – the upright crosier above the large, round and white tonsures of the monks' heads.

At a signal from Father d'Auberoche, clapping his hands softly, everyone rose to their feet; the abbot went over to his throne, around which his three assistant deacons took their place, and the green *prie-dieu* was removed.

The choir was full; the two upper rows of stalls on each side were occupied by professed monks and novices in their black cowls, the lower ones by lay brothers in brown cowls; and below them, on benches, the choir boys in vibrant red cassocks; and in the empty space between it was a coming and going of officiants and of the crosier bearer, a to-ing and fro-ing of the other bearers, the candle bearer and mitre bearer; and these movements were so expertly coordinated that, even in this very limited space, they all changed position and criss-crossed one another without getting in each others' way.

The abbot began the office.

As Dom Felletin had foreseen, the *Invitatorium* immediately cast its spell over Durtal. They were singing the usual psalm, *Venite exultemus*, summoning Christians to adore the Lord, which was intercut after each strophe by its refrain, sometimes shortened: "Christ is born to us"; and sometimes complete: "Christ is born to us, let us worship him."

And Durtal listened to this magnificent psalm, recalling the Lord's creation and his rights over it. Over a slightly sad melody, and with an affirmative and respectful tenderness, the wonders of God were set forth, as were his lamentations over the ingratitude of his people.

The voices of the cantors enumerated his marvels: "The sea is his and he made it, and his hands prepared the dry land. O, come let us worship and fall down, and kneel before the Lord, our

Maker, for he is the Lord our God, and we are the people of his pasture, and the sheep of his hand."

And the choir took up the refrain: "Christ is born to us, let us worship him."

And, after the glorious hymn of St Ambrose, *Christe Redemptor*, the solemn office truly began. It was divided into three vigils or nocturns, composed of psalms, of readings or lessons, and responsories. These nocturns had a special meaning. Durand, the thirteenth-century bishop of Mende, explained them clearly in his *Rationale*. The first nocturn deals allegorically with the time before the law was given to Moses, and in the Middle Ages the altar was hidden under a black veil to symbolise the darkness of Mosaic Law and the sentence pronounced against man in Eden; the second nocturn signified the time that had elapsed since the written law, and so the altar was hidden under a white veil because the prophecies of the Old Testament already shed a furtive light on fallen mankind; the third nocturn expressed the love of the Church and the mercy of the Paraclete, and the altar was hidden under a purple cloth, an emblem of the Holy Spirit and of the blood of the Saviour.

The office unfurled, sometimes chanted, sometimes sung. The whole was splendid, but its supreme beauty was especially reserved for the singing and the responses in its lessons.

A monk would come down from his stall, led by a master of ceremonies, to a lectern placed in the middle of the choir, and there he chanted or recited – it was difficult to know which term to use, because it wasn't exactly chanting, nor was it quite singing. The phrase would unfold over a sort of grave, languid melody, slow and plaintive, and closing one's eyes, listening to these airs which were barely even there, it was like a strange lullaby of the soul, gently cradling the heart, a rocking that suddenly ended on a mournful note as if with a tear.

'Ah, Dom Felletin was right, what a superb service and what a radiant night. While the old world is sinning or sleeping, the Messiah is born and the shepherds, dazzled, come to worship him; and at the same moment, those mysterious men, those dream figures foretold long before St Matthew by Isaiah and the psalmist, who described them as the kings of Tharsis, Arabia and Saba, surging up from who knows where, galloping on dromedaries in the pursuit of a star in the night, in order to worship the infant in turn, and then disappear by a different route than that by which they came.

'What controversies that star has given rise to! But how stupid all the hypotheses of the astronomers seem to me with their inevitable blunders, and how much I prefer the view of the Middle Ages, taken from the Apocryphal Book of Seth and repeated by St Epiphanius and the author of an imperfect commentary on St Matthew. They thought that the Star of Bethlehem had appeared to the Magi in the image of a child seated beneath a cross, in a sphere radiating with fire, and indeed most of the early Flemish primitive painters represented the constellation in this form – Rogier van der Weyden,[5] in one of the panels of his marvellous *Nativity* in the museum of Berlin, to cite one at random.'

Durtal was dragged from these reflections by the ebb and flow of the monks in the choir. The abbot was being vested. A master of ceremonies, standing in front of the altar, lifted up the vestments that had been placed there, the alb, the cincture, the stole and the cope, and handed them to novices who, one after another, after genuflecting in front of the throne, presented them to the deacons assisting the abbot.

Stripped of his long black cape and decked out in a white alb, Dom Anthime Bernard appeared even taller still, he dominated the whole church from his high throne, and after he had girded himself with the cincture, in the movement he made with his arm to replace round his neck his pectoral cross, which one of the liturgists held out to him and which he kissed, the ring on his hand, illuminated by the flames of the candles, flashed briefly. At a sign from Dom d'Auberoche, the mitre bearer, his shoulders now covered by a shawl similar to that of the crosier bearer, the folded ends of which had to cover his fingers when he held out or received the mitre when dressing the abbot, approached the throne; then after donning the stole and cope, the most reverend abbot intoned the *Te Deum*.

Chapter VII

Here, Durtal was forced to moderate his enthusiasm, because he was assailed by memories, and the *Te Deum* of the cloisters couldn't bear comparison with that of the great churches in Paris. 'It's certainly the case,' he said to himself, 'that this hymn is much more imposing at Saint Sulpice, for example, when, supported by thunderous blasts from the organ, the full choir sings it reinforced by the whole body of the seminarists, and it's the same with the *Magnificat royal*, which has a majesty and a fullness lacking in the thin and feeble settings of the *Magnificat* in the Solesmes repertoire.

'Besides, it would need hundreds of monks, all having a voice capable of projecting these vast and magnificent works, and in what monastery could one find a massed choir powerful enough?'

This disenchantment didn't last long, because the abbot, surrounded by cope bearers, masters of ceremony, incense bearers and candle bearers, began to chant the genealogy of Christ from a Gospel, which a monk held in his two hands, supporting it with his forehead; and from this strange, sad chant, monotonous and tender, singular images of the patriarchs filed past, picked out as if by a flash of lightning with the recitation of their names, and then falling back into the shadows as soon as another succeeded them.

And when the reading was finished, while they were removing the abbot's cope and substituting it with a chasuble, the choir sang a short hymn of Greek origin, the *Te decet laus*, and then the office came to an end with the prayer of the day and the *Benedicamus Domino*.

The four principal cantors who had gone to robe themselves in the sacristy now returned and Father Ramondoux, the precentor, placed the insignia of his office, the baton cantoral, a copper staff on top of which was a statuette of St Benignus, in a brass ring next to his seat.

And he and the others were seated on low-backed chairs, installed on a raised step behind the communion rail at the entrance to the choir, opposite the altar. Their backs were therefore turned to the public, splendid backs of shimmering silver moiré, ocellated with circles of cherry silk, inside which the Gothic monograms of Jesus and the Virgin were embroidered in gold thread.

Leaving their seats and standing in a semi-circle in the middle of the choir, they sang the *Introit*, while the abbot, surrounded by his entourage, began the Mass.

When they reached the *Kyrie Eleison*, the congregation came alive, the girls and boys of the village, led by the priest, supporting the monks. It was the same with the Creed. At that moment, Durtal had a clear vision of the past, of a hamlet singing the melodies of St Gregory in the Middle Ages. Obviously this didn't have the perfection of the singing at Solesmes, but it was something. In default of artistry, it was an effusion of the soul, a little raw, the soul of a crowd carried away by emotion in that moment; for a few minutes, it was as if an early church had come back to life, where the people, vibrating in unison with their priests, were truly taking part in the ceremonies and praying with them, in the same musical dialect, in the same idiom; and it was so utterly unexpected in this day and age, that Durtal, on hearing them, thought he'd slipped once more into a dream.

And the Mass unfurled amid a great flood of sound from the organ; the abbot, sometimes at the throne, sometimes before the altar; the abbot, in white shoes and gloves, bareheaded or wearing the gold mitre, then the mitre sewn with gems; the abbot, his hands clasped or holding the crosier which he then returned to the kneeling novice who kissed his ring. Incense smoke veiled the spear-like flames of the altar candles, and the nightlights on either side of the relics darted two topaz-coloured flames into the blue cloud. Through these billows of smoke which were rising beneath the vaults, one could make out at the foot of the altar steps the motionless golden statue of the sub-deacon, holding the paten covered by a cloth, which he lifted before his eyes at the end of the Paternoster, symbolising in this way the Old Testament – of which he was the image, just as the deacon was that of the New – and showing how the synagogue was unable to see the mysteries of the Church being fulfilled; then the Mass continued, all the choir boys kneeled in a row, with lighted candles in their hands during the elevation of the host, which the sound of bells proclaimed to the night outside; finally, after the *Agnus Dei*, the abbot gave the kiss of peace at the altar to the deacon, who went down the steps and gave it in turn to the sub-deacon, who, led by the master of ceremonies, went to the monks' stalls, and there embraced the senior monk who transmitted the kiss to the others, each embracing and bowing to each other, as they joined hands.

Here, Durtal ceased to watch; the moment of communion was near, a peal of bells rang out in the apse; the novices and the lay brothers began to set off, two by two; the deacon, stooping before the abbot, chanted the *Confiteor* in a way that seemed more bizarre than contrite, and, in front of a large cloth held at each end by a monk, everyone kneeled to take communion. Then the abbot came down the altar steps, followed by his cortege of officiants, and distributed the Eucharist to the faithful, while behind him, candles in hand, a troupe of small choir boys lined up.

The noise of boots and clogs filled the church almost drowning out the abbot's voice. One could catch the words '*Corpus Christi…*', pronounced in the Italian fashion, but the rest was lost in the clatter of feet; coming back to his place, Durtal forgot the liturgy and the Mass, and contented himself with imploring the Lord to pardon his faults and deliver him from evil.

He came back to himself when the abbot, wearing his mitre, stood leaning on his crosier, and began to sing the pontifical blessing:

"*Sit nomen Domini benedictum.*"

And all the monks responded:

"*Ex hoc nunc et usque in seculum.*"

"*Adjutorium nostrum in nomine Domini.*"

"*Qui fecit coelum et terram.*"

"*Benedicat vos omnipotens Deus, Pater et Filius et Spiritus Sanctus.*"

And at the invocation of each of the three persons, he made the sign of the cross in the air over the people, to the right, middle, and left of the altar.

As lauds began, Durtal withdrew. His could no longer feel his feet they were so cold. Madame Bavoil came to join him with the lanterns, which they lit on the way out. The night was glacial and snow was falling.

"Wait for us!" It was Mlle de Garambois, muffled up in furs and accompanied by her uncle, who was calling them.

"I'll take you to the house," she said, "not for supper, that would hardly be very monastic, but to have a glass of hot punch in front of a good fire."

They set off, one after the other, along a path already half hidden under the snow; one could make out lights running in every direction, and in the distance inns sprung up out of the darkness, with the red glow of their square windowpanes.

Under the pretext of giving them punch, their kind hostess had loaded a table with pastries and cold meats.

The dining room was quiet; it was a bourgeois dining room, with a sideboard and chairs in the style of Henry II, but the pine cones burned merrily in the hearth, and the smell of resin filled the room; Durtal sat toasting the soles of his shoes.

"We're the victims of an ambush," said Mme Bavoil, laughing, "it's a veritable supper that our friend is threatening us with; but when all is said and done a little gluttony is allowable on the day of the nativity."

But despite all attempts at persuasion, she contented herself with just a morsel of bread and cheese.

The snow continued to fall; the lights of the lanterns on the road had disappeared; drunken shouts resounded on all sides; in the inns, the peasants were getting tipsy.

"What a pity! They were so good just now when they were singing with the monks," said Madame Bavoil.

"Ah," exclaimed Durtal, "don't get too carried away. Those who were singing in church were those who the monastery employs. They go to Mass to please the fathers, but wait until the monks are gone..."

"In any case," said Monsieur Lampre, "even if one allows, against all probability, that these fellows are in good faith, it would still be in the tradition of the Middle Ages, because among our ancestors, especially in Burgundy, piety didn't exclude a slightly crude exuberance. Whatever imbeciles may say about the Middle Ages, that period was not one of prudery. Do you know, Madame

Bavoil, that in the past, before the Mass of the present day, they solemnly celebrated a feast in honour of the donkey in certain churches, and the author of the words and music of this office, would you believe, was none other than Monsignor Pierre de Corbeil, archibishop of Sens. But yes, from the thirteenth to the fifteeenth century the poor donkey shared in the triumph of the Redeemer."

"When I think that he bore Jesus on his back," murmured Madame Bavoil, "I want to kiss him on the nose when I meet him."

"There was also a feast of fools," continued Monsieur Lampre, laughing. "The actors elected a 'bishop' who they enthroned in a ridiculous ceremony, and this buffoon gave his blessing to the people gathered in the church and presided over farcical services, while the peasants, smeared with wine juice and disguised as jugglers or strumpets, swung censers around, burning incense made of old shoe leather."

"I don't see what such drunken revelries have to do with religion," observed Madame Bavoil.

"On the contrary, the origin of these parodies was liturgical. The donkey was honoured because of the ass that spoke, and by its remonstrances called forth Balaam's famous prophecy before the king of the Moabites about the coming of the Messiah. The donkey, which was one of the heralds of Christ, attended him beside the cradle from the moment he was born, and it carried him in triumph on Palm Sunday; it therefore has its reserved place in the Christmas festival.

"As for the feast of fools, it was called by its real name the feast of the deposition, an allusion to *Deposit potentes de sede* from the *Magnificat*. It aimed at humbling pride and exalting humility. On that day, bishops and priests counted for nothing, as if they'd been deposed. It was the common people, the menials and serving lads of the monasteries who were the masters, and they had the right – and used it – to reproach monks and prelates for their transgressions, their simony, their favouritism, and more else besides perhaps… it was the world turned upside down, but by tolerating these public displays of protest – until the moment they degenerated into pure farce – the Church surely showed her superiority and broad-mindedness; by smiling on such follies, did she not prove how indulgent she was towards the small and lowly, and how she was happy to let them alleviate their grievances, by rendering justice themselves, before having fun."

"The fact is that it was funny in those days," cried Mlle de Garambois. "Imagine this, to make fun of me no doubt, my uncle lent me a book by a Benedictine nun, from I don't remember which century…"

"From the tenth," said Monsieur Lampre.

"It's called *The Plays of Hrotsvitha of Gandersheim*.[6] I foolishly believed it was a mystical work; now, these are pieces that this nun wrote for her cloister and there's one, I don't really know how to explain the subject without laughing, called 'The Passion of Saint Gandolphe, Martyr.'"

"Well?" asked Mme Bavoil.

"Well, Saint Gandolphe, who was a prince, married a dissolute woman who deceived him. The poor prince discovered his misfortune and said nothing; but the princess, irritated at seeing herself found out, murdered him. Miracles immediately started to occur around his grave. She made light of it, saying she cared as much about it as she did about one of those little choux pastries they have so unfairly named nuns' farts.[7] And she was immediately punished with a retribution appropriate to the very terms of her contempt. For as long as she lived she was driven to distraction by breaking wind loudly and without stopping, as the happy Hrotsvitha calmly recounts.

"That just proves," said Durtal, "assuming that the works of this nun are not apocryphal, the simple humour of the Benedictine cloisters in the tenth century. Note, moreover, that scatological jokes are still dear to churchgoers and that's quite natural; other jokes, those about women, which amuse the laity when a meal is over and the men are alone, are forbidden to them; they make up for it therefore with these jokes, which are moreover neither dirtier or more stupid than the others – and they at least have the advantage of being innocent."

"A slightly uncouth ingenuousness was one of the charms of the abbeys of yesteryear; try and find that quality today in our monasteries!" resumed Monsieur Lampre.

"I'd have been surprised if you hadn't found a way to get a dig in at our monks," said Mlle de Garambois. "Fortunately," she continued, smiling, "these calumnies are only the sacrilege of love, and you'll still be only too happy, if the Benedictines come to be expelled from here, to go out of your way to help them whenever they have need of it."

"I'll no doubt be silly enough to do that," said Monsieur Lampre, laughing. "Deep down, it doesn't stop me being annoyed by the pettiness of their intelligence and their holiness, because I love them too much not to want them to be better, and God knows these scamps are resistant enough to being pushed!"

"Suppose we go to bed," said Madame Bavoil, "it's rather late, and we still have to get up tomorrow…"

"Today, if you don't mind, because it's just struck three o'clock," replied Durtal as he re-lit the lanterns.

"That Monsieur Lampre is a very learned man," said Madame Bavoil as they trudged through the snow, "and I've no doubt he has a good heart, but it seems to me that he's really too critical of others and not critical enough of himself."

"Ah, you too, you want people to be saints. Alas, the die is almost broken and the master of the mint stamps very few coins now… here and there, perhaps, in provincial retreats or in the obscure corners of a town. There are certainly some in the cloisters. I've known a few personally among the Trappists at Our Lady of the Hearth; there are some in other hermitic retreats, but these latter never mix with the outside world, and how can we ever hope to know them since they are precisely those we never see?

"One of them, who enjoyed a certain notoriety, however, died recently in a Benedictine monastery in Belgium," Durtal continued, after a pause, "but the details I've been given on his account are contradictory, so take them for what they're worth.

"This monk, Father Paul de Moll, is said to have been one of the most extraordinary miracle workers of our time. He healed all illnesses as if for fun; he took on everything, he eradicated toothache and migraines, as well as consumption and cancer; he subdued incurable diseases and ulcers without seeming to attach the least importance to it; he treated men and animals without distinction, and would practise very unpretentiously and modestly, simply prescribing the use of water in which a medal of St Benedict had been dipped.

"This monk, who was our contemporary, because he was born in 1824 and died in 1896, belonged to the abbey of Termonde; he re-established the abbey of Afflighem, and founded the priory at Steenbrugge; he was, moreover, a monk who loved to mortify the flesh and was very keen on self-sacrifice; but you would have to know it, seeing this man calmly smoking his pipe, so joyful and so kind, no one would have suspected a thing.

"Now, of all these miracles, which can be numbered in their hundreds in Flanders, how many can we believe? Some seem to be supported by evidence, others require further examination, because they rest solely on suppositions and hearsay.

"His life, written in all good faith by a man named van Speybrouck, is so incoherent and so far from any concern for history that it can't be trusted. Let's hope, for the honour of the Order, that Father de Moll wasn't a simple sorcerer, but a true saint. The Church alone is able to decide the question and enlighten us."

Chapter VIII

There was a break in the weather, and the wind became less bitter; the sun, which seemed to be lost, made fitful reappearances in the iron-grey sky and bleached the earth with its furtive rays. There was a momentary awakening in the garden; living shrubs emerged from a soil that appeared to be dead. Boxwood, with its small orange leaves that were hollowed out like spoons and brittle to the touch, and juniper, with its bluish needles and rumpled berries of black indigo, started to appear, like a sort of layer of muscovado sugar streaked with white threads by the melting frost; the evergreens, spindle wood, laurel, yew, rosemary, and firethorn, whose vermillion berries were now turning a tan colour, brightened the flowerbeds with their greenery, flowerbeds in which all the other plants were now nothing but stalks, shrivelled and scorched by the icy fire of the north wind; but even so, there was something sickly about these plants, they had the air of convalescents, just risen from their bed of snow.

A single family thrived comfortably in the cold, the hellebores. They swarmed the whole length of the paths; some species, like the Christmas rose, were in full bloom and their flowers of a purplish pink, the shade of sickly scar tissue or of a closing wound, strongly evoked the idea of a dangerous plant, sweating venomous juices and stinking of poison; other black hellebores, with ragged leaves, sawn and serrated at the edges, with flowers like rolled-up shells, were even worse. If you pulled them up, you discovered they had slender roots, like the hair that hangs from a ball of onions. The old botanists of the sixteenth century praised them, saying they evacuated phlegm and yellow bile, and cured the itch, impetigo, ringworm, scabies and other impurities of the blood; but they nevertheless retained a sinister look, with their funereal leaves and the unripe apple-green colour of their flowers, which, like their sisters, the Christmas roses, all hung their heads, and lacked the fresh, cheerful look of a healthy flora.

At this time of year, the garden was far from attractive, with its thickets of shrivelled plants and its clumps of dubious flowers, and Durtal hardly ever went down there. But that morning he was walking there as he had ten minutes to kill before catching his train. For once the weather seemed propitious, he was planning to go to Dijon – to buy ties and boots, a plan hitherto postponed by the prospect of freezing in a railway carriage and of not being able to walk about the town – and he said to himself: 'I can justifiably be excused from attending High Mass here, because I practically know it by heart. It's been the same for the last six days, the Octave of Epiphany[1] having pushed back for a week the procession of saints' days. The Mass is certainly delightful in spite of its rather poor *Introit*. The *Kyrie* is very fine, plaintive, if a little affected; the *Gloria* is lively and respectful, and the second phrase of the *Gradual*, *'Surge et illuminare, Jerusalem'*, and the *Alleluia* are exquisite; the *Reges Tharsis* during the offertory flies as straight as an arrow and you listen to it until the last vibration fades away; but I've still got tomorrow to hear it; a low Mass will suffice for me today, so let's profit from this liturgical occasion and the benevolence of the weather.' And he headed to the station.

Once seated in the train, he called out the door to Dom de Fonneuve, who was looking for a seat, and so the prior joined him in his compartment.

After having chatted of this and that, the monk, speaking of the new parish priest who had taken up his duties a few days ago, asked Durtal if he'd seen him.

"Yes, he honoured me with a visit yesterday, and if you want to know my opinion, I must admit the impression he made on me was rather unfavourable. He seemed to me like a young peasant girl, somewhat ill-bred, who was trying to give himself airs, as they say in Paris.[2] He had a way of squirming on his chair, of being coquettish, of being coy, of making faces like a little girl who's scared of being ravished but drawn to it at the same time, which I didn't think much of. During our conversation, I tried to weigh up his soul and see what he was made of, and I discovered that in addition to an absolute incomprehension of mysticism and of the liturgy, he has a vanity that will, I'm afraid, cause you a lot of trouble. But tell me, father, those repairs to the presbytery are they progressing?"

"Yes, the mayor and the town council proved to be quite amenable once they realised it wasn't about the monks. They've always refused to put so much as a slate on the roof while we occupied the presbytery, but now, socialists though they be, they're all smiles and are trying to butter up their new pastor. Their game is evidently to make us quarrel with him, but I hope they won't succeed; indeed, we're resolved to yield to him as much as possible in order to avoid any conflict. Besides, if this young priest is – and I agree with you – a little pretentious and full of himself, he's nevertheless pretty well disposed towards us and very kind. You are judging him on a few grimaces, but we, who have observed him over the eight days he's already spent with us in the monastery, where we offered him bed and board while waiting for the presbytery to become habitable, we're satisfied with him and are convinced he's a good lad."

"Father, I sometimes think that you're too kind; you think everyone's a good lad."

"Not at all, we're too inclined, you know, to judge others severely; nothing is more unjust, because ultimately, even when a man does you harm, that doesn't necessarily prove he's not right up to a certain point. In acting that way, he may be obeying motives that he believes to be fair; he sees things from a different angle, but that's not to say he's in the wrong; and one should always assume there's an honourable cause for the persecutions to which you may be subjected, so as to be sure you're not in the wrong. Besides, suffering and humiliation are excellent things. You have to let Jesus take up his abode inside you; how can you do that if you don't endure the knocks and insults of the *praetorium*?"

"Agreed, but are you quite sure that if it comes to a fight between the presbytery and the monastery, your monks wouldn't rather have, as you put it, Jesus take up his abode in the parish priest instead, rather than accept him into themselves? In truth, it would be very charitable of them, because the knocks and insults would be for the priest's own good..."

"What a wicked boy you are this morning!" said Dom de Fonneuve, laughing. "But here we are at Dijon, I'm going to my Carmelite sisters, won't you come with me?"

"No, father, I have some shopping to do in the town."

They walked along together as far as the Place St Bénigne, and here the old historian could not leave Durtal without first reminding him of the monastic splendours of the ancient abbey, of which only the sanctuary remained, the rest of the building having been cobbled together and refitted from other parts.

"This is one of the grandest monuments of the Benedictine Order," he said, as he took Durtal's arm and drew him closer, shoulder to shoulder, a habit of his when speaking to friends; "it was in the monastery of Saint Benignus that the Dukes of Burgundy, who came here to take formal possession of their duchy, swore on the Gospels, at the foot of the altar before the shrine of the saint, not to interfere with the privileges of their subjects; and after this oath, the abbot placed a ring on their finger to symbolise the marriage of their towns.

"This cloister, which flourished in the tenth century when the Venerable William, sent from Cluny with twelve monks by St Mayeul, managed to rouse its torpid inmates, degenerated again when it became an abbey in *commendam*.[3] Its superb collection of manuscripts was dispersed no one knows where; one had to wait until the reforms of Saint Maur to see real monks again and Saint Benignus could then boast such indefatigable scholars as Dom Benetot, Dom Lanthenas, and Dom Leroy, who mined the archives of the abbeys in the region. Especially Dom Lanthenas, who was one of Mabillon's collaborators; and it's also fitting to mention Dom Aubrey, who amassed the materials that allowed Father Plancher[4] to write his great *History of Burgundy*, the bulky folio volumes of which you've seen in our library.

"Finally, like everywhere else, the monastery was destroyed in the Revolution; only the church was spared, but what a funny idea it was to cover its towers with multi-coloured tiles, which make it look like a piece of esparto work! The best thing though, is that they've restored the crypt, which was discovered one fine day while excavating the ground.

"For us Benedictines, this cathedral is a blessed spot, a place of pilgrimage. The apostle of Burgundy, a disciple of St Polycarp who baptised him with his name, St Benignus is not very well known;

nevertheless, in his monograph on the cathedral, Abbé Chomton seems to prove that this saint suffered martyrdom around the beginning of the third century. The old hagiographies have at any rate preserved the details of his martyrdom; they tell us that he was first stretched on the rack; then awls were inserted under his nails; next his feet were sealed with molten lead into a stone, which was still in existence in the time of Gregory of Tours; finally, he was mauled by angry dogs and beaten on the neck with an iron bar, and as he still refused to die they pierced him with the point of a spear to finish him off, and it's on his very tomb that the church was built.

"As one of the elect, he was naturally a great saint, but naturally our devotion also goes, and perhaps more directly, to that abbot of our Order who was the glory both of Burgundy and of this abbey, the Venerable William.

"He was raised as a boy oblate at Lucedio Abbey in Italy; from there he went to Cluny, and as I mentioned to you just now, he was sent by his abbot, Dom Maycul, to reform the monastery of Saint Benignus, which had been reduced to a band of undisciplined monks whose liturgical observances were practically nil. Along with the practice of the Rule of St Benedict, he brought a passion for symbolism and the liturgy, a love of art and science, that was truly extraordinary. He established free schools for clerics and for the common people, and he revised the Gregorian chant, the texts of which had been changed by the cantors: he wanted the offices to be impeccable, and that services to God should be magnificent.

"He also proved to be a first-rate architect, because this monk knew everything! He built his own abbey church, which has, alas, disappeared, and which was replaced by the one in front of us. It had nine towers and all the symbolism of the scriptures unfolded around its structure; it was built over an underground church, the form of which reproduced the mysterious T of Ezekiel,[5] an as yet imperfect image of the cross, and which recalled a period prior to the Messiah, while the nave, higher and lighter, represented the light of the gospels, the church of Christ; and every night, to confirm the symbol, they went down to the crypt to chant matins, while the daily services were, on the contrary, celebrated in the church above.

"Everything was in proportion; the capitals, the pillars, and the statues were in keeping with the general idea of the edifice. It was the monks that sculpted them, and the name of one of them, Hunald, has come down to us.

"The abbey was huge; after having sent out more than a hundred monks to various religious houses, William presided over a similar number at Saint Benignus, and in spite of fatigue and in spite of his age, he travelled far and wide in order to regenerate monasteries that had fallen away from God. We see him at Fécamp, at Saint Ouen, at Mont Saint Michel, at Saint Faron in Meaux and Saint Germain des Prés in Paris; we also find him in Italy at Saint Fruttaria, where he added a convent of nuns to a Benedictine monastery; he was to be met with everywhere until the moment when, worn out by these endless journeys, he died in Normandy, and was buried there in the abbey at Fécamp.

"William was an artist, a scholar, and a prodigious administrator, and what is better still he was an admirable saint. I must lend you his biography written by Abbé Chevallier, but I'm preventing you from going to Mass, and I'm making myself late, too. My God, how talkative one becomes when one gets old – goodbye, my child, say a prayer to the Holy Virgin for me, and I, on my part, will pray to her for you, when I'm with my brave Carmelites."

Durtal watched him walk away in his still brisk stride, and thought: 'What a beautiful life that good monk leads, devoted to study and prayer. And what a beautiful life, too, is this Benedictine life, which soars so high over the centuries and beyond time; truly, you cannot walk towards the Lord with a more enthusiastic step or to a music that's more noble; this life achieves the most perfect initiation one can have here on earth into the life of the angels such as it's practiced and such as we will practise it ourselves in heaven. When the walk is over, you arrive before God no longer as a novice, but as a soul prepared by assiduous study for the function it must forever exercise in the eternal beatitude of his presence. How unstable and vain the occupations of man seem in comparison to this.

'That Dom de Fonneuve… I remember the feeling I had so many times in his cell, during the summer or autumn, when paleographers from Paris or the provinces would come to consult him on certain points of ecclesiastical history, or about the authenticity of certain texts. It made me think then of another cell in Saint Germain des Prés, where Dom Luc d'Achery and his pupil Mabillon would discuss with their visitors the principles of diplomatics,[6] the reliability of such-and-such a charter, or the value of such-and-such a seal. Dom de Fonneuve is as learned as Dom Luc d'Achery, but who among his pupils can be compared to Mabillon, let alone the obscurer devotees of the Congregation of Saint Maur?

'In stature, he stands alone here; but then again, among his lay peers who is there who can approach the prodigious du Cange, or even Baluze or that family of learned booksellers, the Anissons?[7] The standard of learning has therefore gone down on both sides and it's not fair to blame the monks alone.

'That lay scholars are, in general, more learned than monks seems incontestable; but it's equally certain, taking into account the state of knowledge in each period, that they too are undoubtedly much inferior to the scholars who frequented the abbey of Saint Germain des Prés in the seventeenth century, so we should be more modest, more indulgent…

'Meanwhile, with my mania for soliloquising about everything and nothing, I'll end up missing the service,' he said to himself as he entered the church. A Mass at the high altar was coming to an end; he checked the timetable near the sacristy. Another was due to follow it. He took advantage of the few minutes' interval between the two services to stroll around the cathedral.

It had three naves of regular width and appropriate height, but by the side of the great cathedrals it seemed small, almost insignificant. It contained a certain number of statues from the seventeenth and eighteenth centuries, respectable works that, after having once seen them, one had no desire ever to see again; the old stained glass had disappeared and been replaced by squares of plain glass or, what was worse still, by that visual emetic: modern stained glass. In the left transept towered a gigantic, bottle-green cross, on which a Christ, seemingly dyed grey, was stretched, and two angels stood on either side, one showing the Saviour an act of consecration to the Sacred Heart, and the other a plan of the church.

In short, as interesting as this cathedral was for the monastic memories it provoked, it was lifeless from an artistic point of view; certainly not equal to the rotunda building erected by the Venerable William of Cluny; and two of its ancient bas-reliefs, now relegated to the archaeological museum of the town, were of a very different quality to Bouchardon's reliefs[8] in the tympanum, which came from the old Church of Saint Étienne and which decorate it today.

As they were ringing the bell, Durtal took a seat to hear the service; despite the fact that he knew it by heart, this Mass never failed to delight him; the truth was that this Feast of the Epiphany meant more to him than any other.

Whether it was the proper season to celebrate it or not, he kept returning to it because, aside from the manifestation of the three kings and the baptism of Jesus in the Jordan, the Church also commemorated, by glorifying it, the miracle of the marriage at Cana. This miracle, whenever he thought about it, elicited long reveries in him.

'In fact, it was the first miracle that Christ accomplished, and the only one prompted by a joyful event, because all those that followed were carried out with the aim of relieving hunger, of healing the sick or assuaging grief.

'Jesus, who we see weeping but never laughing in the scriptures, here manifests his divine power, before its appointed time, during a wedding feast, simply for the pleasure of the guests, for an insignificant motive, for something that really doesn't seem to deserve it.

'His first impulse, when the Holy Virgin says to him, "They have no wine," is the recoil of a man caught unawares, embarrassed by an indiscreet request, and he replies: "Woman, what have I to do with thee? Mine hour is not yet come." And Mary, usually so eager to divine his slightest wish, doesn't even listen to him. She leaves his question unanswered and turns to the cupbearers, telling them to carry out the orders her son is going to give them.

'And after that Jesus doesn't refuse to perform the miracle and changes the water into wine.

'This scene, unique in the gospels, in which one sees the Virgin dispense with Jesus' assent and force his hand as it were to obtain the miracle she desires, is extraordinary when you extract the symbolic meaning it conceals.

'In fact, it's not about satisfying the guests, whose appetites are already sated, by giving them a wine better than that which they'd previously been served, nor is it about the marriage of a man and woman, whose names St John didn't even think it necessary to write down; it's about the union between God and the Church, about the nuptial joys of our Lord and the soul; and it's not about water being changed into wine, but wine being transmuted into blood.

'The marriage feast at Cana is simply a pretext and an emblem, because all the exegetes concur in seeing this scene as a symbol of the Eucharist.

'It's recognised that the Old Testament prefigures the New, but could one not also conjecture that certain passages in the gospels prefigure, in their turn, others in the same books? The wedding feast at Cana is really a foreshadowing of the Last Supper. The first miracle wrought by the Messiah at the commencement of his public life announces the one he will perform on the eve of his death; and we can even see that they reflect each other, in a kind of reverse mirror, because St John, who wrote his gospel to confirm and to complete the work of his predecessors, St John, whose book was written after those of St Matthew, St Mark and St Luke, is the only one who records this miracle. The others don't mention it, while he, on the other hand, is silent about the transubstantiation of bread and wine during the Last Supper. There is in this story a strange inversion; it's the last of the evangelists who anticipates the first, who shows in a veiled fasion, as in the Old Testament, the figure of the sacrament that the synoptic gospels reveal.

'But,' Durtal continued, 'the marriage feast at Cana provides even more food for thought. Just as we saw the Redeemer perform his first miracle in this scene, so in the same way we see Mary, for the first time, availing herself of her right to mediate and intercede for those new children she will adopt at the foot of Calvary, while her son, lying on the bed of the cross, gives birth to the Church.

'And she didn't wait until the prescribed time had passed; in her impatience, she anticipated time and claimed everything straightaway; she didn't proceed by gradation, she didn't first limit the subject of her requests, she got straight to the point, asking simply and clearly for the greatest of all graces; she wanted and obtained the promise of that *magisterium* – the Eucharist – which could heal and save the souls of the children she would be called on to take under her care.

'And Christ yields to this gentle firmness, and if he hesitates, if he shows a certain reluctance, it's because he wishes to teach us that all that he grants is granted only through the intercession of his Mother.

'This episode of Cana is therefore, in short, the starting point of two primary and essential devotions of Catholicism: the Blessed Sacrament and the Blessed Virgin. And the office which is specially dedicated to this mystery, the office on the second Sunday after Epiphany, doesn't even celebrate it! It limits itself to reading the prayers and the gospel at the end of the Mass.

'It seems to me that they should have conserved it, put it, if need be, on a different day, in the place of a saint. But it's strange,' he continued, leaving the cathedral and making his way in his big strides via the Place d'Armes, then the Place Rameau, to the museum, 'it's strange how miracles that have such a supreme importance go unnoticed, or at any rate are hardly explored by priests in the pulpit, or by the faithful.

'What an abject effigy that is,' he sighed at the bottom of the stairs leading to the painting galleries, looking at a statue of the Republic, represented by a girl with the shoulders, arms and breasts of a fishwife, and the tired-looking face of a shop girl, beneath which was engraved a motto that was both blasphemous and stupid: *Stat in aeternum* ('It stands forever'). It had been perpetrated by a man named Coutan.[9]

Durtal browsed the galleries of contemporary painting, where, in a prominent place, lounged a bleak portrait of the wet-looking President Carnot by Adolphe Yvon;[10] a portrait of Marshal Vaillant by Horace Vernet,[11] where the ingenuity of this dyer of military subjects was revealed by a tiny detail: the Marshal, whose head was that of a bewigged notary in the time of Louis-Philippe, didn't know where to put one of his arms, and Vernet had deemed it original to place it on a pile of breastplates, which in turn were resting on bundles of firewood heaped to the requisite height to serve as an armrest, and the whole was set against a fantastical landscape in thin and acidic colours; then there was an early work by Gustave Moreau,[12] *The Song of Songs*, a really mediocre canvas in the style of Chasseriau, which gave no hint of the future talent of the painter of *Hérodias*; finally, there were the lurid absurdities of a certain Anatole Devosge;[13] this last named, together with François, his father, were among the farcical glories of Dijon, and a bust of the former of these two grotesques, with the face of a beadle and whiskers on his cheeks like rabbit's feet stood on a plinth in one of the halls. This Anatole Devosge had daubed an incredible tarpaulin called *Hercules Saving Philo*. It depicted a woman in chains, clutching her son and trying to flee the fangs of a lion, which an angry Hercules was about to strangle.

The lion looked like someone had draped a lion-skin rug over a fire dog;[14] it was sticking out its tongue and seemed surprised at being manhandled in such a way by this man who seemed to be tightening a tie round its neck just a little too forcefully. Hercules himself was huge, with the physique of an Auvergnat maddened by drink; he sported extravagant muscles and above his naked legs, as fat as the beams of a timbered ceiling, protruded a formidable backside, like a couple of balloons, two hot-air balloons of pink percaline. As for the woman, dressed in an apricot-coloured robe and a gooseberry-green peplum, she was rolling her eyes as a sign of her terror, while the child was conventionally crying what looked like beads of tin, following the formula laid down by the odious Jacques-Louis David, whose pupil the painter was.

'Oh, what an absolute nonentity this Devosge was, what an epic imbecile!'

So the modern portion of the museum was unspeakably bad, and yet amid this heap of outlandish freaks and bizarre failures, a superb picture stood out from the wall: *Ex Voto* by Alphonse Legros.[15] It was laid out in this way:

Nine women were praying before a small Calvary scene, in a landscape like a tapestry of bright coloured wool. Of these nine women, seven were kneeling side by side; and in the foreground, one stood dressed in white, leafing through a book, while another in the background also standing and wearing a straw bonnet, was holding a taper.

These women, almost all of them old, wore white caps and were in mourning clothes, with their hands clasped together in black fingerless mittens.

The faces and hands of these old women were of a precision and artistic honesty that was astonishing, when you think of the hurried, slapdash painting of the present day. The simple and concentrated expressions of these praying women, gathered together before the cross, absorbed and oblivious of the world, gave off a real religious flavour. The features were charcoaled in, as if etched with an engraver's needle; and in this powerful, sober work, which seemed to have been executed by a painter-engraver of the school of Albrecht Dürer, the woman in white evoked the memory of Manet, but a Manet who was firmer, wiser and more balanced.

This was certainly the finest picture by Legros that Durtal had yet seen. But what was it doing here, lost amid this jumble of remnants and rubbish, when it might have so triumphantly figured among the masterpieces of the French School in the Louvre? The catalogue stated that it was a gift of the artist to his native city. Well, that aforementioned town seemed to be prouder of its Devosge, whose name lingered on a street sign, than of the author of this present work relegated to a lumber room of failures.

Leaving aside the rooms devoted to the modern French school, the Museum of Fine Art in Dijon was, as provincial museums go, abundantly stocked. It had truly admirable collections of ornaments, earthenware, ivories, enamels, engravings and woodcuts. Monsieur His de la Salle[16] had also endowed it with some very curious drawings by the old masters; but where the museum became regal, the equal of the great museums, was in the old Salle des Gardes, which contains the old marble and alabaster mausoleums of Duke Philip the Bold[17] and Duke John the Fearless.[18] These tombs, shattered during the Revolution, had been expertly reconstructed from their ruins, and regilt and repainted.

The first was the product of various craftsmen: the Flemish artist, Jean de Marville,[19] prepared the plan and the drawings, but died on the job. The Dutchman, Claus Sluter,[20] succeeded him and died in his turn, and it was his nephew, Claus de Werve,[21] who completed the work of his two predecessors, though to what extent is fairly difficult to say.

This work was conceived thus:

The body of Philip the Bold lies on a black marble table, between the legs of which stretched, under all four sides, a little Gothic cloister, populated by miniature monks, and nobles in the prince's train. Wrapped in his ducal blue cloak, lined with ermine, Philip the Bold rests his mailed feet on the back of an obliging lion, and his head on a cushion, behind which two angels with outstretched wings are supporting a visored helmet.

The second monument had been commissioned from a Spaniard, Jehan de la Huerta, or de la Verta, called d'Aroca; but he did nothing, or almost nothing, and it was a certain Antoine Le Moiturier or Le Mouturier[22] who finished the cenotaph, if he did not sculpt the whole thing.

Duke John and Princess Margaret of Bavaria, his consort, are lying side by side on a slab of black marble, beneath the four legs of which stretched an ogival cloister, the arcades of which are filled with monks. The heads of the bride and groom rested on cushions and their feet on the flanks of little lions; and angels are kneeling behind them, wings outspread, one holding out the Duke's casque and the other the coat of arms of the Princess.

This monument was more ornate than the first, the sculpture overloaded with volutes, flowers and fleurons; one was immediately reminded of the flourishes, curlicues and curves of the decorations in the church and monastery at Brou, that late Gothic style which, after becoming corrupted in its old age, flung off its robes of stone to die impure and naked under a shroud of lace.

The beasts on these monuments were like the beasts one sees on mantle clocks, all they lacked was a globe between their paws; the recumbent dukes and princess are no different in their conventional pose to other funerary statues of that period. The beauty of the work lies not in these frigid effigies, nor even in those blonde and charming angels, which are also conceived in the typical style we find with most of the Flemish primitives, but in the little figures under the dwarf arcades of the cloister.

They would originally have been intended to portray the monks of the various Orders lamenting the demise of the dukes; and so they should all have been composed exclusively of 'mourners', but the verve of the sculptors had exceeded the narrow frame of their commission, and instead of tearful monks, they had captured the human side of contemporary monastic life, sad or happy, impassive or fervent; and, to tell the truth, the last thing most of these statuettes seem to be thinking about is lamenting the death of a duke.

In any case, those workmen performed marvels of observation, and captured attitudes taken from living models, postures sketched from life; none of these expressive figures – though unfortunately some had been more or less restored and a few had been placed at random when the tombs were reconstructed – resembled any of the others, and so one was truly amazed at the incredible skill of these craftsmen who, faced with models that were almost identical, with almost uniformly shaven faces, and with nearly identical habits, had understood how to discriminate one monk from another, to express in a simple play of physignomy his innermost soul, to bring forth, from the very disposition of his robe or the shape of his cowl, lowered or raised, the precise character of the man who was wearing it.

In short, they wanted less to describe the effect produced on the monks by the announcement of the death of one or other of their benefactors, than to give a snapshot of everyday monkish life; and so we have a portrait of the abbot, with mitre and crosier, who holds open the Rule of Saint Benedict, and with an imperious and distrustful air watches the monks, who are weeping or reading, meditating or chanting, reciting their rosaries or bored at a loose end; one is even blowing his nose, while another is calmly picking his ear.

One could revel for hours in front of this work, sculpted by good-natured artists, who knew their friends the clergy very well and who, without malice, had had fun at their expense, so much did it exude the genial pleasures of art; and Durtal took leave of it with regret, because its cloistered figures evoked those of Val-des-Saints with their often striking similarities of pose and gesture. How like Dom de Fonneuve was that old father, smiling pensively, his cowl pulled up at the back by a hood cut according to the old Saint Maur fashion.

And that young monk, whose neck, on the contrary, was revealed by a less ample hood, fashioned according to a different tradition, was he not the image of Dom d'Auberoche? And that other monk, looking down at his feet, lost in reflection, surely that's Dom Felletin? And there, too, that fat precentor holding a hymn book and opening his mouth, wasn't that the lead cantor, Father Ramondoux? Only the abbot was different. That of Val-des-Saints being neither so imperious or distrustful, but more easy-going and honest.

In comparison with these little figures, the two wooden altar screens from the fourteenth century which furnished the walls of the same room seemed clumsy and stiff. It's true that they had been much restored; certain parts of them were even modern. They were the work of a Flemish artist, Jacques de Bars, or de Baerze, of Termonde.[23]

In one, St Anthony, a beardless youth, has at his side two swarthy, hairy devils and a nobly dressed she-devil with horns on her head, apple-red cheeks, and a round face with a turned-up nose; she was like a buxom barmaid disguised as a queen, and didn't seem at all disposed to tempt him; as for the saint, whose features were as inexpressive as a doll's, he was calmly raising two fingers in the air to bless us.

In another compartment of the same altar screen, there was a beheading of John the Baptist, with a Salomé dressed up to the neck like St Anthony's temptress, a sort of servant-girl Salomé, who, with her blue eyes that were more suited to watching over stews than fascinating men, was regarding with indifference the kneeling martyr, who seemed to be thinking of nothing at all, while the executioner was readying himself to decapitate him. In truth, these painted and gilded wooden figures were really quite poor, but one group stood out as superior to the others, that of Herod and Herodias, the mother of Salomé; the king, overcome with remorse, recoils with a gesture of displeasure, while she reassures him, one hand resting forcefully on his shoulder and the other on his arm.

The second altar screen contained an *Adoration of the Magi,* a *Calvary* and an *Entombment*: the *Adoration,* with a florid-complexioned Madonna, a tall, well-built, stocky Flemish woman, less common looking than the others, with a pleasant appearance and friendly smile; the infant leaning on her lap holds a tiny hand to the lips of a kneeling king, and touches with the other a kind of ciborium that the monarch is offering him; the second king, one hand raised to his crown, is giving an almost military salute; while the third, with the face of a carter, is raising his finger in a gesture of caution and presenting a flask of perfume.[24]

As for the *Entombment*, it was a rather pitiful piece of art: St John had a bulbous nose, and was half-heartedly supporting a Virgin with a runny nose; all of this embellished by two dolls, on either side of the scene, carrying incense.

These altarpieces were, if you will, somewhat naive and amusing, but they lacked any hint of religion, they were more realist rather than mystic, the art of a Fleming who had lost his faith.

Constructed in the form of cabinets, these altarpieces were completed by painted panels on the two folding doors that enclosed them. The artist who was charged with this commission, Melchior Broederlam of Ypres, had decorated an *Annunciation* and a *Visitation* on the left-hand panel, and a *Presentation of Jesus* and a *Flight from Egypt* on that of the right.

These works, painted on a burnished gold background, had been extensively restored, because before being housed in this museum they had mouldered away for a long period in the Church of Saint Benignus; amid all the commonplace figures who looked like peasants dressed as God the Father or as saints; at least the representation of the Virgin attested to a certain delicacy – this was no longer the pudgy, playful mother, the slovenly maid depicted by Jacques de Baerze; no, with her eyes the colour of blue flax blossom, her milky skin, her nose which was already leaner and straighter, becoming more noble and patrician, so to speak, as it grew thinner; she wasn't quite yet the exquisite Virgin of Rogier van der Weyden or Memling, but she was already a little like Mary, the Mother of God.

However, this discerning impulse confined itself to her alone, because the St Joseph in the *Flight from Egypt* remained a complete rustic, an absolute peasant; turning his back to the Virgin, he appears in profile, wearing big leather boots, and with a stick over his shoulder on which hangs a cooking pot and a bundle of clothes, and he is even in the act of taking a big swig from a tiny cask of wine.

In addition to these altar screen paintings, there was a third, dating from the fifteenth century and hailing from Clairvaux abbey, a smooth and overly-varnished painting, which was also exhibited on the picture rail of the wall. Of its panels, each separated from the other by columns, only one was interesting, on account of the very idea that the painter had, to reproduce the glorious body of our Lord at the moment of his transfiguration, by coating it all over in gold. The face, body, hands and robe were rubbed with this smooth gleaming gold that covers the panels of Lancelot Blondeel in the churches and the municipal museum of Bruges.

This naïve interpretation of divine light was pleasing, but the rest of the altarpiece was dry and frigid and quite undeserving of the praise that was lavished on it.

Lastly, there was another panel, also of the fifteenth century, an *Adoration*, which caught Durtal's eye not so much for the value of the work itself, which didn't really interest him, but for the reflections suggested by its origins. This picture, long attributed to Memling, with whose art it had only a very distant resemblance, had ended up regaining a vague fragment of its provenance.

This *Adoration* could be attributed without too much argument to the Master of Mérode, or the Master of Flémalle, thus named because one of his works was formerly in the Mérode Collection and because a whole series of his paintings from the abbey at Flémalle had been acquired by the Städel Museum in Frankfurt.

Who was this artist? According to research carried out in Belgium and Germany, the real name of the Master of Flémalle was Jacques Daret,[25] and he had been the pupil – at the same time as Rogier van der Weyden – of the painter Robert Campin of Tournai,[26] of whose work nothing now remains.

Daret was engaged on the decorations for a feast for the Order of the Golden Fleece,[27] and for the wedding of Charles the Bold,[28] the Duke of Burgundy, his salary being twenty-seven sols a day, including food. He had a brother, Daniel, born in Tournai and also a painter, who was his pupil and whose works have likewise disappeared, and that's almost all we know about him.

One of the Master of Flémalle's paintings, which belonged to the museum at Aix, and of which Durtal possessed a fine photograph, was a very curious picture of the Virgin, seated on a large bench in the Gothic style, hovering over a town and holding a very alert looking infant Jesus; she was a somewhat puffy-faced Virgin whose head stood out against a strange halo of rays, which gave rise to the idea of the fan of a peacock fashioned out of the unequal spines of a golden hedgehog; below her, a Dominican monk was praying on his knees between a seated pope and a bishop.[29]

Another Madonna[30] – and this one Durtal had seen in the Somzée Collection in Brussels – had for years obsessed him, and she surged up now in front of him, evoked by this panel in Dijon.

In her own way, she was truly unique.

In an interior lit by a window opening onto a town square and furnished with a *credenza* on which stands a chalice, and with a bench on which a book is lying on a red cushion, Mary, dressed in a white robe, broken up into large folds, is about to breastfeed her child; and here again, her head stands out against an extraordinary nimbus as if made from the bottom of a wicker basket or a winnowing basket, and the almost sulphur-yellow of this wicker background harmonises delightfully with the muted soft tones and the pale metallic hue of this painting, in which the characters are delineated, as if outlined in black against a greyish aura.

As a type, this Virgin differs entirely from those imagined by Rogier van der Weyden and by Memling. She is less slender, bigger boned and a little bloated, with singular eyes shaped like buttonholes that are turned up at the corners; the eyelids are heavy, the nose long, and the chin short; her face was less like a kite in form than those of Memling's Madonnas, and less almond-shaped than those of Rogier van der Weyden's Madonnas.

The truth was that Daret painted middle-class women who looked angelic, while the other two painted princesses who looked divine. His Virgins were distinguished, but not naturally so, and they look somewhat self-conscious in front of visitors; hence a certain affectedness, a certain embarrassment. They had, by dint of wanting to show that they were good mothers, forgotten to be so; frankly, they were lacking in genuine simplicity and enthusiasm.

This panel was as mannered and charming as it was bizarre and cold. 'Yes, that sums it up pretty well,' thought Durtal. 'Daret lacked the mystical feeling of his fellow student, van der Weyden, and his coloured projections of the soul were weak, but to be fair, it should be added that if his works seem like prayers emanating from a lifeless brush, they at least exude a strange charm; they are truly original, and in the art of that period occupy a place apart.

'This *Adoration* here in Dijon is obviously inferior, and it has suffered moreover from the damp, as well as at the hands of the restorers; but even so, it's still marked with the artist's imprint.

'Mary, kneeling in front of the child and turning her back to the stable, represents his usual type of Our Lady, but she is more bourgeois, more matronly, and less refined than the Virgins at Brussels and Aix; St Joseph, with his little taper, recalls the St Josephs of van der Weyden, which Memling also adopted; the shepherds with their bagpipes, the women who joylessly worship the baby Jesus, who is as puny as almost all the baby Jesus' of that period; the angels who unfurl banners in a landscape the colours of which are fresh and clear – all these are admirable, but here again there's something convoluted and frigid; joy does not spring from the sum of the parts. This Jacques Daret must certainly have been a man of repressed passion and lacklustre prayer.

'And with all that,' he said to himself, 'among this series of paintings by the primitives I don't see any trace of this famous school of Burgundy, which means we get a special room at the Louvre almost exclusively composed of Flemish paintings.

'No matter how much I search the museums or leaf through the accounts of various officials of the Burgundian treasury, I only ever unearth Dutch and Flemish artists; I never find any painters from the provinces of France of that time. Besides, isn't it obvious that if true artists had existed in France during that period, the Dukes of Burgundy wouldn't have gone to the trouble of bringing foreigners into their country at great expense?

'Dreamed up by that special form of irrationality that is artistic chauvinism, this school is therefore nothing but a con, an illusion. But enough of these cogitations,' he added, looking at his watch, 'I have to go.' He took a last look around. 'This museum,' he thought, 'deserves to be applauded; unfortunately everything here is a bit of a mix of old and new; in Dijon, everything has been restored, from the automata, the gargoyles, the frescoes of Our Lady of Dijon, the façades and naves of other churches, to the tombs of the Dukes of Burgundy and the altarpieces; but no matter, to be fair what a delightful sanctuary this Salle des Gardes is, with its tombs and its paintings, with its tapestry of the siege of Dijon – the faded pinks and harsh indigos of which, jumping out against the bluish hue of the wool, is a sight for sore eyes – and with its high Gothic fireplace, whose fireguard was made from the emblazoned back of John the Fearless' throne.'

He left the museum and in a couple of strides he was on the Place St Étienne, at the end of which stood the Church of Saint Michel.

Its Renaissance façade loomed up, with buttressed towers and octagonal cupolas, surmounted by golden balls which, viewed from below, looked like two oranges. Although he wasn't enamoured of this particular style, Durtal had to admit it was one of the purest specimens of its kind; it had been less tampered with than many other churches, which had been mongrelised and whose parentage remained obscure. From the outside, at least, this one had some pedigree. Inside, it was another matter, it was ogival in style and numerous innovations had been introduced after the fact; in any event, on the left it had a small chapel dedicated to the Virgin, a little eclectic in style with its stained-glass windows representing vague sybils and angels with coats of arms, a chapel which was nevertheless intimate, where one could gather one's thoughts in peace.

But Durtal didn't have time to stay there that day. He busied himself with his shopping and then, after having gone to read his newspaper in a café, he returned to the train station.

If the precise news he was looking for about the Law of Associations was, that morning, wholly lacking, the articles in the Masonic press were, by contrast, overflowing with insults about monks and nuns. They were furiously turning the rack, demanding that the government abolish the congregational schools and disperse – in lieu of harsher measures – the cloisters; and the diatribes against the Company of Jesuits, against the seemingly innumerable mendicants and brides of Christ, followed one after another in the language of the gutter, like graffiti scrawled on a wall.

'It's impossible for these lackeys of the gutter press not to be sneaks or adulterers, defrocked priests or thieves, because with these types of people their hatred for God is a reflection of their own faults; the Church is only hated by those who fear its reproaches or those of their own conscience. Oh,' thought Durtal as he walked up and down the platform, 'if we could lay bare the soul of these enraged Monsieur Homais',[31] what an extravagant compost we'd discover in that dungheap of sins!'

At that moment, two monks came out of the waiting room, Father Emonot, the preceptor, and Father Brugier, the cellarer.

"Ah, hello," they said cheerfully, shaking Durtal's hand, "so everyone's in Dijon today." And they immediately started speaking about Monsignor Triaurault, whose infirmities were getting worse and who had decided to hand in his resignation, and they mentioned the possible candidates: Father Le Nordez, or a priest from Paris; then they talked about the new parish priest at Val-des-Saints, and the conditions that were going to be inflicted on the monks.

"But I saw Dom de Fonneuve this morning, and he didn't say anything about it," cried Durtal.

"He didn't know the clauses stipulated by the bishop; we ourselves have only just learned about them, and that by mere chance, because we happened to meet one of the bishop's bigwigs in the street."

"And what are these conditions?"

"They are these," replied the cellarer, a strongly-built fellow with a five o'clock shadow, dark eyes, and thin lips; a southerner who had formerly been a bursar in a seminary: "We are to have the use of the church on weekdays, but we'll no longer be able to set foot in it on Sundays; that day we'll congregate in our oratory, because the sanctuary will belong to the parish priest alone; on top of that, we'll no longer have the right to hear the confessions of people in the village…"

"What! We can no longer confess to the Benedictines? But that's monstrous; they can't compel the faithful to go to a particular priest; every one is free to choose his own confessor; the law is categorical, so this decree of the bishop is null and void;

he'd have done better to resign than play a trick like that on us."

"Oh," said Father Emonot, "you're an oblate, or at least you will be; you can therefore claim that you're under the abbot's jurisdiction, not that of the bishop; so this measure won't affect you; besides, oblate or not, every man is free to come and visit us in our cell, and we only recognise one authority, that of our abbot; so we'll continue, with his permission, to administer the sacrament of penance to our clients as in the past."

"Yes," agreed Father Brugier, "Monsignor Triaurault's interdiction only applies to the church, which is to a certain extent parochial, but whether he likes it or not, it stops at the threshold of our cloister."

"Good, but what about the women? Mlle de Garambois and my housekeeper, for instance?"

"Ah, that's another matter; they can't enter the precincts of the cloister, so the issue is more complicated; but it's easy to resolve; the bishop's ban only extends to Val-des-Saints, and outside the town we retain our rights. Consequently, it'll be easy for each of us to go once a week to Dijon and hear the confessions of our female penitents, either in the Carmelite chapel, or in that of some other Order."

"All the same, you must admit it's a bit stiff, a prelate wanting to impose a confessor by force; it's truly a rape of the conscience; but, come, your abbot must have been consulted, didn't he protest?"

"He was merely informed of the decision," said Father Brugier.

"The reverend abbot is a friend of peace," Dom Emonot added prudently, and he immediately changed the conversation and began to chat with the cellarer about the novitiate.

To Durtal there was something unsympathetic about this Father Emonot, with his big head tilted back on his short neck, his restless eyes darting behind his glasses, and his thin nose and flared nostrils like the ends of a pair of sugar tongs; but what bothered Durtal was not so much his yellow complexion, his sly demeanor, his pompous tone and his harsh laugh, as the nervous twitching which constantly agitated his face.

The truth was that these lines zigzagging across his face could be called tics of scruple.

Dom Enomot suffered, like many priests and numerous

laymen, from this fearful sickness of the soul; and he would start suddenly, tense up, and repress, as with a facial gesture, a vague temptation, assuring himself by a gesture of denial, by a little recoil, that he had repressed it and not committed a sin.

This infirmity was the product of a truly fundamental virtue, of an ardent desire for perfection, and his narrow-mindedness and prudery were explained by the fact that, for him, everything was a source of apprehension, a subject of reproach and complaint.

But that said, it had to be recognised that he was a man of commonsense, expert in leading the souls who could tolerate his regime up the steep climb of a difficult path, and very clear-sighted about the current situation of his Order.

Durtal backtracked a little from his prejudices, hearing him express himself so wisely about his pupils.

"They all laugh," he was saying, "at the famous 'mould' so dear to the Jesuits, without noticing that, though they're all imprinted with the same stamp, no group of men are more unlike each other than the Jesuits. The Rule of St Ignatius planes off faults and prunes the character, but it never kills the personality as so many people think. Would to God that it was the same with us! What we lack is just such a mould in which we could cast the raw metal of our novices. I know that in certain houses of our congregation such methods of education are considered mean and repressive; they talk only of how to let the soul expand. But alas, we don't expand it, we leave it to itself.

"And even though I'd like to believe that, during the period of probation, we succeed in inculcating a sense of spirit and discipline, in arousing a taste for the interior life in our novices – what comes next? When these constrained souls have passed through the trials of the novitiate, when they serve their time and the period of paternal supervision of the young ceases, they'll relax that impulse for restraint, and it's at that moment that the danger begins; we should continue to keep a tight rein on them, to keep them in check with an absorbing occupation, with assiduous work, even with strenuous manual labour.

"But exactly the opposite happens; the so-called mature Benedictine is free, works only if he wants to; and it's very tempting to do nothing; they end up letting themselves go, settling into the leisurely life of the man of independent means; and the monk who doesn't work spends his time talking, disturbing the others and fomenting intrigues. As our father St Benedict put it so well: *Otiositas inimica est animae*: Idleness is the enemy of the soul."

"Yes, they become pious functionaries and the office itself smells of preserves, with its psalms marinated in the pickle of their plainchant."

Father Emonot smiled rather grudgingly.

"As a Naturalist, you have a way of looking at things and summarising them that is very singular…"

"I'm joking," replied Durtal, "but that doesn't alter the fact, father, that you are a hundred percent right: a monk who has nothing to do is a monk who is already half lost, because after all to work is… well, to sin less."

"Certainly," said the cellarer, "but it's easier to point out the danger than to avoid it. It would be good to change the novitiate system, to raise the level of education which is too low; above all, it would be better not to admit the idle. That's Dom Felletin's concern, he's intelligent enough to figure it out."

"No doubt," said Father Emonot, "as a novice master he's remarkable."

"And there's something saintly about him," added Dom Brugier.

"The saintliness of St Peter," muttered Dom Emonot whose eyes glinted beneath his glasses.

'Of St Peter?' thought Durtal. 'What does that signify? Is he being disloyal? Does he mean to say that, before being a saint, Dom Felletin was a traitor?'

But the monk's eyes were now expressionless, and when Durtal looked into them all he could see was a dead blue. Moreover, the preceptor had swiftly passed on to another subject of conversation.

He was now discussing with the cellarer the matter of certain church ornaments and vestments which the new priest was claiming to belong not to the abbey but to the parish church; there was an interminable enumeration of stoles, of chasubles, and copes. This list had no interest for Durtal, he was not sorry therefore, when the train stopped at Val-des-Saints, to take his leave of the two monks and return home.

Chapter IX

I n the countryside, when a boy is sickly and unable to bear the strain of working on the land or in the vineyards, his mother says: "He's delicate, this little chap; we'll make a priest of him," and that's how Father Barbenton was entered into a seminary, then sent successively to various villages as a curate, and finally appointed as the parish priest of Val-des-Saints.

All the priests to whom Monsignor Triaurault had offered the post had declined, being well aware of the awkward position a parish priest would be in, opposite an abbot and his monastery.

Father Barbenton, however, had accepted, on the assurance that after a certain time he would be transferred to a better parish, which was highly unlikely because it was quite clear that if he succeeded in his conflict with the abbey, the bishop would be in no hurry to move him, and if the opposite was the case, he wouldn't promote him, and if he felt he'd been too compromised wouldn't hesitate to crush him.

Inside this vain and sickly being there was an unbounded ambition to succeed. He knew he had the support of the local gentry, who he'd courted, and that the mayor, despite being a socialist and a freethinker, was almost sympathetic, and was inclined to back him out of hatred for the monks. So he'd hardly settled in Val-des-Saints when he began the fight.

And he started with a powerful blow.

From the very first Sunday he determined to wipe the slate clean, to destroy in a single day the work that had been patiently carried out for years by the monks; he declared to the peasant girls who knew plainchant that from now on they would sing hymns, and he handed them these popular tunes which, moreover, the girls liked.

Backed by his highly-placed friends, he deprived the village of that air of a hamlet in the Middle Ages which emanated from it during the services on Sundays, and he transformed what had hitherto been unique of its kind, into a place like any other, where they bawled out jaunty tunes.

Then, when his 'Children of Mary' were sufficently trained to croon this rubbish without too many mistakes, he asked the monks to lend him their organist to accompany them on Sundays, because he was free that day as there was no organ in the abbey chapel.

Fortunately the abbot was absent, because, not suspecting any malice, he would no doubt have consented; but Father Barbenton had to deal with Dom de Fonneuve, who, more suspicious, replied:

"That depends; if you're singing plainchant, yes; otherwise, no."

Annoyed, the parish priest replied that he was master in his own church, and was free to choose whatever music he liked on Sundays.

"And I'm free to keep my organist," retorted the prior.

This was the first cause of discord between them.

The priest then determined to make changes to the interior of the church, erecting new altars topped by plaster saints procured from the Rue St Sulpice. The local gentry encouraged him in this, but disappeared as soon as it came to opening their purses; he managed to extract from them only an insignificant sum, so he fell back upon Monsieur Lampre, Mlle de Garambois and Durtal, but they told him in unison that they saw no purpose in disfiguring the church.

His hatred for these people, who moreover refused to confess themselves to him and would go either to the monastery or to Dijon rather than receive absolution at his hands, increased.

The situation was clear: the monastery and its three friends on one side; the local gentry and the parish priest on the other.

There remained the village, but here the situation was more complicated. The peasants, at first well-disposed towards the priest, and furious with the abbey which was no longer supplying them with medicine since Father Miné's breakdown – because nobody else in the monastery was a pharmacist – quickly grew indignant when their new pastor demanded fees for marriages and funerals from them. They suddenly realised that the Benedictines married and buried them without ever asking for money, and the eligible ladies of the parish discovered that since Father Barbenton had taken up residence in the presbytry he'd abolished the beautiful Sunday services that had attracted so many fashionable people from Dijon.

And soon the strongest defenders of Gregorian plainchant were the innkeepers, whose trade was suffering by its suppression.

In the meantime, his fight with the sacristan monk commenced on all fronts, but the priest came up against a force of inertia he couldn't overcome; Dom Beaudequin eluded him like quicksilver slipping through his fingers; it was always, "Perhaps, it's worth considering, we'll think about it," and never a yes or a no; as the priest couldn't get him to hand over the chalices and the chasubles he coveted, he wanted to at least annoy the monks who, during the days of the week were masters of the choir and celebrated their offices there, and so he asked them to bring forward or delay their timetable, under the pretext that it would then be easier to carry out catechism lessons and funeral services.

"I have no right to change the Rule of St Benedict, nor any power to change our traditions," replied Dom de Fonneuve, "so it's impossible for me to accede to your request."

The parish priest expressed his dissatisfaction at this refusal by never attending the weekday services again. He had extorted from the abbot permission to sit in the choir in a stall next to him, above that of the sub-prior who was thus relegated to a sort of lower rank; henceforth he let his stall remain empty, thinking no doubt that his absence would offend the monks, but no one even seemed to notice this ploy. So, he put an end to the mode of skirmishing he'd adopted since his arrival at Val-des-Saints, and resolved to take his revenge for these small conflicts, which he'd up until now lost, by engaging in a real battle for which he would prepare the terrain beforehand.

And he believed he had found an opportunity. Recollecting that Monsignor Triaurault's Christian name was Cyril, he consulted the monastic calendar and noted that the feast of this saint fell on a Sunday. He called on the bishop and begged him to come and lunch with him that day at the presbytery, as the nobility of the district wished to offer him their congratulations on the day of his namesake, and then if he would deign to preside over vespers.

Monsignor Triaurault was ill and not at all anxious to waste his time in this way, but the priest was so insistent, assuring him of the prestige that would reflect on him in the parish if he succeeded in bringing his bishop there, that his holiness, irritated, finally gave way.

Then the priest, beaming all over, went to Dom de Fonneuve and proposed that, in order to give more splendour to the ceremony and show greater honour to the monsignor, he and his monks should sing vespers in the church which on that particular Sunday he would put at their disposition.

The prior accepted and the priest smiled.

"I would like," he continued, "the ceremony to be truly magnificent and capture the imagination of our peasants. They are so used to the Solesmes plainchant that this kind of music doesn't interest them any more, so I thought of adding a few pieces selected from the best composers of our day. Baron des Atours, along with his son, and backed by one of their servants who has a fine voice, has offered to sing them up in the organ loft…"

"Absolutely not!" Dom de Fonneuve interrupted abruptly, "I refuse, myself and my bretheren, to take part in such a concert. There is a Benedictine liturgy and I will not allow it to be adulterated by such hackneyed warbling. We will celebrate the office in the church as it is, or we won't sing it at all: take it or leave it."

"But I'm not forbidding you to sing your vespers as you intend them," replied the priest. "My comment was aimed only at the Benediction of the Blessed Sacrament which follows it," and then, a little spitefully he added: "You must admit, reverend father, that your little Benedictions, with their two brief chants that usually precede the *Tantum ergo*, and the hymn *Te decet laus,* or the psalm *Laudate Dominum omnes gentes*, which you intone afterwards, are very short and in any case do little to impress a crowd."

"Our Benedictions, like our offices, are liturgical. Their repertoire cannot be changed on a whim, the issue therefore remains the same, and I can sum it up in three words: all or nothing."

"That's devilishly tricky," muttered the priest, who pretended to think the matter over, "I'd sort of promised Monsignor Triaurault that you would honour him with your presence. What will he say if he doesn't see you in church?"

"I don't know. Will you accept my conditions?"

"Impossible, I would offend the Baron and his family, but reverend father, just think how strange his Lordship will find it if you and your monks are not there when he arrives."

"Monsignor has too high a sense of justice not to understand how well-founded our motives are, and I count on your loyalty to make them known to him."

The priest bowed. 'It's done,' he said to himself as he took his leave of Dom de Fonneuve.

"That's very sly of him," said Monsieur Lampre to the prior, who was talking with him about the matter, "the priest prevents you from accepting his offer and compels you to offend the bishop."

"What else could I have done?" replied the old monk, "duty comes first."

The comical part of the story was that though the priest's snare succeeded in trapping the monks, he himself was also caught in it. Monsignor Triaurault never forgave him for having lured him into what he called an ambush of disrespect, and he reprimanded him firmly, reproaching him for his ineptitude, and when he left he was as furious with the parish priest as he was with the Benedictines.

From that day on, relations ceased almost entirely between the presbytery and the abbey; finally, vexed at being kept at arm's length, the priest tried to find a way to defuse the situation; the feast of St Benedict, which was rapidly approaching, seemed to him to be propitious for this purpose.

He first thought of using Durtal as as intermediary, in order to obtain an invitation to dine at the monastery on that day. He contrived a meeting with him, and then said casually:

"Well, well, my dear Sir, so you're going to make your profession as an oblate? I would very much like to attend. If the ceremony can't take place during the monastic offices, I'll arrange it that you'll be free to use *my* church on that day" – and he put the stress on 'my' – "at whatever time you like."

"I'm much obliged to you, father," Durtal replied calmly, "but my profession will not be made in the *abbey* church" – and he in his turn, stressed the word 'abbey' – "but in the chapel of the monastery, which is to say that, except for the monks, no one can attend, since the chapel is situated within the monastery enclosure."

"Oh, but you'll no doubt dine at the abbey that morning?"

"No doubt."

"The refectory being also situated within the enclosure," continued the priest, with a touch of irony, "I wonder if, besides yourself and the monks, other people will be invited to this meal?"

"I don't know. While the abbot is away, the prior has the right to invite or not invite anyone he likes; he's the only one who can answer your question."

"I'm much obliged to you."

"And me to you, father," replied Durtal walking away.

Father Barbenton thought to himself: 'There's nothing to be got from him, just be brave and push on,' and he went to see the prior. There, he played his part well, declaring that he deplored all these misunderstandings, shifting the blame onto the bishop whose instructions he'd been obliged to carry out; finally, he blurted out that his absence on the feast of St Benedict would have a disastrous effect on his reputation in the village, and Dom de Fonneuve, touched, embraced him, and invited him to dinner.

Then the priest asked if the reverend abbot would be present for the ceremony in the cloister.

"It's highly unlikely," replied Dom de Fonneuve. "The abbot is in Italy, at Monte Cassino, where, as you know, one of his brothers is a monk; and from there he has to go to Rome, to see the primate; so he won't be here for another fortnight."

The priest, who feared the monks might put a spanner in the works by informing the abbot of his schemes, left reassured, and moreover decided to make peace with everyone before Dom Bernard's return.

During this time, Durtal was preparing himself for his oblature by making a retreat for a few days. He spent the time alternately between Dom Felletin, the novice master, and Dom d'Auberoche, the liturgy director.

The former examined him in the Rule of St Benedict, and the latter, who wanted the ceremony to be perfect, forced him to learn the various types of bows and movements. He would have liked Durtal to sing the *Suscipe me, Domine, secundum eloquium tuum et vivam et non confundas me ab expectatione mea* three times, raising his voice each time by a tone, accompanied by the *Gloria Patri* repeated by the whole choir. This verse of Psalm 118, enjoined to be sung at the profession of his monks by St Benedict himself in Chapter 58 of his Rule, was admirable when it was clothed in its simple habit of plainchant. Tentative and plaintive until it reached the mediant,[1] it then became more assured, still imploring, but more insistently; and with each repetition it became firmer, encouraged by the resolute accent of the monks who took it up, as if to assure their new brother that his prayer would be heard, and that he would not be disappointed in his expectations.

And this divinely magical arrangement was so effective that even the oldest of the professed monks couldn't help but tremble in the depths of his soul when he heard it sung, or sang it himself at every profession.

Durtal, who was terrified at the thought of having to sing one tone higher each time in the silence of the chapel and without the support of an organ, ended up obtaining Father d'Auberoche's consent to chant it very simply, and it would be the same for the fathers and the novices present at the ceremony, who had to repeat the verse after him each time.

And then there were the perpetual rehearsals, the full or half bows, the genuflections on the first or the last step of the altar, the various ways of unfurling the charter of profession against his chest, like those statues one sees in the displays of religious paraphernalia shops representing a knight holding a banner on which the word *Credo* is written, and there were the physical constraints of manoeuvring his body in the restricted space of the oratory.

Finally, Durtal managed to satisfy Dom d'Auberoche; as for

Dom Felletin, he cared little for ritual gestures or liturgical details, he would explain oblature, skimming over the centuries, happy to have a novice who knew the subject as well as he did, and he would speak of the future, certain of being understood.

"First of all," he would say, "we must resign ourselves to the conviction that the oblatehood of St Benedict will never become widely popular; it appeals only to an elite and consequently it remains a state of exception; indeed, it requires special conditions from its postulants that are difficult to fulfil. Its *raison d'être* is the liturgy; the life of a monk is the praise of God; the life of an oblate will also be the praise of God, but reduced in scale to what he can endure; to achieve this result it is not enough to perform your duties faithfully and attend communion more or less regularly; you must also have a taste for the liturgy, an appreciation of ritual, a love of symbolism; an admiration for religious art and for beautiful services.

"Oblates who can meet these conditions – God grant that they be numerous, though I doubt it – will therefore live as much as possible that part of the monastic life that takes place in the church, in other words they must reside in the monastery or in the surrounding area.

"Indeed, I cannot imagine oblates scattered in towns like Paris, Lyons or Marseilles, having no daily connection to the monastery to which they belong, and therefore not attending the conventual Mass or vespers sung every day, but meeting only once or twice a month at the abbey, as if summoned by a bugle call. Understood in this way, oblature would be nothing more than a small brotherhood, and there's enough of these, I think, that we don't need to add yet another one to those that still remain.

"On the other hand, it would be a grave error to confound oblature with what's called the Third Order,[2] because the Third Order incorporates everyone, even the most uneducated, provided they be zealous Christians and practising Catholics. We, on the contrary, aim at quality, not at quantity; we need scholars, men of letters and artists, people who are not exclusively devout…"

"You don't want sanctimonious churchwardens or pious beadles…" Durtal blurted out.

Chapter IX

"No," said Dom Felletin, smiling. "Our aim is not to duplicate the work of the Third Orders of other institutions, which are useful because they are of service to the people; nor do we want to follow in the footsteps of the Franciscans, who enjoy a power of influence acquired over centuries; besides, we would, from the point of view of organisation and proselytism, be far inferior to them.

"And moreover, let's have the courage to admit it, by acting in that way we'd be deceiving those of our novices who were more interested in being affiliated to the Third Order of St Francis, because it's very dynamic and assures its tertiaries of advantages that we would be quite incapable of offering. Our sole strength, unique to us, can only reside in the efficacy of liturgical prayer and the offices; and how can these be of profit to people who take no part in them, and who aren't imbued in any degree with that Benedictine spirit without which no admission to our Order is or would be possible?

"No, the more I think of it, the more I'm convinced that the only desirable form of oblature is that of the Middle Ages, that of the layman living, as I've already said, in or near a monastery, in short, living more in the community than in the world, regularly following the religious exercises of the monks.

"Understood in this way, oblature is especially practical for artists; it gives them the support of monastic grace, the assistance of the patriarch, and nevertheless leaves them a certain freedom; and in this regard, I must admit my view is that there would be every advantage for an artist not to reside within the enclosure of an abbey, but rather at its door. Indeed, inevitably, even with this mitigated form of internment, constraints are imposed, especially if the abbot or the father charged with the direction of the oblates has fixed ideas about aesthetics – and what ideas they often are! It's a conflict, and in the name of obedience it results in the suffocation of personality, the death of art.

"The failure of Beuron Abbey is, from this point of view, typical. They wanted to cast all the painters who lived in the monastery in the same mould, and they killed the individual talent of each, in that they all produced paintings that were alike, conceived according to the same formula, and therefore destined to become, after a few attempts, clichés.

"The question can therefore be summed up as follows: an energetic, spiritual direction on the part of the monk in charge of oblature, but liberty as regards all the rest.

"Now by way of illustration, I would point to a now-forgotten attempt – even most monks are unaware of it – which took place at Solesmes, in Dom Couturier's time.

"This abbot had dreamed of reviving the art of illuminated manuscripts, that glory of the Benedictine abbeys of yesteryear. It happened that, along with Étienne Cartier, he had living in the abbey an oblate, Luc-Anatole Foucher,[3] the sole artist at that time with sufficient liturgical knowledge and the talent necessary to continue this exquisite art of the Middle Ages.

"He had already trained some remarkable students at the Benedictine abbey of Saint Cecilia, and he was going to begin to teach certain monks who had an aptitude for this sort of work, when, following the decrees of 1880 and the dispersal of the community in the village, Foucher left Solesmes and this project naturally fell through.

"What is the actual number of oblates who live as inmates in the monasteries of the French congregation? I don't know exactly, because my information is already several years old and some have, since that time, returned to the outside world.

"In any case, there was one who had taken the habit, a priest at Solesmes, who is now at the priory in Farnborough, in England; there were two at Ligugé, one in the habit and the other in lay clothes, but both of them left for St Wandrille, where the first became a monk. There was another in Paris, also wearing the habit, at the priory in the Rue de la Source, and then… well, in faith, I think that's all.

"Of those who live near abbeys, in the very villages where they're situated, I only know of five, including a female oblate at Ligugé. On the other hand, there was a small nucleus of affiliates at St Wandrille, but were they constituted in regular fashion? I don't know. At Solesmes, there are a few relatives of the monks who regularly attend services, but are they real oblates, who have made their profession at the monastery? I doubt it. As for those who live where they please and take no part in the liturgical life, they are fairly numerous in Paris, but I repeat, this sort of oblature has nothing to do with the oblature of the Middle Ages, with oblature properly speaking.

"As you can see, the number of oblates is uncertain and very small; the thread has not been broken from the eighth century down to the present day, but how thin it is!

"Ultimately, perhaps it'll get stronger; while waiting for companions to join you, tomorrow you'll become the first modern oblate at Val-des-Saints; you'll benefit more effectively from the store of prayers that has accumulated in this ancient priory over so many centuries; you'll benefit like us, with the same rights as us, from the fruition of those graces with which the community of Solesmes was invested when Pope Gregory XVI made it the heir to all the privileges accorded by his predecessors to the congregations of Cluny, of Saint Vanne and Saint Hydulphe, and of Saint Maur. You will help to protect this patrimony, and you yourself will add to it by associating yourself with our liturgical efforts; and when the time of rest draws close, you will don the monk's habit, in which you will also be buried, and the patriarch, faithful to his promise, will intercede for you before the inexorable judge.

"Even though you do not make any vows, you promise in front of the altar, during the sacrifice of the Mass before receiving the body of our Lord, to reform your morals, you commit yourself to live a holy life in God. In short, you renounce all that for the carnal man constitutes the joys of life, and it's an existence withdrawn from the world that you will henceforth have to lead. May your new life be pleasant and pleasing to you; above all, may it be acceptable through the sacrifices that it demands to the Almighty above.

"So, it's quite settled is it not? The ceremony will take place during six o'clock Mass, and it will be then during the offertory that you'll bind yourself, by a schedule that will be conserved in the archives of the abbey, to the great Order of St Benedict."

"That's understood, father, pray for me."

"You can count on it, my dear child, and I assure you my prayers will not be alone. All the young novices who are looking forward to being present at this Mass will not forget you."

'Well, the die is cast,' thought Durtal, as he left the father's cell, 'but to tell the truth I really don't feel that it's so wonderfully meritorious of me to repudiate what they call earthly delights; for many years past I have, of my own accord, rejected all that flatters the taste of others, but until now I haven't been forced to do it, I acted of my own free will; what's to be feared now is that given the stupidity of human nature, by the very fact I've made a commitment, I'll find it hard to keep.

'Well, so much the better, those merits I don't have I'll acquire, if I can endure the times of temptations and regrets.

'All the same,' he went on, lighting a cigarette, 'it must be admitted that I'm a rather feeble heir to the oblates of the early centuries. The hermit of Mont Cindre, the successor of the hermits of Lyons, and me, the successor of the oblates of Val-des-Saints, we form a pair. It seems to me that we are to real monks what those hideous kids whose parents have dressed them up in military costumes and who march through the streets with trumpets in their mouths and charcoaled moustaches under their noses are to real soldiers.'

When he reached home, he found Madame Bavoil in a state of indignation.

"I don't understand," she grumbled, "why women can't be admitted to the ceremony of profession; I'm a tertiary of St Francis, and they don't resort to such secretiveness in that Order."

"But my good Madame Bavoil, the Franciscan Order is not enclosed…"

"I know nothing about that, all I know is that, tomorrow, myself and – what's even worse – your sister-oblate, Mlle de Garambois, are to be kept outside, forbidden to pray at your side."

"You'll pray at a distance, Madame Bavoil; besides, if you wish to get an idea of the sovereign beauty that emanates from a monastic profession, it's not that of an oblate you ought to see, that's just an abbreviation, a shortcut, a homeopathic dilution of that of the monks – and even then it's not so much the profession of the Benedictine monks that you should attend, which is nonetheless superb, but rather that of the nuns.

"The absolute zenith of liturgy and art is there. The profession of the nuns of St Benedict! There are moments during this extraordinary ceremony when a little frisson of divine splendour makes your soul tremble, and you feel exalted, transported out of yourself, far from the banality of the world that surrounds you.

"Yes, at certain moments, you want to give vent to the admiration that overpowers you. Perhaps the masterpiece of ecclesiastical art is the Consecration of Virgins in the Pontifical.[4] From the very first, it grips you to the marrow; then, after the *Alleluia*, the officiating bishop or abbot sits down on the faldstool – the seat of the prelates – facing the people; then the master of ceremonies or assistant priest intones the verse from the parable of the Virgins in St Matthew: 'Wise Virgins, bring your lamps, behold the bridegroom cometh; go ye out to meet Him!'

"And the virgin, holding a lighted taper, takes a step forward and kneels. Then the prelate, as Christ's representative, calls her three times, to which she replies with an admirable antiphon: 'Here I am', and she moves forward one step at a time. Like a bird fascinated by a fine-looking snake.

"And from beginning to end, the service unfolds, eloquent and almost overpowering, like during that sonorous and powerful *Preface*; enveloping you as if perfumed by all the essences of the East, while the choir of nuns sing these verses from the Song of Songs: 'Come, my beloved, the winter is past, the turtledove sings, the flowers of the vine smell sweet.' Truly delightful, too, is the episode of the betrothal, when the novice acclaims Christ, and affirms herself 'betrothed to him whom the angels serve, to him whose beauty the stars of heaven adore'; then, holding up her right hand, she shows off the glittering ring blessed by the prelate, and in ecstasy exclaims, 'My Lord Jesus Christ has bound me to him by his ring, and adorns me as a bride.' And the ancient prayers sanctify, as if steeping her in celestial spices, the new Esther who, looking back at the road travelled since her probation and thinking that the marriage is now consummated, sings in contentment: 'Behold, here is what I have long desired. I hold him in whom I hoped. I am united in heaven to him whom I loved so much on earth…' And then, after the recitation of the *Preface*, the Mass continues…

"In comparison with this truly divine drama played out between the soul and God, how poor are the plots dreamed up by playwrights, ancient and modern. My God, how silly they are."

"Yes, but unfortunately, there's no Benedictine nunnery here, so I'll never see it," said Madame Bavoil.

"This was simply to tell you that the ceremony of oblature, if you compare it to the profession of a nun, is so minor it's not even interesting to watch. This fact might console you for not being able to attend."

The next morning, after having repeated, like a school lesson, his Latin responses to the questions the prior was going to ask him, Durtal made his way to the cloister.

He felt disturbed, uneasy, and wished the whole ceremony was already over. The whole ritual side of things, the pageantry, of which Father d'Auberoche was so fond, made him nervous. He was afraid of making a mistake, and this fear prevented him from thinking about the act he was about to accomplish and the communion that was to follow. 'Ah, Lord,' he murmured, 'I'm thinking about everything except you; how better it would be if I could pray to you alone, in some corner.'

He met the novices under the arcades; they smiled a greeting, but none of them spoke; it was the period of 'Great Silence', which begins after compline the evening before and doesn't end till after prime, which is to say about seven o'clock in the morning.

They entered the oratory with him and soon afterwards Dom Felletin and Dom d'Auberoche, wearing their cowls, arrived in their turn and walked over to the sacristy where the prior was dressing for Mass.

Then a few more monks, the guestmaster, the preceptor, and the sacristan went and kneeled in the stalls.

The oratory was extremely small, with a vaulted roof and stone floor; it was one of the most interesting remains of the old medieval priory and at one time must have been used as an annexe to the large kitchens it adjoined. Unfortunately, it had been adorned with mediocre statues of the Virgin and the Sacred Heart, which evoked unpleasant memories of the Rue Bonaparte and the Rue Madame in Paris. In this chapel, Dom Felletin and Dom d'Auberoche were not free, as they were in the novitiate, to send these pious horrors to the lumber room, and the other monks put up with them as best they could; they were there, and it never occurred to anyone to change them.

The Mass was served by Brother Gèdre, a small novice with a wily look in his dark mouse-like eyes. Indeed, he was nicknamed the 'Mouse', as he was always scuttling about, smiling and looking around, always pleased, always happy. If ever he escaped from his prayers, it was because he was rushing to study Greek. He was passionate about it, but as good Hellenists were lacking in the monastery he was obliged to study it alone; this was the sole drawback in that existence spent in the perpetual joy of living in God to being a monk.

He had been so little spoiled in the past, this poor child, that, from the material point of view, the monastery seemed to him to be a dream of comfort, a place of luxury and delight.

He had been an orphan, alone, with neither brother nor sister, from his early childhood, brought up out of charity by a congregational establishment; he had always eaten the cheap food and drink served in these places; he had always slept in a dormitory, never had a moment's freedom or a penny even to buy a sacred picture. At the end of his studies he'd passed from his college to Val-des-Saints with no transition.

And here he felt at home, he had a cell of his own; communal life, so difficult for lay people who have renounced the outside world, didn't bother him, since he didn't imagine one could live otherwise; the food of the monastery seemed so good to him that he deprived himself of certain dishes for fear of becoming a glutton; and the freedom of the novices had seemed to him extravagant in comparison to that of the boarding school.

And yet there were times when he was distressed. One day he said to Durtal, who had asked him why he looked sad: "Ah, one suffers so much in a monastery…"

Durtal was lost in conjecture, all the while trying to comfort him. But his suffering was simply due to the fact that instead of the role of master of ceremonies which he was supposed to take at Mass that morning, they'd asked him to be a candle bearer, and for him it was like a demotion.

It was the sadness of a kid having his stick of barley sugar taken away and given to another to suck; it would have been quite laughable if one didn't remember that some people suffer as much over a trivial matter as others do over more serious causes. Moreover, wasn't it proof of the necessity of the suffering from which no one is exempt? Whether the motive was serious or trivial, it nonetheless affected people the same way. Impervious in certain areas that undoubtedly afflicted his brothers in the novitiate, Brother Gèdre was tortured by trivialities, and the fearful Father Emonot, who had noticed it, didn't spare him, striking him in the sensitive spot, inflicting humiliations on him of this kind, as often as he could, in order to crush all vanity in him, to detach him from himself, to mould him on the model of the true monk.

But that morning, the lad was cheerful and gave a little tender smile, watching Durtal kneel, after he came out of the sacristy in front of Dom de Fonneuve on his way to the altar.

Durtal tried to absorb himself in the Mass, but his thoughts wandered during every prayer; the fear of getting confused in his responses dominated him. 'How I wish this ceremony were over,' he said to himself.

At that moment the offertory commenced, and it began.

Dom Felletin and Dom d'Auberoche ascended the altar steps and stood on each side of the prior. Durtal left his place and came and knelt in front of them, on the lowest step of the altar. Then the prior, crossing himself, repeated the *Domine, labia mea aperies,* the *Deus in adjutorium*, the *Gloria*, and then began to recite Psalm 64, *Deus miscreatur nostri,* the verses of which were chanted by the monks and novices alternately.

Then, addressing Durtal, he asked:

"*Quid petis?*" – What are you asking for?

"The mercy of God, and your brotherhood, as an oblate of our most holy Father Benedict."

In a measured voice, the prior replied, still in Latin:

"My son, you well know, not only from having read it, but also from having practised it and experienced it during the whole couse of a year, the Rule under which you wish to serve. You are not unaware of the conditions of your agreement to enter our brotherhood. If therefore you are resolved to observe the salutary precepts of our most holy Father Benedict, approach; if not, you are free to withdraw."

Then, after a moment's silence, seeing that Durtal didn't move, he continued:

"Will you renounce the pomps and vanities of the world?"

"*Volo.*"

"Will you promise to undertake the reformation of your habits, following the spirit of the Rule of our holy Father Benedict, and keep the statutes of the oblates?"

"*Volo.*"

"Will you persevere in this commitment until death?"

"*Volo, gratia Dei adjuvante.*"

"*Deo gratias.* May God be your help. Since you put your trust in his assistance, you are free to make your profession as an oblate."

Durtal rose, and standing in front of the altar he read aloud the charter of profession, which was written on parchment and which began with the Benedictine *Pax* and the formula *In nomine Domini nostri Jesus Christi, Amen.*

And he read in a faltering voice the Latin text witnessing his self-consecration, made of his own free will to Almighty God, to the Blessed Virgin Mary, and to the holy Father Benedict, in the monastery of Val-des-Saints, promising the reformation of his habits according to the Rule of the patriarch, pledging himself to it in the presence of God and of all the saints.

When it was over, the master of ceremonies came up to him and led him to the top step of the altar, and there, on the Gospel side, he placed his charter on the altar and signed it, first with a cross, then with his name and surname, and finally with the new monastic name of Brother John, which he was going to assume.

He descended the altar steps accompanied by the master of ceremonies, and holding in his two hands the parchment unfurled on his breast, he presented it to the monks standing in the stalls, who looked at the signature and bowed.

When he had thus made the round of the chapel, Dom d'Auberoche took the scroll from him, and enclosing it in a corporal⁵ put it back on the altar.

And Durtal then knelt down again on the floor below the first step of the altar, and with his arms crossed in an X and his forehead almost touching the lower step he intoned three times, each time at a higher pitch, the *Suscipe*, which the monks chanted after him.

Then the prior turned towards the altar, and after the *Kyrie Eleison* and the *Pater noster* he began the series of long verses to which those present responded, followed by a prayer imploring the Lord, through the intercession of St Benedict, to grant his servant strength to be faithful to the promises he had just signed, and after Durtal had murmured "Amen", he went on:

"We, prior of the abbey of Val-des-Saints, acting by virtue of the powers granted to us by the most reverend abbot de St Pierre of Solesmes of the French congregation of the Order of St Benedict, by the merits of this same patriarch Benedict, of his sister, the virgin St Scholastica, of St Placidus, martyr, and St Maurus, abbot, of Gertrude, the seraphic virgin, of St Henry, confessor, and of St Frances, widow, and of the other male and female saints of our Order, receive you into our society and brotherhood, giving you a share in all the good works that are done, with the help of the Holy Ghost, in the French congregation of the Order of St Benedict. 'May God receive you into the number of his elect, may he grant you perseverance until the end, may he protect you against the snares of the enemy and lead you to his eternal kingdom, he who liveth and reigneth forever and ever.'"

"Amen," sighed Durtal.

And he bowed lower while the prior, sprinkling holy water over him in the sign of the cross, uttered:

"*Pax et benedictio Dei omnipotentis, Patris et Filii et Spiritus sancti descendant super te et maneant semper.*"

Chapter IX

And the Mass resumed.

Durtal returned to his seat. When the time for Communion came, he was really touched, seeing all the novices who were not priests going with him to the altar. All of them, rather than taking Communion at dawn as normal, had waited for this Mass.

When Communion was over and Durtal had said his thanksgiving he fled from the chapel. He was stifling in this rarefied atmosphere and he was obsessed with the desire to be alone with God for a moment; he crossed the cloister and went to collect his thoughts in a quiet corner of the church.

It was dark, and swept by a bitter draught. He collapsed onto a bench, surrendered himself, and an immense silence descended on him; it was like a void of the senses, like a tomb of thought; he reacted with a violent effort, then everything came out at once in disorder, his mind humming like the snare of a drum; he tried to sift his thoughts, to keep only a few before him, but an idea surged up, sending God, oblature and every other reflection into the shadows of his memory, implanting itself, standing out clear, alone in the full light of day: the idea that he had forgotten to tell Madame Bavoil he would be lunching in the monastery at noon.

And it becamse so tenacious, so ridiculously insistent that, exasperated with himself, he returned home, grumbling: 'When I've had a sip of black coffee and a crust of bread, perhaps I'll manage to pull myself together.'

As soon as he was back, he had to describe, detail by detail, the scene in the chapel to Madame Bavoil.

"Well, you didn't make any mistakes, that's the main thing," she concluded, "as to seeing you here this evening, no, because I really think that after High Mass, which will finish late, you'll go straight to the refectory."

"You're right."

And Durtal did indeed go to High Mass. The Smyrna carpet, the relics and the night lights were there, but the absence of the abbot, whose stall was however draped with red velvet, reduced the gala aspect of the Mass, which was no longer celebrated in pontifical fashion.

Before Mass there was a procession around the cloister. Preceded by the thurifer, the cross-bearer and two acolytes, the lay brothers in their brown cowls walked in front, followed by the postulants and the novices, then by the monks and the cantors; the prior came last, accompanied a few steps behind by Monsieur Lampre and Durtal.

And they advanced slowly, two by two, in a haze of incense, and having completed the journey through the four galleries that formed the square of the cloiser, they re-entered the church where they had come out, and the Mass began.

This St Benedict Mass was, from the point of view of the text, exquisite; it had retained the *Gradual* and the *Tract,* the *Gospel* and the *Communion* of the delightful Mass of the abbots, but it began with the liturgically florid *Gaudeamus*; it included a special epistle suited to the virtues for which the patriarch was revered, but the sequence was less happy, in the sense that if it was adroit at recalling in its brief strophes the characters from the Bible to whom the saint could be compared, it lacked simplicity and its self-consiously elegant Latin didn't ring true.

As for the plainchant, it was that used on great occasions – in other words, it was mediocre and pretentious. The *Kyrie*, with its twisting, finicky ornamentation, the up-and-down *Gloria*, and the *Credo* like a tune played on a dancing-master's fiddle, could all be found there.

'Obviously,' sighed Durtal, 'my conviction only grows each day that the reformers of Gregorian music went off on the wrong track when they doled out different musical adornments to the Mass. They imagined that the more the pieces were filigreed, and towed caravels[6] of fancy trills in their wake, the better they'd be suited to the high rituals of feast days and better able to enhance their brilliance; but for me it's quite the opposite, because the simpler and more naïve plainchant is, the more eloquent it is and the better it expresses, in its own unique language of art, the joy or the sorrow which are, in short, the two subjects treated by the services of the church, according to the Proper of the Season.[7]

'Be that as it may, this Mass, after that of St Joseph which preceded it in the calendar, was all the more welcome as a change from those of Lent, which were repeated the whole week before. Each day the *Ordo* bore the direction *de feria*; which is to say weekday offices from the Proper, different each day, very fine moreover, but brief: no *Gloria*, no *Credo*, no *Ite, missa est*, no organ; the Tract substituted for the *Alleluia*, the *Te Deum* omitted at matins; just two lighted candles on the altar; on days when there was a deacon and a sub-deacon, the deacon wore his violet stole tied like a cross belt, and the sub-deacon a chasuble tucked up like an apron, and the Mass was preceded by the three short canonical hours recited without a break.

These varied Masses broke the monotony of the Masses taken from the Common, and they also had a very ancient *Kyrie*, short, crisp, and rhythmic, which with its curious candour of a spoilt child, its naïve, almost joyful tone of complaint, never failed to please.

Vespers had been transferred to before the midday meal, because logically they had to be begun on a fast and one could not sustain oneself until five o'clock in the evening if the customary schedule had been followed; and these feast day vespers were a surprise, they were recited so rarely. One no longer heard the *Dixit Dominus Domino meo* and the other hackneyed Sunday psalms. They would change, without duplicating the antiphon, every day; and on the Monday, one could finally hear the magnificent *In exitu Israel de Aegypto*, that was hardly ever sung in the Benedictine liturgy.

The vespers of St Benedict's day brought back the usual psalms, but their lack of interest was saved by the splendid antiphons, above all that in the sexte, the *Gloriosus confessor Domini*. They would have been perfect, were it not for a hymn as mediocre as that of the Mass, the *Laudibus cives resonent canoris*, reeking of pagan language, the Latin of the Renaissance, with its Olympus always being substituted for heaven, a hymn that smelt of college homework and the usher.

But, with the exception of the hymns of this feast, the period of Lent was, from a liturgical point of view, admirable; its melancholy grew each day, before bursting into the Reproaches,[8] into lamentations, into the dolorous sobs of Holy Week.

This period of sadness and expiation had itself been preceded by the melancholy weeks of Septuagesima, the start of which used to be a time of abstinence, shrouding the joyous and delirious *Alleluia.*

And Durtal smiled as he recalled how in the past they would have a funeral service for the *Alleluia,* as if it had been a great personage, so much did this cry of joy seem to be living and intimately tied to our Lord, with whom it rose to life again on Easter Sunday.

In the twelfth century there had even been a whole service for these funerals, to be read on the Saturday before Septuagesima. On that afternoon, after nones, the choirboys would come out in procession from the sacristy, with the cross, tapers, holy water, and incense; and they would carry, in lieu of a body, a handful of earth; then crossing the choir of the church they'd go into the cloister, where they would sprinkle the spot chosen for burial with holy water and incense.

It was the death of an expression, the momentary demise of a song; it was the eclipse of the joyous and lavish neumes, and one ceremonially groaned for having lost them; and the fact is that the *Alleluias* in the Gregorian repertoire were, for the most part, so deliberately exquisite that you would be sad not to sing them, and you would wholeheartedly rejoice when they were reborn with Christ's resurrection.

'This funereal liturgical life that we began with Septuagesima – which is the period of probation for Lent, just as Lent is the novitiate for Passiontide and Holy Week – will get darker still with the prelude of Easter and it will finally end,' murmured Durtal, 'and I truly won't be sorry, because these repeated fasts and abstinences wear me out; really, the honest St Benedict should have at least allowed us to eat meat on the occasion of his name day. Damn it, the austere cod is going to hold sway once more,' he went on, falling into line behind the monks, as they filed out into the cloister by way of the little door at the back of the church. A number of local priests, and a few Dominicans, invited by the prior, were strolling under the arcades. There were exchanges of greetings. Durtal was looking for somewhere to go and light a cigarette in the garden, when he was cornered by the parish priest. He led him down one of the paths and there, while waiting until it was time for dinner, the priest told him the gossip of the village. "You know the Minot girl?" he said, and Durtal shook his head. "But you at least know her sister, who married Nimoret?" And Durtal again shook his head.

"Oh… but you don't seem to know anyone here," exclaimed the priest, amazed and a little suspicious.

"No, aside from Madame Vergognat, my former housekeeper, and old Champeaux, who I employ to weed the garden paths, I don't see anybody; I just go backwards and forwards between my house and the cloister. I stroll in my garden, and sometimes I go to Dijon or call on Monsieur Lampre or Mlle de Garambois, but I have no connection with the villagers, who I know to be lecherous and greedy, like all those who live in the countryside."

The *Angelus* bell put an end to their talk; and they made their way back to the arcades of the cloister. The prior washed the hands of all the guests, who gathered in a line in front of the refectory door, and then, to the sound of reading, falling in monotonous waves over the tables, the meal began.

The predicted cod did not appear, instead there was breaded eel, swimming in a watery shallot sauce that tasted of copper, soft poached eggs on sugared spinach, fried potatoes, a caramel cream, gruyère, and nuts; and, the height of luxury, they drank a finger of some excellent wine, harvested in the monasteries of Spain.

After a return of thanks to the church and coffee, Durtal, who wasn't interested in the priests' discussion on politics, the wine harvest, or the bishop's still impending resignation, escaped with Dom Felletin and went to rejoin the novices.

There was a great debate in progress when they arrived. The younger, who weren't priests, deplored the fact that the abbey didn't have enough monks to be able to celebrate – without interruption, from morning to evening, and from evening to morning – the office; but as it would have needed strong teams to carry out the rotation of the *Laus perennis*, it was impossible to consider.

"Eventually, one day, it will happen," affirmed Brothers Gèdre and Blanche, "and on that day we'll be able to proclaim that the

Benedictine Order is the Church's greatest Order."

Durtal couldn't help smiling at their enthusiasm, and he surreptitiously looked at the older novices who were priests, who weren't saying a word. They formed what is called among the novitiates, the 'priestly faction', which is to say, those not particularly enamoured of the liturgy and the offices. They'd had enough of these ceremonies during their seminary days, and so, despite the contrast between the wretched services in parish churches and those in the monasteries, they generally failed to embrace them.

So the Benedictines preferred to have lay people as novices, people from the outside world, and justifiably attracted to the splendour of monastic art, rather than priests who derive a certain pride from the priesthood, whose habits are difficult to uproot and who lack enthusiasm for the *Opus Dei*, for that which was precisely the essence of the Benedictine institution.

Above all, the priests saw in the monastery a peaceful retreat from wordly life, a way to sanctify themselves with minimal effort, and they were willing to accept in exchange the tedium of long ceremonies and the fatigue of matins.

"Isn't it true," Brother Blanche said to Durtal, "that the goal of monastic life should be the uninterrupted praise of God?"

"Certainly, little brother, but you can console yourself for not being able to realise this project with the thought that perpetual praise already exists, not in one particular Order, but in all the Orders combined together; the prayer of the congregations never ceases; the monasteries belonging to the various observances take it in turn among themselves, and collectively they perform together what you would like to practise alone."

"How do you mean?"

"Well, take a closer look at the schedules of the various communities and you'll find that this is the case. During the day, obviously, unless you are undertaking the Perpetual Adoration and always have several monks in front of the blessed sacrament, you'll have gaps in the unfolding fabric of the offices, because you can't repeat the canonical hours indefinitely and you have to work, to eat – in a word, to live. The question therefore only

Chapter IX

arises about the night: it's about praying to the Lord when no one else is praying; well, that's already resolved, and in this perpetual concert, your place is reserved."

"That's true," observed Dom Felletin.

"Explain it to us," said the younger novices.

"Well, roughly speaking, unless I'm mistaken because I haven't got the rules of the different Orders before me. I'm only dealing here, you understand, with the contemplative Orders, and I leave aside the others, who, as soon as morning dawns, also give you the support of their supplications.

"From the moment the last liturgical hour ends, that's to say after compline, which usually finishes at about eight-thirty p.m., the divine service recommences with matins and lauds. From eight-thirty to ten at the Benedictine nuns of the congregation of France; from nine to eleven among the Carmelites; from eleven to one-thirty at the Clarisses-Colettines, and from eleven-thirty to two o'clock with the Carthusians; from two to four or four-thirty a.m., in the Trappists monasteries and convents, and in the Benedictine monasteries and convents of the Primitive Observance, and also in the Benedictine convents of the Blessed Sacrament; from four-thirty to five-thirty in the Benedictine monasteries of the French congregation; from four-thirty to six in the convents of the Poor Clares and in other institutions, and from six o'clock onwards, the service of prayer is assured by all the community; it goes without saying that I'm omitting from this list the Orders whose rules I've forgotten or whose statutes I haven't read, and that this timetable I've just outlined is only an approximate one, since the offices are longer or shorter according to the rite of the feast."

"Added to which," said Dom Felletin, "the Norbertine monastery which has established itself in France recites the office from midnight to one o'clock, and resumes at five in the morning after a short sleep, like that of the Poor Clares and the Benedictines of the Blessed Sacrament; in fact, there's not a single hour of the night that is idle; when the world sleeps or sins, the Church keeps watch; her nuns and her monks are always at their posts, always on guard, to protect the camp of the faithful, incessantly besieged by the enemy."

"And your list overlooks the Benedictine nuns of Calvary," said Brother de Chambéon; "they should be joined to the Trappists and the Benedictine nuns of the Blessed Sacrament, because they too rise at two to chant matins; it's an Order of reparation that follows the precepts of St Benedict in its strictest rigour; they fast perpetually, and like the Poor Clares go barefoot from the first of May until the Feast of the Exaltation of the Holy Cross."

Brother de Chambéon relished talking about the hardships of these ascetics. This good fellow, who would mortify himself in a terrible fashion, was nevertheless as gentle and kind as a man to whom suffering was unknown. In his character he was the most youthful of all the novices. He preached by example, and more effective than the exhortations of the novice master and the preceptor, his good nature appeased the petty quarrels that inevitably occurred between the 'monkish faction' and the 'priestly faction'. He radiated peace around him and all listened to him, as if to a saint.

"It would be interesting to know," continued Durtal, "if these liturgical timetables were agreed on between the various Orders, or whether they were organised, I won't say by chance, because chance doesn't exist, but by a decision of providence, which would have been arranged when it inspired the ordinances of each congregation, so that each one chose a different hour, in order to complete the picture."

"Now that," cried Dom Felletin, "we don't know. It's difficult to believe in a prior agreement, because these various congregations didn't come into existence at the same time. It must be admitted, however, that after having taken cognisance of the observances of those Orders that already existed, those who founded new Orders could have taken up the prayer at the hour the others relinquished it. That is, after all, possible, but where's the proof of it?"

At that moment, Father Emonot, who had been keeping company with one of the invited priests, arrived, gently leading Father Philigone Miné by the arm. He was struggling, now in his second childhood.

Ever since his stroke, he spent his time wandering slowly round the corridors and only seemed content when among the novices.

He would sit down by their side, never saying a word, but watching them laugh with kindly eyes. Although it was against the Rule for monks to associate with the novices, they made an exception in his favour, and the young fellows, out of charity, walked him round their part of the garden when he was so inclined.

Moreover, he was revered by everyone. His case was indeed extraordinary. This doyen, who was a monk of the old school, had never missed an office during his whole life; even after his mind had started wandering, he continued to go, not even missing that of matins from which all those who are sick are exempt. When the abbot said to him: "Father, you are old and in bad health, you don't need to get up till five," he gently nodded his head, understanding very well the meaning of the words, but he'd persisted in occupying his stall before the 'Psalm of the Lazy' was recited.

And this wasn't a matter of habit or routine as one might think, because, finding it difficult to walk, he now rose earlier in order not to be late. He accurately calculated the time he needed, and prayed earnestly in church. His reason, clouded as regards earthly things, had remained intact when it was a question of praising God.

It was touching to see this old man, supporting himself against the walls in order to get to the church. He had been assigned a lay brother, a worthy man, to assist and serve him; but he refused all help, not wanting to be a burden to anyone. One fine morning he fell and cut his forehead. Then the abbot forbade him, under obedience, to leave his cell unaccompanied; he understood, shed a few tears, and after that, when he was alone, didn't go out.

His pharmacy, which had interested him so much when he was in his right mind, was lost to him now; one day, thinking to please him, they took him there; he stared at it blankly, apparently unable to remember that in this cell cluttered with flasks, he had spent his whole life. His memory was dead; in the ruins of that soul God alone remained; and from time to time, when sitting with the novices, he would stammer a few words that no one understood. Thinking he was asking for something, they would patiently make him repeat the words, only to realise that he was talking about our Lord and about the Blessed Virgin.

"Sit down, Father," said Brother Blanche, settling him on a bench, "sit there, next to our new Brother Durtal." And suddenly, as if roused from sleep, the old man examined him with limpid eyes – and he sadly shook his head, studying him with an unspeakable pity – then he stared at him cheerfully, with a gentle smile.

And like everyone seeing them for the first time, Durtal was puzzled by these quirks of physiognomy, and asked him: "What is it Father?" But the monk relapsed again into the impenetrable silence of his features, incapable of expressing any answer.

Chapter X

Never had there been a Holy Week as gloomy as this in the monastery. The Law of Associations, in the reality of which no monk had believed, had just been passed by the Chamber of Deputies, and a resolute optimism had given way to the blackest pessimism.

Apart from a few stunned idealists – who clung to the hope that the President of the Council would save them at the last moment by scuppering the law in the Senate, and that President Loubet,[1] a pious man, would resign rather than lose his soul – all the others agreed that the senile buffoons in the Palais de Luxembourg were as bad as the malicious brutes of the Chamber. They were all lackeys of the accursed Freemasons, and nothing good could be expected from them.

The abbot, back from his journey abroad, had heard the most alarming rumours as to the fate of the religious congregations in France; he didn't breathe a word of it, but the sadness of his expression and the fervour of his prayers spoke volumes.

The novices thought it impossible that the prayers with which the communities relentlessly besieged heaven could be rejected by our Lord; they just had to redouble their zeal, and they all deprived themselves of something, rising earlier or mortifying themselves, in order to avert the blow.

For several weeks now, by order of the abbot, after terce and before nine o'clock High Mass, all the monks, on their knees, would chant the Psalm *Levavi oculos meos in montes*, the *Sub tuum*, and the prayer to St Michael; and despondency started to take hold, seeing so many prayers for deliverance remaining unanswered.

Durtal – who had always been struck by the demonic character that stamped the Dreyfus Affair, and looked upon it as nothing more than a springboard set up by the Jews and the Protestants from which to leap at the Church's throat and strangle her – had long ago lost hope; nevertheless, when the law was passed by parliament, he felt the slight shock of a man who suddenly finds himself confronted by a danger he thought was much further away.

"Just think," he said to Madame Bavoil, "a few rogues, elected God knows how, by means of scheming in seedy back rooms, are going to crucify the bride, just as the Jews in the past crucified the bridegroom. It's the Passion of the Church that's beginning; nothing is missing, it's all there, from the clamour and blasphemy of the freeloaders of the extreme left, to that former pupil of the Jesuits, that Judas whose name is Trouillot,[2] and that new Pilate, Loubet.

"Ah, what can one say about that one! He'd go regularly to Mass in secret, every Sunday at the Sorbonne when he was a member of that disreputable warren, the Senate; and then he signed the law and he washes his hands; I'd be very interested to know what priest would dare absolve him when he goes to make his Easter confession."

"What could this Monsieur Loubet possibly say to the Lord when he prays?" asked Madame Bavoil.

"Well, he asks him to keep him in office, to help bring his stocks and shares to term, and he begs him to protect his children so that they become fearless Christians like himself.

"Since he doesn't keep a dancer as his mistress he thinks himself a good man, because he's probably like the majority of Catholics for whom only the sins of the flesh count; added to which, he probably considers himself to be charitable, because he saved the cool swindlers of the Panama scandal from prison;[3] his conscience is therefore clear, unreproachable, and he lives in peace, honoured by his family.

"Moreover, he's duplicated himself, because he recognises the right of God to busy himself with the private man, but he considers the other, the politician, as a being apart, who doesn't concern the creator; and after all, isn't a politician just a mere typewriter. One touches the keys, and the word Loubet is formed. If Christ isn't happy, it's not him but Trouillot, Monis, Millerand, or Waldeck-Rousseau[4] who are to blame, because they're the ones who manipulate the keys and type out his name at the bottom of the decrees.

"Then, once the job is done, this family man who forbids the poor to give their children a religious education, calls for the priest of Saint-Philippe-du-Roule – the one who says Mass every Sunday at the Elysée – and recommends him to teach his progeny the catechism, and fingers with a certain pride the luxury rosary his Holiness the Pope gave, as a reward no doubt for their virtues, to that other excellent Catholic, his wife."

"But, my friend, the portrait you're drawing is the spitting image of the Pharisee who our Lord denounced…"

"'Likeness guaranteed',[5] I'm afraid, Madame Bavoil."

"Well, it's not all hopeless, Rome could still intervene…"

"And do what? No pope has ever loved France more than Leo XIII; harassed, it has to be said, by the Catholics who devoid of any initiative kept requesting instructions from him on anything and everything, he thought he was doing us a service by interfering in our affairs, and, misinformed and certainly mistaken about the state of our country, he imagined he could tame the wild fowl – a cross between a vulture and a goose – that is this Republic of Jews and atheists; alas, its beak pecked the hand held out to caress it; he was not however discouraged; he fought, step by step, for the few religious liberties that still remained intact, and in exchange he had to put up with the nomination of unworthy bishops, insults and threats. Naturally, the more paternal he was, the more insolent the enemy became; and that led us to the Law of Associations; then he made a final effort, letting it be understood that if the religious Orders were touched, he would deprive France of her protectorate of the Levant; this time, he was spared pecks from their beak, these wounds were far too noble, and the satraps from the suburbs who rule us were content to taunt him, stinging him by what is called in popular slang 'thumbing their noses at him'; and saddened, fearing to make things worse, he has kept his silence. What else do you think he can try? He can't react now, it's too late."

"Certainly, if anyone deserves pity," said Madame Bavoil, "it's this poor old man whose kindly intentions have been rewarded only with mockery and insults."

"Nevertheless, I imagine," said Durtal, "that greater griefs have tortured the holy father's life; in any case, this is one where he's had to drain the chalice to the last drop, and there's nothing more bitter than that.

"The papacy could and should play a magnificent role in our time, and Leo XIII was certainly ready to assume the responsibility for such a historical gesture; but the events which he's had to bear and which we know nothing about, have broken his will, thrown him, exhausted, into the shadows.

"So while this decaying Europe, united against mercy and justice, grovelling before brute force, looked on, smiling, at the Turkish massacres of the Armenians and British banditry in the Transvaal, a single man stood, imposing by virtue of his age and majesty – the Pope – and said to them all: 'I speak in the name of the Lord, whom you crucify by your cowardice; you are the worshippers of the golden calf;[6] you are a Cain among people.' That it had no effect from the political point of view, that's possible, but from a moral point of view it was immense. It proved that there was still justice here on earth; Rome shone like a beacon in this dark night invading the world, and nations in disarray could at least turn in his direction and believe that the representative of Christ on earth was with them, was for them, against the crowned scoundrels and the demagogues.

"For reasons that were of course incontrovertible, his holiness, who must have wept tears of blood over his enforced silence, never said a word. Ah, the poor Pope!"

"The fact is," said Madame Bavoil, "that the life of Leo XIII, interned in the Vatican, robbed of a temporal power which by right was his, has for many years been nothing but a Calvary."

"Alas. But to return now to the hardships inflicted on him by France, the daughter he loves the most, what will he decide to do? Today, when the game he played against the Freemasons has been lost, and his spiritual patrimony is about to be pillaged, will he stand up, and in a thunderous awakening, strike with excommunication, cut off from the Church and curse down to their last descendents Loubet, Waldeck-Rousseau, Trouillot, Monis and all the deputies who voted for the law, and all the senators who are going to vote for it? It would be a solace at least for those unfortunate Catholics who see themselves entirely abandoned by their leaders, and I can assure you that it would be no laughing matter for the excommunicated, because it's on their families, nominally designated in the papal bulls, that the mass of misfortune these furious anathemas entail will fall.

"Will our Sovereign Pontiff unleash them? I doubt it; he will forgive and he will be evangelically right; but where will all these resigned defeats lead us?"

"Ah," cried Madame Bavoil, shaking her head, "let's have done with this sorry business; let's think only of Jesus who is going to be crucified; the hour of darkness is near, let's go and console him."

"Assuming we are worthy of it…" said Durtal, as he put on his hat and jacket.

Once settled in the church, he forgot the sorrows of the present moment. The divine liturgy lifted him up, soaring so high above the mire of this world, and he took in at a glance the panorama of that terrible week, this 'painful week' as the Middle Ages called it.

Before climbing those days that led, in short stages, to the summit of Golgotha, to the very foot of the cross, the Church shows, in the gospel of the Passion, the Son of God reduced to run and hide so as not to be stoned by the Pharisees; and to express this humiliation, it covers its statues and crucifixes with purple veils. Another week passes, and suddenly for a few moments its distress is interrupted by the feast of Palm Sunday.

The evening before, the epistle in the Mass would proclaim the appalling curses hurled against the Jews by Jeremiah, that precursor of Christ; and the next day, in the magnificent offices, to the cry of Hosanna and the triumphal *Gloria laus*, Jesus advances, riding on the foal of an ass as predicted by Zachariah, and he enters, deafened by the cheers of the people, into that Jerusalem which, amid clamours of rage, would kill him a few days later.

And as soon as this glorious march with the procession of the palm branches was over, the anguish of Christ and his Church immediately resumed in the Mass, and wouldn't cease until Easter; the reading of the Passion would begin with St Matthew, and continue on Tuesday with St Mark, on Wednesday with St Luke, and on Friday with St John.

And as he listened to them, Durtal would be entranced, transported outside himself by this strange, thrilling chant; there was a sort of melody running though the story, with its constantly recurring themes; this chant was monotonous and alarming, but also almost caressing; and this lulling, mournful impression was again experienced during the lamentations of the *Tenebrae*, sung to barely a handful of notes, varying with the full stops, the question marks, and pauses in the text.

These cantilenas must have been collected in part from the oldest antiphons of the Jewish people. The Graeco-Roman strand, which the paleography of Solesmes links to the origin of plainchant, made itself felt less than the Hebrew strand in these melodies which recalled, in the chanting of the letters, with their languid lilt and cadence, the naive and yet subtle melodies of the Orient.

In any case, they certainly dated back to antiquity, and the repairs that their fabric had undergone in the seventeenth century and since, had altered neither their colour nor their outline; they were wonderfully suited to the services that also dated from the first ages of the Church, perhaps even from the church of Jerusalem in the fourth century.

And these mournful days at Val-des-Saints were indeed admirable.

Shod in thick slippers, the monks, no longer heralded by the sound of bells, entered like shadows, and as they passed the swish of their large black cowls produced a cold breeze that smelt of damp cellars and tombstones; and the minor hours before the Mass came and went, falling drop by drop, without the *Deus in adjutorium*, which usually precedes them, without the *Gloria*, that usually intersperses them and succeeds them, and at the end of each office the *Miserere* was recited in lugubrious tones, until the final word, *vitulos*, was flung into the air, like a shovelful of earth into a grave.

In the dimly lit church, with the crosses encased in lozenges of purple, the triangle of smoking candles, and the lamb-like bleating of the Hebrew letters chanted at the beginning of each of the *Lamentations of Jeremiah*, it was heartbreaking. On Maundy Thursday, the abbot, with mitre and crosier, and in purple vestments, proceeded to wash the feet of his lay brothers; and on Friday, after the *Adoration of the Cross* and the funereal *Impropere*, interspersed as if with refrains by the imploring strophes of the *Trisagion*, he went, dressed in a black chasuble and white mitre, without candle and without crosier, to take the consecrated bread at the altar, and all the kneeling monks, in two rows, held black lighted tapers and extinguished them immediately after the abbot had consumed the holy species.

The monastic services of Holy Week did not differ from the Roman ones; but in no church, nor even any cathedral, were they celebrated with such splendour; unfortunately, if at Val-des-Saints the ceremonial had been magnificent up until Saturday morning, on that day everything took a turn for the worse.

As a result of a compromise between the abbey and the presbytery, it had been agreed that the monks should occupy the church on Easter Sunday, but that the priest would have the honour of blessing the font on Saturday. He therefore took the service, surrounded by the whole community, but he barely knew his trade, and his French pronunciation of the Latin blended ill with the Italian pronunciation of the monks.

To those who were long accustomed to hearing '-um' pronounced '-oum', '-us' pronounced '-ous', '-ur' pronounced '-our', the 'j' becoming 'y', for those accustomed to the fricative 'c', which transforms the word '*coelum*', for example, into '*tchoeloum*', the Frenchified Latin waa a little embarrassing; nevertheless, it would have been bearable if that was all, but mixed with the other method of pronunciation, it turned into a cacophany; it seemed as if the parish priest and the Benedictines didn't speak the same language, and this confusion was echoed in the Gregorian chant, which the priest sang, not according to the text of Solesmes, but that of the seminary… and Lord how he sang!

Everyone was eager for this now ridiculous ceremony to end. Fortunately, the splendour of the Mass compensated for the failings of this office, which is so wonderful when performed in plainchant by the monks.

After the short Epistle of St Paul, the subdeacon appeared before the abbot standing at his throne, and announced to him the resurrection of the *Alleluia*. And the abbot, joyful at the good news, chanted it three times, and three times the choir responded with an *Alleluia* that was a little timid as if hesitant to take flight; then, after the *Credo*, at the offertory, the paschal lamb, adorned with ribbons and flowers, was led up to the altar rail.

The poor beast, which was being pulled by the guestmaster and pushed from behind by the cook, was getting restive; looking to escape, it was staring defiantly at the man robed in gold who advanced from the back of the choir, escorted by his train of attendants, to pray over it and give it his blessing; the beast seemed to have a presentiment that so much deference directed at it would end badly.

This Holy Saturday morning was interminable. Beginning at eight o'clock, the office lasted til about midday; but Durtal was happy; when the service dragged, he allowed his thoughts to stray from the liturgy, and he mused about Jesus and his Mother.

'Yes, certainly,' he said to himself, thinking of the Virgin, about whom, in this mournful period, the scriptures say so little, 'yes, certainly, the moment when she stood at the foot of the cross must have been terrible; the transfixion predicted by the aged Simeon was fulfilled; but the sword of pain wasn't thrust into his chest in one blow. It hesitated at first, and in Mary's sufferings there was a moment which must have been particularly awful, the period of suspense between the arrest and the condemnation of her Son; it was then that the tip pierced the flesh, prodding and enlarging the wound, without penetrating deeper.

'The wait lasted eleven hours. Jesus was, in fact, arrested and brought to Jerusalem on Thursday night, at about eleven o'clock.

On Friday he was dragged before Annas and Caiaphas from midnight until two o'clock in the morning; brought before Pilate at six o'clock, and transferred to Herod at seven o'clock; then mocked, scourged, crowned with thorns and condemned to death between eight and ten o'clock.

'The Blessed Virgin knew that Jesus must die. She herself had consented to his death and she would even have sacrificed him with her own hand, so Antoninus tells us, if the salvation of the world had required it; but she was nonetheless a woman. She had all the virtues to a heroic degree, possessed the most perfect gift of the spirit, she was the most holy of Virgins. She was unique, but she wasn't divine, she couldn't escape her human condition, and consequently could not but be tortured by the anxieties of waiting.

'Had it been otherwise, she would have imitated her Son, who suspended his divinity, as it were, on the cross, to suffer the more, and she would have asked for and obtained the right to inflict on herself the bitter torment of disappointed expectations.

'What those hours of waiting were like, it's difficult to imagine. Mother of God, wife and daughter of the Lord, and sister of mankind, of whom she would also become the mother, a mother born at the foot of the cross, in streams of blood, she grafted, one onto another, all these relational sufferings; but she wept above all for the perversity of that abominable race to which she belonged, and which demanded that, in a baptism of curses, the blood of the saviour should fall on her.

'Ready to suffer all that she could possibly suffer, she must have hoped against hope, wondering in her overwhelming grief if these villains would, at the last moment, spare her Son, if God, by some unlooked-for miracle, would not achieve the redemption of the world without inflicting upon the Word Incarnate the awful torment of the cross. No doubt she remembered how Abraham, after giving his consent, was spared the fearful task of slaughtering his own son, and perhaps she hoped that like Isaac, his prototype, Jesus would also be released at the last minute and saved from the sacrifice.

'Such thoughts are natural if one considers that Mary knew what was fit for her to know, but she didn't know all; she knew, for example, the mystery of the incarnation, but had no knowledge of the day, the place, or the hour; nor did she know, before the visit of the angel Gabriel, that she was the woman chosen from all eternity to give birth to the Messiah.

'And, humble as she was, never seeking to penetrate the secrets of the Most High, she could easily delude herself.

'What happened during those hours about which the gospels are silent? When she heard that the saviour had been arrested, so Ludolph the Carthusian tells us, she rushed after him with the Magdalene, and as soon as she found him she stayed with him and never left him again.

'Sister Emmerich confirms the Virgin's course of action, and she enters into numerous details, a little confused about the comings and goings of Mary, who according to her, was not only accompanied by the Magdalene, but also by a small troupe of holy women.

'She shows Mary following at a distance the soldiers who surrounded Jesus, and fainting when she saw his arrest. She tells us that they took her to the house of Mary, mother of Mark, and that it was the apostle John who informed her about the brutalities committed by the thuggish guards along the way; she relates that it was also he who escaped from Caiaphas, in order to warn her, while poor Peter, out of fear, lied.

'But she wouldn't stay where she was, so the visionary tells us. She went out again and, near the house of Caiaphas, met Peter, to whom she said: "Simon, where is my son?" He turned away without answering; she insisted and then he shouted: "Mother, question me not, what your son is suffering is unspeakable; they have condemned him to death, and as for me, I denied him!"

'And, heartbroken, never resting, she followed the way of the cross, till at last St John points out to her, at the foot of Calvary, the heart pierced by the seven swords of the deadly sins, swords buried this time to their very hilt.'

When recalling this pitiful story, Durtal always returned to his first idea: before penetrating deeply into the flesh and remaining fixed there, what tortures these implacable swords must have inflicted on Our Lady of the Seven Sorrows, twisting in the wounds, stoking, as it were, the fire of the wounds, with those pangs of despair and hope, and what a subject of meditation is to be found in the reconstruction of the few hours of a life so completely unknown as that of our Mother.

And Durtal groaned with her when, during the reading of the second lesson of the nocturne on Good Friday, the soft, clear voice of little Brother Blanche, standing in the middle of the choir before the pulpit, chanted, like the prolonged and plaintive bleat of a lamb, the Hebrew letter *Mem*, and then continued with the doleful, waddling rhythm of the prophet's lament: "To what shall I compare thee, and to whom shall I liken thee, O daughter of Jerusalem? To what shall I equal thee, that I may comfort thee, O virgin daughter of Sion? For great as the sea is thy wound, and who shall heal thee?"

'Heal thee…' sighed Durtal, 'instead of the oil and wine with which the Good Samaritan used to soothe wounds, it's rather with vitriol and hydrochloric acid that our modern Pharisees would treat her wounds if they had her in their grip. For centuries the Virgin has chosen France for her special home, because nowhere else, in no other country, has she dispensed so many graces, nowhere else has she proved herself as at the present moment by a series of continual miracles like those at Lourdes, and as was the case in Palestine, insults rain down on her and persecution rages against her votaries.

'France invented a way to make the liturgical calendar an eternal Holy Week for the Madonna.'

These thoughts obsessed him. Deep down, truth to tell, the "painful week" was that which was best suited to his aspirations and his tastes; he could only really see our Lord on the cross, and the Virgin in tears. The *Pietà* would spring to his mind before the nativity.

So, when he came out of those long offices of Holy Week he was exhausted, but happy. He felt himself to be truly in communion with the Church, and he had prayed so well.

And he needed to make an effort to change his state of mind when Easter came, to enter into the transports of joy when the *Alleluias* resounded beneath the vaults of the church, when the joyous carillons of bells rang out, with their clusters of novices hanging on their ropes; and yet, what a glorious feast day is that day of the resurrection! What an atmosphere of jubilation would fill the church! It was hung with red velvet, covered with flowers, and the reliquaries, like mirrors of glass and gold, reflected spears of fire from the candles; the pontifical Mass was as full of pomp as that of Christmas, with all the servers in black hoods cast back over white surplices, with a crosier bearer, mitre bearer, candle bearer, and train bearer; after the procession, it blossomed from the *Introit*, where Christ celebrates his resurrection, through the prophetic words of the psalmist, and the group of prayers that rose from the choir; even imploring supplications, such as the *Kyrie*, arrayed in festive purple flowers, seemed to rejoice with the enthusiastic and candid sequence of the *Victimae paschali laudes*, which proclaimed itself triumphantly with that *Alleluia*, so forcefully, so proudly, which follows the *Ite, missa est*, and is taken up again after the *Deo gratis* at the end.

And to complete the mastery of this office, the antiphons of the vespers were quite exquisite, and to the Benediction, added in honour of the Virgin, as well as the marked prayers, after the rousing rustic lament that is *O filii et filiae*, an ancient text, *Salve Mater misericordiae*, taken from the collection *Variae preces*, which had borrowed it from an old Carmelite breviary, there was a text, with a refrain, whose strophes unfolded to a popular melody.

It was a day of musical ecstasy, an orgy of liturgical pleasure; Durtal hadn't left the church and the monastery since the morning, and he had eaten the paschal lamb along with the monks, Monsieur Lampre and the priest.

The lamb had been served whole on a table, with its legs up in the air and its mouth agape, exhibiting rows of teeth and sticking out a black tongue. Swathed in great aprons, the cellarer and Father Ramondoux, armed with huge knives, carved it up.

And Durtal couldn't help laughing.

The younger novices who hadn't eaten their fill since the beginning of Lent, were delighted, even though this lamb had the stringy flesh of an old ram; these monkish cherubs stuffed themselves like ogres; and the older monks furiously wolfed down the less appetising cuts of meat.

'The fact is,' thought Durtal, as he looked at Brother Gèdre and Brother Blanche, 'the fact is that these poor lads haven't tasted a morsel of meat for forty days, and even their bread was rationed, so they had just enough to stop them from fainting; and it's not with spinach and beetroot in white sauce that you can keep these lads, who have been up since dawn, on their feet until evening.

'As for me, whose abstinence has been almost as rigorous – because, for lack of fish at Val-des-Saints, I had to be satisfied with vegetables on days when eggs were forbidden – I feel quite weak, my stomach is out of order, and I'm not at all sorry to get stuck into this mutton in my turn, tough though it is, and I'll be even more pleased to resume my old habits, to go to vespers at four o'clock, which is to say at a more convenient time, instead of at half-past eleven, which left me with an awkward hour gap which I didn't how to fill after Mass had finished at ten o'clock. The only thing I could do, while waiting, was either go back home or wander round the village; but starting from today we're returning to normal, *Alleluia*!'

And after dinner, when he'd got back from the chapel and joined the abbot, Dom de Fonneuve, Dom Felletin, Dom Badole, the priest and Monsieur Lampre in the guest room for coffee, Durtal was overwhelmed by a feeling of well-being, for which he was unable to explain the reasons; they were, in truth, many; there was the spirit of a cloister in the grip of that liturgical joy that had been flowing since the morning offices; there was the satisfaction of a man freed from irksome spiritual exercises and restricted meals; and finally, there was the invigoration of the temperature, which had, with the end of the cold weather, become milder, because nature was also reborn with Christ.

It was almost warm. Durtal had taken a walk in his garden before Mass; the little woodland walk was carpeted with violets, and the sticky brown buds of the chestnut tress were springing up amid the black branches; the fruit trees were in blossom, and the cherry trees and the peach trees looked as if they were sprinkled in white and pink snow; after the harsh bareness of winter and the tiredness induced by massive doses of prayer during the previous week, what an immense relief it was to reach spring and Easter.

And this impression was felt by everyone, even the priest who, legs crossed, was fidgeting in front of the fireplace, where the remains of a log were still smouldering.

But suddenly, with a word from the abbot, who had a concerned tone in his voice, their cheerfulness vanished.

After the obligatory discussion with the guests about the beauty of the service and the grandeur of the plainchant, the abbot, addressing himself to Monsieur Lampre and Durtal, had quoted the words in the Gospel of St Luke, "With desire I have desired to eat this passover with you before I suffer," and, with everyone listening, he added: "Next year at the same time, where will we be, with whom will we eat the paschal lamb?"

"Father," said Durtal, "have you decided to leave us?"

"Decided? I can't decide anything yet; we must first wait until the law is passed by the Senate: it may be a matter of months, then before coming to any decision we have to know what instructions the Pope will give us."

"And if he doesn't send you any," said Monsieur Lampre, "or rather if he sends only vague and imprecise ones, leaving everyone to get out of the muddle as best he can – and between ourselves, he can't really give you clear and firm instructions, because the interests of various institutions differ, and the solution suitable for one would be harmful to another – what will you do?"

"In that case, we will meet up, all the abbots of the Order, at our mother house in Solesmes, and decide what line of action to pursue."

"And it's already marked out in advance," said Dom de Fonneuve, "because we can't submit to a law which openly violates the superior right of the Church and the very principle of religious life. To accept the measures in this sacrilegious law would be, on our part, to surrender.

"And indeed Orders such as ours, which take solemn vows, enjoy the privilege of being exempt as regards the Ordinary, but

Chapter X

this law decrees exactly the opposite, since it wants to place us under the jurisdiction of the bishops.

"Now, this right of exemption was determined by the ecumenical Council of Trent and by the apostolic constitutions, which simply confirmed the decrees of the Council, so it's not up to either the government or the bishops to change it. They can neither approve nor disapprove the statutes of the religious Orders, as long as the Holy Father has given them his sovereign approval. It's therefore an intolerable encroachment of civil authority over the prerogatives of the Holy See, and at the same time it's a denial of the monastic life, since this impious edict refuses to recognise the solemn vows on which this life is based."

"Imagine," cried Dom Felletin, "Monsignor Triaurault substituting himself for St Benedict, and if we consented to hand over our Rule to him, suppressing the articles he didn't like or introducing measures of his own."

"Not to mention," said Monsieur Lampre, "that another bishop, in another diocese in which there was a Benedictine monastery, might do the exact opposite. He might strike out all the clauses that his colleague had kept, and invent new ones in his turn. What a mess that would be!"

"Added to which," continued Dom de Fonneuve, "we would be singularly naive to comply with the requirements of this law and furnish, with our request for authorisation, a statement of our receipts and expenses, and an inventory of all the goods and chattels we possess; because this would be to hand over our wallet to these sharpers, whose only hesitation is over the best means to employ to steal it. After all, what guarantee does this authorisation offer us, even supposing it were granted, since it requires only a simple decree from the council of ministers to annul it? We are also called on to furnish a list of the members of the community, giving their family name as well as their name in religion, their nationality, their place of birth, their age and the date of their entry; this is establishing for monks the kind of heavy-handed police surveillance that was repealed for criminals. The only thing lacking is a form with anthropometric details, proposed by M. Bertillon."

"That was certainly an oversight on the part of that agent of the Freemasons, Trouillot," said Durtal, "let's hope that bringing the law back to the Senate will amend it."

"Moreover," said the guestmaster, "the decree about how it's publicly administered, announced in Article 20, could further aggravate the infamy of this law through the interpretations of Jewish lawyers."

"Yes, you can expect that," said Monsieur Lampre.

"We mustn't delude ourselves," said the abbot, "the congregation of Solesmes will never consent to submit to this torturous yoke. So, supposing the Senate passes the law after the recess – and it certainly will – that will take us to June, and after that we'll have just six months to move. Consequently, by next December at the latest, we will no longer be here."

"And where will you go, your reverence?" asked Durtal.

"I don't know; Belgium is the nearest country and life there is not expensive; it's also the last Catholic country where the pack of Freemasons is still muzzled; if, as is certain, the assembly of abbots orders a departure into exile, I will start searching as soon as I get back from Solesmes."

"Oh, we have to find out first if the ministers will apply the law," said the priest.

"And how they'll apply it!" exclaimed Durtal, "do you really think that these miscreants, have arrived at this result, so patiently and skilfully prepared for so many years, in order to let it drop? You take them for being more stupid than they are; have no fear, they'll see their wicked scheme through to the end, and they're not going to stop with the monks, because I can assure you that the persecution of the secular clergy will be next."

The priest shrugged his shoulders; if, in his heart of hearts, he considered the monasteries to be troublesome and unnecessary, he was convinced that priests were indispensable and that the Republic would never dare to touch them.

"And after the clergy, it'll be the turn of the middle class," said Monsieur Lampre, "after the properties of the Order are transferred to the state, we'll witness the wholesale plundering of our stocks and shares. Will the middle class be roused from its apathy when they start forcing open our cash boxes?"

The middle class? it'll submit with a sigh and that will be that," retorted Durtal; "as for the Catholics, you know as well as I do what a bunch of fools and cowards they are; if, by chance, you found among these intrepid people someone who was determined to resist, the deputies and senators of the party would immediately step in and do the job of the enemy by disarming him."

"So, there's nothing to be done?" exclaimed Dom de Fonneuve.

"No, Father, nothing. I'm not a prophet, but count on it that, during the more or less perilous events that are being prepared, Catholic spokesmen will be all talk; they'll sign petitions which every government when it receives them throws into the bin, and they'll make pathetic speeches at meetings where the audience is specially selected so that no harm comes to their precious persons; then, when the moment comes to go out into the street and show themselves, these pious blusterers will issue more warlike protests, while our lords the bishops will whimper respectfully in high-sounding phrases, after which, they'll all calmly submit and grovel on the ground, convinced, moreover, that they've done their duty and behaved valiantly."

"If that's so, we may as well despair of France."

"I can't see any reason for not despairing," retorted Durtal.

"No, no," cried the others in chorus, "you're too pessimistic; it's just a period to get through; the Orders will go into exile, that's clear; it may even be 1793 over again; but then there'll be a reaction and France will rise up and the monasteries will flourish again…"

"I hope, as much as you do, that there'll be a reaction," replied Durtal, "but without wishing to sound like a bird of ill omen, I have to confess that I can't see, even after a victory by conservatives, the monks being reinstated in their monasteries. To me, it will be with the Law of Associations as it was with the Concordat,[7] which their most Christian majesties were so eager to keep. It's a weapon that no government, of whatever type, will want to part with…

"The best thing that could happen in your scenario is that the new law would be so implacably and so unfairly implemented that it would become difficult to defend; then perhaps they might modify some of its most imprudent clauses; I hope so; if on the other hand it's applied placidly and calmly, if it strangles the Orders in a perfumed snare, it'll be inscribed without reform into the graveyard of our Code, like a *concession à perpetuité*. It's sad to say, but it'll require some blood to dismantle it, and blood is like money, the Catholics are a little stingy with it."

"Alas," exclaimed Dom de Fonneuve, "I'm afraid that this time you're right."

The bell rang. The recreation period was over. Everyone separated.

"That's all very well, my friend," said Madame Bavoil to Durtal, when he repeated this after dinner conversation to her, "but if the Benedictines go what will become of us?"

And when Durtal didn't reply, she added:

"Perhaps the moment has come to pray to one of your favourite saints, St Christina the Astonishing, who one invokes to resolve difficult situations."

"And also to St Benedict, I think, because the profession I made for him and through him at Val-des-Saints is a little bizarre, that of an oblate *in extremis*, that of an oblate of the last days. I will have to bury myself, and lead my own mourning. Even so, it seems to me that the good patriarch will restore me to life somewhere, I don't know where, remote from the busy world. I hope so, but, while waiting for this new direction, we have a lot on our plate to worry about."

CHAPTER XI

A few months had passed; as had been predicted, the Chamber of Deputies had found in the Senate its shameful other half. A second-rate Trouillot by the name of Vallé¹ had filled the pig trough of the Rue de Tournon with a few bowlfuls of his rhetorical slop, and the old boars had wallowed in the slurry of his eloquence and voted, trotters in the air, for the Law of Associations; the congregations were well and truly strangled, and the goal so patiently pursued for so many years was attained.

The Pope had spoken, condemning the provisions of the new law, but leaving everyone free, under certain reservations, to crawl into the wicker cage the state called 'public worship' if they thought it appropriate. No agreement being possible between the various rival congregations, there was no hope of any united resistance which would obviously have been the only dignified response, the only decent position, so the decision taken by Rome was therefore, under these circumstances, wise.

Even the few monks who were stirred by the idea of fighting the measure were obliged to agree. In this cloister of Val-des-Saints, formerly such a haven of peace, concerns that up until then had been relegated to the future began to grow; the fathers invaded the scriptorium where all the Catholic reviews and journals the monastery received were held; they would read them in silence, and during the recreation period talk about them, sometimes embellishing them with amusing comments.

This little world, which knew nothing of contemporary events, and which had, God knows how, been indifferent to politics until then, began to ask itself what evil it could have committed that it should be hunted down in this way.

And these anxieties found an echo in the novitiate.

"What have you committed? Why, in the eyes of your accusers, you've committed the most unpardonable of crimes, that of not sinning against God," said Durtal to Brother Gèdre, who had consulted him, dazed by the buzzing all around him, like a beehive under attack.

All the monks wandered the corridors, eager for news. The reverend abbot was at Solesmes and they were waiting impatiently for him to write to the prior, to say when and how they were to carry out their departure.

"There's no news," said Monsieur Lampre to Durtal as they came out of church together after High Mass, "but it's so perfectly obvious what the resolution of the chapter of abbots will be, that a letter from Dom Bernard won't tell us anything we don't already know; it will be exile after a short delay; the place chosen for banishment is still uncertain, and will be for quite a while, I think."

And as Durtal was preparing to leave him on the steps of the church, he continued:

"Come, since you're lunching with me today, instead of coming at the usual time set for meals, why not come home with me now and by way of an aperitif we can look through some of my illuminated manuscripts."

"Ah, I'd like that very much," said Durtal.

Monsieur Lampre's house, situated two steps from the church and the monastery, was one of those big, ordinary buildings that often thrive in country towns. It smelled of the provinces, a mix of fish glue and apples, but inside, the rooms were pretty well laid out and contained old, comfortable furniture. Monsieur Lampre had inherited it from his family, like the ruins of the old monastery, which he'd given to the monks, along with its vast tracts of land.

He had simply reserved for himself a spacious garden, which he had separated from that of the abbey by a wall, so that each could feel private; and this garden, planted with age-old trees, was crossed by paths bordered with flowers, one contained beds of roses of all shapes and colours, among which figured the green China rose, which was actually quite ugly. His collection of roses, maintained at great expense, was highly regarded in Burgundy.

Chapter XI

"And yet," he said to Durtal one day, "I've got no special affinity with horticulture, I do it out of a sense of duty, and I only spend money on it to keep myself interested."

And as Durtal, who was admiring floral fireworks that sprang out of the ground, looked incomprehendingly at him, he added:

"It's very simple, I'm so lazy, so little of a walker, that I wouldn't leave the house, I wouldn't even go down to stroll in the garden if I wasn't impelled by the very prosaic sentiment of assuring myself, by looking at these bushes grow, that I wasn't wasting the money that buying and maintaining them costs me. I look at a bed of plants here, I scrutinise a border there, and without noticing it I'm walking about; horticulture serves to stretch my legs more than delight my eye; it's an odd way of looking at it, but since it's useful to me that's its *raison d'être*."

'What the devil could he have done in life?' Durtal sometimes asked himself. What was known about him amounted to very little. In his youth, Monsieur Lampre had been a pupil at a charter school, and had long lived in Paris. He had remained a bachelor, and his only living relative was the daughter of his sister, who married a certain Monsieur de Garambois, a prefect under the Second Empire. His sister and her husband had died, and he saw little of his niece, as she had always lived with nuns or near the cloisters at Solesmes. It was only when she settled in Val-des-Saints that their relationship, formerly so distant, became truly close; they were fond of each other, even when they argued, without seeing too much of each other.

If you believed the monks' gossip, Monsieur Lampre, whose fortune had been considerable before he'd made a dent in it through numerous indiscretions, had led a somewhat colourful life during his youth in Paris; then he'd converted, and from that time forth had lived in seclusion in his house at Val-des-Saints, a charitable and irascible man.

He and Durtal got on well; tastes in common brought them together; Monsieur Lampre was not very well up on contemporary literature, and quite behind the time as regards modern art. In his capacity as a collector, he limited himself to a very small number of areas. In painting he stopped short even before the Primitives, preferring illuminated manuscripts, and in monastic history he attached value only to monographs amd cartularies.

Of these he possessed very full collections; in particular he had some beautiful books of hours from the fourteenth and fifteenth centuries, which the monks much coveted, and which moreover he had promised to bequeath to them. In the past, he'd spent imposing sums on these purchases, but times were now a little harder; he'd been obliged to help, during the first few years, with the installation and even the livelihood of the monks he'd brought from Solesmes, and he was both angry with them for preventing him from being able to continue to spend extravagant sums, and satisfied at being able to help them.

On days when he was in a bad mood he would growl his usual complaint: "What do I ask of them in exchange for all the fine bargains I've missed on their account? That they become saints, and now I'm out of pocket because these rascals have tricked me." Then, having let off a bit of steam, he was again ready to be of service to them.

In addition to his passion for cartularies and miniatures, he was, in his capacity as a Burgundian, smitten with another love, that of a well-stocked cellar, and when dining, he would melancholically recall the years when he hadn't been able to acquire a few cases of Beaune Hospice, "because the blasted Benedictines had drunk it all".

These regrets delighted his niece, who he often reproached for her weakness for fine food.

"Look," she would say, "we should be indulgent towards each other, because everyone has their little manias and their pet sins; for me, it's a love of dainties, for my uncle, it's old vintages of Burgundy."

But he wouldn't allow this comparison; the love of great wines, he would say, is an almost noble love, because there's a certain beauty, a certain art in the taste, the colour, and the bouquet of a Corton or a Chambertin, while the greed for sweets and cakes betrays a middle-class sensibility and reveals coarse tastes and vulgar cravings; and he turned his back on her, while she, amused at hearing him grumble, doubled up with laughter.

While waiting for her to arrive – because that morning she was also due to lunch with them – Monsieur Lampre took Durtal to the room where, on oak shelves, were ranged the monastic histories and the cartularies.

The room was large, lined in wallpaper with a poppy flower pattern against a grey background; there were armchairs upholstered in cadmium yellow velvet, mahogany tables and a Second Empire writing desk with a trefoil-shaped lock.

Durtal examined the library shelves, but only a few of these bulky tomes interested him, because, as in all such collections, to make up the numbers and complete the series, there was a mass of unreadable volumes that even Monsieur Lampre hadn't opened.

What captivated Durtal more were the books of hours, these were ranged in cabinets and enclosed in cases. Monsieur Lampre was not generally well disposed to show them off, he guarded them jealously for himself. Nevertheless, he'd already shown them to Durtal on several occasions, but it had to be he himself who suggested looking at them, otherwise he would turn a deaf ear to any request of the sort.

That particular morning he'd proposed examining them, so he had no hesitation and took out a few from their slipcases.

It was always a treat to look at these pristine marvels. "I haven't got many," he would say, "but I think that I snapped up only the choicest specimens at the auctions," and he would sigh, acknowledging that he'd paid thirty thousand francs for one of these books, a magnificent copy of the *Horae beatae Mariae Virginis*, a small in-quarto in sixteenth-century binding, worked in open-leaf tracery, a manuscript of the fourteenth-century Franco-Flemish school, written in Gothic characters on vellum, each page bordered with a decoration of sinuous fronds and branches; and this volume of almost three hundred pages contained some fifty miniatures on gold backgrounds, amazing portraits of barely pubescent Virgins of the Nativity, with melancholy or mischevous faces; there were young and beardless St Johns, writing next to eagles, in charming interiors illuminated by leaded windows which opened onto green landscapes with pale roads that led to tiny castles; and grander scenes, such as the annunciation to the shepherds, the visitation, and Calvary, which were treated with such a good-natured realism and such naive piety as to be truly touching.

"Here," said Monsieur Lampre, "is a diurnal which didn't cost as much, but is nevertheless very curious; notice the way the artist has depicted the Holy Trinity; it's quite different from the familiar model adopted by the majority of illuminators in the Middle Ages; the Holy Spirit is soaring in the form of a dove above the Father and the Son. Here, the Father, crowned with a sort of papal tiara, and seated on the edge of a golden halo shaped like an almond, with his feet resting on the world as his footstool, holds Jesus in his lap, who himself holds, in the same manner, the Paraclete, portrayed as a smiling, fairhaired boy. Isn't that strange?"

"And what's no less strange either is the state of preservation of this manuscript; the colours are as brilliant as when they were first put on," cried Durtal, amazed indeed by these fresh, clear tints, by these reds untouched by time, by these untarnished golds, by these still limpid pale blue skies.

"Oh, they didn't get their colours from paint shops, and synthetic oils hadn't been invented then," replied Monsieur Lampre. "They themselves had to grind their colours, which they extracted from certain minerals, clays, and plants.

"We know a little about their recipes; that rather pasty white you see there is made of calcined bone, that other lighter shade is white lead; that black is made from charcoal crushed with vine shoots, that blue is lapis lazuli; those yellows come from soapwort and saffron; that brilliant red is minium, and that brownish red that corresponds to ochre is from loamy soil such as the volcanic soil of Naples; this green is extracted from the flower of the iris or the buckthorn berry; that blue turning to violet is not, as you might think, obtained by mixing blue and pink, it comes from the sunflower and is composed of disparate elements, such as the urine of a man who's been drinking wine.

"Their formulas were strange, but effective, since none of

their colours have faded. For the white of an egg, which was the ingredient most used for tempera, they broke down its viscosity with two-week-old water from the laundry, and its frothiness by adding a little cerumen or ear wax. To fix gold leaf they first rubbed the parchment with spit, taking care to use only that of a man who had fasted or who hadn't eaten recently; then, as a size, they used a confection comprised of gum tragacanth, bole armoniac and honey; according to a recipe found in Dijon among accounts relating to Jean Malonel the painter, they also used a gelatin extracted from a cod's fins."

But Durtal was no longer listening to him; he was staring at the dazzling blooms on these vellum pages. "Ah," he said, closing the book, "Illumination is like a delightful, frail girl, blue-eyed and golden-haired, who after a long labour gave birth to an enormous daughter, Painting, and died in the process!"

"Yes, but she didn't expire before having reached the supreme apogee of her art, with artists such as Fouquet, Jacquemart of Hesdin, André Beauneveu, Simon Marmion, the Limbourg brothers, and in her final years with the astonishing Jean Bourdichon, who painted a book of hours for Anne of Brittany.[2]

"We have some knowledge of those who worked for princes and kings, because their names and details of their work are found in archives and treasury registers, but many more remain unknown. And in the cloisters, where miniature painting was born and where monks didn't always mention the names of these artists in their writing, how many lost or anonymous masterpieces there must be, and how many attributed to laymen who were really only their imitators or their pupils.

"Certainly," Monsieur Lampre went on after a pause, opening a book of hours of the Virgin, "this manuscript is a marvel, but, to be frank, my dream would be to possess examples that were less perfect perhaps, but earlier than these, whose monastic origin was more certain; that Bible mentioned in the chronicles of Cluny, for instance, which was copied and illuminated by Albert of Treves and adorned by the monastery's artists in an ornamented binding set with gold, and bejewelled with beryls and rubies; or better still, a volume by the monk named Durand, who so magnificently illustrated the abbey's liturgical books that, as a token of gratitude and admiration, the abbot wanted the community to double, after his death, the office that they chanted for every dead monk.

"I would have sold my house, my land – the whole lot – to get them. Who were these monks whose work so delighted their contemporaries? I don't know. Histories of Cluny and the biographies of some of the abbots are sometimes quite detailed, but they tell us little about the life of these miniaturists, who they merely mention, lumped in with architects, jewellers, bookbinders, fashioners of sacred images, stained-glass workers, and all the other craftsmen from every region who filled the monastery, because Cluny was a veritable school of mystical art in all its forms."

"Not to mention the writers," said Durtal, "such as St Majolus, St Odilo, St Hugh, Peter the Venerable, and others who weren't canonised but who left behind instructive biographies, such as Syrus' life of St Majolus, Jotsald's life St Odilo, and the famous Rodulfus Glaber, whose comprehensive History has been quoted many times since the Middle Ages.[3]

"But the glory of Cluny Abbey was above all assured by its architects. I remember visiting the remains of the abbey, which had become a training school and stud farm; the ruins of the church suggested the contradictory idea of gracefulness and vastness; this gigantic church, with its forest of bell towers, its porch as big as Our Lady of Dijon on it own preceding the church proper, which was immense with its five naves, its groves of pillars whose capitals were carved with leaves, birds and chimerical beasts, its three hundred stained-glass windows, whose figures burned in coloured flames, its two hundred and twenty-five stalls for monks in the choir; all gave the impression of a colossal monument, revealing the model of a style that only survives there, and the proportions of which have never been surpassed by the Gothic."

"There can be no quibbling, the two monks who built that giant church were grand fellows: Gauzon, who drew up the plans, and Hézelon, who carried out the work."[4]

"And it wasn't just those two," said Monsieur Lampre,

CHAPTER XI

"architects whose names are now forgotten but who were also Clunyists, spread further afield and built those superb sanctuaries at Paray-le-Monial, Saint Étienne at Nevers, Vezelay, Charité-sur-Loire, Monteneuf, Poitiers, Souvigny, and many more.

"The abbots had imposed no formula, no aesthetic template on their workshops; they respected the temperament of each monk and this deference explains the extreme variety of the buildings, and proves that Viollet-le-Duc[5] was wrong when he spoke of a Clunesian style – because no such thing ever existed, there was only the Romanesque style which the Cluny architects utilised, though each in a different fashion, working for the glory of God, according to their personal ideas, and according to their strengths."

"Ah, Cluny!" exclaimed Durtal, "that truly was the ideal of divine labour, the dreamed of ideal, in it was realised the artistic monastery, the deluxe house of God; I've said it before, it's the source to which the modern congregation of France should return if it wants to preserve its *raison d'être*."

"It's all very well talking about it," said Monsieur Lampre, "but you have to find pious people who are talented in all fields of art, or create them, and that's no easy task."

"Evidently, but just imagine if we had a monastery and church in Paris built by Dom Mellet, the monastic architect of Solesmes, and that a colony of monks from the same abbey, led by Dom Mocquereau sang plainchant; and imagine if there were magnificent ceremonies, ornaments, and statues to match. The success of the Benedictines would be prodigious; snobbery would get mixed up in it, just as it did with the choir of Saint Gervais, but it would help to attract the crowds.

"And the Benedictines would certainly have seeded many a vocation among artists fascinated by the splendour of such surroundings, and harvested all the money they could have wished for. Added to which, they would have singularly advanced the hour of Gregorian chant's triumph, by establishing it in the very heart of Paris, and they would have occupied a position in art such that no government would have dared to touch them.

"In order to obtain a result such as this, it would have been necessary, to use the language of industry, 'to go big', to exhibit an impeccable mastery, to unfurl beneath imposing vaulted ceilings, a skilful procession of sumptuous liturgies. Only Solesmes was big enough to realise such an idea, but owing to a series of disastrous circumstances quite beyond his control, the abbot was unable to establish a monastery in Paris. The same bad luck occurred at Solesmes itself, when Dom Couturier wanted to revive the art of illumination."

"So you know about that?"

"Yes, Dom Felletin told me about the scheme, and mentioned the name of an oblate who was a real expert in that forgotten art…"

"Anatole Foucher? Yes, I used to see him at one time…"

"And he trained the nuns at Saint Cecilia, didn't he?"

"Yes, and also the Benedictine nuns of the Rue Monsieur in Paris, because miniatures are now the preserve of the female cloisters of the Order. Moreover, I've seen coloured designs on vellum by these nuns in Paris, and also by those in Dourgne Abbey, and in addition to an attractive dexterity in the work, they revealed a Godly spirituality that was truly delightful.

"Many ladies have turned their hand to illumination, but I don't need to describe the mess they made of the liturgy and the insipidity of their designs, which were only fit to grace a gift box for a child's baptism, or figure among Eulalie Bouasse's infantile chromos of religious scenes."[6]

"Yes. I know the ones you mean; I once saw some in Paris, when a group of aristocratic lady-painters exhibited them in an elegant drawing room; but there's worse still, a new school that applies techniques of the Middle Ages to contemporary secular subjects; it comprises inept amateurs whose muddy gold backgrounds serve as a setting for cheap gemstones and third-rate pearls. It's a travesty of the art of illumination, I doubt if it could ever be treated with worse taste or a more execrable design."

"As I mentioned just now, before it completely disappeared the art lived on in Foucher and in a few of his pupils, forgotten behind the grilles of the cloister. Also of note, I remember having read somewhere that the Benedictine nuns of Marédret in Belgium illustrated a superb manuscript of the Rule of Saint Benedict, which the abbot of Maria Laach presented to the German emperor, but that's all I know."

"I'm late," cried Mlle de Garambois, entering the room like a gust of wind, "but it's the fault of Dom Felletin, who I'd asked to talk to…"

"Lunch is ready," said Monsieur Lampre, seeing the maid open the dining-room door, "let's go in, you can make your excuses afterwards."

"I'm furious," she said when they were seated, "I couldn't go to Communion this morning because Dom Felletin, despite his promise, wasn't there yesterday to hear my confession in Dijon. He has just explained to me that he'd been called for at the last moment which made it impossible to catch the train… you must admit that since the appointment of the new priest our situation at Val-des-Saints has become quite ridiculous!"

"You're right," replied Durtal, "when I think that on Whit-Sunday, the Feast of the Holy Spirit, the fathers couldn't officiate in the church because it was a Sunday, and the priest didn't see fit to let them borrow the building… it's unheard of! We had to put up with a Mass sung in that paltry little chapel where you can hardly breath and there's no room for any kind of ceremony.

"When I recall the same feast day a year ago, with its pontifical Mass, and the notions conjured up by the monks whose black cowls and white albs stood out against the purple and gold of the vestments; when I recall the *Veni creator* taken up by all the monks and raised to the very vaults by the thunderous waves of organ music… and then to think of the pitifulness of what I saw and heard in that stuffy little chapel, I get so angry and I wish five hundred devils would make off with the bishop and his priest."

"But you could go to Mass and vespers in the parish church…" said Monsieur Lampre, laughing.

"Oh, picture this," cried Durtal, "last Sunday, I slipped into the church for Benediction and I witnessed one of the craziest performances I've ever seen. Baron des Atours was standing in front of a harmonium, while his big lout of a son was smearing the keys with his clammy fingers.

"And the Baron, after nonchalently stroking the back of his bald pate with his be-ringed hand, twirled his stubbly moustache, and glancing heavenwards sang in his acidic voice an astonishing verse, of which I only remember the end:

"Jesus will be my ambrosia,
My sweetest honey too,
I will be his beloved home
His little sky of blue."

"Can you imagine the Baron as Christ's 'little sky of blue'? The mouths of the gobsmacked peasants gaped like oyster shells, while our priest nodded his head, and smiled a deferential, happy smile."

"Yes," replied Monsieur Lampre, "with his haughty demeanour and his pretensions as a singer, Baron des Atours is certainly rather ridiculous, but aside from that it's only fair to say that he's a good fellow and does a lot to help philanthropical societies in Dijon. And his son is also less of a ninny than he seems. He's an honest lad, and hardworking, but by heaven he's so very provincial. But look, here's something provincial I can thoroughly recommend," he continued, as he uncorked with infinite care a bottle of wine. "This wine is a Clos de la Commaraine; it's produced in the vineyards of the Pommard region; our fathers described it as 'loyal, rosy and saleable'. In any case, its bouquet speaks of age and good cellaring; look, it pours like liquid rubies."

"And he reproaches me for being a gourmand…!" exclaimed Mlle de Garambois.

"My dear niece, fine wines are works of monastic art like architecture, like illumination, like all that is beautiful and excellent here below. Clos Vougeot and Chambertin, the pride of this Burgundy of ours, have been cultivated, the first by Cistercian monks and the second by the monks of Cluny; the monks of Citaux had vineyards at Corton and La Romanée; records held at Volnay mention the vineyard of St Andoche, which belonged to the Benedictine abbey of that name, as being within the territory of that commune. The Cistercian monastery at Maizières developed

Chapter XI

a number of domains at Savigny-les-Beaune, as did the Carmelites later on, and as you know Beaune wine attracted the laudatory epithet of being 'nourishing, theological and wholesome'; there's no denying it, the most renowned wines of our region are due to the viticultural art of the monks.

"And it's only natural, after all. Wine is a sacramental substance. It's extolled in many pages of the Bible, and our Lord himself could find no more noble liquid to change his own blood into. It's therefore meet and just, right and salutary[7] to love it!"

"Doctors are beginning to forbid it now..." said Mlle de Garambois.

"Doctors are imbeciles," replied Monsieur Lampre, "aside from the fact that wine rejoices the heart of man, as the holy scriptures put it, it's a tonic more potent and certain in its action than iron pills and drugs of that sort which one can't digest; nowadays people who complain of stomach upsets are forbidden to drink it, but our fathers used it to treat such complaints, witness Erasmus who tells us that in his day they would cure this type of ailment with repeated doses of an aged Beaune; the truth is that our Lord chose rightly, in pointing them out to us and ennobling them, the two substances he deemed the most precious and which he intended to ensure the health of body and spirit: bread and wine; to not make use of them is to contemptuously ignore his teachings."

"Very well, uncle, but there's another point of view that it seems to me you're forgetting: the liturgical point of view; you agree with me, do you not, that the sublime ideal of Cluny, of celebrating the praise of God with pomp, of dedicating to him what is most beautiful and the best we have, is an ideal that is right and proper, 'elevated', as our brother Durtal might say..."

She paused, waiting for her uncle to give some sign of approval. But sensing that she was preparing some sort of attack he remained silent.

Taking his silence as a sign of assent, she went on:

"Doesn't it seem to you that the wine offered to our Lord to transubstantiate his precious blood should be in keeping with the sumptuousness of the liturgical ceremonies observed by our Order? Consequently, the best vintages of white wine should be given to the monks for use in the Mass, and you, who are well stocked with genuine Montrachets and Pouillys, you would certainly be doing a pious act by depriving yourself of them for the sake of the altar.

"You would also be setting me an example of contempt for dining on fine food that would no doubt be very profitable to me..."

"Ah, so that's what you're getting at, fine dining in the service of the good Lord, I recognise you in that; well, I don't want, under the pretext of honouring the Most High, to instill in his priests the distractions of a gourmet during the Mass; sin for sin, all things considered, it's better, because it's less serious, less offensive to God, if it's me who commits it sitting in front of a glass at the table, than a priest standing in front of a chalice in the church. So, with all respect to you, in the interest of religion itself, I will keep my Montrachets and my Pouillys, and with the piety and commonsense that characterise you, my niece, you will surely, on reflection, say I'm right."

"I can't win," said Mlle de Garambois, laughing, "to tell you the truth I wasn't expecting to; but come, my dear Durtal, to return to the subject of our unfortunate situation at Val-des-Saints, how does poor Madame Bavoil manage to fulfil her religious obligations, because she's in the same boat as me?"

"Well, not being able to go to Dijon to see Dom Felletin very often, because otherwise there would be no housekeeping or cooking done here, she has to put up with the priest, but she goes under protest and moans about having to confess – as she puts it – to a boy who knows nothing; I try to console her by pointing out the perfect wisdom of God, who deprived the priest of all tangible grace so that she doesn't have mystical discussions with him – but to no avail!"

"Perhaps it's just as well, because such annoyances will make it easier for her to leave here, if you have to follow in the wake of the monks."

Durtal shifted awkwardly.

"The idea of moving all my books and carting away all my things and my furniture stupefies me so much," he sighed, "that I prefer not to think about it."

"But," said Monsieur Lampre, "not all the fathers will leave the area."

"How's that?"

"Well, first of all there's the vineyard, which is the principal resource of the abbey, and they'll have to leave Father Paton and the lay brothers he employs to look after it. One or two monks will also have to remain to look after the buildings, so necessarily there'll be a few left here."

"And if the government takes over the buildings and the vineyard?"

"Nonsense! I may have offered the old priory and the adjoining land to the abbey, but I wasn't such a fool as to not take precautions against any such attempt at legal spoliation, either of the fathers or myself; in other words, I had the house rebuilt and I lease it to the Benedictines, the indentures and invoices are in my name, and it was me who personally settled the accounts of both builders and architect. The Benedictines, according to the leases granted and registered in due form, pay me every quarter, against receipt, one-fourth of the annual rent of ten thousand francs. I give them back the money afterwards, or never receive it," Monsieur Lampre went on with a smile, "but the documents are there; I'm the sole owner of the house and the lands; and as this is my family property, and they can't say that I specially acquired it in order to settle monks here, no legal quibbling by any third party is possible.

"The same goes for the vineyard; it was bought in my name, and paid for by me through a lawyer – the deeds prove this – and I'm also nominally renting it to them for the purpose of cultivation, so my rights from a legal point of view are incontestable."

"Yes, but they could prevent the Bendictines from being your tenants."

"Anything's possible with scavenging dogs of this sort, but nobody could prevent Father Paton, once released from his vows, from joining the secular clergy of the diocese of Dijon where he was born, and renting my vineyard, not as a monk but as an ordinary citizen; it's the same for the lay brothers, who would likewise take off their monastic habits and be engaged as farm labourers.

"I've already talked this over with the reverend abbot and we both agreed to take this course of action. Therefore, whatever happens, even if I have to go to law and the case drags on for years, the monastery will not be completely empty, and perhaps there'll be a way of holding services and organising things."

"Who's this Father Paton? I've never met him. He appears during canonical hours, then he goes out by the sacristy door; nobody seems to have anything to do with him."

"Father Paton is a former priest, an authority on viticulture, and a monk who mortifies himself very strictly; would that there were more like him at Val-des-Saints! Moreover, he's an excellent man who slaves away from morning till night like any peasant, and who, because of his work, keeps himself to himself. I would add that he has the secular virtues, which is to say he doesn't inform against his fellow monks, nor does he consider denunciation a virtue…. in him we will have a tough but devoted director, a man who really loves the soul."

"Ah, what you're saying is balm to my heart; perhaps we won't leave after all. If you knew what a nightmare the prospect of going to Paris, or wherever it might be, is for me now…"

"Just wait, things will turn out better than you think; you'll see, we'll hang on somehow."

"Basicallly, uncle, it's you who hold the key to the situation," said Mlle de Garambois.

"Yes, in part at least; I'm a windbreak, a windbreak protected by procedural law, and I swear to you that they'll have to unleash a hell of a breeze to blow me down!"

"I once visited the monastery vineyard in the course of a walk," said Durtal. "It's spacious and well situated; do they use it for making altar wine?"

"Yes, and moreover it's not bad. The hillside on which the

vineyard lies is of limestone-clay soil, reddened by the presence of iron oxide; it's like that of some of the Pommard vineyards; Father Paton has planted some pinot grape vines there, and in a few years, if the seasons are good, it'll no longer be altar wine they produce, but a quite passable table wine; on that day, the abbey will be rich.

"In the meantime, the sale of white wines is almost enough to cover the outgoings of the community; so this vineyard has to be saved at all costs, because if the monks settle abroad it'll help to support them, otherwise it'll be a case of starvation, and then utter collapse."

"Well, let's say that the government can't confiscate the vineyard; even so, it would still be impossible for Dom Paton and his helpers to live there in the cloister, because they would be prosecuted on charges of forming or re-establishing an unauthorised association."

"It wouldn't be advisable for Father Paton and the lay brothers to live in the monastery itself. They would be quartered outside; each of us will take one in, and even if the police put seals on the doors of the novitiate chapel and the oratory, the office will take place in some room arranged for that purpose in one of our houses."

"I hope God is listening to you," said Durtal, as he rose to take his leave.

"What, you're leaving, but it's not even four o'clock."

"Yes, we've talked so long it's almost time for vespers. Listen, you can hear the first bell."

"Time for vespers? Why, so it is," said Monsieur Lampre, with a stern glance at his niece, "and you dare to wear white ribbons in your hat and a kerchief of the same colour! What about the holy liturgy?"

"But," his niece replied in amazement, "today is a simple feast day of the Virgin, and the colour of the day is white."

"I beg your pardon, but the vespers are twofold today; they are like that ice cream, half vanilla white and half pistacchio green; in the *Ordo* you will see that from today's chapter reading until the next, that's to say tomorrow, Sunday, the colour is marked as being 'of the following day,' i.e., the ninth Sunday after Whitsun, that is, green. Now, a liturgist of your calibre ought to know that the veil of the tabernacle is changed halfway through the service, and bears a different colour in the second half. Therefore, at that moment, you should put on a green ribbon and a green kerchief… you've brought them with you, I presume, so you can change?"

"That's his revenge for you demanding he use his Montrachet and Pouilly as altar wine," laughed Durtal.

"I'll pay him back for that," said Mlle de Garambois, laughing in her turn.

"If Monsieur Lampre manages to keep us living here, neither the monks nor you will pay him back, on the contrary, we'll all bless him in unison."

"Oh we certainly will," she replied, putting on her hat, "because to live without my daily office would be impossible, and if I can I'd rather follow in the wake of the monastery to Belgium."

"She'd be quite capable of it," growled her uncle, putting on his overcoat to go with her to vespers, just as the second bell began to ring.

Chapter XII

'Evidently, the glory of Dutch sculpture is here in Dijon,' thought Durtal as he walked round *The Well of Moses*, which he had come to look at again in the lunatic asylum built on the site of the old Carthusian monastery,[1] about ten minutes' walk from the station.

This establishment where you could, in certain places, wander around in peace far from the inmates, would have been an ideal refuge for dreaming about art if only one could sit down quietly in front of this *Well* without always being dogged by the attendant waiting for you to finish looking at the statues so he could close the grille that enclosed them and lead you back outside by the shortest route.

The town of Dijon's habitual hospitality wasn't tolerated here.

So, when he'd gazed his fill on this masterpiece by Claus Sluter and his pupils, Durtal went off to think about it further away, in the delightful botanical garden that borders the road to Plombière, opposite the railway embankment. In the morning sunlight, the leaves of the tall trees in the asylum grounds were speckled with beads of gold that turned into bluish drops on the gravel of the paths; one walked through the alleyways beneath this screen of light and shade, and a close-set hedge of cypress trees, which you had to go past to reach the courtyard containing *The Well*, perfumed the air with a faint scent of resin.

It was in this lonely courtyard that stood the monument commissioned by Philip the Bold from Sluter, who was assisted by the most skilful artists of his time.

The monument emerged from the very interior of the well, supported by a hexagonal pedestal, on the sides of which stood statues of the six prophets who had foretold the passion of Christ, and this was surmounted by a platform supported by six weeping angels above the prophets. On this platform, this 'terrace' as the ancient texts call it, there formerly stood a Calvary, now lost, some fragments of which had been collected by the town's museum of archaeology. The whole thing was housed in what looked like an enormous iron aviary, topped with a roof, and furnished inside with a wooden floor that was raised up above the coping of the well itself, and that had a railing running around it, beneath which one could look down at the stagnant water that the moss-covered base of the pedestal was standing in.

And you would walk on this balcony around life-size effigies of the prophets, hewn out of blocks of stone which had formerly been painted by Malouel[2] but had subsequently become, with age, a uniform colour in which a little white was mixed with a lot of grey.

The most astonishing of these statues, the one that instantly captured you by the unforeseen vehemence of his appearance, was that of Moses.

Wrapped in a cloak whose fabric looked as flexible as that of real cloth, undulating in supple folds, falling in limp waves from his belt to his feet, with one hand he grasped the Tables of the Law, and with the other an unfurled scroll on which could be read a verse from Exodus, a portent of the times: "And the whole assembly of the congregation of Israel shall kill the lamb in the evening."

The head was hirsute, enormous, its forehead bulging with two bumps, as if with horns, and wrinkled above the eyes, which had a hard, unblinking, almost insolent look, with circumflex accents; the beard was parted, flowing down in two huge waves over his chest, leaving stranded a nose like an eagle's beak and an imperious mouth, which showed neither indulgence nor pity. Beneath this wild beast's mane, his face was tilted upwards, peering out implacably; it was the face of a stern judge and a despot, the face of a bird of prey; Moses seemed to be listening to the embarrassed excuses of the guilty tribes, ready less to forgive than to punish this Hebrew rabble who he knew to be capable of all manner of betrayal, all manner of idolatry, all manner of shamefulness.

This face, like a storm which one felt was about to break, had an almost superhuman aspect, it was, in any case, more eloquent and, it should be said in passing, more haughty, than that other Moses created less than a century afterwards by Michelangelo, a Moses equally furnished with horns and a flowing beard; but the latter artist only embodied an attitude, sculpted nothing more than an impassive colossus, robust in form, majestic even, if you like, but a colossus that was spurious and hollow.

Unfortunately, it has to be admitted that Sluter's Moses was the only figure among the statues as a group that testified to an art that rose above mere realism, that had a certain elevation; the others were, in fact, simply down-to-earth, admirable, but without soul, without anything that lifted them out of the common. The most typical in this precise but ordinary genre was that of King David, which suffered all the more in the contrast with Moses.

His head encircled by a crown, his hair long and curly, his beard divided under the chin into two tentative tufts, he posed with one hand resting on a lyre while the other unrolled a scroll on which were engraved the words: "They have pierced my hands and feet; they have numbered all my bones."

David had the placid features of a fair-haired or red-headed Dutchman, of an honest bourgeois, a little puffy, fed on smoked and salted meats and fattened up on strong beer. He was the future model for Jordaens' painting, *The King Drinks*, but done before Twelfth Night and before the meal. He revealed himself, in short, to be more distracted than distressed, more of a sleeper than a dreamer; as a portrait of a rich, rather supercilious man from the north, more adept at wielding a tankard than a lyre, this statue was perfect, but it was completely insufficient to represent the precursor of Christ and the author of the Psalms.

The prophet Jeremiah, placed next to him, was more serious, more collected; his head covered by a hood, his cheeks and chin clean-shaven, his nose hooked and his eyes closed, he was holding a wide-open book in his right hand, and a banner in the left with this inscription: "All ye who pass by, behold and see if there be any sorrow like unto mine."

The face was less sad than thoughtful, that of one of the monks of the Champmol monastery, who had no doubt served as a model in any case, or that of a priest in the act of meditating; it must have been sculpted from life and was obviously a striking likeness, but what connection has this tranquil monk or priest with Jeremiah, whose life of trials and sorrows was considered to be a living prophesy of the sufferings of Christ?

And the same question could be asked as regards Zachariah, who was wearing a strange kind of hood that looked like a cross between the capital of a church column and a pie; as for him, he was bowing his head in a vaguely distressed way, the head of a country wine seller, with a flowing beard and his upper lip shaved. Surely we have seen this old man behind a counter or in a cellar, preparing his shipment of casks and barrels for the retailers of the town; this face of a rustic tradesman was a little heightened by tribulation and ennobled by suffering; but even so it gave off a whiff of his trade. Was it really these words inscribed on his unfurled parchment scroll: "They weighed for my price thirty pieces of silver," that distressed him so much? He seems rather to have the air of someone deploring the loss of a grape harvest than the death of the Word.

Different again was his neighbour, Daniel, sternly pointing his finger at his phylactery on which is written: "And after sixty-two weeks Christ shall be slain." He stands there, arguing furiously with the unbelievers. Among this silent group, he alone was speaking, and he didn't look afflicted in the least, but rather agitated. He was a quick-tempered Burgundian, who brooked no contradiction. Topped by a loose cloth turban, and wearing an ample robe held in place by a belt, and draped in a magnificent cloak with studiously embroidered adornments, he stands out in profile, his nose like a billhook, his hair wavy, and his beard curled into little knots. He looked at once like a lawyer and a well-to-do merchant. Had he bought Zachariah's wines, he would have forestalled the objections of his clients by his aggressive tone, and hastened sales by the enthusiasm of his sales pitch.

Lastly, Isaiah demonstrated as much, if not more than the others, the all too certain discrepancy that existed between these statues and the characters they were supposed to represent. Isaiah appeared in the guise of an old Jew, a rabbi of the Judengasse, a patriarch of the ghetto. A round, bald head, creased with wrinkles at the brow, cheeks furrowed as if slashed with a sabre either side of the pointed shears that served him as a nose, a forked beard and equally long, drooping moustaches, like those of a Chinese man, and heavy-lidded eyes that are almost closed, he sadly lowers his head, a book under one arm, and a scroll hanging from the other on which this sentence is written: "He is brought as a lamb to the slaughter, and as a sheep before her shearers is dumb, so he openeth not his mouth." At no time had there ever been extracted from stone an image more acute and more lifelike, an effigy more truthful, a portrait more beautiful, but here again the same question arises: what similarity was there between this sad, weary octogenarian and the evangelist of the Old Testament, that prophet in turmoil, the impetuous, vituperative Isaiah?

With the exception of the Moses, whose leonine face and grandiose appearance really did capture the extraordinary being this man was, Sluter's other prophets embody nothing more than a fasting Gambrinus,[3] a Carthusian monk or priest, a wine-merchant, a tradesman and a Jew.

And Durtal still wandering round them, thought to himself: 'Yes, but if the link between these characters and the predictions that they announce isn't obvious, if the lamentation of the events they prophesy doesn't sufficiently move these harbingers of divine symbolism, it's because Claus Sluter deliberately decided to do it that way. His faces are more or less engaged, more or less mournful, but the expression of their sorrows stops there. The prophets are sad, but it's the angels that surmount and separate them who are crying.

'Indeed, in this work the role of the 'weeper' has devolved on the angels, and if one looks closer one can vaguely perceive the motive for this decision.

'The prophets foresaw the Passion of the Messiah, to the extent that God was willing to show it to them, and each repeats the detail that was specifically given to them; they all complement each other, the Lord having divided the visions between them, not having allowed a single one to comprehend the whole; they must have been dismayed by the growing certainty that this incorrigible people, who they were commanded to warn and rebuke, would commit the most abominable of crimes by crucifying Christ; but once the messianic revelations were received and propagated among the tribes of Israel, they had to live in the present, in their own epoch, and it's understandable why this future which they weren't called on to witness with their own eyes, and which moreover they only perceived in fragmentary form through a divine light, didn't cast them into a permanent state of tears. Sluter was perhaps right, therefore, to limit the signs of their emotions and to entrust more manifest evidence of mourning to the pure spirits who, though they cannot themselves see into the future, have a more subtle mode of knowing than our own, and who are, in any case, in their very being, independent of time and space.

'Another point to be cleared up would be that of determining which parts of the monument were assigned to his assistants. In addition to Claus de Werve, who we know carved the angels, several sculptors worked under his orders – Hennequin de Prindale, Rogier de Westerhen, Pierre Aplemain, Vuillequin Semont, to cite just four whose names occur to me. Another, called Jean Hulst, seems more particularly indicated in his role as an ornamentalist, as the carver of the foliage on the capitals. To what extent did they contribute in completing the figures of *The Well*?

'According to the records of the Champmol monastery, preserved in the departmental archives of the Côte d'Or in Dijon, it appears that Claus de Werve and Hennequin de Prindale sculpted certain portions of the statues of the prophets.

'But which ones? Did they execute the decorative, ornamental part of the work? If so, one must admit that they were the most amazing craftsmen of their kind, because the embroidered harps on David's mantle, the festoons, the foliage, and the Greek crosses braided on those of Daniel and Isaiah, the carved metal buckles of their leather belts, the books held by Jeremiah and Isaiah, with their stone pages as pliable as pages of vellum, and their elaborately embossed bindings, with clasps and mitred corners, are all executed with a skill, a sort of *trompe-l'oeil* that is disconcerting. Never in the art of sculpture have accessories been more cleverly wrought or more patiently rendered.

'But nothing proves that they confined themselves to reproducing inanimate objects, or that they didn't also work on the living parts of the model. But Sluter's name covers everything, and for want of more precise information he arrogates to himself alone the glory of the humbler craftsmen who assisted him.

'And they weren't just simple workmen, but real artists, because after Sluter's death one of them, Claus de Werve, became sculptor to the Duke of Burgundy, and it's to him that we owe the completion of a work begun by de Marville and Sluter, the tomb of Philip the Bold, which is now in the town museum. He worked on it, assisted like Sluter by other "shapers of stone" whose glory he likewise monopolised in his turn, and this work lasted five years.

'It's strange,' murmured Durtal, looking at the ensemble of this group of prophets one more time before leaving, 'how this Sluter, who lived at the end of the fourteenth century, gives us a hint of the Renaissance long before the death of the Middle Ages. His art is strangely in advance of the ideas of his century. If he no longer shared the mystical conception of the image makers of previous centuries, if he repudiated that era's emaciated, ecstatic faces, its hieratic poses, its slender almost fluid figures sheathed in rigid garments pleated with long folds, he gave us in exchange poses that were less constrained, the heavier, more natural faces of people who lived on this earth; he brought in draperies that were more malleable, clothes that were more supple, and above all he revealed a gift of observation and a power of breathing life into his work which makes him one of the greatest artists of all time.

'He was certainly pious, since he ended his days in a cloister, and yet his art reveals only a superficial piety, a piety on command; his portraits are those of people who are more concerned about their own affairs than those of God; his prophets are prophets of the marketplace and of the fireside; his work was not prepared by prayer, nor does it prompt people to pray in front of it; and that's the flaw in this sculpture, if you consider it from the very point of view it wants you to see it from, because it's meant to be understood in this way. If Sluter hadn't presented these figures to us as biblical characters, if he'd simply labelled them, on some civic monument, as shopkeepers or priests or magistrates, then one could not but admire, unconditionally, the immense talent of this man.

'Was the Calvary, which formerly stood on the plinth, and of which a few fragments remain, of a more religious feeling? I doubt it,' continued Durtal, 'I saw the recovered head of Christ in the museum; it was correct, deferential, sympathetic in expression, and soundly devout, but it wasn't otherworldly, it wasn't divine, and as for the Virgin, now standing over the doorway of the chapel a few steps from here, she looks like a mean woman, ready to whip a crying child.

'I refuse to believe that this Virgin is by him; this man, who if he lacked mystical feeling nevertheless knew how to capture the epic grandeur of a Moses, could never have conceived of a Virgin as false and vulgar as that.

'No, what I prefer is the little Madonna of the fresco, fading away on the wall of Our Lady of Dijon; and deep down the thought strikes me that the real sense of the divine is neither here nor at the museum, but in the painted prayers of that church.

'Yes, I know I'm annoying you,' he thought as he looked at the concierge, who was starting to jingle her bunch of keys, 'you don't give a damn about Sluter or Claus de Werve, whose names you've learned in order to recite them to tourists, nevertheless these craftsmen are worth an extra ten sous to you; you should think of them, those brave Dutchmen who inspire me from beyond the grave to give you your tip, and it's only fair, because everything here below, even daydreams have to be paid for,' he thought as he left the asylum.

He walked slowly towards the botanical garden, which was formed by joining the old Promenade de l'Arquebuse to the Jardin des Plantes; and it was charming, with its secluded paths, its high trees, its flowerbeds, and its lawns with grass strewn with daisies and buttercups.

Certain trees reminded him of La Trappe at Our Lady of the Hearth, and some of the stone benches, backing onto the eighteenth-century house that stretched out in front of the garden, recalled the old nursery in the Jardin de Luxembourg.

This morning, a few maids were knitting near a huge poplar, whose hollow trunk formed a wooden grotto, low to the ground. This tree, which figured in old views of Dijon, bulged like the gnarled hide of an elephant, and was encircled by bandages, corseted by cast-iron stays, propped up with crutches, and held in place by wires in every direction.

And here and there, priests were reading their breviaries, and gardeners were wheeling barrowloads of flowers; near the edges of the flowerbeds you breathed in the smell of iris, like honey and freshly cut grass, but now and again this sugary perfume was swept away by the breeze which brought with it the pungent odour of the Bohemian olive, of which you could see specimens at the other end of the garden, three or four trees, with inky-black trunks, silvery leaves and golden blossoms.

And the smell reminded him of over-ripe melon, of stale strawberries, of a poultice when you take it off.

Before sitting down, Durtal walked along the paths that separated the trees. There were groups of conifers: blue cedars, various larches, and pines, the boles of which were almost white, and the needles almost black; and in the flowerbeds were salmon-pink roses, white and yellow tea roses, Maltese crosses that were as red as bichromate of potassium, and magnificent bushes of aconite, with dark leaves standing out in sharp linear outline and blossoms of a celestial blue like a turquoise gemstone, but a turquoise from which every trace of white had been removed.

'That's true,' thought Durtal, 'these aconites are vegetable turquoises, only of a lighter and purer shade of blue; but if nowadays the plant is a boon to actors whose overstrained vocal cords it soothes, how it was hated by our ancestors, who believed that it was engendered by Cerberus' slaver and who ranked it as the quickest acting of all poisons. By contrast, here's one with a better reputation, and monastic at least,' he continued, looking at the white blossoms that sprang up like jets of water from enormous clumps of crimson stalks, the ends of which bore large leaves of dark, shiny green, 'it's the sour and stimulating rhubarb, the herb of the monks, so-called because it abounded in monastic dispensaries, of which it was the favourite remedy; and the fact is that Father Philigone Miné used to distribute it profusely, in powder form or made up into pills, to the peasants of Val-des-Saints who complained of feeling tired or unwell.

'As for those poor beggars over there,' he went on, looking at some succulents, lined up in pots out of the way in a corner, 'they can't claim any monastic ancestry, and their ugliness justifies their classification alongside those plants of ill-omen that flourish in forest clearings, where witches would hold their sabbaths in the Middle Ages.'

Some looked like hairy snowshoes, giant earlobes bristling with hair; others assumed the contours of snakes with peeling skin studded with horsehair; others again hung down like the flabby jowls of old men with unkempt beards, and still others were rounded like discuses,[4] discuses endowed with short, white eyelashes; and they paraded in the sun their horrible colours, mouldy greens, jaundiced yellows, muddy violets, burned pinks, and browns like decaying mushrooms or mildewed chocolate.

This exhibition of monstrosities amused him, and he would have mused about their changes in colour, but that particular morning he was obsessed by the sculpture of *The Well,* and above all by Claus Sluter, whose personality haunted him. So he moved away from the succulents, and sitting down alone on a bench recollected the few details he'd read about this artist.

'We know he was born in the Netherlands, and may, like his nephew Claus de Werve, have been a native of Hatheim in Holland. He settled in Burgundy – for what reason no one knows – and during the year 1384 he entered the studio of Jean de Marville, a master image maker and valet to the Duke, to study sculpture. After Marville's death in 1389, he inherited his teacher's titles, and worked on the tomb of Philip the Bold, sculpted the gateway of the Chartreuse monastery, *The Well of Moses,* and various statues for the châteaux of Germolles and Rouvres.

'What kind of man was he? Should we believe Cyprien Monget, who in his scholarly and well researched book on the

Carthusians of Dijon, advances the opinion that Sluter was a difficult character who was never satisfied, because he was constantly repairing or modifying the lodgings he occupied after Jean de Marville, a house belonging to the Duke, and above all because he was given to changing his workmen as one changes one's shirt? It's quite possible, but it has to be said in his defence that the dilapidated or badly-built house was in danger of collapse, according to the actual estimates of the architects, and that the workmen who he brought in from Flanders and Holland to a land of vineyards where wine was cheap were most likely unmanageable at certain times.

'We are, in fact, very poorly informed about his way of life and the docility, or lack thereof, of his character, but it's safe to say that his ideas were sometimes rather singular; indeed, a receipt from the bailiwick of Dijon informs us that he ordered a pair of spectacles from a goldsmith to adorn the nose of his statue of Jeremiah, and one is entitled to wonder what he intended to signify by giving this object to one of the prophets of the Bible.

'In any case, it's probably better to see this as a touch of eccentricity, than a desire to make his portrait of the monk or priest who evidently served as a model more lifelike, because this would be certain proof of an incomprehension of, or an indifference to, the religious subject he was engaged to treat, in favour of an overly naturalistic approach.

'If we know little of his earlier life, and if his mature years are practically unknown, his old age is, by contrast, better understood.

'Even before he'd finished the works commissioned by the Duke, he retired to the abbey of Saint Étienne, an Augustinian Order in Dijon, where after a stay of two years he died in 1405.

'The contract drawn up between himself and Brother Robert de Beaubigney, a doctor in canon law and the abbot of the monastery is in the departmental archives of the Côte d'Or, and reading it gives a good idea of Sluter's mode of life during his last days.

'For the sum of forty gold francs, half of which was paid in advance, he had at his disposal – for life – a room and a cellar in the cloister, for himself and a servant; every Sunday they would give him twenty-eight little loaves, or four every day if he chose, plus a pint and a half of wine, Dijon measure; and every time there was a special allowance of food, such as a feast day, the monastery was bound to give him a canon's portion. He was free to take his meals in his room, or in the town, or in the refectory with the monks, but in the last case he had to bring his own bread and wine, and be content with the ordinary food of the community, "without any other pittance or provision".

'Lastly, according to the terms of the contract, he became "a feudal vassal of the abbot and his monastery", and he had to take part in the Masses, prayers and orisons of the said monastery, which would, in its turn, benefit from his prayers and orisons.

'In short, he was an oblate in an Augustinian abbey. He lived there, he took his meals there when he pleased, and he was free to work as it suited him and supervise his workshops, which were situated outside the monastery in the ancient stables belonging to the Duke.

'And all this naturally brings to mind the "Brethren of the Common Life",[5] who were thriving at the same period in Holland, and who had also been placed by their founders, Gerard Groote and Floris Radewyns, under the Rule of St Augustine.

'Their little lay cloister in Deventer was composed of scholars and artists who would copy manuscripts and illuminate them, occupy themselves with religious art, and at fixed hours meet together to pray.

'That's the true *raison d'être* of modern oblatehood,' said Durtal to himself.

'As Dom Felletin puts it so well, there's no need to extend it into a Third Order, which it isn't, in the strict sense of the word. Contemporary Third Orders – which are moreover excellent and no doubt constitute, given the events we are currently theatened with, the germ of a new sort of monasticism for the future – already suffice. As long as it comes under Benedictine control, oblature, aside from the personal sanctification of its members obtained by liturgical means, can only have one aim: to revive Catholic art that has fallen so low. At first sight it might seem that this task is more appropriate to the monks, but it's quite clear that the monasteries rarely recruit artists, because with the day being broken up by the offices, sustained artistic work is impossible; the work can therefore only be carried out if it is entrusted to laymen who are subject to certain ritual formalities, but who are living freely outside the cloister.

'Yes, that's the true, authentic oblature, the one we find in the most distant past, the one that I myself am leading at Val-des-Saints; it's going to disappear in France along with the monks; Dom Felletin's plans, which were also mine, have all fallen through; consequently, it's now a matter of either renouncing this mode of secular monasticism or transforming it in such a way that it can adapt itself to the demands of the present day, while at the same time retaining its medieval character.

'Is this achievable? I believe so – if one allows that it's possible for oblature to organise itself and have a life of its own, under the direction of one or more fathers left behind by the abbot in order to continue this work in France.

'Obviously, this institution wouldn't be easy to establish; in order for it to function properly it would need many things… first of all, pious artists with talent. Where are they? I don't know; but if there aren't any it's up to the Lord to bring them forth, and if there are some, unknown, scattered here and there in the remote corners of a town, to bring them together; next it would be necessary to create a kind of small monastery; the oblates, no longer being able to even settle near one and participate in the offices, will have to form one themselves and carry out, to a certain degree, the exercise of the canonical hours; but that would have no chance of success without adopting a few precautions which, to those familiar with it, sustain the daily routine of the cloister.

'So, to avoid the inconveniences of a life in common and the idle gossip which is a constant source of quarrels and disturbances, it would be necessary for each oblate to occupy a little house of his own, like those of the Carthusians, the only recluses who since their foundation have never needed reforming, so wisely and cleverly devised was their regime of solitude.

'Indeed, it prescribes silence and isolation, but at the moment it becomes too oppressive, it's broken by the offices, and on certain fixed days by meals that aren't eaten alone but communally in the refectory, and also by the long weekly walk, called the *Spatiamentum* in Carthusian phraseology.

'It's obviously not a question of affiliating, directly or indirectly, to the Rule of St Bruno, which is far too severe and too time-consuming for laymen who don't wish to fast perpetually, or to get up in the night, and whose aim is not to live in a monastery. It's very spirit is different from our own. It's a matter simply of borrowing, in a milder and even more relaxed form, its system of solitude, while in all other things following the Rule of St Benedict taken in its broadest sense. In other words, a monastery not in a single building, but cut up into little houses; a life less conventual and more personal; the freedom to come and go, and a reduced timetable of services allowing one to work in peace for hours at a time.

'This wouldn't be, as some people might imagine, a new thing, but on the contrary a regression, almost a return to the early times of monasticism, when each monk lived in a separate hut and only met the others at a special place in order to pray. It takes us back to the conventual parish that held sway in the fourth century, with St Severin of Agaunum in the Valais; it would be a mixed system, a little bit Carthusian and a lot Benedictine; it would, for people fond of analogies, be like the type of nunnery as it exists for women in Belgium, a series of small houses in which each lives on their own and where everyone comes together in a chapel when the hour for the offices sounds.

'One can't help dreaming,' sighed Durtal, 'of a life immersed in God, and culminating, with the aid of liturgical prayers, in the colourful orisons of art, like when you find yourself in Ghent or Bruges, when you enter those small towns set within a larger one, so calm and collected; in those pious and charming convents, with their cheerful facades, with their red brick or whitewashed walls, their stepped roofs, their windows with frames painted Veronese green and hung with pale-coloured blinds or light curtains behind the panes, their discreet doors opening onto wide lawns planted with rows of old elm trees and crossed by paths leading to the ancient church, where nuns pray with outstretched arms.

CHAPTER XII

'It doesn't seem as if there could be any place more restful and, at the same time, more inspiring for a painter or a writer who wishes to work on a picture or a book for the greater glory of God...'

And still dreaming, Durtal recalled the statutes of these retreats, summing them up in a few words. The nun, on entering, would promise obedience to the superior, to the 'great lady' as they call her, and pledge to observe the rules in the strictest fashion; she had to undergo a novitiate of two years before being definitively received, but she wasn't bound by any vow and could leave the enclosure when she wished; she also had to prove that she had a yearly income of one hundred and ten francs and provide, with the help of this money and her work, for her necessities. She wore a religious uniform, like that of a nun, was obliged to attend certain services and be home before nightfall, and that was about all.

'Yes,' Durtal reflected, 'but these little sheepfolds have never been able to thrive except in northern Europe. They flourish nowadays only in Belgium and Holland, there are no more in France now.

'Why? No one knows. The dispassionate, sensible temperament, the calm and deeply-held religious feeling of the northern races, their love of domesticity rather than the wandering life outdoors, perhaps explains this anomaly. It seems, moreover, that even in the Middle Ages, when faith was ardent in the south, no convent of this type took root in that region. These kinds of convents, whose origin goes back to the end of the twelfth century, only blossomed in fact in the regions of the north, the west, the east, and even the centre. We find numerous examples in Cologne, Lübeck and Hamburg; they flourished in the territories of Flanders; they abounded in France, but their habitat seems to stop immediately below the Loire.

'In an article on convents in Paris, Léon le Grand gives a list of houses of this type, which are almost everywhere except in the south – he mentions those in Picardy, at Laon, Amiens, Noyon, Beauvais, Abbeville, Condé and Saint-Quentin; in the east, at Reims, Saint-Nicholas-du-Port, and Châlons; in the west, at Rouen, Caen, Mantes, Chartres, Orleans and Tours; in the environs of Paris, at Crépy, Melun and Sens; and finally in Paris itself, where Louis IX, the saint and king, founded one in the parish of Saint Paul.'

'This convent, which differed but little from the contemporary ones at Bruges and Ghent, fell into ruin after two centuries, due to lack of members. By 1471 only two remained, and since then I know of only one attempt to revive these sisterhoods in France, and a recent one at that: in 1855, Abbé Soubeiran tried to found a house in Castelnaudary on the model of the Belgian ones, but he failed.

'He obviously hadn't realised that the soil of Languedoc wasn't at all suited to this variety of conventual plant, which needs silence and shade to grow.

'Nevertheless, it seems to me,' Durtal thought, 'that by transferring this semi-monastic system for women to that of men, something might be done. You can easily imagine the setting in a large city such as Paris: a big town house like those that already exist for sculptors and painters on the Boulevard Arago or in the Rue de Bagneux, for instance, roads lined with flowers, bordered by little houses and workshops; it would be easy to set up communal rooms and an oratory in the back, and that would suggest pretty well the idea of a miniature convent, of a little institution of nuns or lay Benedictines.

'Especially Benedictines, because the Order of St Benedict, unlike many others, admits artists; its Rule is formal on this point, and besides, artistic work is the logical continuation of its offices, the culmination of its theory of luxury for God, the flower, so to speak, on its stems of prayer and its groves of orisons. In essence it's purely Benedictine – or Clunesian to be more precise.

'But could or would the modern Benedictines be able to realise it? That's another question. Not that I subscribe to the theories of Monsieur Lampre, who claims that the good fathers would be profoundly annoyed if they saw laymen and secular monks complete a work which they themselves would be incapable of accomplishing; that's to attribute to the sons of St Benedict sentiments they don't have and to judge them very unfairly. Besides, in the old days, did they not encourage authors like Bulteau, the oblate of Saint Germain des Prés, who left behind a history of the Order and also a history of Eastern monasticism?

'There's no reason to believe that, in the absence of an equal passion for the work, the congregation of Solesmes would be more narrow-minded in its ideas, more stick-in-the-mud, than their Saint Maur ancestor; but in the end, if, as a result of the difficulties caused by its exile, it hesitates to claim its artistic heritage, if it can't find among its personnel a monk able to organise and direct the oblates, then evidently the only course would be to go forward and proceed without it.

'After all, when you think about it, oblature such as I imagine it could be created and developed without the help of the cloisters, if it had at its head a priest who loved mysticism and the liturgy, who was eloquent enough to explain them to his listeners and therefore put them in a position to use them in their work, and who was saintly enough that his management would not be disputed and would be accepted by everyone without demur.

'Moreover, he might affiliate himself as an oblate to one of the Benedictine monasteries in France or abroad, and the occasional help from a monk would be sufficient in order to teach psalmody, ritual and plainchant, so as to imprint on the oblates, from its earliest days, the particular mark, the monastic stamp of the Order.

'The difficulty doesn't lie there, but in the choice of the priest responsible, in lieu of an abbot, for steering the ship. Well, providence will certainly find one, if she wants the place that has remained empty in her church for centuries to be filled.

'Because in short, all other types of work are thriving, except that of art for God; the congregations have divided all the others up between them, except that one.

'Some, indeed, like the Jesuits, the Franciscans, the Redemptorists, the Dominicans and the missionaries preach, arrange retreats, and evangelise unbelievers; others run boarding schools and colleges; others, like the Sulpiciens and the Lazaristes, run seminaries, most of them even combine these different jobs; others still care for the sick, or, like the Carthusians and the Cistercians, make amends for the sins of the world, are reservoirs of atonement and penitence; finally, others, like the Benedictines of the congregation of France, devote themselves more particularly to liturgical services and the divine office of praise.

'But none of them, not even the Benedictines, to whom it belongs by right, has claimed the heritage of religious art, which has fallen into disuse since the passing of Cluny.

'Yes,' Durtal continued after a pause as he rolled a cigarette, 'I know very well that people will say: "Is art really useful? Isn't it a luxury, like a dessert after a meal?" Well then, why wouldn't we offer it to Christ? He's been deprived of it since the Reformation, or even before; wouldn't it be fitting to give it to him again?

'Moreover, one must be pretty ignorant to deny, even from a practical point of view, the power of art. It was the most reliable aid to mysticism and the liturgy during the Middle Ages; art was the Church's favourite son, its interpreter, the one it entrusted to express its thoughts to the masses, to exhibit them in books, on cathedral porches and on altar screens.

'It was art that offered a commentary on the gospels and set the crowds ablaze, which threw them laughing in joyous prayer at the foot of a crib or which racked them with sobs before the weeping groups in scenes of the Calvary; art which made them kneel, trembling, during marvellous Easters, when Jesus, risen again, smiled at the Magdalene;[6] art which uplifted them, breathless, crying for joy in front of extraordinary scenes of the ascension, Christ rising up into a golden sky and lifting his pierced hand, flowing with a ruby red, to bless them.

'All this is far off, alas. What a state of abandonment and feebleness the Church has found itself in since it lost interest in art – and since art withdrew from it. It has lost its best mode of propaganda, its surest means of defence. So it would seem that now she's assailed on all sides and taking on water, she must beg the Lord to send her artists whose works would certainly inspire more conversions, and bring her more supporters than those empty refrains which her priests, hoisted up in their pulpits, pour over the resigned heads of the faithful.

'Religious art, however extinct, however dead it might be, can be revived, and if Benedictine oblature has a mission, it's to create it anew and elevate it.

'Obviously, certain conditions are necessary for it to succeed.

Chapter XII

First of all, of course, it has to be the will of the Most High – but let's admit that's the case – well, considering it from the human perspective, such an institution would hardly be possible except in Paris or its environs, because men of letters, historians, scholars, people who are specialised in the study of diverse sciences, as well as painters, sculptors, architects, and craftsmen of all the artistic trades that could be fostered in a house of oblates, would need to maintain relationships with editors and art dealers, and to frequent libraries and museums. One would need to arrange life in such a way that each could attend to his own business and work without being continually disturbed by services. The timetable would be easy to establish: prayer and Mass early in the morning; complete freedom during the day; vespers at five or six for those able to attend, and compline for everyone in the evening.

'Nevertheless, I'm not hiding from myself that, by the very fact it would be redemptive and truly decent, there's a chance this work would incur all manner of hatred, but it seems impossible to me that, in spite of all the mockery, of all the bad faith, that it won't take shape one day, because the idea of it is in the air, as they say; there are too many people waiting for it, who desire it, too many people who cannot, by reason of their occupation, their state of health, or their way of life, intern themselves in a monastery, for God not to establish some haven of mercy, a port, where souls haunted by a longing for monastic life, by a yearning to live apart from the world could moor themselves, and work near him and for him in peace.

'I'm daydreaming,' Durtal said to himself, looking at his watch, and he headed towards the station. 'Let's admit that the moment is poorly chosen to think of founding, or even imagining, such a convent, precisely at a time when the chambers of the Senate are bent on exterminating all religious brotherhoods and Orders.

'But,' he continued, as he walked, 'it's perhaps not as badly chosen as all that. Well, think it out. I'm more and more convinced that the Law of Associations will not be repealed for many years to come – so what will become of the Benedictines who will themselves be banished from France? Will they have sufficient spiritual stamina to endure such exile? I want to believe it. Will they be able to find recruits abroad, where other abbeys of the same Order already exist? I doubt it. Even supposing that they don't die from a lack of resources, the houses of the Solesmes congregation will be condemned to vegetate, and perhaps to disintegrate in the long run, into an insurmountable ennui; in any case, the Benedictine spirit is bound to disappear from France, if we don't discover some subterfuge to conserve it; and it's here that oblature reveals itself to me as that subterfuge and that expedient; will the Benedictines, for the very honour of St Benedict, make use of this ruse, this last resort?

'I hope so; moreover, I can't see that the government has the power to oppose such a scheme, indeed, no law can prevent artists from each renting an apartment in a town house fitted out accordingly, or from living there as they please, coming together at certain moments to talk about art or to pray – in a word, to do as they please. They're not priests, they have a recognised civil profession, they are not bound by any vow, they are not dressed in any visible monastic garments, since the great scapular is worn underneath the clothes. Their association would therefore fall under the category of literary societies, which are exempt from requesting prior authorisation.

'Furthermore, it's not impossible that one of the lodgers could offer hospitality to a monk, dressed, if need be, as a secular priest, because there's no law yet that forbids one to host a friend; and so from that an oblature would be formed.

'While waiting for these beautiful dreams to be realised for others, I – who will no doubt never see them – would like our abbot to leave us a few monks here, as is also the hope of Monsieur Lampre; of course it'll be very dismal, we would have only a meagre office, but in the end, as long as Mass and vespers are chanted every day, a life of oblature would be possible; besides,' he sighed as he got onto the train, 'I have no other choice, unless I leave Val-des-Saints... but to look for what? To go where? To Paris? Ah, I'm not looking forward to that.'

Chapter XIII

The Feast of the Assumption was over; since dawn the pontifical office had been unfolding with all the glory of the plainchant, and with the solemn coming and going of mitred bishops, with the pomp of the finest vestments, and the church, now empty, exhaled its natural odour of the tomb mixed with the soothing perfume of stale incense and extinguished candles; it symbolised pretty well the sepulchre where the beshrouded Virgin rose to take her place next to her son, amid celestial fragrances and singing, effortlessly climbing the unfurling stairway of the clouds, a shining figure attended by a throng of angels and saints who came to meet her.

All day the heat had been overwhelming. After the Benediction, preceded by the solemn procession instituted by Louis XIII in memory of the consecration of his kingdom to the Madonna, Durtal, on his return home, sat down in the shade of the great cedar tree in his garden.

There he meditated on the festival which for him was a feast of liberation, of freedom from pain, the chief festival of Our Lady; it prompted him to contemplate the mother under a special aspect, because it brought him face to face with the terrible problem of Sorrow.

Indeed, did it not play a strange role, both huge and at the same time limited, in the life of the Virgin?

To try to understand the reason for this appalling benefactress, for this salutary goddess of vengeance, one must go back to the first ages of the world, to that Eden, where the moment Adam became conscious of sin, Sorrow was born. It was the first born of man's work, and it had pursued him on earth ever since, beyond the tomb, to the very threshold of Paradise.

Sorrow was the expiatory daughter of disobedience, the one that baptism – which effaces original sin – could not prevent. To the water of the Sacrament she added the water of tears; she cleansed souls as best she could with two substances borrowed from man's own body: water and blood.

Despised and detested by all, she martyred generation after generation; from father to son, antiquity handed down a hatred and fear of this representative of the divine work, this torturer, incomprehensible to a paganism that turned her into an evil goddess, unappeased by prayers or by gifts.

For centuries she marched under the weight of humanity's curse; weary of eliciting nothing but anger and abuse from her work of reparation; she, too, awaited with impatience the coming of the Messiah who would redeem her of her terrible reputation and remove the hateful stigma she bore.

She awaited him as her redeemer and also as her betrothed, destined for her since the Fall, and she reserved for him the frenzy of a lovesick Maenad, which had long been repressed, because until she fulfilled that ghoulish mission, that holy and dreadful mission, she could only hand out tortures that were just about tolerable; she reduced her grievous caresses to the size of mankind; she did not unleash herself completely on those desperate souls who repulsed and insulted her, even though they could only sense her pacing around, without ever coming too close to them.

She was never truly the magnificent lover except with the Man-God. His capacity for suffering exceeded all that she had known. She crept towards him on that awful night, when, alone, forsaken in a cave, he took on himself the sins of the world, and she rose up as soon as she embraced him, and attained a grandeur that was never hers till then. So terrible was she that he swooned at her touch; his death agonies were his betrothal to her; her sign of alliance was, as it is with all women, a ring, but larger, a ring in form only, which was at the same time a symbol of marriage and an emblem of royalty: a crown. She placed it on the head of her bridegroom, even before the Jews had braided the thorny diadem she had ordered, and his forehead was encircled by beads of ruby-red sweat, adorned by a circlet of pearls of blood.

She showered him with the sole blandishments that were hers to offer, atrocious and super-human torments; and like a faithful spouse she devoted herself to him and never left him again. Mary, the Magdalene, the holy women, could not follow in his footsteps to the end, but she accompanied him to the *praetorium*, to Herod, to Pilate; she counted the barbs on the whips, she adjusted the thorns of his crown, she made sure the iron hammers were heavy, that the vinegar was bitter, that the spear was sharp, and she jealously filed the iron nails to a point.

And when the supreme moment of their wedding feast had come, when Mary and the Magdalene and St John stood weeping at the foot of the cross, she, like the poverty St Francis speaks of, deliberately climbed onto the bed of the gibbet, and in the union of these two outcasts of the earth, the Church was born; it came forth in a torrent of blood and water from the victim's heart and then it was over; Christ, impassive, escaped for ever from her embrace, she became a widow the very moment she had finally been loved, but she descended from Calvary rehabilitated by that love, redeemed by that death.[1]

Spurned, just as the Messiah was, she was raised up with him and she too dominated the world from the top of the cross; her mission was ratified and ennobled, and henceforth she was comprehensible to Christians and she would be loved until the end of time by those souls who appealed to her to hasten the expiation of their sins, and by those others who loved her in memory and in imitation of the Passion of Christ.

She had held the son in her grip for eleven hours – the number of transgression[2] – if you count from the arrival in the Garden of Olives to the moment of his death; over his mother, her grip was of longer duration.

And it's here where the strangeness of this unwarranted possession reveals itself.

The Virgin was the one human creature who, logically speaking, she had no right to touch. The Immaculate Conception should have put Mary beyond her reach, and what's more, having never sinned during her earthly life, she should have been unassailable, exempt from her reparative ills and sorrows.

So to dare to approach her, Sorrow required special permission from God and the consent of the mother herself, who, to be the more like her son and to co-operate as far as she could in our redemption, agreed to experience and to suffer, at the very foot of the cross, the sovereign agonies of the final catastrophe.

But in no way did Sorrow have free reign with her. No doubt she left her mark on her from the very moment when, responding to the angel Gabriel's "*Fiat*", Mary saw a premonition of the tree of Golgotha standing out against the divine light; but after that Sorrow had to step back and keep her distance. She saw the nativity from afar, but could not enter the cave of Bethlehem; it was only later, when Joachim's daughter came for the presentation at the temple, that, given permission by the prophet Simeon, she leaped from her ambush and implanted herself in the Virgin's soul.

From that moment on she took up her abode there. She had, to use a vulgar phrase, got her foot in the door; however, she wasn't absolute mistress there because she didn't live there alone. Joy cohabited with her; the presence of Jesus was enough for the mother's soul to overflow with pleasure. She therefore had little room to manoeuvre, only a limited power at her disposal. It was certainly like this until the treachery of Judas Iscariot. Then Sorrow took her revenge, showing herself to be despotic, absolute, and she overwhelmed the Madonna so terribly that it might have been thought she had drained the cup to the last dreg. But it was not so.

If for her the blinding grief of the Crucifixion had been preceded by the sly, stabbing pain of the trial, it was followed by yet another period of all-consuming, persistent suffering, the uncertain expectation of that day when she would finally rejoin her son up above, far from this earth which had so despised them.

It was therefore, in the soul of the Virgin, like a sort of triptych. All-powerful Sorrow, attaining its most intense state filled the centre panel, while on either side was anguish and the pangs of suspense; the two side panels differed, however, in this sense, that the suspense before the crucifixion was one of fear, while that afterwards was one of hope.

Even so, for the Virgin there could be no going back. She had accepted the heavy task bequeathed to her by Jesus, that of bringing up the child born on the cross. She received it and, for twenty-four years, according to St Epiphanius, or for twelve as other saints affirm, like some gentle grandmother she watched over this weakling, who the world, like another Herod, would search to destroy; she conceived a little church and taught it to be a fisher of souls; she was the first pilot of that bark which began to sail forth upon the ocean of the world; when she died, she had been both Martha and Mary;[3] she had united the privilege of the active life and the contemplative life here on earth; and that is why the gospel for today's Mass is aptly taken from the passage in St Luke recounting Christ's visit to the house of the two sisters.

Her mission was thus accomplished. Entrusted to the care of St Peter, the Church was now strong enough to sail alone, without towing.

Sorrow, who had not left Mary's side during this period, was now forced to flee; and indeed, just as she had been absent at the moment of Our Lady's childbirth, she likewise withdrew when the moment of death came. The Virgin died neither from old age nor from sickness; she was carried away by the vehemence of pure love; and her face was so calm, so radiant and happy, that her death was referred to as 'falling asleep'.

But before attaining that longed for night of eternal deliverance, how many years of torments and desires she endured! Because being a woman and a mother, how could she not have longed to be rid of her body, which however glorious it was to have conceived the Saviour, nevertheless kept her attached to the earth, and prevented her from rejoining her son.

Also for those who loved her, what a joy it was to know that she had at last been exonerated from her prison of flesh, resurrected like Christ, crowned, enthroned, so simple and so good, so far from our worldy filth, in the blessed regions of a celestial Jerusalem, in the endless beatitude of the heavens.

'No, never have the naïve raptures of the *Gaudeamus* been so justified,' Durtal said to himself, 'as in this Assumption Mass, in which, from the beginning, the grateful Church gives itself up to joy. The breviary repeats, as if scarcely able to believe it, the triumphal news, which it sums up, all the better to bear witness to it, in a clear and short sentence, that of the antiphon in the *Magnificat* of the second vespers: "Today, the Virgin Mary ascends into heaven. Rejoice, for she reigns with Christ forever."

'Ah, Lord,' continued Durtal, 'it's true, when I invoke your Mother, I forget in that moment her sufferings and her joys; I see her only as my own mother to whom I can say what I'm thinking and to whom I can tell my petty problems, who I implore to keep me and those who are close to me from stumbling on the path. But when, having nothing to ask of her, I think of her, who is so present to me, so alive, that I cannot pass two hours without her coming into my mind, I always picture her as anxious and suffering, I always imagine her as Our Lady of Tears. When I contemplate her in the scene at Golgotha, though she has the consolation of your visible presence and can adore you, I see her unhappy. The sword of compassion is there. Today, by an effort of will, I'm able to see her in a different light; so content – in spite of her dedication to and love of sacrifice – to be near you at last, forever rid of pain, that if it was possible for me to forget my own anxieties I would be truly joyful. Yes, I felt cheerful when singing the *Gaudeamus* and listening to the offices which I follow as best I can; I, who am usually so easily distracted, I was only with you, and only with her on this day of liturgical joy; but now that the candles are extinguished, that the plainchant is silent, that everything has fallen back into the darkness, here I am invaded again by a flood of sorrow, submerged by a rising tide of troubles.

'The fact is that everything is ruined; how can I ignore events that may change my life once again? And if you only knew, my dear Lord, how tired I am, and that now I've found a seat here how much I would like to remain seated.'

In alarm, he recalled the now rapidly approaching threat of an

Chapter XIII

exodus from Val-des-Saints. The abbot had rented a château for his monks near Moerbeke, in Waes, Belgium, and had decided not to wait until the 2nd of October, the latest date allowed by the Law for their departure. On his return to the monsastery he'd despatched the cellarer and the guestmaster to Moerbeke to go and fit out the premises, and as soon as they came back a first contingent of monks would be sent to take possession of the place, and then little by little the rest of the monastery would follow. It was therefore only a matter of days.

The vacant choir stalls of the two monks reminded Durtal, as soon as he entered the church, how imminent the day of departure was, and he couldn't help smiling a little bitterly when, before the High Mass, everyone, monks and novices, persisted in chanting the prayers for preservation from exile; but they chanted them without enthusiasm now, those prayers had, alas, been poorly received.

'Instead of Psalm No, 121, *I will lift up mine eyes unto the hills,* they will soon be singing No. 136, *By the rivers of Babylon I sat down and wept,*' he said to himself, thinking that their stay abroad would be a long one, and that homesickness and lack of money would no doubt break up many communities.

Added to which, Monsieur Lampre was now anxious and seemed much less sure that the abbot would leave several fathers at Val-des-Saints to continue the office, and so the question came up again as to whether he in his turn would be evicted.

Lastly, Mlle de Garambois was in tears, and Madame Bavoil took a gloomy view of everything. She imagined great disasters and would read every line in the newspapers that were already announcing the start of the exodus, and which would reproduce extracts from Belgian papers listing properties either bought or rented in their country by congregations resolved to emigrate from France.

And closing her eyes, she would sigh: "The venerable Jeanne de Matel said that the saviour had been suckled on the cross with gall, and now we in our turn are going to savour its sacred bitterness. Good God, what will this villainous government do to us next!"

'Whether I leave the cloister or stay here, it will be a sad draught to swallow,' murmured Durtal, who pictured one more time the balance sheet of his sorrows. Feeling pins and needles in his legs, he got up from his seat and went for a walk in the garden.

'To leave Val-des-Saints at the very moment when the garden is so shady and becoming so charming, what a misfortune,' he thought as he looked around him; all these shrubs that he had planted were shooting up into a mass of green stalks, brimful of sap. Never had the flowers seemed more lively or more beautiful. Sunflowers, their black monastic tonsures encircled by a golden mane; roses and snapdragons of every colour were springing up in flowerbeds, overflowing onto the paths; elders were showing off their black berries, bryonies their pink berries, rowans their vermilion berries and medlar its berries of burnt sienna. Dazzling nasturtiums were climbing the trees. In the thickets of the wood, reseda swayed their green candle-like heads, a corkscrewing wick hanging down; the calycanthus, a small shrub which the year before seemed dead, had taken on a new lease of life and was, by reason of the variety of its perfumes, most peculiar. Its bark smelt of varnish and pepper; its blossom, like a big spider lying on its back with a brick-red belly and lemon-coloured legs, gave off a smell like camphor; and its jujube brown fruit exhaled a whiff of apples and old barrels.

'My poor calycanthus,' said Durtal, smiling as he sniffed its aroma, 'I don't think we'll be living together very much longer, because the more this goes on, the less I have the courage to simply vegetate here with no office and no monks. You're not exactly what one might call a nice and attractive tree, and Madame Bavoil hates you, because she says you're not only useless, you stink. I've always stuck up for you, but the next tenant will no doubt be less friendly and you run the risk of being dug up one fine morning and like other more common trees turned into firewood; so you, too, will fall a victim of the Law of Associations.'

'Oh, there's Dom Felletin,' he said; he walked towards the novice master, who, seeing him came to meet him.

"What's new?"

"Nothing."

"Is the abbot going to keep a few monks here? I'm asking you straight out because this question is driving me mad."

"I don't know for certain, and you can be sure that at the present time the abbot himself doesn't know either. To be frank, I confess that the majority of the chapter is against the scheme, but it could very well be that we'll have to adopt it. It seems that the château rented in Belgium isn't big enough to house all the monks. It's possible that while waiting for it to be enlarged, a small colony would stay here in the country for a few more months. In any case, it's already been agreed that in order not to interrupt the liturgical services, two or three of us are going to remain at Val-des-Saints and won't leave until the other monks, having arrived at Moerbeke, start up services there."

"And then?"

"Then the little rearguard will join the main body of the troops."

"And it'll just remain for me to slip away…?"

"It's no good tormenting yourself in advance; if it's necessary, as I believe, to build an annex to the château that we've rented, you'll have plenty of time ahead of you… the time it takes to draw up plans and raise money, the time it takes to finish the new buildings… but we may have returned to France by then, the elections are not far off, and after all it could be that things turn out well…"

Durtal shook his head.

They took a few steps, without speaking, into the garden.

"What feast day is it tomorrow?" Durtal finally said, to break the silence and say something.

"St Hyacinth, a confessor, a double Mass, the *Os justi*… so white ribbons for Mlle de Garambois," Dom Felletin, added with a smile.

"Since I've got you here, I'd really like to get some information from you about your technique. Imagine that, to forget my worries, I immersed myself in the Roman breviary and the monastic breviary, and that I came out of this experience a little bewildered. It seemed to me at times that I was wandering through large empty rooms whose shutters were closed. They may well have had high ceilings, but you know they weren't always easy to make out…"

"Not easy to make out? What's your difficulty?"

"Well, the incoherence I encounter at every step. For instance, will you explain to me why St Hyacinth, whose feast day we're celebrating tomorrow, is given the Mass *Os justi* rather than the Mass *Justus ut palma,* which also figures among those suitable for saints of his status and importance? It's the same, moreover, for the hiero-confessors[4] and the martyrs, to whom alternative Masses are also assigned. Why choose one in preference to the other? What's the motive that determines this choice?"

"None, most of the time; these substitute Masses simply serve to vary the office, so we don't always have to recite the same words."

"So these substitute Masses are assigned haphazardly?"

"If you like."

"Another question, let's take the Roman breviary and stick to that. I'm only talking about it, you understand, from the point of view of history, literature and art. Now, here's St Bernard, St Benedict, St Claire, St Teresa, and St Norbert – that's to say the founders of the great Orders – they don't have special Masses; the first three haven't even got a prayer that's specific to them; conversely, others who established institutions that were comparatively insignificant, such as Francis Carracciolo, one of the creators of the Minor Clerks Regular, Joseph Emilianus, founder of the Somaschi, Joseph Calasanctius, of the Regular Clerks of the Mother of God, to name just three, each have their own Mass.

"Others still are midway between two stools, they don't have a special Mass, but they are rewarded with a collect, a 'secret' prayer or a post-communion prayer which is personal to them: St Angela Merici, St Françoise de Chantal and St Bruno for instance; why such differences which nothing seems to justify?"

"It all depends on the epoch and the moment when they were canonised; the liturgy is an alluvial soil to which each century has added a layer, according to the spirit of the times. There were periods when proper Masses were unusual, and others, by contrast, when they were numerous. No hard and fast rule exists on this subject.

"And then you must remember this: the founders of the Orders you just mentioned – and you forgot St Francis of Assisi and St Dominic, who both have new Masses, and also St Augustine, who besides a collect, a secret prayer and a post-communion prayer, has a special verse after the Alleluia which is different from that of other doctors of the Church – are not deprived of a special office by the fact that this office hasn't been inserted in the Roman breviary. Nearly all of them have an office of their own in the missal or breviary of their congregation; like St Benedict, who, lodged along with other abbots in the Roman breviary, has a mansion of his own in the Benedictine prayer book.

"Moreover, in questions of this sort it's not enough to look at only one breviary; on the contrary, it's necessary to consider them all and then a view of the whole can be formed; with the monastic breviaries and those of the different dioceses, it all balances out. A saint who has no place in one location finds it in another; the liturgy is an eternal feast to which an ever-increasing number of saints flock, and the mother Church is very hospitable, she accommodates everyone and places them where she can."

"Fine, but still on the subject of these Masses and religious communities, how is it justified that two Franciscans – St John Capistran and St Joseph Cupertino – each have an entire Mass of their own, while their brother in St Francis, St Bernardine of Siena, who I presume is their equal in heaven, has only a gospel reading and a separate prayer?

"No, father, it's all very well saying that the building is a bit chaotic. But can you explain how a saint like Pope Gregory VII is given a furnished apartment in a communal lodging, while the young Louis de Gonzagua has his own house? And can you also tell me why the formula of the great feast, the *Gaudeamus,* reserved for Our Lady of Mount Carmel, for St Anne, for the Feast of the Rosary, for the Assumption, and for All Saints, is also granted to St Agatha, to St Thomas of Canterbury and to St Josephat? Why is this honour given to these three, and not to any others? Note that we are dealing with doubles, and that this distinction clashes with their lower status. It's like a general's ostrich-plumed hat being worn with the simple uniform of a lieutenant."

Dom Felletin began to laugh. "My answer will still be the same: it's a question of opportunity, and a question of time; and I'll add, so as not to omit anything, it can equally depend on the influence of the congregation or diocese from which the candidate came. Look, take two saints who follow each other in the calendar and whose work was the same: St Vincent de Paul, founder of the Lazarists and the Sisters of Charity, and St Jerome Emilian, founder of the Somaschi. St Emilian, who lived a century earlier than St Vincent, has a special Mass, but St Vincent hasn't; he's only been granted, instead of an ordinary gospel reading, that of the feast of St Mark. Why, you will ask me again, why everything for this one, and almost nothing for that one, even though both are classed under the double rite? Probably because the wind was blowing in a different direction when the process of canonisation of each of them was being heard.

"No, there's no use searching to find tiny cracks in the great edifice that is the liturgy, its naves are magnificent, even if some of its chapels, built at a later date, are second-rate.

"If there's some pure gold, there's also some shiny gold plate; some of the Masses devoted to saints are masterpieces, others are more commonplace – if you look at them as you do from the point of view of art; take for example that of St John Damascene. As a result of the calumnies of which he was a victim, this doctor of the Church had his hand chopped off, but he was healed by the Blessed Virgin. Now, notice how his whole Mass – *Introit, Epistle, Gradual, Gospel, Offertory and Communion* – continually allude to this miracle. It's a Mass with a leitmotif, truly charming and very cleverly woven together. Look also at that of St Gregory, the miracle worker; it is not a personalised Mass, as he shares it with other hiero-confessors, but it's enriched in his honour with a special gospel reading; it alludes to the faith that moves mountains. Now, according to his biographers, St Gregory actually succeeded, through his prayers, in shifting a mountain that prevented him from building a church. So you can see the reasoning and how apt the choice was.

"In contrast to these two Masses, now look at that of St Anthony, it's the usual Mass for abbots, with another gospel reading; let's consider it a bit more closely.

"The breviary tells you that the vocation of this hermit was due to the words of the gospel: 'If thou wilt be perfect, go, sell what thou hast and give to the poor.' So it would seem logical, if they weren't going to keep to the 'common' gospel for him, that they would allot him that one, but not at all, he was given that of the confessors, which has no bearing on his case at all.

"But for every office of middling composition, there are a hundred that are admirable; and from the three examples I've just given you, you can understand how some saints, by reason of their miracles, or by certain outstanding events in their lives which it's useful to keep in mind, have a better right to a special Mass which other saints, whose lives were duller so to speak, don't quite deserve.

"And besides, I'll say it again, the breviary is a kind of ecclesiastical geology; it's formed of strata of varying ages and varying thicknesses, and that accounts for the incongruities you find in it. Do you think a Mass, composed at the present day from various elements in honour of a newly canonised saint, would be written in the same language and conceived in the same way as certain parts of the Mass for the Dead, such as its Offertory for example, which dates back to the first era of the liturgy, from its 'primary formation' to use the geologists' expression?

"So one has to allow for these strata. They are seen, moreover, not just in the liturgy, but also in plainchant, where very often the old weft has been newly darned and refurbished, and the whole thing so expertly blended that you'd have to feel the underside of the tapestry to recognise the dubious age of the wool or the premature aging of the gold thread. But no matter, provided the work is beautiful. It's a product, a composite of the anonymous art of the times, all that energy has converged towards the same goal, to glorify God with the musical incense of its notes!

"But the question of liturgial discrepancies doesn't lie there. In the time that we've been chatting, we've only circled the issue without going deeply into it; your criticisms, which are more or less justified, are nothing in comparison to the ones that really preoccupy those who job it is to recite the office; they are far more serious, and have recently been summarised in a pamphlet by the Bishop of Annecy, Monsignor Isoard.

"The situation is this:

"On the one hand, there's a rising tide of saints, and as the new saints are almost all classed as doubles when they are introduced into the calendar, they push back the earlier saints, some of whom were nevertheless of a greater stature, but who in those far off times were only inscribed under the rite of a semi-double, or a simple; for example, St George, St Margaret, St Edward, St Elizabeth of Portugal, St Casimir, St Henry, St Alexis, Saints Cosmas and Damian, St Marcellus Pope, and numerous others besides.

"These, most of the time, no longer have Masses or vespers, and they have to be content with a small commemoration in the office of a more fortunate rival.

"In a word, the newcomers drive out the old. St Christopher and St Barbe, for whom our fathers had so much veneration, are now dispossessed of their ancient inheritance, and their only remaining refuge is in the churches of which they are the patron saints. They are exiled in the Proper of the Saints[5] for certain dioceses, providing it doesn't create a vacancy in the columns of the *Ordo*.

"On the other hand, this army of saints raised to the dignity of a double, also displaces the weekday services, and so it comes about that the magnificent offices of the seasons have given way to ordinary Masses from the common; only commemorations and gospel readings are read now during Sunday Mass, and it's the same for vespers; the same psalms are repeated over and over again, so that one tires of listening to the everlasting antiphons of the *Ecce sacerdos magnus* of the hiero-confessors, and the *Domine quinque talenta* of the confessors. As Monsignor Isoard justly observes, of the hundred and fifty songs of which the psalter is composed, only about thirty are usually read. This monotony turns it into a

Chapter XIII

mere habit, and the recitation of the psalter becomes, under these conditions, a burden, a chore."

"There are too many saints…" exclaimed Durtal, laughing.

"Alas, there'll never be enough! But a revision of their ranking is needed, a reform that would restore the broken balance between the different classes of saints on the one hand, and the saints and feast days on the other.

"Dear me," the monk continued after a pause, "we're a long way from the *Ordo* of earlier times. To go no further back than the time of Charlemagne, months such as March had only two feast days, and April, four; others, a bit more crowded, such as January and August, had eleven. A figure that has multiplied ever since with the saints we worship…"

"You must admit all the same, father, that this regimentation of the saints is rather funny when you think about it. They're subjected to a completely military-style hierarchy; for them the protocol is implacable.

"There is in this army, of which we are the lowly rank and file, officers of all ranks: field marshals, generals, colonels, and captains, right down to the poor second lieutenant, to whom just a simple rite is allotted.

"The insignia of their rank, as I see them here, are lighted candles, varying from two to six; for superior officers, one adds a deacon, a subdeacon, two masters of ceremonies and four cantors descending down the middle of the choir, all in copes, or two in copes, or else all four in cowls; eminence is precisely quantified, homage weighed out by measure; two masters of ceremonies! You would have to be St Benedict or be pontifically famous for them to employ such elaborate pomp in favour of a saint.

"As for the smaller offices, two candles are thought enough, and for a High Mass only one server accompanies the priest; and if by any chance the inferior officers are given a section of vespers, it'll be a dull and dry bit; the antiphon is not doubled for them, and even the very tone of the prayers diminishes and becomes more common; they are rewarded according to their status, and they are made to feel it too!

"The unfortunate thing, as you remarked just now, is that the promotions are so unequally distributed, because it's not the oldest or the most revered saints who have the highest rank.

"And what about those special divine offices, those deluxe hotel suites that are booked for some, versus the hotel rooms with communal furniture that are reserved for others; what about the battle that you yourself refer to in technical terms as 'concurrence', which is to say the conflict that breaks out at vespers between two offices of equal rank, and in order to get everyone to agree they split the office in two, dividing it up like an ice cream, at the reading…?"

"The notion that the breviary needs to be reformed is nothing new," replied Dom Felletin, "for centuries people have been considering an overhaul. Read Dom Guéranger's *Liturgical Institutions* and Abbé Batiffol's *History of the Roman Breviary*, and you'll see that there are few periods when the complaints of the clergy have not been heard in Rome.

"An anonymous work, a product, like plainchant itself, of the genius and piety of the ages, the Roman breviary had reached a state of perfection by the end of the eighth century. It preserved itself practically intact until the end of the twelfth. Amended in the thirteenth century, for the use of Friars Minor, by their head, Father Aimon, it spread through his influence to all the dioceses and ended up replacing the original text. Now, the modifications made by the Franciscans were simply deplorable. They stuffed the office with interpolated or dubious phrases, encumbered it with useless or apocryphal stories, and inaugurated a system that succeeded in sacrificing the temporal to the personal. Such as it was, this office lasted until the sixteenth century. Then Pope Clement VII decided to overhaul it from top to bottom. He turned to a Spanish cardinal who was also a Franciscan, and from the work of this eminent personage came that which is called the Quiñones breviary,[5] a hybrid compilation, with neither head nor tail, and quite outside any tradition. They had to put up with it, but not for long this time, because twenty-two years after its publication Pope Paul IV's rescript forbade it to be reprinted.

"The Sovereign Pontiff submitted a new project for the canonical office to the Council of Trent, but he died and it was his successor, Pius V, who took it over. It was his intention to restore the ancient *Ordo* and prune it of all the parasitical prose that was suffocating it; he also posited the principle that new feast days for saints should not be too readily included, for fear of not leaving enough room for subsequent ages, and when the work was finished he decreed it obligatory for all, decided that it could never be changed, and with a stroke of his pen suppressed any breviary that was less than two hundred years old.

"His own breviary wasn't perfect, but how superior it was nevertheless to those it replaced! At least it restored the antiphons and the responses from the time of Charlemagne, and pushed back the sanctoral office and brought the temporal office to the fore.

"Thirty years afterwards, in spite of the prohibition of Pius V about modifying any or all of it, his immediate successor, Pope Clement VIII, deeming the breviary incorrect and incomplete, modified and corrected it in his turn; and acting in the opposite direction he gave preference to the Proper of Saints, to the detriment of the weekday services, so what we gained with Pius V we lost with Clement.

"So already that's a lot of revisions of the breviary. If we add to this another by Urban VIII in the seventeenth century. This pope, being a Latin poet, endowed the office with two hymns of his own composition, the hymns of St Martina and St Elizabeth of Portugal; two more mediocre additions wouldn't have changed much, but what was worse was that he gave orders for the antiphons to be tampered with, and these reworkings, alas, are still sung in the Roman breviary today.

"The story of the Roman breviary ends there, because I don't count the various innovations recently introduced to the translation of feast days; indeed, they don't affect the heart and very lifeblood of the office.

"As for the Gallican liturgy, by studying its structure one can well believe it derived, at least in part, from the churches of the

East. In short, at its beginning it was a rather savoury mixture of the rites of the Levant and those of Rome; it was dismantled in the reigns of Pepin the Short and especially of Charlemagne, who, at the urging of Pope St Adrian, propagated the Roman liturgy among the Gauls.

"During the Middle Ages it was augmented by some admirable hymns and delightful responsories; it also created a whole series of symbolic prose pieces, embroidering the most innocent flowers onto the old Italian fabric. When the Bull of Pius V was issued, the French liturgy, which had been in existence for nearly eight centuries, was free not to recognise the reformed Roman breviary. But out of deference it was accepted. The bishops destroyed the work of the native artists, burned, so to speak, their Primitives, or at any rate only saved a few, which they locked away in the little sacristies of their own dioceses. The city of Lyons preserved its heritage intact, and we are indebted to it to be able to hear, in the old basilica of Saint John, truly archaic exhortations and venerable prose pieces.

"The loss of ancient customs and the destruction of traditional prayers, were, if you look at it from the point of view of archaeology and of art, acts of real savagery, of pure vandalism. All originality disappeared from the offices…"

"Yes," Durtal broke in, "it was as if a steamroller had flattened all the liturgical roadways in France!"

"In the end," the monk continued, "this edifice, constructed of bits and pieces, lasted as best it could till the reign of Louis XIV. Then Gallican and Jansenist ideas intervened, and it was resolved to demolish this building which had been repaired so many times.

"The Roman breviary was knocked down and reconstructed on a new basis. We then had the works of Harlay, Noailles and Vintimille. These prelates upended the whole psalter from top to bottom, admitting only antiphons and responsories taken from the scriptures; they cut out the legends of the saints, reduced the cult of the Blessed Virgin, ousted a series of feast days, and substituted the old hymns with verses by Coffin and Santeuil.

CHAPTER XIII

Jansenist heresies were dressed up in the Latin of paganism. The Parisian breviary became a kind of Protestant handbook, which the Jansenists in Paris hawked about the provinces.

"In a very short time this created absolute pandemonium in the dioceses; each one invented a service for its own use, and all sorts of personal whims were permitted. We were living under a regime of the goodwill of the Ordinary, until Dom Guéranger managed to bring about a unity of worship in our country by having the rites of the Church of Rome adopted once and for all.

"At the present time, therefore, Christianity – except for those religious Orders whose offices were, like ours, more than two hundred years old when the Bull of Pius V appeared – is subject to the force of the Roman breviary such as it was adapted, and ruined, by Urban VIII.

"It leaves much to be desired, but in the end, despite the incoherence you accuse it of, and, if I say so myself, despite the more than mediocre choice of its homilies and lessons, it nevertheless forms an ample and magnificent whole. It contains pieces of great beauty; think of the penitential Masses at Lent and Advent, of the Ember Day Mass, and Palm Sunday; think of the admirable office of Holy Week and the Mass for the Dead; think of the antiphons, the responsories, the hymns for Advent, for Lent, for the Passion, for Easter, for Pentecost, for All Souls, for Christmas and for Epiphany; think of matins, lauds and the marvellous office of compline, and you have to agree that in no literature of the world does there exist such radiant and splendid pages."

"I agree, father."

"Let's also admit, in defence of those poor saints who so often trespass on the Proper of the Seasons, that from a liturgical point of view – if we limit ourselves to that – they're very useful, because ultimately, in the ecclesiastical cycle, the life of Christ unfolds in six months, during winter and spring. From Pentecost onwards, during summer and autumn, it's nothing more than padding, and there our good saints form a glorious group around the great feast days, such as Assumption, All Saints and the dedication of churches. With regard to this dedication, you should read, in the Pontifical, the liturgy for the consecration of a church; there, in the text of this ceremony, you'll find the art of symbolism transported to its highest degree."

"I've read it, and also the *Consecration of Virgins* in the Pontifical; we are of the same opinion, father, they're sublime; but it's precisely because I love the liturgy that I want to see it without spot or blemish; moreover, it wouldn't be impossible to achieve, because there are untold treasures in the forgotten caskets of the liturgy. All that's needed is to open them, and replace the dross with which the holy office is cluttered with pieces of the first order."

"Well, that's easy for you to say, but the experiment has been tried and proves you wrong. You can see how many times our books have been amended, and they're still not complete, still not right."

"Because the people who revised them were undoubtedly clever, but they weren't artists."

"Well, I hope you'll be more indulgent to our Benedictine missal and breviary. Certainly, it's not above criticism, but you must admit that in its broad outline it's superb. Less overloaded with extraneous feast days that replace the Sunday offices and the weekday services, feasts likes those of the holy family, the prayer in the Garden of Olives, the holy crown, the holy shroud, the five wounds, and the spear and the nails, it has retained a delightful flavour of antiquity. It was the first to bring together the hymns that now figure in the canon. Indeed, it was St Benedict who first introduced prose or sequences into the main body of the offices. His children have made of the Christian prayerbook an anthology that contains the most beautiful songs by St Ambrose, Prudentius, Sedulius, Fortunatus, Paul the Deacon and other poets. In any case, there's no renovated stuff there, the re-heeled pieces of the Roman br…"

"Now, now," said Durtal, laughing, "you're cheating, father. Our monastic hymnal also has its poems composed in pretentious and really bad Latin, and these aren't so very old either. And like the Roman breviary, we go on endlessly repeating the prose of the confessors and the hiero-confessors, the *Iste Confessor*, embellished in each *Ordo* with the cryptic letters 'M', 'T', and 'V' to indicate the days when one has to change the third line of the first verse, because these days don't accord with the date of the saint's death. Now this anonymous hymn, which I believe was written in honour of St Martin, isn't in the least relevant to the majority of the saints on whose feast days it's employed. It alludes to the miracles wrought at St Martin's tomb and to the cures effected by him, but a number of the holy pontiffs and non-pontiffs for whom it's now used have never performed any cure or worked any miracle after their death that I know of... so, I return to my point, the ancient repertoire of the Church is stuffed with pieces that, in many cases, could advantageously replace these ones.

"And it wouldn't even be necessary to spend much time looking; you'd simply have to open Dom Guéranger's *Liturgical Year* or Canon Ulysse Chevalier's *Liturgical Poetry of the Middle Ages* to discover prose and verse that is simpler in its art and more mystical in flavour than those all-purpose sequences with which our diurnal is full."

"Well, if they lack variety at least admit that our hymns, spared the adulterations concocted by Urban VIII's liturgical chemists, are authentic, and that they smell of the soil in which they've grown and the century in which they were born."

"Yes, moreover, I went to the trouble of comparing the two texts, the genuine and the spurious, in that little book by Abbé Albin which you lent me, *The Poetry of the Breviary*. Of its kind, this volume is, after the two rather massive tomes by Abbé Pimont, a marvel of concise clarity, with its comparative texts, its variants, its French translations, old and modern, and its notes on versification and history. How is it that it wasn't a Benedictine who took on and succeeded in such a work?"

"OK, now you've changed the angle of attack," exclaimed

Dom Felletin, laughing. "You've let go of the office in order to pounce on the monks!"

"As far as that goes, father, I'll never leave you in peace, because it makes me so angry, even loving the Benedictines as I do, to see them so uninterested in work that really belongs to them. What about a menology, a register of saints belonging to your Order? All religious institutions have their own: look at the Franciscans, the Dominicans, the Carmelites, all have written works in which the lives of their saints are narrated to some degree or other: but you, nothing! And, while we're on this subject, your breviary is incomplete too. You barely celebrate the feast days of some of your own saints, and as for your elected female saints, such as Austrebertha, Walburga and Wereburga – all your '…bertha' and '…burga' saints – where are they?"

"If they were included in the Proper of our congregation, you'd reproach us for neglecting the temporal office," retorted Dom Felletin. "It's precisely because our roster of saints is not full to overflowing that we can still recite a votive office to the Blessed Virgin and to St Benedict. I presume you're not complaining about that?"

"No, because they use the old plainchant, which is so simple and truly exquisite."

"As for a menology, in the past Dom Onésime Menault, who died at Silos, began a series of Benedictine monographs; if they'd been collected together these little pamphlets would have formed one or two interesting biographical volumes about the history of our Order. But only two pamphlets appeared: the life of St Benedict of Aniane and that of St William of Gellone. They didn't sell and the publisher withdrew the advance.

"Nevertheless, it's clear that the menology you spoke about would be very useful, but it's too late to saddle ourselves with such a task; it's not the right moment, what with the upheaval of going to live outside France, to think about preparing a long-term project like that now…"

They both fell silent. They had returned to the starting point of their long discussion, to their exile, and it was impossible for it to be otherwise, because this departure haunted them all like an obsession. Every conversation however unconnected led back to it.

"Ah," said Durtal, "who knows? You may find some studious novices abroad suited to research and capable of writing; the more evil the times, the more monastic vocations we see."

The monk nodded his head.

"No doubt," he said, "but what worries me is this heaping together of refugee monasteries in the same country. With the exception of the community at Solesmes, which is going to live on the Isle of Wight, and that of Marseilles, which is going to Italy, all the other abbeys are going to Belgium, and Belgium is not a big country. If my information is correct, Saint Wandrille, Saint Maurus of Glanfeuil and the Priory of Saint Anne of Kergonan have taken houses in the province of Namur. In short, all three will be on top of one another; for its part, the abbey at Ligugé is going to settle a little further north in Limburg; the Wisques Priory is moving to Hainaut, and we are going to East Flanders.

"We can only suffocate in such a limited space, but what's worse is that, above us, there will stand the imposing and very beautiful Belgian abbey, Maredsous Abbey. It's famous and prosperous, and is directed by an abbot who is the head of the Order.

"Obviously we will be crushed by it, because it's clear – even taking into account that a Frenchman would always prefer to live in a French environment rather than a Belgian one – that every postulant will want to pass their period of probation in a real abbey, rather than whatever ramshackle place where we'll end up. There's no disguising the matter, the ambience of a place and its décor are essential to sustain a religious vocation; where there's no cloister, no real church, no separate novitiate, no proper cells, there's nothing for the soul. Do you know they are actually thinking of fitting up a sort of a chapel in a tiny drawing room... it'll be the death of solemn ceremonies – deprived of its framework, the liturgy will disintegrate, and that means our very purpose, our *raison d'être* will disappear... my God, and that's assuming that we don't end up falling to pieces ourselves, dwindling away into mere nostalgia or depression if the exile endures!"

Durtal didn't have the courage to protest, because he didn't foresee anything good coming from the Benedictines move abroad.

The silence became oppressive. It was a relief when Madame Bavoil impatiently came into the garden to remind them that it was time for dinner.

CHAPTER XIV

"Will you explain to me what all this means?" exclaimed Madame Bavoil, who was brandishing a newspaper above Durtal's head as he sat in front of a cup of coffee after lunch. "Because either it's me who's crazy or it's the others who are mad. Here are all these Carmelite nuns who, having refused to apply to the government for authorisation, have now run away. It's been a proper stampede, apart from a convent in Dijon, and one or two in other towns, a whole host of them have all buckled up their trunks and made off – take a look at this – can you understand it all?"

"I don't understand it any more than you," replied Durtal, handing the newspaper back to Madame Bavoil. "The Carmelites received a letter from Cardinal Gotti, their superior in Rome, instructing them to go, and now Father Grégoire, the assistant general of the Order in France, is making a formal statement to the press that the cardinal's letter is a forgery. What is one to believe? I don't know."

"Whether it's a forgery or not is not the issue. The Carmelite convents are houses of expiation and penance; they ought to welcome persecution, not flee from it; weren't the Carmelites of Compiègne sent to the scaffold by the Tribunal of Paris during the Revolution? Were *they* afraid? Did *they* run away?"

"You are becoming very belligerent, Madame Bavoil, what's come over you?"

But without answering, Madame Bavoil sat on a chair and continued:

"I'm exasperated by what I'm reading. Ah, Jeanne de Matel[1] was right when she said that we gain God in losing ourselves. If these nuns had lost themselves in him, they would just calmly wait until they were kicked out. But these nuns are running away, and your Benedictines too; and the Carthusians, the Dominicans, the Franciscans and even the Benedictines of Pierre-qui-Vire, are seeking authorisation. Why these discrepancies?"

"I don't know. The Pope allowed the congregations to conform to the law, with certain reservations, so those institutions that submit to it can't be wrong, but I also think that those who refuse to obey such an iniquitous edict are right."

"That's what they call a Norman answer,[2] my friend; if Rome consents, why are some Orders trying to appear more Popish than the Pope himself?"

"You'd better ask them; but since you want to know my very honest opinion, here it is: I think that, apart from the charitable institutions which the government is unable to replace, the petitions by the convents will be rejected en bloc by the chambers, and after that I don't see that there's any reason for the monks to inflict fruitless and humiliating procedures on themselves."

"But, bless me, a monk is made to be humiliated; if he doesn't accept affronts humbly and gladly, tell me in what way is he better than other men? Ah, I'm going to get this off my chest, because it chokes me up; there's a weakening of the religious spirit; the monasteries are in a state of decline; you told me one day that if a catastrophe such as the fire at the Charity Bazaar[3] could happen, it was because there weren't enough convents of reparation, enough sanctuaries of penance; the balance of good and evil was broken and the lightning conductors for God's wrath were insufficient."

"Yes."

"Well, are you quite sure that the lightning conductors that remain are not, how can I put it…?"

"Rusty…? or demagnetised, if you prefer…"

"That's it; well, are you sure that, if the Lord has punished us, it was because the quantity was insufficient? Don't you think it was rather the quality that was lacking? I'm greatly afraid that it's the monastic reservoirs of expiation, disrupted by the spirit of the devil, that are failing."

"That I don't know."

"If what I suspect is true, we must expect that the good Lord will call on us to give him a helping hand to put matters right; and you know how he acts in such cases, he overwhelms you with trials and tribulations. The Catholics who now calmly watch their few defenders go into exile will have to endure all sorts of ills, all sorts of afflictions, all sorts of misfortunes; whether they like it or not, they will suffer, because there'll be nothing to counterbalance the rabble that are running France."

"The fact is that this exile of the Carmelites is a very sad affair. And indeed, even supposing that the strict Orders had as much need of reform as the others, they were nevertheless still useful as lightning conductors; but it's not fair to blame the monks who carry out their mission as best they can for the perilous state we find ourselves in – we should blame the bishops, the clergy, the faithful: in a word, all Catholics.

"I'm not going to talk about the bishops, apart from the older ones, who were promoted in better times, nearly all the others have been tamed and had their claws trimmed in the cage of the Ministry of Public Worship; as for the clergy, they either lean towards rationalism, or else they reveal themselves to be in a sorry state of ignorance and slackness. The truth is that they are the product of useless and out-of-date methods, methods that are moribund. The education in seminaries is only fit for the rubbish bin, candidates suffocate in these classrooms where not a window has been opened since the death of Monsieur Olier.[4] The teaching is obsolete, and the studies are useless, but who will have the courage to smash the windows and let a little fresh air into these rooms?

"The faithful, too, have contributed to making Catholicism what it's become, something soft, emasculated, neither one thing nor the other; a sort of brokering system for prayers, a stock market for devotions, a sort of holy lottery where you haggle for grace by slipping petitions and pennies into sealed boxes beneath holy statues.

"But to tell the truth, the issue is a long-standing one and goes back further than these recent forms of devotion; for many years now in France religion has been steeped in a mixture of that old stain of Jansenism which we've never been able to get rid of, and the lukewarm infusion the Jesuits injected us with in the hope of curing us. Alas, the remedy didn't work, and to a desiccant they added a depressant. Idiotic prudery, the fear of our own shadow, a hatred of art, an inability to understand anything, an intolerance of other people's ideas; we owe these things to the disciples of Cornelius Jansen, the 'appellants'.[5] A passion for petty devotions, prayers without the liturgy, the suppression of the office – supposedly compensated for by the great salvation of music – a lack of substantial nourishment and a milk diet for the soul, we've taken these things from the priests of the Society of Jesus. The ideas of these two irreconcilable enemies have ended up merging in our souls, into that strange amalgam of sectarian intolerance and effeminate piousness into which we're dissolving.

"Of course, now that they're treated as pariahs, I pity the Jesuits, who are good and saintly people, and who – between ourselves – count among them spiritual directors and scholars who are much superior to those of other Orders. But what of it? What's been the result of their teaching? People like Trouillot or Monis, or else colourless young men who may be more secretive than other people when it comes to womanising, but who would never run the risk of a slap in the face to protect their masters or defend the Church.

"Experience tells us. No man of surpassing ability has ever emerged from these forcing houses; their colleges will disappear like those of other institutions which were, moreover, no more successful than the Jesuits; and what will we lose?"

"It's not their fault," said Madame Bavoil, "you can't cut a good coat out of bad cloth."

"No doubt, but let's leave that aside and admit that, in general terms, the claims we're now making are a bit hypocritical. Today, we're demanding freedom, but we've never granted it to others. If tomorrow the wind changed, if one of those sad vegetables harvested in our Catholic allotments were to take the place of Waldeck-Rousseau, we'd be even more intolerant than him, so much so we'd make him seem almost sympathetic. We've annoyed everyone, Madame Bavoil, whenever we've been in even the least position of authority, and now the favour is being returned; everything has to be paid for, and the moment for repayment has come.

"And moreover, you'll notice that the Jacobins who oppress us aren't the product of some temporary growth; they're the result of a particular state of affairs, they were engendered by the weakness of our faith, by our anemic prayers, by the feeblness of our religious instincts, by the selfishness of our tastes. Oh yes, the Catholics deserve everything they get, and we should repeat this to ourselves every morning and every evening on our knees, before God and before man!"

"How can we get ourselves out of this mess, my friend?"

"I don't know, but I'm nevertheless certain that our Lord will extract some good from this evil; if he allows his Church to suffer persecution it's because he wants to prepare her, through persecution, for the reforms that are necessary; the death knell is tolling for the Orders; the cloisters will disappear. He'll replace them with something else. The monastic idea can't perish any more than the Church can, but it can be modified. Either he'll create new institutions more in accordance with modern conditions or he'll graft new branches onto the old ones; no doubt, we'll see a development of affiliation schemes and of Third Orders, which by their secular appearance will escape the constraints of the law. I'm not worried at all from this point of view, the Blessed Virgin knows how to bring people together when she wishes to.

"On which, I'll wish you a good evening, because I'm going to the abbey to say goodbye to Dom de Fonneuve who leaves tonight for Belgium, and then after vespers to attend the final taking of the habit."

"Who is taking the habit?"

"A young novice who was a seminarian, Brother Cholet."

"Do you know him?"

"No, I only know he's from Poitiers, which isn't exactly a recommendation, because if he has the vices of that part of the country he'll be singularly lazy and sly; anyway, let's hope that this one, by not being a good-for-nothing, will be an exception to the rule."

The Oblate

When Durtal entered the cloister, he was deafened by the noise of hammering, coming from all sides. The din came from every floor, through the open windows. Crates were being nailed down everywhere. The guest room into which he went was crammed from floor to ceiling with deal tables, legs in the air, students' desks painted black, repaired stools and rush-bottom chairs; it was pitiful to see all this wretched furniture, which not even the poorest working man would have wanted.

And in another room he saw a heap of cast-iron fireplaces, rusty coal scuttles, sheaves of fire tongs and fire shovels, a pile of stovepipes, angled chimney flues, commodes for the use of the sick, washbasins, and jugs, chipped, broken or without handles.

"Why the devil are you taking all this rubbish with you, it's not worth the straw you're packing it in," he asked Father Ramondoux, the precentor, who was in the process of making an inventory of these paltry items, which the lay brothers and novices carried away as soon as they were registered.

And in his deep voice that seemed to come from a barrel, came the touching reply:

"Clearly, from a financial point of view it would be better to leave all this junk behind, as the cost of transporting it is more than it's worth; but exile will seem less painful if we have things around us which we're used to; we'll feel more quickly at home there with our old furniture than with new things."

And when Durtal asked him about Dom de Fonneuve, he replied:

"He's in the library; he's superintending the packing of the books."

As he passed through the corridors Durtal bumped against more barricades of old furniture. Folded iron bedsteads and bottle racks were lined against the walls; mattresses were piled up next to slop pails, stoneware jugs, china chamber pots, and zinc bowls; bits of crockery lay on the straw. He met several monks with whom he silently shook hands; amid all this confusion of objects, they seemed alone; preoccupied by their own sadness, no one said anything.

He reached the fifteenth-century spiral staircase, and went up to the second floor, to the sound of hammering; the door of the library was open; from the landing you could glimpse a succession of high-ceilinged rooms, full from top to bottom with books. Along the white wooden bookshelves ran ladders on wheels, laden with novices, among whom Durtal recognised Brother Gèdre and Brother Blanche.

In a corner, his face distraught, sat Dom de Fonneuve. He pointed to the lower shelves filled with old folios, and tears came into his eyes.

The shelves he was pointing at contained the great collected works of the abbey; these were the prior's favourites, dusty tomes, bound in parchment, vellum or yellow calf, their gilt worn off and their titles faded.

He led Durtal over to them, and made him bend down to examine them more closely, pulling a volume from the shelf.

"This is a rarity," he sighed, pointing to the ancient volumes of Wadding's *Annales minorum*; and Durtal ran his eye along the rows: the *Monasticon anglicanum*; the *History of French Literature* by the Benedictines of Saint Maur, the *Rerum gallicarum et francicarum scriptores*, the *Gallia Christiana*, the *Acta Sanctorum* in a very old edition, Martène's *De antiquis ecclesiae ritibus*, the *Annals* of Mabillon, an edition of Bulteau, the collected works of Le Nain de Tillemont, of Dom Ceillier and of Muratori, and Mansi's *Concilia.*[6]

"Look, my dear boy, look how beautiful this edition of Baronius in forty-two folio volumes is. It's the 1738 edition, to which are joined Tornielli's *Sacred Annals*; it's the best edition, because that of Bar-le-Duc doesn't include any indexes. And here's the *Patrologia Latina* and a whole series of Migne's works, Canon Ulysse Chevalier's *Index of Historical Sources from the Middle Ages*, du Cange's *Glossary*, and La Curne de Sainte Palaye's *Dictionary*[6] – solid tools for working in the cloister."

Dom de Fonneuve was speaking in an undertone and his hands were shaking as he listened to the sound of the hammers. It seemed as if with each crate they nailed down, they were burying someone he loved in a coffin.

"What will become of all this abroad," he murmured, "in a château where there's no room to house them, where no library is ready to receive them?

"Yes, take them," he said to Brother Blanche, who came up with his face smiling to warn him that he was going to move the big folios.

He caught hold of Durtal's arm. "Let's go downstairs," he said. They passed through another room; this one was already more than half empty. There were gaps in the shelves next to the crates, and some of the books, no longer propped upright by the others, lay on their sides, sprawling in a mass of dust.

He quickened his pace and led Durtal down to the cloister, but here, too, he bumped into crates and pyramids of assorted objects that had been taken down from the attics and placed under the arcades while waiting to be packed.

"Let's go to the garden, away from all this hustle and bustle." They were heading for the door when they met Monsieur Lampre. He was just leaving the abbot; he looked depressed, and his wild beard seemed even more straggly, as if he'd been feverishly pulling at it with his hands.

"Well," he asked, "is the packing up of the books progressing?"

"Yes," replied the father with a sigh.

"And are you still leaving for Belgium this evening?"

"Yes, but I'm not stopping there long and will rejoin Val-des-Saints without delay, because I want to personally see that the crates are properly labelled. Ah, it'll be a long while before this library is relocated and classified in some attic room, God knows where."

There was a silence, then speaking more to himself than to his two companions, the old monk continued:

"What a wake-up call it is for us, who have been enclosed in a monastery for years, little aware of the events happening outside, but when you're passing through your seventy-third year, and a good night's sleep is becoming more and more rare, you're forced to lie awake at night, and to examine your conscience; and then you ask yourself if the Lord, dissatisfied with his religious Orders, has allowed this persecution to punish them.

Chapter XIV

"Yes, this idea haunts me during my nights of insomnia, and I'm starting to believe that we deserve the punishment the Saviour inflicts on us.

"You see," Dom de Fonneuve went on after a pause, "we certainly love the good Lord in this abbey; I can assure you, no word of a lie, that there's not one bad monk among us, but is that enough?

"A few years ago, something was said by a postulant, a man of the world, who, by the way, we dismissed for not having a vocation; I'll never forget his words, they haunt me; this is what he said: 'You eat pretty well in this monastery, you get enough sleep; you don't have to work and you still gain salvation for your soul: that suits me fine.' He was obviously exaggerating, but still…"

"Come, now, father," said Durtal, "you don't eat as well as all that!"

"We don't eat well…?"

"Well, to be fair, it's eatable, but it's not a feast; you're safe from the sin of gluttony."

The prior seemed surprised.

"You're very fussy about what you eat," he said, "personally, I find the food good, too good in fact; this question of cooking is only a subsidiary one, but it relates to a whole set of things that worry me.

"Indeed, suppose that I'd never entered the monastery, that I'd remained in the world like you. I would certainly have had many trials and many hardships that I've avoided by being in a cloister. I would have had to earn my living, pay my rent, raise children if I'd married, perhaps take care of a sick wife; on the other hand, supposing I hadn't remained a layman, that I'd become a priest or a vicar in the provinces, I would then have had to take care of people's souls, I would have had to run about the villages of my parish dispensing aid, to fight with my bishop and the often hostile municipal governments – to lead the life of a dog, in a word.

"Instead of all that, I live like a pig in clover, a life of leisure; I don't have to concern myself about food, my rent, or children; I don't have to travel, often great distances and at night, to give the last rites; I know nothing about life's cares; and I think that in exchange for avoiding so much hassle, I haven't given very much to God… it seems to me, to tell you the truth, that I've profited from the sacrifice of others."

"Oh, father, you're going too far," exclaimed Durtal. "You've worked all your life, without ever taking any rest. And what about the hardships of communal life, which everyone else avoids; and getting up at four o'clock in the morning during winter, the long services in a cold church, the lack of freedom, and the mortifications which you never speak about?"

"But that's just child's play in the art of the Lord, my dear friend; as for me, I see now that, personally, I've listened to myself too much; whenever I've felt a little unwell, I too easily invented excuses for not going down to matins."

"You?" said Monsieur Lampre, "why, it was the abbot himself who had to forbid you to attend the early office on several occasions; you fainted from weakness in the choir and they had to take you back to your cell."

"It's clear," continued the monk, who wasn't listening to them, "that we lack an inner life here in the cloister; we imagine that when we've finished reciting the office we're quits with God; that's a serious error; it's also necessary to work and suffer, and instead of which we're lazy and don't practise self-sacrifice. Where is the divine madness of the Cross in all this?"

"Ah now then, father," said Monsieur Lampre, "with all due respect, you're making fun of us. You have your full share of infirmities; there are months when you can't even put one foot in front of the other, where you drag yourself along, leaning against the walls to get to chapel. Self-sacrifice? But there it is. What more do you want?

"That there aren't enough monks in monasteries who live a unitary life or who are at one with God, I quite agree, and I've been shouting it from the rooftops for long enough. But at the end of the day, as you said just now, there are no bad monks at Val-des-Saints; that's already something; moreover, the spiritual situation here is better than in many richer abbeys where money, as it does everywhere, pursues its work of destruction and demoralisation. Fortunately, the Benedictines here are poor, and consequently not afflicted with the craze for building monastic palaces and buying up land. Your novitiate is full of pure, guileless souls; it seems to me that you suffer and make reparation for the faults of others rather than for your own."

Durtal smiled at this reversal of roles. Here was Monsieur Lampre actually defending the Benedictines, even though it was usually he who would attack them.

"We also have to expiate the pride we take in our Order," said Dom de Fonneuve in a lower voice, "we're living on an ancient reputation which we're no longer worthy of; it's time to make our *mea culpa*, now that the good Lord is chastising us."

Durtal was looking at him. The old man's eyes were full of tears; he spoke so humbly and with such conviction.

Durtal, who admired him and loved him for his great learning and his great kindness, couldn't help embracing him, and the old man began to sob against his friend's shoulder.

Then he pulled himself together.

"You see what a fine monk I am," he exclaimed, trying to smile, "even a little girl wouldn't be so pathetic; ah, I could say I don't know what came over me, but deep down, it's because I saw them packing up the books I'm so fond of that I feel so moved; that'll teach you, you silly fool, not to follow your own rule that forbids you to get attached to things, whatever they are.

"Now, goodbye, I'm going to pack my suitcase; I'll be back in a few days. You're coming to the taking of the cowl this evening, aren't you?"

"Certainly, father."

The old prior left them.

"Have you spoken to his reverence?" Durtal asked Monsieur Lampre.

"Yes, he's made his decision. No monks except Father Paton will remain at Val-des-Saints; it's the complete collapse of our plan to continue the office here. Moreover, the abbot wants to speak to you about it himself, because he has a proposal for you."

"What is it?"

"He didn't tell me."

The bells rang for vespers and both made their way to the church. After the service, which was nothing out of the ordinary, being that of a simple hiero-confessor listed under the double rite, the abbot put on a white stole, and following the procession of monks – preceded by Brother Blanche carrying his crosier, and Brother Gèdre his mitre – he walked back by way of the nave to the cloister.

Monsieur Lampre and Durtal followed behind him under the galleries, and in their turn made their way to the Chapter House, a huge room with oak beams in the ceiling, furnished with plain benches along the walls, and with a throne on a raised dais at one end, above which was nailed a crucifix. Two stools were placed on either side of this throne, and on the right stood a table on which a basin, a ewer, and some towels had been set.

In the middle of the room, facing the abbatial seat, there was a carpet, two lighted candles, and two chairs, one for the novice and the other for Dom Felletin; and in front of the novice's chair was a stool with a red velvet cushion.

When all were seated, Dom Felletin approached the abbot, and after bowing said to him in Latin:

"Reverend Father, the Rule has been read a first time to our Brother Baptistin Cholet; is it your pleasure to invest him with the novice's cowl?"

"Go and fetch him."

Dom Felletin went out and came back a few minutes later with Brother Cholet, who was staring, intimidated, at the ground. He prostrated himself at full length on the floor.

"*Quid petis*? What are you seeking?"

"The mercy of God, and brotherhood with you."

The abbot replied:

"May the Lord number you among his elect."

"Amen."

Then the abbot resumed:

"*Surge in nomine Domini*. Rise in the name of the Lord."

The brother raised himself, and then knelt down; the abbot held up the Rule of St Benedict and asked him if he wished to observe it, and on receiving a reply in the affirmative, he said:

"May God complete what he has begun in you."

Then he spoke a few words, thanking the saviour for giving him, during this distressing period he was going through, the consolation of seeing a vocation to persevere in his abbey, and when he'd finished his address, he put on the plain silver mitre, intoned the antiphon, *Mandatum novum do vobis,* the alternate verses of which, like those chanted for the washing of feet on Maundy Thursday, were exchanged by the two choirs of monks.

As soon as the antiphon began, the postulant, after saluting the abbot, sat down in the chair alloted to him opposite the throne, took off his shoes and socks, and placed his bare feet on the footstool.

And then the abbot, a cloth round his waist, followed by his assistants and by Father Emonot, replacing Dom d'Auberoche the master of ceremonies who'd gone to Paris to raise money, knelt down on the velvet cushion. One of the servers held the basin, while the other poured some lukewarm water perfumed with aromatic herbs from the ewer, and the reverend abbot washed the brother's feet and then wiped them with a towel, which he then used to cover just the toes, leaving the rest of the feet bare; then he kissed them, and each monk came up in turn to kneel down and kiss them.

From the way in which such kisses were given one could guess the degree of fervour and affection between the fathers and brothers; some pressed their lips and really kissed, seeing in the newcomer, as in every guest, the image of Christ; others kissed with equal force out of brotherly affection; some, on the contrary, brushed their lips lightly, confining themselves to fulfilling a duty, without attributing any more importance to it. As for Durtal, he was thinking about this custom, perpetuated by the Church since its earliest ages, about this lesson of humility which St Benedict inflicted on all his monks… and all of a sudden, he couldn't help smiling; Father Philigone Miné, who had been seated in a corner lost in his thoughts, suddenly came to, as was his habit when it was a question of the office. He struggled up, and supported by two brothers was heaved over to the footstool, where, smiling, he left a fine big kiss on little Cholet's feet, after which he was lifted up again with difficulty and led back to his bench.

When all the monks had filed past, and while the choir was chanting the *Ubi charitas*, on a sign from the master of ceremonies the novice put his socks and shoes back on and knelt in the middle of the floor; the monks knelt likewise at their places.

The abbot took off his mitre, and turning to face his seat he intoned a series of verses, recited the *Kyrie Eleison* and the *Pater*, and finished with three prayers, the last of which borrowed from the office of the patriarch: "Renew, O Lord, in thy Church, the spirit by which thy servant, Blessed Benedict, abbot, was inspired, that we, being filled therewith, may love that which he loved and accomplish the work which he hath given us to do. Through Jesus Christ our Lord."

All the monks having responded "Amen", the reverend abbot withdrew, this time at the head of the procession.

The ceremony would be completed the next morning at High Mass, when, after the Communion antiphon, followed by the *Veni creator*, the abbot would invest the novice with the cowl, whereupon he would go the round of his brother novices and then take a seat in the choir that was henceforth to be his.

This preliminary solemnity of the *Mandatum* was always touching, with the abbot prostrating himself in front of the young lad he was welcoming into his fold; Durtal had attended the ceremony a number of times, but in the circumstances in which this one was taking place, on the eve of their departure into exile, it became singularly moving.

He was brooding over these reflections under the arcades of the cloister when Father Ramondoux came up to tell him that the abbot was waiting to talk to him.

He went up to the first floor where the reverend abbot's room was located. It differed little from the cells of the other monks except that it had, in addition, a little study, very dark, in which there was an iron bed similar to all those in the community; the rest was equally shabby, whitewashed walls, a desk, painted black, a wicker armchair and chairs, a deal cupboard, and on the partition an oak cross without a Christ on it and a yellowing print of the Virgin in a frame.

Dom Anthime Bernard shook hands with Durtal, who kissed his ring, and when they were seated he said to him:

"My dear son, for nearly two years now you have been living among us and with us, everyone loves and respects you; in a few days we will be leaving you, as Dom Felletin tells me you have no intention of accompanying us to Belgium; I daren't say you're mistaken, because I myself don't know how we're going to organise ourselves in Waes, the inhabitants of which only speak Flemish, but once we're settled I will let you know and you must promise me that, as soon as your room is ready, you'll come and see us; that's agreed is it not?"

Durtal nodded.

"Now, another question. Monsieur Lampre would have been pleased, and you too I believe, if I could have left a few monks here to look after the monastery and to continue the office. That's not possible. Besides the trouble this might draw down on us from the government, which might see it as a pretext to take over the abbey, I need all my monks over there, as their number is going to be considerably reduced by the leave I've had to grant to several of them, who are eager to visit their families before heading into exile.

"I wanted to tell you this myself, so that you would know it was impossible for me to act otherwise; there only remains one more thing to ask you: you're aware that it's our stict duty never to interrupt the office, at any cost; the liturgical services must therefore continue here, until we can resume it in Belgium. In addition to Father Paton, who can't quit Val-des-Saints because of our vineyards, I'm leaving the father sacristan and a novice, Brother Blanche, for the handful of days necessary. That makes three. But I haven't got a fourth essential to form a choir, the few I had in mind have just asked for leave of absence during this period. Now, it occurred to me that you'd consent to be the fourth. You know the office as well as we do, since you've been reciting it for two years. You're an oblate, a Benedictine like us, so there'll be no difficulties."

"That depends; if it's just a matter of reciting the office, I might be able to manage it, but if on the contrary it's a question of singing or serving Mass, I'd be absolutely useless."

"No, there's no question of any of that; the lay brothers who are staying on with Father Paton will serve Mass, and even supposing they were all delayed in the vineyard, Brother Blanche, who I'm delegating specifically to help the two fathers, will take care of it. As for singing, there'll be none, as neither of the fathers can sing. They'll limit themselves to chanting."

"Then it's agreed."

"Thank you. Life here alone will be very dull for you," the abbot continued after a pause. "Don't you intend to leave Val-des-Saints after we've gone?"

"Definitely, I've never been fond of the countryside, and if I came here it was only because of the abbey. Now the abbey's going, there's nothing of interest for me here. After thinking it over, it seems to me that the wisest thing would be to leave the provinces, which moreover I have a horror of, and go back to Paris. I'll try and choose a quiet neighbourhood, and find an apartment that's simple and clean, not too expensive, and if possible near a church."

"Why don't you take rooms near our friends, the Benedictine nuns in the Rue Monsieur? They have High Mass and choral vespers every day; they're saintly women, and you could follow the office in their sanctuary."

"That's an idea, certainly; but as regards that, allow me, your reverence, to ask exactly when your monks are leaving, because I need to know for certain myself so I can arrange my affairs?"

"Next week, the novitiate will leave en bloc with the lay brothers, under the direction of Dom Felletin. On their arrival they'll do most of the work and prepare the oratory and the rooms. A team of monks, along with Dom de Fonneuve, will go next, and when they're settled I'll take the rest of the abbey with me. I aim to be the last to leave the ship."

"Very well, as soon as the liturgical services start up again in Belgium, I'll take a train to Paris."

"That's settled, then."

Durtal kissed the abbot's ring again, and as soon as he left the monastery he bumped into the parish priest who was on his way there. The latter at once began to moan about the political situation and to deplore the banishment of the monks. He kept talking in an unstoppable stream.

'My God,' thought Durtal, when he was finally rid of the tiresome priest, 'I should be fair to him. I find it difficult to forgive him for having abolished plainchant and dinning his silly tunes into our ears, but if, against his own interest, which is to have the church of Val-des-Saints to himself, he's as genuinely sorry the monks are going as he says he is, then it's true, I'd gladly shake hands with him, because it would prove that in spite of all his schemes he's really a good man. And with that, let's go and have dinner."

And that evening at table, when Madame Bavoil, who had calmed down, asked about the departure of the Benedictines, Durtal told her all about his interview with the abbot.

"Who is he," she said, "this father sacristan who's going to stay with Father Paton?"

"I don't really know him. Dom Beaudequin is a sturdy Norman; he has a reputation for being sly and pigheaded. The abbot probably chose him because he's on good terms with the parish priest. At first, he tricked him with his indifference and his evasions; but then, no one knows why, from a need for company perhaps, he became his partner in arms, his best friend. But it's all the same to me, I'll only see him during the hours of the office, and outside of that not at all. As for Father Paton, he's the opposite, straight as a die, an honest monk and a saintly monk it seems; but he's always working in the vineyard, and up until now I've hardly seen him."

"Ah, you'll soon get to know him... by the way, Mlle de

Garambois came to see you; she can't stop crying and keeps saying that, if it weren't for her uncle, she too would go off to Belgium."

"When you think about it," Durtal replied, "those most to be pitied in this affair are ourselves. Indeed, after the first shock of being uprooted from their former cloister, the fathers will find, once installed at Moerbeke, their cells and their services just as before. A true monk belongs to no country, only his monastery. Whether it be in France or abroad matters little, since he never leaves its precincts; so exile won't change him; except for the fact that he'll drink beer instead of wine during meals, his life will be the same; and as for the novices, they'll console themselves with seeing a new country, they're like children who are amused by a voyage; but as for us, this is our daily existence; we've been knocked sideways by this damnable law, it means having to move somewhere else, a complete upheaval."

"Yes, we'll be living on spiritual short rations from now on…" concluded Madame Bavoil with a sigh.

Chapter XV

S ad days and still sadder nights followed. The stalls of the monks in the choir grew emptier each day. They all went off before the deportation to their families, and had to rejoin the abbot in Paris, in order to make their way from that city to Belgium.

In default of the necessary elements, there was now only one server at Mass, and the status of the feast day could only be worked out from the number of lighted candles.

Editorials in the newspapers were rife. They spoke of nothing but the return to Russia of the Czar,[1] who seemed to have come to France only to divert the public's attention, and play the part of organ-grinder drowning out the cries of the victim in the Fualdès affair;[2] but now that the Russian emperor's visit was over, the exodus of the two abbeys at Solesmes was the subject of all the talk in the cloister.

The novices were full of admiration for their method of retreat in so grand and spectacular a style, and regretted that it couldn't have been the same at Val-des-Saints, where everyone was dispersed in small groups; the older monks shook their heads saying: "Solesmes has a more devoted population than Val-des-Saints, and it still remains to be seen if, once the Benedictines have their backs turned, people won't ally themselves with their enemies." They also discussed the departure for the Isle of Wight of the nuns of Saint Cecilia; it was the complete abandonment of Dom Guéranger's beloved Solesmes.

'And with no hope of coming back,' thought Durtal, 'because it won't be long before the abbey of Saint Peter will be sold by the government and taken over.'

The time for the departure of the novitiate at Val-des-Saints was approaching. It was decided before the first group left the cloister, to at least celebrate a final pontifical Mass; the parish priest offered the use of the church the Sunday before the novices set off, the feast of Our Lady of the Seven Sorrows; and this sad feast day seemed well chosen to bid a final farewell to the church, because beginning the next day the monks would have to chant the office in their own oratory, being too few to fill the choir.

On this Sunday, the peasants from the surrounding area turned up. Almost all of them were socialists and had always clamoured for the suppression of the congregations, but they felt that the closing of the monastery would be the ruin of the countryside. They all made their living from these hated monks, especially the poor, who would leave their empty baskets at the porter's lodge, then carry them away full, and were thus assured of having food every day.

The peasants were half saddened, half angry; their view was that the Benedictines should have submitted to the new law, and continued to let themselves be sponged off by them.

The difficulty was to organise an imposing ceremony for this last feast day, because the number of servers was limited. Nevertheless they succeeded, even though the Smyrna carpet, the green *prie-dieu*, and the draperies usually hung behind the abbot's seat and on either side of the altar had already been packed. They made up for them with pots of shrubs and flowers. The abbatial throne was set off by a background of green leaves, and the relics that weren't yet packed away sparkled in the candlelight. Father Emonot was promoted to master of ceremonies, Dom Paton and another monk assisted the abbot as deacon and sub-deacon; three young novices were chosen to be crosier bearer, mitre bearer and incense bearer, and a lay brother as a train bearer. The role of candle bearers was confided to choirboys and it was understood that Brother Gèdre and Brother Blanche, who had very nice voices, would replace the two absent cantors and stand in their robes in the choir.

And so the ceremony unfurled with vestiges of its former splendour; the abbot, in *cappa magna*, blessing the faithful on his entry, before celebrating the Mass himself.

The Mass was beautiful, with a very special liturgy, opening with an image of the Cross between the Blessed Virgin and St John, and the singing of the *Stabat*, revealing a glimpse of the hill of Calvary.

There was no more touching sequence than this, because it was in some sense the Magdalene of prose, washing with her tears the feet of the mother, in the same way that the Magdalene had bathed those of her son; and the tremulous, clear voices of Brothers Gèdre and Blanche, who were nervous of singing in front of everyone in the choir, added still more emotion to those stanzas appealing to Mary for the grace to weep with her and share in her sorrow.

The Mass, so naively and tentatively treated in this way, had a note of tenderness, an accent of adoration that it wouldn't have had if the precentor, Father Ramondoux, had been present, as he would have crushed all the other voices with the steam-hammer blows of his bellowing.

'How lucky it is that he was given a leave of absence!' thought Durtal, but he added melancholically, 'alas, that's the last bottle of plainchant I'll get to drink because tomorrow the cellar of Gregorian melody will be empty.'

After the gospel reading, the parish priest ascended the pulpit, asked for the abbot's blessing, praised the monks, and expressed on behalf of his parishioners his regret at seeing them leave.

He spoke clearly and well.

'That redeems everything, even his hatred for plainchant,' thought Durtal, and at the end of the Mass, he shook hands and congratulated him; then he went to see Dom Felletin in his cell.

He wanted to make his confession one last time with his friend, but there was neither a *prie-dieu* nor a chair in the room; everything had gone, even the crucifix and the coloured print of the Virgin; the only thing left was a bare straw mattress on the floor to sleep on that night.

The monk sat on the window ledge, and as the floor was covered in dust from all the upheavals, Durtal spread out an old newspaper and knelt on it. After confession, he got up and they talked.

Dom Felletin tried to resist the feeling of sadness that overwhelmed him; he talked of his faith in the future, of the providential designs that were certainly leading to a purification of the Church, of the unconscious role played by the fanatics of the two chambers of government whose destiny it was, without them even knowing it, to accomplish a useful task, and he said:

"Tomorrow, we'll leave at dawn, and in the evening we'll sleep in Paris at the Benedictine convent, where they've prepared a dormitory for us. In the morning, after Mass, I'll take all the novices and lay brothers to Our Lady of Victories and in the afternoon, if we have time, we'll make a pilgrimage to the Basilica of Saint Denys, or in any case to Saint Germain des Prés, because it's only right that we pay homage to the Virgin, who is revered there, and that we also visit our great ancestors, Mabillon and Monfaucon, whose memorial stones have been let into the wall of the new chapel dedicated to St Benoit Labre. Saint Germain des Prés is the Paris church that means the most to us. Besides having been once the abbey church of our monastery, it now contains Our Lady in White, the consoler of the afflicted. Her statue, on the right of the main entrance, was offered to our abbey of Saint Denys in the fourteenth century by Queen Joan of Evreux, and after a short stay in the museum of the Petits Augustins during the Revolution it returned to settle in Saint Germain des Prés, in an ancient church of our Order. It's therefore a Benedictine relic, though quite forgotten, alas, because no one, not even in our monasteries, knows of its existence."

"The poor church," exclaimed Durtal, "hasn't it been vandalised enough! Initially, it has to be said, by our brethren of Saint Maur, who in the seventeenth century bedizened it in the gaudy style of the day; since then, it's got worse, its walls have been covered Saint Sulpice fashion with the pious and banal effusions of Flandrin's paintbrush.[3] They reworked the nave from top to bottom, replaced the eleventh-century capitals with crude gilt reliefs, and painted the columns and vaults in hideous colours, Tripoli reds mixed with mud browns, pepper greys, and the washed-out greens of a well-boiled lettuce.

"But even so, I know one thing, father. However disfigured, however defiled it is, the church is admirable if we compare it with those built by the stunted nonentities of the present day; with its twelfth-century choir, whose contours have been fortunately spared by inattentive architects, it is even worth exploring from an artistic point of view. So if, as seems likely, I'm left stranded in Paris, it'll be a chance to go there and recite my office, to say a prayer to our father St Benedict and the short hymn *Te decet Laus*, which we alone have in our breviary. For more than two centuries our patron saint hasn't heard them beneath those vaults; so I'll show him that there's still someone in Paris who recites his liturgy and remembers both him and those close to him.

"I will, and this goes without saying, also visit the Benedictine Virgin; in the absence of the monks she'll have to be content with the prayer of a layman of the Order, who at least knows who she is and how she got there; with her, I'll be on familiar ground straightaway."

"Yes, do that, my dear son, and don't forget me in your prayers to the Madonna. I have great need of them because despite being a monk, I'm also a man, and it's dreadfully hard to tear oneself away from all this…" he murmured, pointing through the window at the church, the surrounding buildings and the gardens.

Durtal came up to the window and looked at the paths that stretched out before him; one bordered by hornbeams reserved for the fathers; and the other covered with a trellis of vines for the novices. They were deserted; everyone was busy with the final preparations. Life had already departed from the gardens, solitude was settling in even before the exile.

"And what about the ravens of St Benedict and the doves of St Scholastica?" asked Durtal, who noticed in the distance the grill of the grotto topped by the statue of St Joseph.

"Father Paton will look after them. What else can you expect, having to move like this we can't take the poor animals with us."

A little discreet knock was heard at the door, and Brother Gèdre's head appeared.

"Father, we're about to pack up the relics."

"Come," said the monk to Durtal, as he put on his cowl.

They went upstairs to the novices' classroom; piled up on the tables were bronze and silver-gilt reliquaries of all shapes, tiny churches and castle keeps, and round or oval medallions. Two novices were holding lighted candles. Dom Emonot was wrapping each reliquary in a strip of white linen and placing them on straw in the packing crates.

When the work was done, they all reverently bowed, and then closed the crates and blew out the candles.

Durtal said goodbye to everyone because they wouldn't see each other again, and then returned with Dom Felletin to his cell, where they took affectionate leave of each other.

"I'll arrange to meet you in Paris," said the monk, "I'll have to go there from time to time on business connected with the novitiate. I'll ask you to dinner; be strong, everything will turn out better than we think."

"May God hear you," sighed Durtal.

And the same scene of farewell was repeated a few days later with Dom de Fonneuve. Durtal had looked for him in vain, in the cloister, the library and his cell; finally, he found him in the oratory, weeping in front of the altar, his head in his hands. The old man seemed haunted by gloomy forebodings. "We'll meet again in Heaven," he said sadly.

"And before that, at Moerbeke when I come to visit you, or in Paris, when you go there," replied Durtal, with forced cheerfulness.

"Come quickly, if you wish to see your old prior again," replied the monk, and he hugged his friend and blessed him.

'This is the end of everything,' thought Durtal, when these two monks who he loved the most had gone. With their disappearance, he broke down, discouraged; he would kill time wandering from room to room, walking through the garden, ill at ease and unable to do any kind of work.

And an absolute loathing to do anything whatsoever, even to go out, overwhelmed him. If he finally decided to return to Paris it was because there was no other choice. Not wanting to live at Val-des-Saints without the Benedictines, there was nothing left to do but head for Paris, because to pay rent for another term in a provincial town where there were neither the charms of the countryside nor the advantages of the capital would have been absurd. No, it was one or the other.

Once he'd made up his mind, the idea of getting on a train, of looking for lodgings and moving, panicked him.

'It would be better to bury myself here,' he'd moan, 'rather than start a new life again, rather than go back to where I was a few years ago.'

'When I left Paris, God knows I had no thought of ever going back. But I'm driven to it, because in the end it's stupid to think of staying here even for a second. No, I've seen quite enough two-faced aristocratic idiots and country yokels here – anything, rather than that.'

And he tried to work up an enthusiasm for Paris.

'There'll be a hard phase to get through, that of the move, but afterwards when I'm settled, it should be possible to arrange a quasi conventual, truly peaceful life.

'Paris is full of churches, steeped in prayer, more pious than all the provincial churches put together; and its chapels devoted to the Virgin – Our Lady of Victories, Saint Sèverin, Saint Sulpice, the Abbaye-aux-Bois,[4] and the sisters of Saint Thomas de Villeneuve – are like welcoming dispensaries where the Madonna heals one's wounds with a smile.'

In summer he could walk along the quays looking for old books, stopping off at Saint Germain l'Auxerrois, in the chapel of Holy Souls, so quiet and self-contained at the far end of the sombre apse; at other times he might go as far as Saint Sèverin or Notre Dame, or linger on his return in Saint Germain des Prés; weren't there sanctuaries in Paris for every passing state of the soul?

Added to which, by way of distraction between visiting the two churches, there were the Louvre and Cluny museums. Lastly, from the Benedictine point of view, now that all the monasteries of the Order were about to disappear from France, wasn't Paris the final refuge?

If the nuns of the Rue Monsieur had, as Dom de Fonneuve affirmed, already been authorised for a number of years, it would still be possible to follow the offices and hear plainchant; and for its part, was there anywhere more apt for recollection or suitable for prayer than Saint Germain des Prés, with its Lady Chapel, its tombs of the monks of Saint Maur, and its choir where monks had prayed for so many years?

'What more could you want?' he said to himself

And he encouraged himself with thoughts of these walks along the quays, spurred himself with thoughts of these churches; he would try to look forward to them, listening to see if any positive response to these exhortations rose up within him. But he heard nothing; the prospect of going back to Paris didn't appeal to him.

He would then look at the garden, which was now in the full bloom of autumn. Birds were chirping in the coppices; basil and lemon balm were starred with little white florets. The Michaelmas daisies, mints, and sages were populated with bees, which trampled over them and pumped their nectar, then raised their wings and flew off; the leaves of the chestnut trees were turning copper, and those of the maples were transforming their blood-red into bronze; the tiny spikes of the cedar were turning blue, and its branches were covered with little brown pods, and if you touched them, a sulphur-yellow dust, like that of club-moss spores, coated your fingers.

Was it the perfumed shade of this garden, its quiet wooded pathways and its beds of flowers, that kept him from desiring Paris? No, because he felt no attachment to this land or to these woods; no regret clouded the thought of leaving this countryside where, nevertheless, he'd believed he would end his days. He aspired neither to live in Paris, nor to stay in Val-des-Saints; so what then?

'What I'd like would be to stay here, but with the office and with the monks!' he exclaimed; and he started daydreaming about a sudden change in government putting things right, allowing him to stay and the monks who had left to return. It was mad, but these wild dreams only served to deepen his depression, and each time he fell back to earth after these flights of fancy, he suffered still more.

Painful as they were by day, these bouts of delirium became truly appalling at night.

As soon as the candle was out, his troubles would plague him; the darkness acted on his mind like a mirror magnifying phantasms, like a microscope making wisps of straw as large as beams. All his difficulties were exaggerated. As for the move, he'd need to bring a van from Paris. One? More like two, because his fifty boxes of books would make a vanload on their own. How much was all this going to cost?

And then to find an apartment, it was easy to say, but where? Moreover, how could he fit in all his books and objets d'art? It was no use thinking of a newly-built house, which as far as walls went, had glazed partitions and sliding doors, all with cream-coloured wainscotting and distempered ceilings. Apartments of that sort were built for people who had no furniture and even fewer books!

So it would be necessary to find a niche in some old building, but then there was the humidity, the lack of daylight, the inconvenience of poorly arranged rooms that were difficult to heat; it would be like an icebox, a cell...

'What's more, my search will be limited to the sixth and seventh arrondissements, near the Rue Monsieur if possible. Will I find the desired haven, at a reasonable price, in that neighbourhood?'

And if, when ruminating on these thoughts, he happened to doze off, his sleep would be broken and fitful, and he'd wake up again, shattered, at three in the morning; he forced himself not to open his eyes, to try and go back to sleep, in order to forget things and not to return to hateful reality; but it was no good; once awake, life's problems battered his mind like a military tattoo, and in despair he'd sit up in bed. He would light a lamp as quickly as possible to dispel these black thoughts, but the panic of the trials and tribulations to come raged like a storm; the machinery of his imagination had been set in motion and was going full steam ahead. To pull himself together he tried to recite the rosary, but the beads would run through his fingers, powerless to divert his thoughts which constantly turned on the same track.

The bells would strike four o'clock, and it was awful. Nothing was heard after that last strike. The abbey bells hadn't rung since the departure of the novices, and there was no summons to call the monks to prayer; the *Angelus* too was silent, it was as if death was in the air.

And when he'd really chewed over his troubles and fears, Durtal railed against those Catholics who continued to amuse themselves, to live as if nothing had happened, while the monks were being driven away. Newspapers, like *Le Gaulois*, with its reports of dinners, receptions and balls, left no doubt about the heartless indifference of these people. They don't care about the poor monks. Unless it's to try and get rid of them, they're too busy with the Panama scheme, and bribing the chambers.

'I'm afraid,' sighed Durtal, 'that Madame Bavoil is right when she predicts some terrible punishment; God's patience must be near its end. Moreover, nothing holds any longer, everything is collapsing; bankruptcy is everywhere – the bankruptcy of materialistic science, the bankruptcy of education in the great seminaries and Orders – a universal bankruptcy won't be slow in coming. The anarchists are perhaps right. The social edifice is so rotten, so worm-eaten, that it would be better if it collapsed, then it could be rebuilt anew afterwards.

'In the meantime, it's much to be feared that the Lord will leave us to simmer in our own juices and intervene only when we're completely cooked; if only we were like that gold in the furnace which the Bible talks about, but damn it we're only lead scrapings in a kitchen saucepan; we melt without being purified.

'Come on, I suppose I'd better get up, it's five o'clock at last.' He dressed, and went down to attend Mass in the cloister.

Like the other services, this early morning Mass in the oratory was a singularly gloomy one, lit only by candles. The abbot no longer celebrated it with his usual two assistants and the candle bearer. A single lay brother served him, the same as for any other monk.

In this small barrel-vaulted room, simply furnished with a few stalls and benches, Durtal knelt on the ground, feeling overcome with such distress that he could hardly pray; his one consolation was to take communion with the monks who weren't priests and the lay brothers. He prostrated himself with them at the feet of the abbot, while one of them recited the Confiteor, and it was very quiet this communion meal of outlaws, passing the communion cloth among themselves in brotherly fashion. And then a great silence ensued; each one crouched in the gloom, asking the Lord for the strength to endure this trial, and after the Mass, everyone went out without exchanging a word.

'My God,' thought Durtal on the way back home, 'wouldn't it have been better to cut the mooring in one stroke, rather than to drag it out and split up bit by bit like this?'

Finally, the day of departure for the abbot and the last group of monks was set. The evening before, at vespers, it unsettled

Durtal to see the old man, holding his head in his hands, without moving. When he raised his head, his face was strained, his lips trembled. He gave the signal for the beginning of the office, tapping on the pulpit with his small gavel.

And while they chanted the preliminary nones, Durtal said to himself as he listened to the psalm *In convertendo*, 'How ironic this psalm which celebrates the joy of return would be, if it weren't for the verse that says "They who sow in tears shall reap in joy." Will we ever see joy here again?'

And after vespers, at that moment when, before leaving the oratory, everyone lowered their heads in silent prayer, their faces buried in their scapulars, Durtal couldn't keep back his tears, crying to himself, 'Ah, holy mother Virgin, and you poor St Benedict, it's over, the lamp is out!'

He returned home, heartbroken. Madame Bavoil, who was reading an old book near the stove, was also overcome by a wave of sadness. They looked at each other and shook their heads. Madame Bavoil took up her book and read in a low voice:

"'Why is it, do you think, that so few reach perfection? It's because so few resolve to embrace the privations that contradict their nature, and which make them suffer, because no one wants to be crucified. Our life is spent in a spiritual theory that is seldom put into practice. Providence takes most care of those to whom it gives the finest opportunities to suffer, but God bestows his favours only on his best friends, and gives them both the occasion and the grace to endure suffering.'"

"Very true," sighed Durtal, who glanced at the volume. He recognised a very rare work of mystical theology, belonging to Abbé Gèvresin's library: *The Spiritual Works of Monsieur Bernières-Louvigni*.[5]

"My God," said Madame Bavoil, putting down her book, "who will deliver us from those workers of iniquity, from those under the spell of the synagogues and the lodges?"

"No one. There are two pretenders to the throne, Madame Bavoil, but they are waiting for France to be brought to them on a plate."

"A hot one, perhaps?"

"No, because they'd be afraid of burning their fingers. There are no real men left. Humanly speaking, there's nothing to hope for. France is like one of the vineyards around here that Father Paton was telling me about. It's infected by what they call 'root rot', it's one of the oldest diseases of the vine in Burgundy; it's not phylloxera, but it's not much better. Root rot is a fungus that rots the vine stems. They grow weak, their branches get more and more bent, like a weeping willow; finally they die and their roots are so rotten that you only need to pull lightly on the stump with your fingers to pull it out.

"At the present time they've found no effective remedy against the ravages of this parasite, any more than we know of one to stop the damage of this parliamentary root rot that's attacking us.

"This, like the other one, leaves behind it only corruption and decay. It eats away at France and putrifies it; it's the destruction of all that was honest, of all that was clean. This root rot has turned our country into a vineyard of lifeless consciences, a plantation of dead souls."

"The devils' harvest, my friend; but tell me, what time is the abbot leaving tomorrow?"

"At five o'clock."

"Are we going to the station to see him off?"

"Of course."

Early next morning they went to the station, and were joined on the way by Monsieur Lampre and Mlle de Garambois, and depressed though he was Durtal couldn't help smiling when he noticed that his sister oblate, in spite of her sadness and her eyes full of tears, hadn't been able to forget her liturgical finery. She was decked out in the colour of the day, Virgin white, but given the circumstances she'd allowed herself to break the rules a little, adding a touch of mourning to the white by sporting a violet cravat.

When they entered the waiting room they saw Baron des Atours, his wife, his daughter, and other members of the gentry from the surrounding chateaux, who were talking with the parish priest in a corner.

Durtal shook hands with the priest and greeted the other gentlemen, and for the first time they all mingled. Their shared sense of distress made them forget their squabbles and their quarrels, and brought the two groups together.

There was no doubting the sincerity of these people; they were good Catholics, and though for petty, parochial reasons they weren't fond of monasteries, under these circumstances they couldn't help deploring this odious persecution and regretting the departure of the monks.

They spoke about it sadly, and were no more hopeful than Durtal that the Benedictines would soon return to the country. To put an end to this mournful discussion, the priest announced a great item of news which he'd just received, the resignation of Monsignor Triaurault had finally been sent in and accepted, and his successor, Father Le Nordez, had been appointed.

"I know this churchman," said Monsieur Lampre in a whisper to Durtal, "and I can assure you that with him we'll be under the cosh of the Ministry of Religion, so much so that Monsignor Triaurault, who prostrated himself before the government, will look like an independent bishop in comparison to him. It's just as well the Benedictines are leaving, and I'd advise them not to return to the diocese, because he's quite capable of forbidding them to celebrate Mass."

"Here they are," exclaimed Durtal.

The door opened and the abbot appeared at the head of his monks. He looked pale and bent with grief. Behind him crowded the fathers carrying their bags and suitcases. They were barely recognisable with their clerical hats on, one was so used to seeing them bareheaded. Father Titourne had lost something of his look of a lanky Pierrot in black, though his face was paler than usual and he was fussing around two monks from the infirmary, who were leading in Father Philigone Miné, supporting him under his arms. He wanted to take off the hat they'd put on him and which was annoying him.

Baron des Atours came forward to meet the abbot and made excuses for the absence of his son, who'd gone to take his exams for naval school; then, on behalf of those with him, he offered his condolences.

Dom Bernard bowed, and especially thanked the baroness and her daughter for having come such a long way so early in the morning, for coming from their chateau to the station to bear witness to their pious sympathy for him; then at that moment, he was pushed away from them by a crowd which invaded the room. A group of peasant women from the neighouring hamlets surrounded him, moaning. "Don't lose heart," he said, "don't lose hope," and he smiled at Mlle de Garambois and Madame Bavoil, who knelt down to kiss his ring.

The sound of whistles pierced the station, the train was approaching, and for a moment there was general confusion. Father Titourne scrambled in search of the reverend abbot's suitcase, which he'd left somewhere; Dom Paton and little Brother Blanche embraced all the fathers in succession, while Dom Beaudequin, the sacristan, taking advantage of the confusion, slipped into the parish priest's party in order to pay court to the nobles.

Everyone threw themselves onto their knees. As he gave them his blessing, the abbot, usually so well able to control himself, quivered and tears sprang into his eyes. It was a relief for poor Mlle de Garambois, who was repressing her emotion, and she began to sob along with Madame Bavoil.

The stationmaster hurried the monks to get on board. It was pitiful: Father Philigone Miné had to be hoisted into the carriage. He was moaning and refusing to go. He only calmed down when the abbot seated himself beside him.

"Goodbye, my children," said his reverence, holding hands with Durtal and Monsieur Lampre through the door window, "have courage, we will meet again."

The train moved off; they knelt down on the platform and for the last time he blessed them, making a big sign of the cross, and amid clouds of steam and to the din of rolling wheels, everything disappeared.

Durtal stood up, and feeling sick with sadness saw that Brother Blanche was crying so hard tears fell from his eyes onto the ground, like drops of rain in a storm.

Father Paton came up to hug and console him.

Unable to bear any more, Durtal, fearing he might break down, left before the others and walked swiftly home.

Chapter XVI

L ife in Val-des-Saints became grim. The clock had been stopped at the very moment the abbot crossed the monastery threshold to go to the station. The hours were no longer rung, no peals, no bells. The funereal impression given off by the village was such that the peasants instinctively began to speak in an undertone, as if in a sickroom.

The inns, whose best customers had been people visiting the monastery from Dijon and the surrounding environs, were suddenly empty; the barber, whose main income came from shaving the tonsures of the monks and the beards of those on retreat, was able to close his shop every day except Saturday evening; but the tradesmen who were most directly and most promptly affected were the baker, and especially the butcher, who, for lack of sufficient sales, had to start preserving his meats, otherwise it wouldn't have been worth killing his animals. Throughout the village there was general discontent; the mayor and the municipal councillors adroitly used this against the monastery. To the complaints of the inhabitants, who reproached them for having ruined the town by their anticlerical policy, they replied: "We didn't expel the monks; if they'd asked for authorisation we would have supported their request with the prefect. They chose to rebel against the law; we had nothing to do with it, take it out on them."

And indeed the peasants did turn their indignation against the Benedictines, and even against the parish priest, who for lack of money couldn't help the unfortunate; but most of all they hated Father Paton, who put an end to their final attempt to make money by refusing to allow strangers to explore the now abandoned cloister; he wasn't easily roused, however he was cautious enough to dress the three lay brothers, who were to stay permanently with him in the empty buildings, in civilian clothes. Like Durtal, they concealed the great scapular of the Order beneath their clothes; one acted as gatekeeper and would prepare the food for the little camp, the other two worked like hired labourers in the vineyard, and lodged in an outbuilding adjoining Monsieur Lampre's house. As for Dom Beaudequin, he lived with his friend the priest, while little Brother Blanche had been taken in by Durtal.

Mlle de Garambois gave Madame Bavoil a hand with her preparations for the move and they tied up parcels together; as for Monsieur Lampre, he went backwards and forwards between Dijon and Val-des-Saints, consulting solicitors and businessmen, organising work for the defence of the abbey, fortifying it with legal procedures and precautionary measures against a possible attack.

Indeed, the police were not slow in arriving, but they found that all the papers were in order and that only one monk was living in the monastery, along with a lay gatekeeper, and so they left. Such was the state of things a few days after the departure of the abbot.

Durtal listed like some dismasted vessel, and if he hadn't had that angelic being Brother Blanche with him, he would certainly have sunk into a depression. He would never have believed that the monks had taken him so much to their hearts; the result was a sort of mirage. He no longer saw the faults, the absurdities, the blemishes, the all-too-human side of the monastery; the honest but mediocre group of monks in the middle receded into the shadows, while the two extremities, old age and youth, stood out in bright light: the old monks, those brought up according to the ancient model, who were truly imposing and truly pious, and the young novices in all the first fervour of their vocation. Thanks to these two elements, a virtue emerged from this monastery, and this virtue was akin to the power of the liturgy; its force, through daily habit, became imperceptible, like swimming with the tide, and you only realised its real power and your own weakness when its influence was removed.

In recalling the abbot, so indulgent and so kind, Dom de Fonneuve, Dom Felletin, and Father d'Auberoche, all those fathers with whom he'd spent his time and who he loved, Durtal stirred up his feelings of regret, and also stimulated his aversion to those peasants who, he knew, hated him as much as they did the Benedictines, whose friend he was.

The slogans traced in charcoal and chalk on the abbey walls and on his own – "Down with the monks! Down with the church rats! Down with the Jesuits!" – were proof of the unjustified animosity of these beggars.

'Ah,' he said to himself, 'if I hadn't promised his reverence to stay on here until the office was resumed at Moerbeke, I'd be off to Paris in a flash, and never set foot in this horrid place again.'

However, he didn't spend much time brooding over his troubles, because he never had a minute to spare. He had to go to the oratory first thing, having carefully read over the office beforehand for fear of making a mistake, and then, when he was back home, he and Brother Blanche would wrap up the most fragile of his books in paper, sort out his notes, and pack up his curios – in a word, organise everything so that the removal men had only to fill their crates and load them in their van.

Inevitably, the number of services had been reduced. Father Paton was overwhelmed with work, so he would say his matins and lauds on the way to the vineyard, and he would come back at six o'clock to celebrate a Mass which was attended by all. It was preceded by prime and terce and followed by sext recited together. After which, everyone went about their own business, and would return to the little chapel at five o'clock to chant none and vespers; compline would be recited privately at home before going to bed.

The hours of services were announced by Brother Blanche, who would ring a muffin-man's bell in the cloister; the monks would then put on their cowls and entered the little church two by two, the two fathers at the head, and the novice and the oblate behind them.

There, they split up, and after genuflecting in front of the altar they nodded to each other. Durtal would sit next to Father Paton in the stalls, Dom Beaudequin and Brother Blanche sat opposite them, on the other side of the choir.

How melancholy it was, droning the offices in the discomfort of this dark cellar! Durtal would produce a stump of a candle from his pocket which he would light and place on the edge of his desk, and then strain to read his little diurnal, the letters of which swirled around, dancing a *saltarello* of red and black before his eyes.

There were no difficulties with the little hours; besides, he knew by heart the hymns and psalms of the week, which didn't vary from Tuesday to Saturday. He had to study only those of Sunday and Monday which differed; but vespers complicated things; they were easy enough to recite, even when they were cut at the chapter and passed from one saint to another, but in the end it all got into a tangled mess; sometimes there were three commemorations and you had to remember their order, and then jump from one end of the book to the other in order to pick out the right antiphon and choose the proper prayer. In spite of all the bookmarks and all the pictures inserted between the pages, there was always a chance of mixing up the saints. With its perpetual cross references and its mistakes in pagination, what a defective instrument, what an absurd tool of prayer this diurnal was!

If only one had the time to look properly, to recover one's place, but no, in order not to spoil the office, the antiphon had to be ready and recited in time; and with the tiring business of the bows required by the doxology, with the continual leaping around of the text in the uncertain light of the candle, the liturgical exercises were a painful business.

Eventually, Durtal more or less found his way through it, but his anxiety to avoid any blunders, prevented him from praying or even from understanding the meaning of the words he was chanting. He only managed to collect his thoughts again when, just before leaving the chapel, a short moment of private prayer was allowed.

There was, however, after sext, a solemn moment when the common prayer brought everyone back to the reality of their surroundings, the moment when, to close the office, Father Paton would say in a low voice:

"*Divinum auxilium maneat semper nobiscum.*" (May God's help always be with us.)

"*Et cum fratribus nostris absentibus, amen*" (And with our absent brothers, amen), replied the three others, also lowering their voices.

In less troubled times this prayer would simply have referred to brothers who happened to be travelling; today, it applied to all the monks who had left their home, perhaps for ever; and there was a silence after this response, a reminder of the scene of boarding the train, and of the abandoment of the four of them who now found themselves in a deserted abbey; and then everyone left without having the courage to confess the sadness of his thoughts.

In the morning, when sext was over, Durtal would often wander around the gardens of the abbey and smoke a melancholy cigarette.

Neglected even before the exodus, because all the lay brothers had been employed in packing things up, the garden was already growing a little bit wild; grass was covering the paths; there were crushed tomatoes strewn all around, and bruised pears on the ground. The flowerbeds were invaded by straggly yellow weeds, wild mustard, herb bennet, silverweeds, and especially yellow rocket, a ragged-looking plant with its criss-crossing skinny stalks that resembled tiny perches for parrots; even brambles were starting to come up. Nature, no longer under surveillance, was starting to reassert herself.

Sometimes, he would walk under the novices' vine trellis with Brother Blanche. At the end of the path, they would reach the grotto where the doves and the ravens were kept. The ravens were venerable birds, having been brought from Monte Cassino, where they were bred in honour of St Benedict; as for the doves, on the feast of St Scholastica they enjoyed the privilege of being let loose in the refectory at the end of the meal, where in among the monks they would peck at the crumbs left on the tables.

These birds, who could see nothing in front of them now but a silent and deserted path, seemed bewildered. The ravens huddled together without moving, looking sullen; but the doves, recognising the young monk who usually spoiled them, fluttered against the grille in front of him; and he would open the cage and take them one by one, give them some corn to eat, and, after kissing them and assuring them he wouldn't forget them, he would put them back into their cage again, almost in tears.

"Ah," he said, "if I didn't have to travel with Father Beaudequin, who has a horror of animals, I'd bring them with me, and I'm sure his reverence wouldn't scold me too much; luckily, Dom Paton won't let them starve."

Other times, when this father wasn't going back to his vineyard after the service, the two would stay with him and help to clear up the mess in all the rooms; the floors were strewn with wood shavings, bits of paper and straw, and they would sweep them, and then fill up a wheelbarrow which they empied on a compost heap at the bottom of the vineyard.

When the cells and corridors were a little bit tidier, the monk took them up to the loft; he planned to set them in order, too, but they lacked the courage to attack the barricade of piled up pieces of furniture with which it was filled.

All the rubbish accumulated by the monastery over the years was here. The cellarer had a mania for keeping everything, and in this junk room he'd deposited all sorts of disused things and broken objects. There were sick-beds and watering cans that had lost their spouts and with leaky bottoms, dented oil cans, dead lamps; there were tables without legs, broken chairs, cracked saucepans; there were even decapitated statues of saints, everything heaped up higgledy-piggledy under a layer of dust criss-crossed by the trails of rats.

Dom Paton pulled a chair by its sole remaining leg, whereupon everything started to collapse. There was a sound of broken glass and of bits of old iron, and they were covered by a cloud of blinding dust. They braced themselves.

"It would need a squadron of skilled sappers to make a way through this jungle of rubbish!" said the monk, dusting himself off.

Durtal liked the monk for his dignity and his simple kindness; with his tall stature, his face tanned by the sun, his steel-grey eyes hidden behind large horn-rimmed spectacles, he had a somewhat gnarled and stern appearance; but a shy gentleness lay beneath this hermit-like exterior. Durtal went to him for confession, and admired his discretion, his wisdom, his self-effacement and his almost childlike love for the Virgin; he also admired the fatherly affection he showed for Brother Blanche. Had he been his own child he couldn't have treated him with more indulgence.

It's fair to say that it would have been difficult not to like this young monk, who was so naïve and so candid with his attractive face, his bright eyes, his natural laugh, and his untiring joy at serving the Lord and being a Benedictine; but, the lad's perfect innocence, his inherent, unstated piety, didn't preclude a very clear vision of his surroundings; he had a calm outlook on life which he expressed with absolute frankness, without ever worrying about the consequences.

And he was drawn to Father Emonot, who he revered and who he even approved of when he inflicted long penances on him for having spoken too freely.

"He's very fair," he said; "he often catches me without my knowing why. He explains it to me, but I don't always understand the gravity of the mistake I've committed; but if he is sure that I'm guilty, it's because I am. Ah, he never messes around, our father preceptor, but if he's strict it's because he wants to purify us, and you know if you listen carefully to his advice, if you truly consent to mortify yourself, you end up becoming a true monk."

"But it seems to me, Brother, that you do follow his advice."

"No, when I believe I'm innocent and he punishes me, deep down inside my initial reaction is to rebel. I suppress it afterwards, but I still have it. I submit, but I don't want to be humiliated; that shows you I haven't slain the old Adam inside, and how far I am from the precepts of our holy rule, which says in Chapter 5, on obedience, that 'if the disciple submits with bad grace, if he demurs not just outwardly but even in his heart, his work will not be acceptable to God, who sees the reluctance in his heart.'"

And then, after a short reflection, he added: "I'm not eager for servitude, I'm no good.

"Then, you see," he went on, "I have a cousin who was very educated and who became a Trappist; well, he wanted nothing more than to be a lay brother. Between ourselves, this is the touchstone of the two branches of the Benedictines: among the

White Monks, no one wants to be a father out of humility; among the Black Monks, none of us wants to be a lay brother."

"But… but…" cried Durtal, "everyone has their own vocation; you'll be more useful here as a monk in the choir than as a brother."

"No doubt, but it doesn't alter the fact that if I was really humble, I wouldn't have aspired to the rank of a professed monk."

"With that system, there'd be no more offices… of course, if anyone is an enthusiast for the Trappists it's me, because it was in one of their monasteries, Our Lady of the Hearth, that I encountered a saintliness I've rarely seen elsewhere; but ultimately the Cistercians have a special mission that's different to yours. There's room for all in the Church; the Orders complement one another, so let's take them for what they are, and be on our guard, brother, not to be so ambitious to be humble, because that's not so far removed from having an air of pride."

Another day, as they were both tying up bundles of pamphlets, Durtal spoke to him about the novice with freethinking proclivities who had ended up being placed in a seminary short of students, and the lad very lucidly explained this unfortunate's state of mind.

"Brother Sourche," he said, "has a true heart, but his mind is wrong; he used to read and read, but he never digested anything; his poor brain was a tangled mass of doubts and scruples; sometimes he'd rush around the corridors like a bull in a china shop; at others, he'd shut himself up in the lavatory and sob; it was all very sad, but they couldn't keep him here because his agitation created trouble all around him. He truly loved God, but in his fear of completely losing his faith he fabricated for himself a religion that was almost Protestant, without realising that by skimping on the supernatural, he ran the risk of not believing in anything at all.

"Poor Brother Sourche, if his brain wasn't quite right, his heart was excellent. There couldn't be a more affectionate or more charitable being; we were good friends, so when he left we exchanged mortification flails."

'Of course,' thought Durtal, somewhat taken aback by the strangeness of the gift, 'that's the only thing novices can call their own; they can't give each other anything else as a souvenir.'

Chapter XVI

"And what about Brother Gèdre?"

"Him? He's a model of wisdom and reason, brother 'Mouse' as we call him; together with our old saintly Brother de Chambéon he's the best of all the novices when it comes to being utterly forgetful of self and surrendering to God; and do you remember what a fine voice Brother Gèdre had? I've never heard anyone sing the second phrase of the *Gradual* in the Mass for the Blessed Virgin, the *Virgo Dei genitrix*, as he did. How well he prayed singing like that."

And he himself began to sing the passage, and hearing him, Mlle de Garambois, who was downstairs helping Madame Bavoil with the packing, recognised the plainchant immediately and rushed upstairs like a horse from the starting line.

'What a good soul she is, too, and always kind and ready to help.' Durtal regretted having to leave Val-des-Saints, however hateful it had become to him, because of her and her uncle. Monsieur Lampre obviously couldn't be expected to live in Paris, but she was different, she had always lived in the vicinity of convents, so why not settle herself there? And Durtal tried to persuade her to at least spend the winter in Paris.

But, to the great joy of little Brother Blanche, she replied:

"You've known me long enough to know that I'd spend hours on end at the patisserie; here, I can't commit the sin of gluttony because I don't have any chance to, but in Paris…"

"Are the cakes so very good, then?" asked the boy, who had hardly ever tasted one in his life.

"Yes, very good," and turning her eyes heavenwards she added, "especially with a sip of port wine afterwards." Then, recovering herself and blushing slightly, she exclaimed, "That's wicked of you, you're undoing my confession. I've just finished my penance, I wasn't thinking of anything like that, and now you're making my mouth water, talking about my gluttony…

"No," she continued, a little more calmly, "as for me, I'm a fixture here. If I were to move, it would be to go and live in the environs of an abbey; and by that I mean an abbey of monks, because among the nuns there's no ceremonial, no pontifical feasts, none of the things I love. To get them I'd have to go into exile abroad, and even then I'd be disappointed because there most probably wouldn't be, as there is here and in all our monasteries in France, a church outside the cloister and therefore accessible to women.

"So could you see me in a country where I didn't know a soul and where I couldn't follow the office? And besides, my uncle is old and this isn't the time, now when he needs me, to leave him."

"Will you at least come to Paris from time to time?"

"Ah, as to that, yes."

"And at the risk of leading her into temptation, I'll cook her a nice meal," said Madame Bavoil, who had come upstairs looking for her.

Days flowed by, but no telegram from the abbot announcing the definitive resumption of the offices at Moerbeke came.

Durtal was ready; his plan of departure decided. As soon as Dom Beaudequin and Brother Blanche had received the order to rejoin the others in Belgium, he was resolved to go to Paris. Once there, assuming that he was lucky enough to find a suitable apartment, he would make arrangements with the furniture removers; one could reckon on three days for the vans to get to Val-des-Saints, and during those three days he'd have the rooms re-papered, if necessary, leaving them to dry for the four or five days it would take to bring the furniture back to Paris.

He would therefore not return to Val-des-Saints, which would save him the cost of a railway ticket, and Madame Bavoil could take the train as soon as the vans were on their way. Mlle de Garambois had kindly offered to put her up at her home after the beds had been packed.

As he stared sadly at the flowerbeds and the trees in the garden, he said to Brother Blanche:

"I don't know if any of us will ever come here again, but if we do, what changes we'll find. Some of these old trees will be dead and some of the small ones will have grown huge; it'll all be unrecognisable; my successor will undoubtedly be less merciful than me to these poor plants, which I kept because they were dedicated to saints," and he listed them, pointing them out to the boy: "That's the primrose dedicated to St Peter, the valerian to St George, the coltsfoot to St Quirinus, the ragwort to St James, the wallflower to St Barbara, the wormwood to St John the Baptist, the fleabane to St Roch, and how many others…

"Except for the valerian growing in the wall, with its pretty blotting-paper pink blossoms, dulled by a white that seems to have been transferred to the green of its leaves, the others, which for the most part have vulgar yellow flowers, like all the plants not considered fit for flowerbeds, are ugly, and the gentleman who rents the house after me will never understand why I tolerated them."

"To leave all this is going to be painful," murmured Brother Blanche, "because you're so comfortably settled here; but what would upset me the most if I were in your place would be not being able to see Our Lady of Good Hope at Dijon any more."

"The Black Virgin exists under another name in Paris," replied Durtal, "and in her chapel in the Rue de Sèvres she's worshipped with as much fervour as that of Our Lady in Dijon; as for the White Madonnas, there's no equivalent in Burgundy of Our Lady of Victories, of Our Lady of Good Hope in Saint Séverin, of Our Lady of Paris, of Our Lady in White in Saint Germain, and the Madonna of Abbaye-aux-Bois, to name but five,"

"The fact is that, from this point of view, you'll have nothing to complain about," said the novice.

Finally, one morning, when the two of them arrived at the oratory, Father Paton showed them the telegram he'd just received. It notified them that the office had now been resumed and instructed the two monks to leave.

Even though it was expected, it was a big blow for Durtal to be parted from his little Brother Blanche; they had lived together for a week, and if the atmosphere had not been so heavy with sadness and regret their existence would have been one truly devoted to God, and truly sweet.

'Ah, Father St Benedict,' said Durtal to himself, kneeling in the chapel as the last office of the day, vespers, came to an end, 'the lamp is rekindled in Belgium, it only remains for us to blow out our poor candle,' and indeed he extinguished his little stump of a candle, a perfect symbol of the poverty of these canonical hours, chanted by only four people.

The next morning, after accompanying Brother Blanche to the railway station and giving him a goodbye hug, he went to see Monsieur Lampre, who had invited him to a farewell lunch; but the meal was a depressing one; in spite of the choice wines, they were both silent and absorbed in their thoughts. The fiasco of the abbey would end with that of the oblates; their dispersal would break all ties; both of them knew they weren't likely to see each other again.

And Durtal experienced this tenacious, haunting sensation again when he climbed aboard the express train at Dijon; his friends had accompanied him to the station platform; they shook hands, and promised to return to Val-des-Saints and to visit Paris, but when the train started off, Durtal, leaning back in his seat, had no illusions and felt himself to be truly alone, forever apart from these kind people.

And he said to himself:

'The experiment is over; Val-des-Saints is dead; I attended the monastery's funeral and I was the assistant gravedigger of its offices. That's the extent of my role as an oblate; it's over now because, today, torn from my cloister, it no longer has any reason to exist.

All the same, it has to be admitted that life is strange. Fate has ordained that I should spend two years here, only to send me back to Paris no better than I was before. Why? I don't know, but one day no doubt I will. Nevertheless, I can't help thinking there's been a blunder in this affair, that I got out at an intermediate station instead of stopping at the terminus, at the end of the line.

'Perhaps I made a mistake, a wrong assumption.

'In any case, my Lord, it's not good what I'm going to say to you, but I'm starting to distrust you a little. It looked like you were guiding me to a safe haven. I arrive – after considerable hardship – I go to sit down and the chair breaks! Does the untrustworthiness of terrestrial workmanship have an echo in the workshops of heaven? Do the celestial cabinet makers also manufacture cheap seats that collapse as soon as you sit on them?

'I'm laughing though I don't really want to, because these tunnels, of which I can't see the end, scare me. That you're acting in my best interests I'm not permitted to doubt, and I'm also very sure that you love me, and that you'll never forsake me; but – and excuse the impropriety of the proposal – put yourself in my position for a moment, and confess my dear Jesus that I'm not rambling when I swear to you that I no longer know what to do.

'Did I obey your will, or did I not obey it? I know you to be a great hunter of souls, stalking and beating them like you did mine at La Trappe. Now there, there was no mistake; by taking refuge in asceticism, I was certain to please you; the indications were clear and the responses precise. Today, you're no longer herding me, I no longer hear the echo of your orders and I'm reduced to guiding myself according to the dictats of human reason. And how little I care about that, but it's all I can hear, in default of anything better.

'Also bear in mind that I'm not alone, that I had to tow Madame Bavoil behind me and that neither of us know where we're going; it's the parable of the blind leading the blind, and perhaps the ditch is not far off.

'In a few days, if you ordain things in this way, we'll be reinstalled in that Paris which we really thought never to live in again. What will happen to us there? Will the chairs be more solid than at Val-des-Saints, or will this, too, be a stop on the way?

'All the same,' he resumed after a moment's silent thought, 'what a disaster this departure is in terms of tranquility, money, liturgical piety, friendships – of everything. I'm grumbling, but I'm not the one most to be pitied. Think of the others, those who remain, of poor Mlle de Garambois, alone, without her beloved offices; think of Monsieur Lampre, who is fighting against legal chicanery in order to save his monks; above all, think of the unfortunate Father Paton, abandoned in this hole, far from his fellow monks, with no monastic life possible.

'But their misfortune doesn't alleviate mine; alas, it only makes it worse and I shudder at the thought of returning to Paris and all that hubbub! How depressing!

'Instead of a quiet house, I'm going back to that domino box of a building divided into apartments, with threats to my peace both above and below; with hysterical women banging on pianos, and noisy kids dragging things about in the afternoon and howling at night – unless someone takes it into their head to strangle them; in summer it'll be a stuffy hothouse, and in winter, instead of my blazing pine cones, I'll have to look through a mica grill at an evil-smelling fire imprisoned in an iron stove. As for views, I'll no doubt have a landscape of chimneys. Well, in the past, I got used to thickets of tin stovepipes on zinc roofs standing out against the brackish backdrop of drizzly days. I'll get used to it again; I'll get back into the stream of things.

'And then… and then… there are so many things to atone for. If the divine chastisement is being prepared, let's offer our backs and at least show a little willingness. Even so, in the spiritual life it isn't the same as it is in real life, you can't be like the man who marries a washerwoman or a midwife, the man who just looks on and twiddles his thumbs!

'Ah, my dear Lord, give us the grace not to haggle like this; to forget ourselves once and for all; to live at last, no matter where, so long as it be far from ourselves, and close to you.'

NOTES

1 Huysmans first visted the abbey of Saint Peter at Solesmes, situated some 150 miles west of Paris, in September 1896. Although he found the relaxed rule of the Benedictines at Solesmes more conducive than the stricter rule of the Trappists (see Note 2), he felt the monastery was too large and its abbot, Dom Delatte, too authoritarian. He would make several visits to what he called the 'barracks' of Solesmes before settling on the smaller Benedictine monastery of Saint Martin in Dijon, which he depicted in the novel under the name Val-des-Saints.

2 La Trappe was Huysmans' name for the Trappist monastery Notre Dame d'Igny, which he portrayed in his fiction as Notre Dame de l'Âtre (Our Lady of the Hearth). He would make three retreats there, but ultimately found the discipline too strict.

3 An offshoot of the original Benedictine Order, the Cistercians were monks and nuns who sought to return to a stricter application of the teachings of St Benedict. They were known as White Monks because they wore a white cowl, to distinguish them from other Benedictines, who wore black habits.

4 Saint Bernard of Clairvaux (1090-1153) was a Burgundian abbot who was instrumental in the renaissance of Benedictine monasticism in the Middle Ages, and particularly in the formation of the Cistercian Order.

5 There is usually a distinction in monsteries between 'fathers' and 'brothers', though both are considered monks. The former are priests, ordained by a bishop, who have subsequently become monks; the latter are lay brothers who are attached to the monastery but who haven't been ordained. I have generally used the term 'priest' to refer to a parish or diocesan priest, and 'father' to refer to a monk who is also a priest, as Huysmans was careful to distinguish between the two, and point out the antagonisms that often existed between the two religious factions.

6 Huysmans uses a mixture of real and fictional names in the course of his post-conversion novels. All three monks mentioned here are references to real individuals: Paul Delatte (1848-1937) was a Benedictine monk, and abbot of the abbey of Saint Pierre, Solesmes, from 1890 to 1921; André Mocquereau (1849-1930) was a monk and Gregorian musicologist at the abbey of Solesmes who had a great influence on the restoration of Gregorian chant; Paul Cagin (1847-1923) was another monk at Solesmes who made his name through his work on the liturgy.

7 See Note 2.

8 Walafrid Strabo (c. 808-849), was a Benedictine monk and theological writer, known for his treatises on herbals and medicine.

CHAPTER II

1 Benedict of Aniane (*c.* 747-821), known as the 'Second Benedict', was a Benedictine monk and monastic reformer.

2 Prosper Louis Pascal Guéranger (1805-1875) was a French priest and reforming Benedictine monk. He founded the monastery at Solesmes on the ruins of a former priory, and was the abbot there for nearly forty years. He was also the author of *L'Année liturgique* ('The Liturgical Year'), a popular commentary covering every day of the Catholic Church's liturgical cycle.

3 The *Ordo Divini Officii recitandi Sacrique peragendi* was a list or directory of offices and feasts for each day of the year.

4 A character in Victor Hugo's novel *Les Misérables* (1862), Mademoiselle de Blemeur was the prioress of Petit-Picpus convent, a short, stout, sixty-year-old woman who was "lettered, learned, competent, versed in the curiosities of history, stuffed with Latin, Greek and Hebrew, and more a monk than a nun".

5 The canonical hours mark the divisions of the day in terms of fixed times for prayer. A book of hours, chiefly a breviary, normally contains a version of, or a selection from, such prayers. In general, the canonical hours are as follows: vigil (eighth hour of night: 2 a.m.); matins (from 3 a.m. to dawn); lauds (dawn; approximately 5 a.m.); prime (early morning, the first hour of daylight); terce (9 a.m.); sext (noon); nones (3 p.m.); vespers (approximately 6 p.m.); compline (end of the day before retiring, approximately 7 p.m.).

6 The Exaltation of the Holy Cross is a liturgical feast celebrated on 14 September to honour the cross on which Christ was crucified. The Roman Catholic Church adopted the feast in the seventh century.

7 The nomenclature for ranking the various feast days of saints and Christian mysteries is a somewhat complex and confusing one, and includes 'Simple', 'Semi-Double', 'Major Double', 'Double', 'Double of the First Class', and 'Double of the Second Class'. The term probably derives from the fact that matins was 'doubled' on a particular feast day i.e. the first matins being for the day of the week, the 'double' being that for the feast day.

8 This refers to the tradition of having two lecterns on either side of the altar, one containing the Epistle, the other the Gospel, from which readings are made during Mass. The Gospel side is to the right of the priest, or the left-hand side of the altar as seen from the congregation.

9 Khosrow II (*c.*570-628) was the last significant king of Iran before the Muslim conquest five years after his death. Huysmans' fanciful version of his life has only a faint parallel with actual historical events.

Notes

10 The True Cross refers to the physical remnants claimed by various churches to be from the cross on which Christ was crucified. These relics were believed to have healing or mystical properties. A reliquary in Notre Dame in Paris supposedly contains fragments of the True Cross.

11 *Vexilla Regis* by Venantius Fortunatus (530-609) is considered one of the greatest hymns of the liturgy. It was written in honour of the arrival of the True Cross sent to Queen Radegunda by the Emperor Justin II.

12 Fernand Cabrol (1855-1937) was a French theologian, associated with the liturgical revival. He was the co-founder of the *Dictionnaire d'archéologie chrétienne et de liturgie*, which he published with Henri Leclercq. His *Livre de la prière antique* was published in 1900.

13 Two statues in Chartres cathedral representing a seated Virgin Mary with the child Jesus on her lap. The original Our Lady of the Cave dated from the eleventh or twelfth century, but was burned during the Revolution and replaced in the nineteenth century. Our Lady of the Pillar dates from the early sixteenth century, it was known as the Black Virgin due to the colour of the wood or the patina it had aquired, but in 2013 it was restored to its original colours and no longer appears black.

14 Louis II de la Trémoille (1460-1525) was a French general who served under Charles VIII, Louis XII and Francis I.

15 Joseph Gaudrillet was the author of *Histoire de l'image miraculeuse de Notre Dame de Bon-Espoir*, first published in Dijon in 1733. The original book describes Gaudrillet on the title page as a *mépartiste*, which signified a community of priests who were attached to a particular parish but who didn't derive their income from it.

Chapter III

1 The abbot of a Benedictine monastery traditionally washed the hands of guests.

2 Jean-Baptiste-François Pitra (1812-1889) was a French cardinal and theologian. He joined the abbey at Solesmes in 1841 and made numerous voyages to Belgium, Netherlands, Britain, Germany and Switzerland in the course of his studies.

3 In the original Huysmans uses the word 'neume', a group of notes sung to a single syllable. I've substituted the word 'trill' here as it implies the flourishes and embellishments that Huysmans felt were spoiling the plainchant neume.

4 The 'Common of Saints' is the part of the Christian liturgy that consists of texts common to an entire category of saints, such as apostles or martyrs. The term is used in contrast to the 'Ordinary', which is that part of the liturgy that is reasonably constant, or at least selected without

regard to date, and to the 'Proper', which is the part of the liturgy that varies according to the date, either representing an observance within the liturgical year, or a particular saint or significant event. Commons contain collects, psalms, readings from scripture, prefaces, and other portions of services that are common to a category of saints. This contrasts with propers, which contain the same elements as commons, but are tailored to specific occasions or feasts. Commons may be used to celebrate lesser feasts and observances in the Church calendar.

5 The Dreyfus Affair was perhaps the most divisive issue in French politics at the end of the nineteenth century. Centred around an accusation of treason against a Jewish army officer, it became the locus of antisemitic invective, a *cause célèbre* in which conservative Republicans, militarists, royalists and Catholics were ranged against left-wing Republicans and progressives. Zola's famous *J'accuse* (1898) denounced the persecution of Dreyfus as illegal and antisemitic.

6 Henri Brisson (1835-1912), was a French statesman. As a leader of the radicals he actively supported the ministries of Waldeck-Rousseau and Combes, especially concerning the laws on the religious Orders and the separation of Church and State. He was prime minister during the Dreyfus Affair, and spoke out in favour of the latter's innocence.

7 The Congregation of Saint Maur, also known as Maurists, was a congregation of French Benedictines, established in 1621 and known for their high level of scholarship. The congregation, which took its name from St Maurus (d.565), a disciple of St Benedict, was suppressed and its superior-general executed during the French Revolution.

8 Dom Jean Mabillon (1632-1707) was a French Benedictine monk and scholar of the Congregation of Saint Maur. He is considered the founder of the disciplines of palaeography and diplomatics.

9 The National Charter School is a French institution of higher education, founded in 1821. It is located in Paris in the Latin Quarter and specialises in supporting historical disciplines.

10 Nitrated lemonade: nitric acid diluted with water and sweetened. It was used as a mild laxative.

CHAPTER IV

1 Jacques Paul Migne (1800-1875) was a French priest who published inexpensive and widely distributed editions of theological works. Migne's *Patrologia Latina* ('The Latin Patrology') is an enormous collection of the writings of the Church Fathers and other ecclesiastical writers which was published between 1841 and 1855.

2 Rabanus Maurus (*c.*780-856) was a Benedictine monk, theologian and

Notes

author. Although he was subsequently qualified as a saint, he is not the St Maurus (512-584) referred to elsewhere, who was St Benedict's disciple and the inspiration for the Congregation of Saint Maur.

3 The Court of Miracles (*cour des miracles*) referred to slum districts of Paris where unemployed migrants from rural areas resided. Victor Hugo used the term in *Les Misérables* and *The Hunchback of Notre-Dame*. The name stemmed from the observation that many of those begging pretended to be blind or crippled, but at the end of the day would return home able to both see and walk.

Chapter V

1 The decorative gargoyles on the western façade representing human beings, animals and monsters were made in 1880-1882, during the restoration of the church. According to the archives, they were the work of seven Parisian sculptors: Chapot, Corbel, Geoffroy, Lagoule, Pascal, Thiébault and Tournier.

2 In the original, Huysmans refers to *poires d'angoisse*, a medieval form of torture in which a pear-shaped metal ball was inserted in the mouth, it was made of rounded segments which when progressively screwed opened out, painfully stretching the mouth and throat.

3 The automata represented a man with a hammer who would strike the hours on the bell of a clock located on the exterior wall of the church.

4 Épinal prints were prints on popular subjects rendered in bright sharp colours, sold in France in the nineteenth century. The first publisher of this type of image – Jean-Charles Pellerin – was born in Épinal and named the printing house he founded in 1796, *Imagerie d'Épinal*.

5 Aloysius Bertrand was the pen name of Louis Jacques Napoléon Bertrand (1807-1841), a French Romantic poet, playwright and journalist. He is credited with introducing prose poetry to French literature, and is considered a forerunner of the Symbolist movement. His collection of prose poems, *Gaspard de la Nuit*, was published posthumously in 1842.

6 Louis-Joseph Yperman (1856-1935), born in Bruges (Belgium), he studied with Maillot, Bonnat and Bouguereau.

7 Gérard van Caloen (1853-1932), born in Belgium, was a Benedictine monk in Maredsous. He was the founder and superior of several abbeys, including Notre Dame de Monserrat in Brazil, of which he was abbot.

8 Saint Pantaleon was martyred during the Diocletian persecution of 305 AD. Information about him is scarce and some consider the stories of his life and death to be purely legendary.

9 The term 'octave' is usually applied to the eight days during which certain major feasts, such as Christmas or Easter, came to be observed.

10 *Délectation morose* in the original. The Latin concept on which it is based, *delectatio morosa*, is found in Thomas Aquinas' *Summa theologica* and can be defined as 'the habit of dwelling with enjoyment on evil thoughts'.

11 The *Hôtel de Vogüé* is a seventeenth century townhouse, situated at 8 Rue de la Chouette, close to the church of Notre Dame de Dijon.

12 The *Maison des Cariatides* is a historic house dating from 1603, situated at 28, Rue Chaudronnerie.

13 *Échauguette* in the original. This is a kind of fortified oriel window, protruding from the main façade of a house and supported by corbels. The example in the Rue Vannerie dates from the sixteenth century and has an ornately sculptured base.

14 The *Touring Club de France* (1890-1983) was a French social club dedicated to travel, founded by bicycle enthusiasts. By the turn of the century there were branches all over France.

15 In the original, the name used is *La Menagère*, which was a branch of a Parisian store called *À la Ménagère*, created in 1863 and intended mainly for women. The Dijon store located at 73 Rue de la Liberté was set up by Georges Maugey and opened in 1897.

16 The brand *Au Pauvre Diable* was created in 1831, but the department store in the Rue de la Liberté in Dijon was erected in 1875 by a former department manager of Printemps in Paris. It was one of a number of shops, such as *Au quat'sous, Au diable par la queue, Au bon marché*, and *Au Gain Petit*, that targetted a less wealthy clientele during the nineteenth century, and which marked the rise of department stores and mass trade.

17 *Aux Cent Mille Paletots* in the original. This was another discount clothing store. In 1901 it was involved in a scandal after it was accused of being little more than a sweatshop. The socialist leader Jean Jaurès was caught up in it as he edited a newspaper that had connections with the store and refused to criticise its exploitative practices.

18 The monument was put up in honour of those in Dijon who resisted the German army during the 1870 invasion.

19 Before famously spending forty years on top of a pillar, the ascetic Simeon Stylites lived at the bottom of a well or cistern.

20 Dom Luc d'Achery (1609-1685) was a French Benedictine monk in the Congregation of Saint Maur, and librarian at the abbey of Saint Germain des Prés. He wrote on the ecclesiastical history of the Middle Ages but his most important work was a collection of ancient texts, *Spicilegium, sive Collectio veterum aliquot scriptorum qui in Galliae bibliothecis, maxime Benedictinorum, latuerunt* (Paris, 1655-1677).

21 Grimlaicus was a cleric who lived in the ninth or tenth century, known

only for his book on how to lead a solitary life in a monastic community, *Regula solitariorum*, which drew heavily on the Rule of St Benedict.

22 Louis-Antoine Augustin Pavy (1805-1866) was a French Catholic priest. Huysmans is probably referring to his early books *Les Cordeliers de l'Observance à Lyon* (1836), and *Lettres sur le célibat ecclésiastique* (1851).

23 The Camaldolese was a monastic Order founded by the Italian monk, Saint Romuald (*c*.950-c.1025). It sought to integrate earlier eremitical traditions with monastic communal life.

24 Aelred of Rievaulx (1110-1167) was a Cistercian monk, abbot of Rievaulx Abbey in Yorkshire. The work Huysmans alludes to is *De institutione inclusarum* ('The Formation of Anchoresses'), which was written in 1160–62.

25 Hippolyte Hélyot (1660-1716) was a Franciscan friar who wrote on the history of religious Orders. *L'Histoire des ordres monastiques, religieux et militaires, et des congregations séculaires de l'un et de l'autre sexe, qui ont été établis jusqu'à présent* was his most important work, eventually being published in eight volumes, with Hélyot writing the first five.

26 In the original Huysmans uses the phrase *passer à la coupelle*, which means to go through a severe examination or a rigorous trial.

Chapter VI

1 Jean-Gaspard Deburau (1796-1846) was a celebrated Bohemian-French mime, whose most famous pantomimic creation was the white-costumed and white-faced clown, Pierrot. Huysmans had first written about Deburau in *Croquis parisiens* (*Parisian Sketches*) in 1880.

2 Jean Mabillon's *Annales Ordinis Sancti Benedicti* appeared in 1739; Gian Benedetto Mittarelli (1707-1777) was an Italian monk and monastic historian, a member of the Camaldolese Order at the monastery of Saint Michael, on the island of Murano in the Venetian Lagoon. Along with Anselmo Costadoni (1714-1785), he published *Annales Camaldulenses ordinis S. Benedicti, ab anno 907 ad annum 1770* (Annals of the Camaldolese of the Order of St Benedict, 907-1770) in nine volumes between 1755 and 1773); Charles du Fresne, sieur du Cange (1610-1688) was a philologist and historian, his most important work was his *Glossarium ad scriptores mediae et infimae Latinitatis* ('Glossary of writers in medieval and late Latin') which was published in three volumes in 1678; Ursmer Berlière (1861-1932) was a monk at Maredsous monastery, and a prolific author. The journal *Messager des Fidèles*, founded in 1884-5, was renamed the *Revue Bénédictine* in 1890.

3 Angelo Manrique (1577-1649), his *Cisterciensium seu verius ecclesiasticorum annalium* ('Cistercian Annals') was published in Latin in four volumes;

NOTES

Pierre Le Nain (1640-1713) was a Trappist monk and author of *Essai sur l'histoire de l'Ordre de Citeaux* ('An essay on the history of the Cistercians'), published in 1696; *Annales de l'abbaye d'Aiguebelle: de l'ordre de Citeaux* was written by a monk at the abbey, Hugues Séjalon (1824-1890), and published in 1863; Henri d'Arbois de Jubainville (1827-1910) was a French historian, philologist and Celtic scholar. His book *Etudes sur l'état intérieur des abbayes cisterciennes, et principlament de Clairvaux aux XIIe et XIIIe siècles* was published in 1858.

4   There seems to be little information about the term *converti barbati*, which appears to have been used during the Middle Ages to refer to masons or builders under ecclesiastical control.

5   Félicie d'Ayzac (1801-1881) was a French poet and historian, who wrote mostly on ecclesiastical art and sculpture. Her *Histoire de l'abbaye de Saint-Denis* was published in 1860.

6   Étienne Cartier (1813-1887) was the author of *Études sur l'art chrétien* (1875), *Les Sculptures de Solesmes* (1877), and *L'Art chrétien, lettres d'un solitaire* (1881). His *Vie de Fra Angelico de Fiesole de l'ordre des frères prêcheurs* was published in 1857.

7   Bernhard Pez (1683-1735) was an Austrian Benedictine historian and librarian. His *Thesaurus anecdotorum novissimus* (1721-29) is a collection in six volumes of theological, historical and literary sources.

8   An Ordinary was an officer of the church, such as a diocesan bishop or his equivalent, and applied to someone with ordinary authority in church law over a group of clergy, over the members of a religious Order, or over certain pastoral concerns in a specific geographical area.

9   The monastery of Tor de' Specchi ('Tower of Mirrors') is the home of the oblates of St Frances of Rome. It was established in 1433, by the foundress of the community, St Frances (1384-1440).

10 The Benedictine monastery of Pierre-qui-Vire in the Yonne was founded in 1850 by Jean-Baptise Muard (1809-54).

11 See Chapter III, Note 2. *Spicilegium Solesmense* was a collection of manuscripts and documents in Latin covering the ecclesiastical history of Solesmes, published by Dom Pitra in four volumes between 1852-58.

12 Jean-Martial Besse (1861-1920) was a Benedictine monk and writer. He was also Huysmans' spiritual director. His book *Les moines d'Orient antérieurs au Concile de Chalcédoine* was published in 1900.

13 A seventeenth-century movement closely linked to Jansenism, the *Solitaires* were Frenchmen who chose to live a humble and ascetic life in retreat at Port Royal des Champs.

14 A light breakfast allowed on fast days in the Roman Catholic Church.

15 The whip used for mortification of the flesh, referred to as a 'discipline',

had seven cords, to represent the seven deadly sins that were to be expiated, and the seven virtues that the monk worked to emulate.

16 Louis Duchesne (1843-1922) was a French priest and philologist who adopted a critical approach in his histories of Christianity and Roman Catholic liturgy, and applied scientific methods in his research; Elphège Vacandard (1849-1927) was a French Catholic priest and the author of several lives of saints. Like Duchesne, he adopted a more rigorously scientific or critical mode of research. His *Vie de Saint Bernard abbé de Clairvaux* was published in 1895.

17 The 1901 Law of Associations abolished all restrictions on the right of association for legal purposes, with the exception of religious associations because they were directed from abroad. The Law effectively suppressed many of the religious associations in France and confiscated their property.

CHAPTER VII

1 The Samoyedic people are a collection of several semi-nomadic peoples in Siberia, Their traditional way of life revolved around hunting, fishing and raising reindeer.

2 The Beuron school was founded by Benedictine monks in Germany in the late nineteenth century and sought to emphasise the spiritual or mystical aspect of a scene, rather than its psychological or visual realism. It often incorporated elements of ancient Egyptian, Greek, Roman, Byzantine and early Christian art.

3 The O Antiphons are *Magnificat* antiphons used at vespers on the last seven days of Advent. They date to at least the sixth century in Italy, as Boethius refers to them in *The Consolation of Philosophy*.

4 Henri des Houx was the pseudonym of Henri Durand Morimbau (1848-1911) a French Catholic journalist. He wrote for *Le Matin*, which had a moderate Republican agenda and was opposed to socialist ideas.

5 Rogier van der Weyden (*c.*1400-1464) was an Early Netherlandish painter whose surviving works consist mainly of religious triptychs and altarpieces. Along with Robert Campin and Jan van Eyck, he is considered one of the most influential Northern painters of the fifteenth century.

6 Hrotsvitha (*c.*935-973) was a secular canoness at Gandersheim abbey. She was one of the few women who wrote about life in the early Middle Ages whose work survives. The book Huysmans refers to, *Théatre de Hrotsvitha, religieuse d'Allemande*, is a translation into French of Hrotsvitha's six plays by Charles Magnin, published in 1845. The book doesn't include 'The Passion of Saint Gandolphe, Martyr', which is

actually an elegiac poem not a play, but Magnin gives an outline of it in his preface, the details of which Huysmans relies on.

7   Huysmans' reference in the original is a little obscure, referring to a small pastry like an eclair known as a *beignet*, or *pets de soeurs* (literally nuns' farts). I have made the allusion slightly more obvious.

CHAPTER VIII

1   Until 1955, when Pope Pius XII abolished all but three liturgical octaves, the Latin Church celebrated Epiphany as an eight-day feast, known as the Octave of Epiphany (6 January to 13 January).

2   In the original Huysmans uses the expression *faire sa tata*, which can mean to make oneself look important, or to play the busybody, but which was also a slang expression implying homosexuality. It's not exactly clear whether this is what Huysmans is implying here, but the other phrases used – *coqueter, jouer de l'eventail, apprehendant…un rapt*, do seem to reinforce this, as does his reference to the priest as a *jeune paysanne* (young peasant girl).

3   In canon law, the term *in commendam* was originally applied to the provisional occupation of an ecclesiastical benefice, which was temporarily without an actual occupant.

4   Urbain Plancher (1667-1750), was a French historian and a Benedictine belonging to the Congregation of Saint Maur, and the Saint Bénigne abbey in Dijon. He was the author of *Histoire générale et particulière de Bourgogne,* which appeared in three volumes in 1739, 1741 and 1748.

5   In Ezekiel 9, God ordered the foreheads of those to be saved in Jerusalem to be marked with the last letter of the Hebrew alphabet, shaped like a T.

6   Diplomatics is the critical analysis of historical documents, focussing on the conventions, protocols and uses of a document and its creator. The word was coined by the Benedictine monk Jean Mabillon, who published his treatise, *De re diplomatica* ('On the Study of Documents') in 1681.

7   Laurent Anisson (*c.*1600-1672) was a printer who produced some important collections, including works by the Church Fathers. His son Jean Annison (1642-1721) also directed the *Imprimerie royale* at the Louvre.

8   Edmé Bouchardon (1698-1762) was a French sculptor. His bas-relief representing the stoning of St Étienne was originally in the old Church of Saint Étienne in Dijon, but after the church's destruction in 1794 it was integrated into Saint Bénigne.

9   Jules-Félix Coutan (1848-1939) was a French sculptor and educator. A student at the *École des Beaux-Arts*, he would later teach there. His work was in the Academic tradition and he was hostile to Rodin and the Impressionist sculptors who followed him, hence Huysmans'

contemptuous attitude.

10 Adolphe Yvon (1817-1893) was a French painter known for his paintings of the Napoleonic Wars. Yvon studied under Paul Delaroche, rose to fame during the Second Empire, then finished his career as a teacher.

11 Horace Vernet (1789-1863) a French painter typically of military and Orientalist subjects. Huysmans criticised his work in *L'Art moderne* (*Modern Art*) in 1883.

12 Gustave Moreau (1826-1898) was a French artist who was emblematic in Huysmans' earlier work, most notably *À rebours* (*Against Nature*) of 1884.

13 Anatole Devosge (1770-1850) was a French painter. Born in Dijon, he was the son of the painter François Devosge and grandson of sculptor Claude François Devosge. He studied under Jacques-Louis David.

14 Huysmans' original description uses a more convoluted phrase: *Le lion était issu, en droite ligne, d'une lionne de tête de chenet et d'un lion de descente de lit* ('The lion was a straight cross between an andiron lioness and a lion-skin rug').

15 Alphonse Legros (1837-1911) was a painter, etcher, sculptor and medalist. Huysmans had praised Legros as an artist as early as 1876, but he gets a number of details wrong in his description of the picture: the woman in the foreground is kneeling not standing and only one of the women is wearing fingerless mittens.

16 Aimé-Charles-Horace His de la Salle (1795-1878) was a French art collector who specialised in drawings by the old masters, including Poussin, Fra Angelico, van Leyden and Géricault. He donated a large number of paintings and drawings to French museums, including 450 drawings to the Louvre.

17 Philip II the Bold (1342-1404) was Duke of Burgundy and *jure uxoris* Count of Flanders, Artois and Burgundy. He was the fourth and youngest son of King John II of France and Bonne of Luxembourg, and was the founder of the Burgundian branch of the House of Valois.

18 John the Fearless (1371-1419) was the son of Philip the Bold and ruled the Burgundian State from 1404 until his death. He was behind the murder of the king's brother, his uncle, the Duke of Orléans, an act which ultimately led to his own assassination in 1419.

19 Jean de Marville (d. 1389) was a sculptor known for his work for Philip the Bold, Duke of Burgundy, in the Champnol monastery, where the Duke is buried. He also established an important school of sculpture at a time when Burgundy was becoming a major cultural centre.

20 Claus Sluter (1340-1405 or 1406) was a Dutch sculptor who became court sculptor to Phillip the Bold. As well as the duke's tomb, he was also responsible for *The Well of Moses*, which Huysmans talks about in

Chapter XII, and which was considered his most important work.

21 Claus de Werve (*c*.1380-1439) was a Dutch sculptor. In 1396 he became the assistant to his uncle, Claus Sluter, at the Burgundian court in Dijon and helped to carve the mourners on the tomb of Philip the Bold.

22 Both Jehan de la Huerta and Antoine Le Moiturier were sculptors who worked in Jean de Marville's studio.

23 Jacques de Baerze (active *c*.1384-*c*.1399) was a Flemish sculptor in wood, two of whose major carved altarpieces survive in Dijon.

24 Huysmans' description is not quite accurate; the king making what appears to be a salute is the one holding the container and who has a more rustic looking face, while the third king holding his finger up carries nothing in his other hand.

25 Jacques Daret (*c*.1404-*c*.1470) was a Netherlandish painter born in Tournai, now in Belgium. He was a pupil in the studio of Robert Campin alongside Rogier van der Weyden, and afterwards became a master in his own right.

26 Robert Campin (*c*.1375-1444) is now usually identified with the Master of Flémalle, though at the time Huysmans was writing this was not the case. Although he is considered to be the first great master of Flemish painting, the attribution of Campin's paintings has been a matter of debate for many years, as he did not sign or date any of his works.

27 The Order of the Golden Fleece was a Catholic chivalric Order created by Philip the Good in 1430.

28 Charles the Bold (1433-1477) was the Duke of Burgundy from 1467.

29 *The Virgin in Glory* (*c.* 1440) at the Granet Museum, Aix-en-Provence is now attributed to Robert Campin.

30 *Virgin and Child Before a Firescreen* is now attributed to Robert Campin or to his workshop.

31 A character in Flaubert's *Madame Bovary* (1857), Monsieur Homais became a byword for the hypocrisy and moral posturing of the middle classes.

CHAPTER IX

1 The third note, essentially the note halfway between the tonic and dominant scale.

2 The term Third Order signifies the lay members of a religious Order who don't necessarily live inside the community but can wear the habit and participate in its activities.

3 Luc-Anatole Foucher (1851-1923) studied painting in Paris and became an oblate in 1883. He moved to Ligugé in 1885, where Huysmans himself would move in 1899.

4 In the Roman Catholic Church the Pontifical is the liturgical book that

contains the rites and ceremonies usually performed by bishops.

5 The corporal is a square white linen cloth on which the chalice and paten are placed during communion.

6 The caravel was a small, highly-manoeuverable sailing ship, developed in the fifteenth century by the Portuguese. It is surprising how many metaphors and allusions to the sea that Huysmans makes, given that he had little affinity or connection with it, and lived his whole life inland.

7 The liturgical feasts throughout the year as given in the Roman Missal.

8 From the Latin *Improperia*, the Reproaches refer to Christ's 'reproaches' to his people for having rejected him. They are sung in the Catholic liturgy as part of the Passion, usually on the afternoon of Good Friday.

CHAPTER X

1 Émile Loubet (1838-1929) was President of France during the period the Law of Associations was being promulgated.

2 Georges Trouillot (1851-1916) was a French Radical politician who along with Pierre Waldeck-Rousseau played a central role in developing the 1901 Law of Associations.

3 The Panama scandal erupted in 1892, with accusations of corruption that involved a number of prominent French government ministers and officials. Linked to a French company's failed attempt to construct the Panama Canal, it was perhaps the largest monetary corruption scandal of the nineteenth century. Due to the involvement of the Jewish banker, Baron Reinach, the scandal became a catalyst for antisemitic feeling, which was further exacerbated by the Dreyfus Affair, and those on the right used it to attack left-wing Republicans in government.

4 Ernest Monis (1846-1929) and Alexandre Millerand (1859-1943) were both socialist politicians during the Third Republic, who held positions in Waldeck-Rousseau's cabinet (1899-1902), the former as Minister of Justice, and the latter as Minister of Commerce, Industry, Posts, and Telegraphs; Pierre Waldeck-Rousseau (1846-1904) was the Prime Minister of France (1899-1902). His administration put forward the 1901 Law of Associations which would eventually lead to the official separation of Church and State in 1905.

5 Huysmans uses the phrase *Avec ressemblance garantie*, the words which formed the advertising slogan for early photographic portraits.

6 Alongside the reference to the golden calf, a symbol for idolatry, Huysmans also uses the term *vache à Colas*, which was a French expression from the beginning of the seventeenth century. It referred to an anecdotal story in which a cow belonging to a Catholic peasant strayed into a Protestant temple and was butchered and eaten by

Notes

Huguenots. Among Catholics, the phrase was emblematic of the predations of Protestants.

7 The Concordat was an agreement executed by Napoleon Bonaparte and clerical and papal representatives from Rome and Paris, on 15 July 1801. It determined the role and status of the Roman Catholic Church in France, and also gave Napoleon the authority to nominate bishops, redistribute parishes and bishoprics, and establish seminaries. Although it restored some autonomy to the Church after the French Revolution, its provisions were largely favourable to the state.

Chapter XI

1 Ernest Vallé (1845-1920) was a French lawyer and politician who was Minister of Justice from 1902 to 1905.

2 Jean Fouquet (c.1420-1481) was an influential French painter and miniaturist; Jacquemart of Hesdin (c.1355-c.1414) was a French miniaturist working in the Gothic style; André Beauneveu (c.1335-c.1400) was a Netherlandish sculptor and painter known for his naturalistic work in the sculptural style for King Charles V and Duke Jean de Berry; Simon Marmion (c.1425-1489) was a painter of panels and illuminated manuscripts whose patron was Philip the Good; the Limbourg brothers (Herman, Paul, and Johan) from the city of Nijmegen, were painters active in the early fifteenth century in France and Burgundy, who worked in the International Gothic style; Jean Bourdichon (c.1459-1521) was a French miniature painter and manuscript illuminator at the court of France.

3 St Majolus of Cluny (c.906-994), the fourth abbot of Cluny monastery; St Odilo (c.962-1049), the abbot of Cluny who oversaw the monastery's rise in the tenth century; St Hugh of Cluny (1024-1109), an influential leader of the monastic Orders and abbot of Cluny for over 50 years until his death; Peter the Venerable (c.1092-1156), abbot of Cluny; Syrus was a monk at Cluny whose life of St Majolus was composed c.1010; Jotsald of St Claude (died c.1052), a monk who had accompanied St Odilio on his travels; Rodulfus Glaber (985-c.1050), his best known work was the *Historiarum libri quinque ab anno incarnationis DCCCC usque ad annum MXLIV* ('History in five books from 900 AD to 1044 AD').

4 Little is known of the architects Gauzon and Hazelon. According to legend, St Peter revealed the plan of the monastery to the monk Gauzon when he was asleep.

5 Eugène Emmanuel Viollet-le-Duc (1814-1879) was a French architect and author who restored many prominent medieval landmarks in France. His most significant projects included Notre Dame de Paris, the Basilica of Saint Denis, Mont Saint Michel, Sainte Chapelle, and

NOTES

the medieval walls of the city of Carcassonne.

6 Eulalie Bouasse-Lebel (1809-1898) was a French publisher, the daughter of Jacques-Auguste Lebel, a Parisian printer. In 1845 she founded her own printing firm under the name 'Madame Bouasse, née Lebel' which focussed on religious imagery using modern printing techniques, including chromolithography. The firm was subsequently run by her son.

7 The preface to the Eucharistic prayer begins with the words, "It is very meet and just, right and salutary".

CHAPTER XII

1 The Chartreuse de Champmol was a Carthusian monastery on the outskirts of Dijon. It was founded in 1383 by Philip the Bold to provide a dynastic burial place for the Valois Dukes of Burgundy, and dissolved in 1791 during the French Revolution.

2 Jean Malouel (*c*.1365-1415) was a Dutch artist who worked in the International Gothic style. He was the court painter of Philip the Bold and his successor, John the Fearless.

3 Gambrinus was a legendary figure, celebrated in Europe as an icon of beer, brewing and joviality. He was traditionally represented as a stout, bearded duke or king, holding a tankard.

4 *palettes pour battre les bouchons* in the original. The *jeu de palets* was a traditional game involving wooden discs that had to be thrown close to a smaller disc (*le bouchon*).

5 The Brethren of the Common Life was a Catholic pietist community founded in the Netherlands in the fourteenth century by Gerard Groote (1340-1384) and Floris Radewyns (*c.* 1350-1400). Although there were no formal or irrevocable vows, the Brethren gave up their worldly goods and aimed to live chaste, regulated lives in communal houses. They attended divine service, worked, and took communal meals that were accompanied by readings from the scriptures.

6 In the original Huysmans adds a detail about Christ leaning on a spade, because when he first appeared to Mary Magdalene she mistook him for a gardener. In paintings of the resurrection from the Middle Ages, Christ is often shown holding a spade.

CHAPTER XIII

1 This powerful image of Sorrow consummating her love for Christ on the cross undoubtedly owes something to Félicien Rops' transgressive and 'pornographic' images of crucifixions featuring naked women, which Huysmans had also written about in *Certains* (*Certain Artists*) in 1889.

2 In the symbolism of numbers eleven was seen as transgressive because it

both broke the perfect ten, and was less than the equally perfect twelve.

3   This refers to a story in the Bible where Jesus was at the home of two sisters, Martha and Mary. While Martha went to make food, Mary sat and listened to Jesus speaking. When Martha complained at being left alone to do the physical work, Jesus replied that Mary had chosen the better path and that only one thing was needed i.e. the Word.

4   The title 'Confessor' is usually given to someone who has suffered for the faith; the term 'Hiero-confessor' usually applies to someone who has suffered for the faith, but who was also a bishop.

5   The Proper of the Saints (*Proprium Sanctorum*) lists the feast days of a range of saints.

6   Named after Francisco de Quiñones (1482-1540), this simplified breviary, undertaken by the order of Pope Clement, eliminated elements such as hymns and antiphons.

CHAPTER XIV

1   Jeanne Chézard de Matel (1596-1670) was a French mystic who founded the Order of the Incarnate Word and Blessed Sacrament, a religious community for women that had houses in Avignon, Grenoble, Lyon, and Paris.

2   The origin of this expression is thought to have come from an old Norman law giving someone who had signed a contract the right to retract within twenty-four hours.

3   The *Bazar de la Charité* (Charity Bazaar) was an annual charity event organised by the Catholic aristocracy in Paris. In 1897 there was a huge fire at the Bazaar in which over 120 people died, including a number of high profile donors. Some people, such as Léon Bloy, saw in the event a sign of God's disapproval of the materialism and irreligion of the epoch.

3   Jean-Jacques Olier (1608-1657) was a French Catholic priest and the founder of the Society of Saint Sulpice which established seminaries throughout France known for their moral and academic teaching.

5   Cornelius Jansen (1585-1638) was the Dutch Catholic bishop of Ypres in Flanders and the father of Jansenism, a reformist theological movement that tried to reconcile divine grace and human liberty, but which would eventually be deemed a heresy by the Catholic Church.

6   Luke Wadding (1588-1657), was an Irish Franciscan friar and historian, his *Annales minorum* was published between 1625 and 1654 in eight volumes; *Monasticon anglicanum* by William Dugdale (1605-1686) was first published in 1655; the *Rerum gallicarum et francicarum scriptores* (1738) was a collection of histories of France and the Gauls; the *Gallia Christiana* is a catalogue of all the Catholic dioceses and abbeys of

NOTES

France first published in 1626; the *Acta Sanctorum* is an encyclopedic text of the lives of Christian saints running to sixty-eight volumes, the first of which was published in 1643; *De antiquis ecclesiæ ritibus editio secunda* (1736-8) was a collection of writings by Edmond Martène (1654-1739), a French Benedictine historian and liturgist; Jean Mabillon' *Annals*, see Chapter VI, Note 2; Louis Bulteau (1625-1693) was the author of *Histoire de l'Ordre de St Benoît*; Louis-Sébastien Le Nain de Tillemont (1637-1698) was a French ecclesiastical historian; Dom Rémy Ceillier (1688-1763) was a historian of the Catholic Church and the Benedictines; Lodovico Antonio Muratori (1672–1750) was an Italian historian, notable for his discovery of the 'Muratorian fragment', the earliest known list of New Testament books; Gian Domenico Mansi (1692-1769) was an Italian prelate, theologian, scholar and historian, known for his *Concilia*, a work on Church councils.

6　Agostino Tornielli, (1543-1622) was an Italian monk, his *Annales sacri et ex profanis praecipui ab orbe condito ad eumdem Christi passione redemptum* was published in 1610; Philigone Migne, See Chapter IV, Note 1; Ulysse Joseph Chevalier (1841-1923) was a French Catholic priest, bibliographer and historian who specialised in the Middle Ages; Du Cange, See Chapter VI Note 2; Jean-Baptiste de La Curne de Sainte-Palaye (1697–1781) was a French historian, classicist, philologist and lexicographer.

CHAPTER XV

1　The Russian emperor, Nicholas II (1868-1918), made a state visit to France between 18-21 September 1901, during which he met French president Émile Loubet in Paris.

2　The Fualdès affair was a court case dating from 1817-18, but which continued to arouse passions long after due to suspicions of political interference and a cover-up. Antoine Fualdès, the former imperial prosecutor, was assassinated in 1817 in Rodez, and his body thrown into the waters of the Aveyron. During the trial it was said that the victim's cries for help were muffled by the sounds of an organ grinder.

3　Hippolyte Flandrin (1809-1864) was a French painter, known mostly for his religious paintings in the neo-classical style. Huysmans had criticised his work in *L'Art moderne* (*Modern Art*) in 1883.

4　Abbaye-aux-Bois was a Cistercian convent at 16 Rue de Sèvres, Paris. Huysmans lived for a large part of his life at 11 Rue de Sèvres.

5　Jean de Bernières-Louvigni (1602-1659) was a French mystic who lived as an ascetic. A collection of his work, *Oeuvres spirituelles de M. Bernières-Louvigni*, was posthumously published in 1677.

Books by J.-K. Huysmans available from Dedalus:

Translated by Brendan King:
Marthe
The Vatard Sisters
Parisian Sketches
Drifting
Modern Art
Against Nature
Stranded
Certain Artists
Là-Bas: A Journey into the Self
The Oblate

Translated by Clara Bell (revised by Brendan King):
The Cathedral

Translated by C. Kegan Paul:
En Route

Dedalus has also published Robert Baldick's *The Life of J.-K. Huysmans*, edited by Brendan King.